No Fox Given

Collector's Edition

Aimee Easterling

NO FOX GIVEN

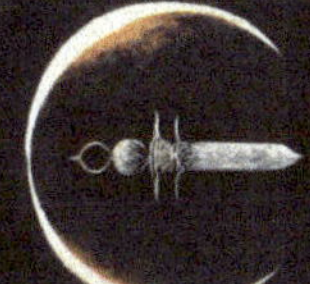

AIMEE EASTERLING

Table of

Contents

FULL MOON SALOON
KIRA FAIRWOOD: BOOK 1
USA TODAY BESTSELLING AUTHOR
AIMEE EASTERLING

Full Moon Saloon

Chapter 1

G irls' night out in a shifter bar?

I cocked my head at the cursive neon lights that glowed above the door of the blocky, three-story building. Then I checked my phone. Yep, this was the address Charlie had provided in her emailed invitation.

She just hadn't included the establishment's name—Full Moon Saloon. And her nose wouldn't have picked up on the scent of fur that overwhelmed car exhaust and autumn leaves while I lingered on the busy sidewalk out front.

The question was—why would my entirely human friend pick this place? Charlie had no concept that some of us went furry on occasion.

Or so I thought. Given the dangers to Charlie of learning about shifters' existence, so I hoped.

I shrugged away the trickle of concern and pushed the heavy door open, blinking as my eyes adjusted to the dim, throbbing interior. The scent of fur was stronger here, but a quick scan suggested no one was four-legged at the moment.

Danger, however, infused the space. Someone was hunting. But who and hunting what?

The establishment was smaller than it had appeared from outside, a closed door off to my right and one behind the bar leading to apparently non-public parts of the building. But that didn't mean it was easy to find the hunter. Shifters were everywhere, elbows planted on polished wood tables, booted feet invading walkways, husky chuckles nibbling into the back of my neck.

My eyes settled on the broad shadow of the proprietor. Separated from his customers by a bar that ran the length of the room, his right hand caressed the long counter as if it wasn't a hunk of dented and scarred wood but was instead a woman's hip.

Wait, no, he wasn't caressing the bar. He was wiping down its surface.

And he wasn't hunting. The trickle of cold in my spine came from somewhere else.

I found Charlie before I spotted the hunter. Or rather, she found me.

"Kira!" Her greeting trilled above the music and chatter. Her hug struck like a rattlesnake and for one split second I let old memories bite.

Swords, camaraderie, and cascades of laughter. Cramming for finals while lounging knee to knee atop a white, fluffy rug in the twins' dorm room.

Then emptiness. Silence. Friendship disappearing without explanation.

I swallowed, forcing myself out of the past to focus on the present. On a friend redolent with chemical reagents and bunsen-burner fuel, just like she'd smelled way back when.

Charlie squeezed me tighter before pushing me back to arm's length. "You look exactly the same."

Of course I did. My half-Japanese heritage meant I was often mistaken for a teenager even though I was actually midway through my twenties. Speaking Charlie's language, I shrugged. "Blame it on the genes."

"Hmm." She squinched her eyes half shut. "You're starving. Better feed you before something breaks. Thom, can you nuke us a pizza?"

Bar pizza was vile. Still, my stomach growled and Charlie released her customary peal of horse-snort laughter while drawing me toward the puddle of light above two empty bar stools.

"That what you want?" The bartender—Thom—didn't look in my direction. But he was closer now, or so my nose informed me. Close enough that I could tell he wasn't much older than Charlie. That his scent wasn't mere shifter fur but instead carried the headier musk of dominant alpha werewolf.

Still, his question came out gentle. Not subservient, but protective. As if he'd smelled my initial caution and wanted to make sure Charlie wasn't steamrollering over my wishes.

She wasn't. Tonight, vile bar pizza with Charlie was exactly what I wanted.

And, without me needing to turn that thought into a verbalization, Thom nodded. Dropped the cloth onto the counter then headed away from us through a door into what was presumably a kitchen, leaving me alone with my once-friend.

"It's been too long," Charlie said as I sank down onto the bar stool beside her.

I nodded but kept scanning the room. Because the scent of the hunter had rebounded even stronger as Thom stepped away from us. And, being human, there was a good chance Charlie was the one in the predator's sights....

Well, make that a slight chance. The bar wasn't just full of werewolves the way I'd initially assumed; it also contained a healthy helping of non-shifters. For example, a man and a woman, clearly on a date, were laughing at a table only feet from three snarly werewolves. The combination, loosened by alcohol, seemed problematic at best.

But as I turned my head, seeking danger, the certainty that a hunter stalked the premises faded from my hair follicles. And Charlie's words snagged my attention instead.

"I'm glad you emailed."

My brows drew together. I hadn't emailed.

Well, I guess I had. I'd sent out a group request for contributions to the alumni magazine last winter. "I—"

She spoke over me. "Can we not talk about what happened? At least not tonight."

Charlie and her twin had been adorable as teenagers, all big blue eyes and glossy curls. Now, at twenty-eight, her prettiness had matured into elegance. If she'd wanted, she could have used that beauty the same way I used my understanding of human psychology—to wrap everyone around her little finger.

Which wasn't why I nodded. I nodded because those usually wide eyes were squinting painfully. Charlie's smile wasn't as broad as I remembered it being.

And, frankly, I didn't want to sully the present with the past any more than she did.

"So you're a chemist," I guessed based on the parts of Charlie's scent that had carried over from college. "What awesome discoveries are you on the trail of?"

And just like that, the awkwardness receded. Charlie waggled her eyebrows, her voice turning confidential. "I work on a military base. If I told you more, I'd have to kill you. But here's a hint—Gate City ghost!"

Her arms waved wildly, as if including me in a well-known secret I wasn't actually aware of. Or maybe she thought there was a specter present in the bar beside us. Never mind that ghosts, I was pretty sure, didn't exist.

I hummed noncommittally, the time we'd spent apart yawning wider. And Charlie deftly changed the subject, pointing her chin at my sword then tossing out a conversational gambit that I could run with.

"And *you*. I'll bet you're still charming your way out of trouble while wearing the cutest, sharpest sword this side of the Mississippi. Let me guess." She bit her lip, gloss catching a glint of lamplight. "Pirate?"

"Law enforcement," I told her, which was only sort of a lie.

"Ooh, adventure. Dish, please."

So I regaled Charlie with the tale of my latest escapade, leaving out bits where the trespasser had gone furry and tried to nibble his way through my trousers. We were both laughing when Thom slid dinner between us, a pizza that he'd somehow dressed up to become more than thin layers of toppings atop wheat-based cardboard.

"Full Moon Special," he said, eyes remaining hidden. This close, his presence was hotter than the molten cheese that drew my fingers and made me forget about the danger of a scorched tongue.

Something unfamiliar and heady fluttered through me and I shivered. Charlie, never one to miss a physical reaction, poked at the goosebumps beading on my forearms.

"You don't want to go there," she whispered, her tone low enough so the human two bar stools down wouldn't hear. "Thom doesn't date. Doesn't hook up either."

Unfortunately, Charlie didn't understand the superior auditory abilities of werewolves. The scent of amusement emanating from the alpha werewolf roiled between us in a wave of spice.

"Good. Great." I took my slice with me as I spun the stool all the way around so my back was to the source of my chagrin. "Why don't you tell me about them?" I asked, waving vaguely at the other bar patrons before biting into the Full Moon Special. It had real parmesan on top, along with fresh pepperoni that sparked my taste buds wide awake.

"The best part of moving here," Charlie agreed. Picking up her own slice, she used it to point at two women parked at a table in one corner. "Officers' wives rubbing shoulders with scientists and locals. Never a dull moment in the Full Moon Saloon."

For a moment, the buzz in my brain made it impossible to focus. Then Thom's scent receded, the gentle whoosh of the kitchen door promising he'd taken pity on me.

And, at the same moment, the scent of active predator reasserted itself. Someone *was* hunting. Nearby. Intently. And they were very close to the kill.

Luckily, Charlie seemed content to chat about the people around us, giving me further opportunity to peer past my pizza into the room. As best I could tell, the so-called locals were evenly split between werewolves and farmers. Other than the oblivious dating couple, most of the humans seemed to have chosen spots far from danger. Which made sense—humans usually sensed shifters' predatory nature at an instinctive level and took steps to preserve their own skins.

Well, no, the couple on a date weren't the only ones lacking hairs-on-the-back-of-your-neck sensitivity. A young human's reed-thin arms shook as he braced himself one-handed against a wobbly walker. Beside him hovered a very rough-round-the-edges werewolf, young yet bulky. The shifter's gaze riveted on the human as if the latter was a juicy rabbit just waiting to be snapped up.

"That's my boss's son, Eli," Charlie explained, catching the direction of my gaze if not the purpose for it. "He makes friends with everybody."

In fact, Eli appeared to be telling the werewolf beside him about the history of bar games even as he struggled to pick up a dart. The tiniest hint of a smile fluttered across the werewolf's lips and I relaxed.

Yes, this werewolf was hunting. But not blood. I suspected he intended to fleece Eli for all the young man was worth.

For his part, Eli's stream of chatter was so relentless that I blinked and nearly missed the moment his laboriously lifted metal projectile landed dead center in the dart board. "Looks like you're paying," Eli crowed, his jubilation resembling that of a ten-year-old winning a heated round of Monopoly. "I'll take Pepsi. In a glass. With a cherry on top."

What do you do when a rabbit turns on you with teeth bared? I would have been tempted to laugh and accept failure. The hunting werewolf didn't share my approach.

Instead, a fist thudded onto the table between them, rattling empty glasses. The werewolf growled something wordless that, to a shifter, would have come across as a threat to rip out throats.

"Don't feel bad," Eli offered, leaning in closer so he could pat the irate shifter's shoulder. "I've been practicing." Then, as if reciting truisms from a parent: "Losing just means you need to try harder. You're still a worthwhile person inside."

Beside me, Charlie snickered. She thought Eli was tweaking the nose of a rough-around-the-edges bar patron. What she didn't realize was the sharpness of that bar patron's teeth.

Sure enough, Eli's pat turned the werewolf's muscles stiff. Then he made everything much, much worse.

Leaving his walker behind entirely, Eli flung himself into a hug that wouldn't really have been considered appropriate even among humans. With an irate werewolf, the gesture was deeply unwise.

I dropped my pizza and drew my sword as the werewolf's scent turned dark and dangerous. He shoved Eli hard at the same instant Charlie muttered, "Oh shit."

Chapter 2

We weren't close enough to catch Eli as he was flung backwards, but someone else was. One of the military wives scrambled forward, perfume seething around her person as she sank down to her knees with Eli's head cradled in her lap.

"He's fragile!" she warned.

And the shifter picked up the nearest table. Hefted it as if the metal and wood weighed no more than a soccer ball and would be just as easy to toss toward Eli's head.

Unlike a soccer ball, however, the heavy furniture wouldn't bounce harmlessly away when it made contact. Instead, features would shatter. Blood would fountain. Bones would break.

Luckily, Charlie and I were able to prevent that disaster from unfolding. "Pied Piper?" my friend murmured. "You don't happen to have another sword handy, do you?"

"Always," I lied, tossing her the non-magical weapon I'd been holding. As she tested its balance, I mentally massaged my star ball to create another blade in a newly materialized scabbard running the length of my spine.

Because a kitsune's star ball was one of our greatest assets. Made up of immaterial energy that helped us shift in the blink of an eye, the star ball could also be solidified into physical objects both visible and very, very tangible. The only danger being that separation from the result sapped my strength as quickly as water drained through a yanked bathtub plug.

I didn't intend to be separated from my star-ball sword, however. Instead, I twisted the blade until it caught a glint of light from the dangling ceiling lamps, shining warning into the shifter's eyes.

He curled back his lips, snarling. I cocked my head, grinning at the haze of adrenaline fizzing through my veins.

I didn't speak to the werewolf, however. Instead, I addressed Charlie in a voice loud enough to catch everyone's attention. "Wanna do it? Right now? Outside for all the world to see?"

Charlie wiggled her eyebrows just like she had in the college cafeteria when we were trying to catch cute guys' attention. "I can't wait to see who ends up on top, you or me."

The werewolf, bless his heart, panted. He really was pretty far gone into his animal self. The never-to-be-flung table clattered to the ground as my sword curved towards Charlie's.

Just a tap. A clang of steel on steel to solidify any wandering attention.

Then I was sidling backwards while Charlie ushered me doorward, her sword nudging mine when our trajectory needed a tweak. We'd perfected this dance years ago, so I was able to let my muscles drift into autopilot while I scanned the interior of the space.

The formerly irate werewolf wasn't the only one following after us. As best I could tell, we'd attracted the attention of every red-blooded male in the Full Moon Saloon.

Every male...including Thom. He slammed out of the kitchen like a storm cloud, taking in the scene with one glance before vaulting across the bar. Hard boots gashed a new dent in the surface of the wood he'd so lovingly polished earlier. His gaze, when it met mine for the first time, was like an icepick to the brain.

Blue eyes boasted the hue of a submerged glacier. Luminous yet hooded. Wild and dangerous and dark.

For one split second, I fell into the Antarctic Ocean. Then Charlie's sword clanged into mine a little harder than necessary. Flinching back to reality, I noted that Thom had picked up his pace.

Which was when I realized he thought Charlie and I needed rescuing. *"We're fine,"* I mouthed. *"Check on Eli."*

Because Charlie's boss's son—man in stature, boy in behavior—seemed unharmed from a distance. He was on his feet, being guided back to his walker. But that fall hadn't looked good....

Thom hesitated then swiveled away from me. The icepick eased up into a strange sort of yearning. I shook my head, refocusing on my friend.

"I wonder if one of these big guys would like to have a go with the winner?" Charlie mused, eyes sparkling. Then we were dancing out the door into the crispness of October in Virginia, two dozen hungry werewolves at our back.

Ten minutes later, we were still dancing, even though Charlie's and my positions had reoriented so we could fend off the werewolves who'd piled on all at once. Their behavior was reprehensible...and deeply gratifying. Because it gave me permission to press my back up against the back of an old friend and whack sense into those who deserved whacking in perfect unison with someone not in my pack.

"I'm gonna drag you behind that car," the werewolf in front of Charlie snarled, his words not quite words but still getting his point across. "Then..."

Charlie snorted before he could finish, twisting her blade and tapping him on the forehead with the flat so hard he yelped. "I suggest you go home."

A human usually wouldn't have been able to make headway against a shifter, but these werewolves had reflexes dulled by drinking. Plus, even though they wielded swords, I didn't get the impression they trained with them. Typical of outpack wolves gathering in a bar like this.

No wonder the guy Charlie had struck mumbled something I pretended not to hear then turned away into the darkness. Returning my attention to my own fight, I slid beneath a hulking werewolf's guard, locked the hilts of our swords, and flicked his off into traffic. A car's brakes squealed and the shifter made a very similar noise as he hightailed it out of my blade's reach.

In the lull as our remaining opponents realigned themselves, I checked on the real purpose of our endeavor. Yep, there was the slow-moving huddle I'd hoped for, skirting the edge of the battle. Eli in his walker, flanked by Thom and the overly perfumed military wife. The unlikely collaborators helped the young man into the back of a car, then Thom leaned his head in after to offer a few words.

"You're safe here, Eli. I won't let this happen again."

The bartender's words rumbled with werewolf danger, but Eli just laughed. "I know I'm safe. I don't get nightmares."

Then the military wife was easing the vehicle away into traffic and Thom's icepick eyes met mine above three werewolves' bobbing shoulders. His eyebrows rose, a question. I shook my head, a reply.

No, I neither needed nor wanted any help. This was all fun and games.

Behind me, Charlie disarmed another of her opponents just as ably as the first one. "You've been practicing," I called over my shoulder.

"Not quite enough," she answered, only slightly more out of breath than I was. "Swords don't play a big role in lab work. Actually, I'm surprised they do in law enforcement. Since when do cops rely on blades instead of guns?"

"New thing." My mouth puckered with the sour taste of the lie and I almost missed the shifter, not so wobbly as the others, who leapt up in my blind spot. I tried to parry, but the angle was wrong. Words, more instinct than expectation, barked out of my mouth.

"Charlie! Cobra!"

Even as I spoke, I rejected the expectation of assistance. After all, the term was a throwback to the days when Charlie, her twin, and I had all taken lessons under my sister. Ancient history. Unlikely to work today.

So I counterattacked, knowing as my arm lashed out that the wild blow wasn't going to be effective.

To my surprise, our code was remembered. Charlie's sword came stabbing back over her shoulder while I tossed myself sideways. And the werewolf who'd invaded my blind spot grunted in distress.

Charlie's blind blow had only been a glancing one, but the guy still sheathed his sword, backing away from us with hands raised. The chance of an easy lay might have tempted him initially. But neither Charlie nor I was easy, not when we clenched swords in our fists.

And now the air between us sweetened. Moving in perfect harmony, only a few words were necessary to unite us in reminiscence.

"Remember that summer?" Charlie asked, referring to her twin's kidnapping when I was in grade school and they weren't much older, a trauma that had tugged us all so close together that we remained friends until college. After the event, the Raven twins had signed up for swordfighting lessons with my sister, which might explain why Charlie brought up the distant past now.

"Of course," I answered. Then, broaching the topic I'd never been mature enough to ask at the time: "Do you think Jessie has flashbacks about it?"

"Nah." Charlie's blade flashed into my peripheral vision. We were almost out of werewolves to unite against. "Swords made us both strong."

Then there were no opponents left. Just an empty sidewalk and the tentative germination of an old relationship turned new.

Assuming reality didn't squelch that tender sprout of connection.

"We haven't lost our touch," I observed, swiveling to revel in our triumph.

But Charlie's back was all that met my gaze. Her shoulders were tense the way they hadn't been in battle.

"I need to visit the lady's room," she muttered. "I'll be right back."

Chapter 3

Here in front of the bar, there were three small round tables directly beneath a streetlight, each boasting two rusty metal chairs. Rather than following Charlie the way I wanted to, I sank into one of the latter. At least I could keep an eye on the werewolf who'd seemed most upset about losing to ensure he didn't sneak inside and waylay Charlie while she was alone.

Nope, he was stalking off across the street, crossing against traffic. A horn blared and he shook a fist at the driver. Venting aggression at cars—great move, werewolf.

I was still chuckling at the loser's misplaced testosterone when a deep, gritty voice curled out of the darkness right beside me. "Your drinks."

Someone had slipped past my guard, which meant I should have sprung to my feet with sword extended. Should have swirled around until my blade bit into his throat.

Instead, I turned slowly, knowing who I'd see even before two of the pinkest, cutest beverages imaginable settled onto the table in front of me. I mean, there weren't just umbrellas stuck into the neon-colored liquid. There were candy lips kissing each rim.

This was exactly the sort of frou-frou fun Charlie adored. Someone knew his clientele's taste.

The bartender who'd carried them out to us, however, was ten times as enticing as the beverages. Tall, broad, well-muscled. Dark facial hair that formed a well-cropped shadow around a square jaw. Eyes that no longer averted themselves from mine, and a smile that softened crags like sun slipping through a break in a mountain range.

Add in the flannel shirt and I expected Thom to pull out an ax and go Paul Bunyan on me. No wonder I let flirtatious banter dance off my lips. "These are adorable. But could you possibly leave them for Charlie and make mine a virgin?"

I *did* want a non-alcoholic drink, but I'd also found that tossing the V word around tended to pique guys' interest. Only...this time my effort backfired. The sun left the mountain and Thom's question came out hard and cold. "Virgin?"

And banter eluded me. Words eluded me. Thom hadn't repeated my request as a sexy rejoinder. Instead, his voice had gone gruff, his body language proving that I'd made a major faux pas.

Did Thom think I was making a dig about his refusal to date? Insinuating that he was a virgin because he couldn't find a willing partner?

"No, no, no! That's not what I meant!" Diarrhea of the mouth. How embarrassing. And I couldn't quite make it stop. "This is about me, not about you. Bad idea to drink tonight."

Someone laughed inside the bar. A car rolled past on the street in front of us, teenagers bobbing along to the beat of way too loud music.

Thom still didn't speak.

So I did. "Why, you might ask, did I come to a bar if I don't want to drink? That's an excellent question. The deal is, I haven't seen Charlie for six years, since I was a freshman in college and she ditched me without explanation. She sent me this address yesterday and I had the afternoon off. So of course I showed up."

I slapped one hand across my face, covering up my eyes so I didn't have to see Thom's reaction. "And, yes, I did just air all my dirty laundry to a stranger. Kill me now."

For another moment, the night hung heavy around us. Then soft flannel brushed my cheekbone. A gentle hand pried my fingers loose from their stranglehold grip on my forehead. I blinked and peered up, half hoping and half fearing that the icepick would reignite.

Only, Thom wasn't watching me. Instead, his gaze turned to the spot where Charlie and I had fought just a few minutes earlier. The scent of fur seethed around us, leftover from aggression released in battle. "I understand your caution," Thom rumbled, the words vibrating like honeybees in my stomach. "But I, personally, will ensure your safety in my town."

His town. So Thom *was* an alpha.

Filling in the blanks settled my crazy emotions. Helped me forget about the icepick and see what Thom saw.

He thought I was a female werewolf outside her pack showing understandable caution around a horde of riled shifters. "No, that's not it," I corrected. "Unfortunately, I have promises to keep. And miles to go before I sleep."

And, apparently, no ability to come up with succinct replies that hadn't first been written by dead poets. Argh!

Wait, that argh hadn't emerged from my throat. It had instead come from Charlie as she dropped down into the other chair, formerly sweat-streaked hair reformed into its usual perfect waves through her entirely human sort of magic.

"No!" she continued, the joy of winning against so many opponents sloughing off her. "You're staying the night. I have a guest room. Actual clean towels. Come on, Kira. Don't let me down."

And now, finally, ordinary words became available in my jumbled brain. "Family. They're expecting me."

I shrugged, realizing as I did so that Thom had slipped away, his absence allowing me to carry on an understandable conversation at long last. Which, after all, was why I was here.

So Charlie and I conversed while someone other than Thom delivered more drinks to our table. I tried not to be disappointed that his alpha musk didn't reassert itself while I sipped something with no kick but great flavor. And, gradually, I lost myself in the recital of family business.

I told Charlie about my sister's six-year-old son—"I call him Grub"—and current pregnancy with my first and only niece. She reciprocated with the tale of her twin sister's job teaching fencing in the same school all three of us used to attend. Jessie had two-year old and four-year-old girls.

"Wow," I murmured. "Babies everywhere."

"Yeah. But you and I are single and out on the town!" Charlie, who had gulped down her first two drinks and sipped her way through a third and fourth, now grabbed her borrowed sword off the table and brandished it at the nearest streetlight.

The blade circled dizzily before tumbling back toward her upturned features. "How about I take that?" I pried the hilt out of my friend's fingers one second before sharp steel made contact. Settling the weapon back into its sheathe at my hip, I added: "And take you home."

"Already?"

"It's two AM."

And the bar was closing around us. While Charlie and I had been deep in conversation, the hot bartender must have turned things over to a less brain-fuzzing human woman. She was the one who had brought us drinks and who was currently locking the door to the Full Moon Saloon.

The *empty* Full Moon Saloon. I hadn't noticed everyone else dribbling away while Charlie and I relived our past adventures. Hadn't noticed the street turning somnolent. Now, the only illumination flickered out of streetlamps and a few porch lights.

"You two good to get home?" the closing bartender asked.

I nodded and returned my attention to Charlie. She'd relented and was doing her best to lever herself upright. Unfortunately, she kept canting sideways before she achieved a vertical state.

"Oopsie," my friend murmured, catching herself just before she tumbled back into her seat a third time.

"Here." I offered my arm and we stumbled through the night to the cute little house Charlie had clearly been fixing up for some time now. I settled her onto the sofa and promised: "We'll stay in touch."

"Always!" Charlie's promise would have been more believable if a line of drool hadn't already soaked into a throw pillow.

Still, the possibility of a rekindled friendship warmed me as I drove the long hours to the territory of the werewolf pack who'd propped me up when the Raven twins let me down so many years ago. Sneaking into my childhood bedroom through an unlocked window so as not to wake the inhabitants, I embraced my return to the place that would always be home to me.

Here I was happy. Part of something bigger. Completely at peace.

What I didn't learn until later is what else happened in Gate City that night. A woman who'd enjoyed herself in the Full Moon Saloon was found torn apart by animal teeth at a private zoo a few miles deeper in the countryside. My first instinct had been right. The uneasy alliance between humans and shifters at the Full Moon Saloon had been a powder keg waiting to ignite.

Chapter 4

But murder wasn't on my mind the next morning when fifty pounds of wannabe werewolf cannonballed into my bed. "Auntie Kira!"

I cracked both eyes open with an effort, my voice rusty as I demanded. "What time is it?"

"Time to get up!" Grub bounced, jiggling the mattress so enthusiastically the liquid in my stomach sloshed. "I waited outside your door last night but you never came!"

I was so very glad I hadn't imbibed alongside Charlie. Because, if I'd been hungover, I wouldn't have been able to roll onto the floor, straighten up...then swoop my nephew's feet out from under him before he could evade my grip.

Swinging his upside-down body gently then faster, I strode toward the open window I knew for a fact I'd shut behind me last night. Grub had clearly used the same route I had to enter. "How'd you know I was here then?" I asked.

"Pack bond!" hooted my favorite nephew. In further proof that he took after his alpha werewolf father, the six-year-old wiggled his fingers around an invisible connection that tied the two of us together, prompting a ferocious tickle in my gut.

"You little monster." I swayed his body even further out over the shrubbery then back in while Grub giggled so hard I could barely understand his words.

"I had to use the window! Daddy locked your door! He said not to bother you!"

"So uncool," I agreed, carting my nephew over to the door in question. "My hands are full. Guess you'd better do the honors."

"Sure thing, Auntie Kira!" He twisted his body around so he was more of a tuning fork than a pendulum, then his chubby fingers fumbled with the lock.

And even though my phone rang just as he twisted the knob and pushed the door open, I ignored its demands. Instead, I took in the welcome sight of Grub's mother, my sister, tapping her foot in the hallway outside.

"Grub." Mai looked the way I'd look in another decade, her brows crunching together exactly as mine had when my nephew landed on my bed. "Really?"

"Kira doesn't mind," my nephew observed, as if blood wasn't pooling in his head and making his eyes bug out. "If she minded, she'd...."

"Guess I'd really better take this call," I said, raising the kid up as high as I could, then dropping him. Hands free, I could now pull my still-ringing phone out of the pants I'd never bothered taking off before falling into bed far too few hours ago.

"Aaaaaaaaah," shrieked my dramatic nephew as he plummeted floorward.

Mai made no move to catch him, so I snagged his ankle with one hand a millisecond before his head struck floorboards. Swiping my phone awake with the other thumb, I lowered the kid to the ground as I answered. "Kira here."

Grub was still shrieking, which might be why my boss actually asked a personal question for the first time ever. "Is everything alright there?"

"Peachy. Except I suspect you're about to tell me my weekend off is canceled."

"How soon can you be back in the office?"

I looked at Mai. She looked at me. Thirteen years my senior and my sole support since I reached double digits, Mai was more mother than sister.

Added to that close relationship was the fact that we hadn't seen each other in weeks. But she nodded anyway. "Do what you need to do. We'll be here when you land another free weekend."

So—"Three hours" I told Scarlet. Then I swung through the kitchen to accept breakfast-to-go from Mai's mate Gunner before heading back to my car.

My family stood in a tight huddle, the view receding far too rapidly in my rearview mirror. The tallest was Gunner, a burly werewolf who somehow made

Mai's spark shine brighter rather than stifling her with his overwhelming alpha presence. Next came my sister, slender except for the gentle curve of her pregnant belly, any matronly vibe countered by the sword belted at her hip. Finally, cradled between Mai and Gunner so he wouldn't sprint down the shortcut to the end of the driveway then hitch a ride on my roof the way he had last time: my nephew and the apple of my eye.

I couldn't see the pack bond, but I could feel it wrapped around them. Could feel it tugging against my departure as I drove away.

But, in a way, I was still there with my family. After all, Grub and my niece existed because of me.

I hadn't understood that at first, even though Mai and Gunner waited to have a kid until I achieved my legal majority. The event occurred six long years after the pair met each other and changed the name of Gunner's pack to Fairwood, a compilation of Mai's maiden name (Fairchild) and Gunner's bachelor name (Atwood). If creating a new surname out of nothing wasn't commitment, I don't know what was.

Still, no offspring had materialized until precisely nine months after my eighteenth birthday. A clue I hadn't paid attention to at the time.

Instead, I'd accepted the awesomeness of having a nephew without wondering about the timing. I doted on Grub during breaks from college, only later realizing how carefully Gunner had planned that aspect of my life. In retrospect, the way he'd gone stingy on funds when I considered a far-flung institution was totally out of character. But it had the desired effect.

Rather than graduating shoulder-deep in debt, I'd fallen back to the college within pack territory my brother-in-law suggested. Never once did I consider the oddity when an older pack member offered to be my roommate and signed up for all the same classes I took.

Yeah, it was obvious now that the larger world had never been safe for me. That I was being guided and guarded through my young adulthood. At the time, however, I'd just embraced the independence I did have.

I might never have caught on if I hadn't heard my own name rumbling through my sister's closed door in Gunner's deep voice less than a year ago. "You think Kira's keeping herself small because of the kitsune issue?"

"How could she not?" Mai had answered. "I've barely left pack lands for a decade, which I now realize was a mistake. It's time for me to force the issue, get the other clans used to having a fox among them. Kira's life shouldn't be so constrained."

"There's another way to rock the boat," Gunner countered. "We could always try again."

A pause, during which Mai hummed her pleasure and my face went hot. If they were going to canoodle, I'd leave them to it....

But then Mai, a little breathless, observed, "Bring another kitsune into the world, you mean."

"It's your body. Your choice." Gunner's voice turned wistful. "But, yeah. We either get another Grub or a daughter. A cute little fox to keep us all on our toes...and to take the other packs' focus off Kira. Both options sound nice."

"Our neighbors would erupt." Despite her words, Mai wasn't putting her foot down. Instead, she sounded as dreamy as Gunner.

I liked my brother-in-law in his own right, but my favorite thing about him was the way he moved mountains for the sake of my sister. So I wasn't surprised when his answer came out full of alpha bite. "I'll deal with anyone who takes offense."

Two months later, Mai informed me I was going to be an aunt again. Another season and it was confirmed—the baby in her womb was a girl.

A girl. A kitsune, like me and Mai. Bane of werewolves. Safe only when hidden deep within one of the few packs who accepted us as equals.

And here's the deal. Mai had spent half her life protecting me, even when I did stupid, crazy shit that I'm now too embarrassed to even talk about. I'd fledged but stayed close to the nest. And, in response, my sister had stuck her neck out once again to make sure my life didn't always consist of in-state tuition with a bodyguard werewolf sharing every minute of my wing-stretching time.

Which meant it was time to turn the tables. I could be the one making things better for kitsunes outside the Fairwood bubble. I could pound my head against that glass ceiling until it shattered into heaps of rainbow-tinged confetti. I could ensure my niece grew up able to backpack through Europe or run for president or do anything else she darn well chose.

Which was why I'd taken this job. Why, today, I fought traffic and breezed into the Lawkeepers' Roanoke office instead of staying home to tease my favorite (and only) nephew.

Because when I decided to make a name for myself among werewolves, I'd figured I might as well head straight to the top.

The long, cautious route toward acceptance outside the Fairwood pack would have been winning over alpha after alpha, each of whom was god within his own territory. The short, bold way to the same destination consisted of proving my worth among the overarching group that kept the existence of shifters under wraps.

Nowadays, if rogues went off the rails and came to the attention of the human government, the issue was swept under the rug...then dealt with quickly and harshly by Lawkeepers drawn from various packs. Lawkeepers like me.

And like Rupert, who glowered from his cubicle as I breezed through the bullpen. Although short and weedy by werewolf standards, Rupert's appearance wasn't the reason he'd landed the role of everyone's least-favorite coworker. It was his behavior that made seeing him on a daily basis so unpleasant that we'd banded together and begged for him to be given a perennial weekend shift.

So, yeah, Rupert's existence here on a Saturday was ordinary. Scarlet's and mine...not so much.

But a light beckoned from inside my boss's office. "Close the door behind you," Scarlet ordered in lieu of a greeting when I followed that glow into a space full of sleek furnishings and a distinct absence of gewgaws. My boss's physical appearance matched her office in every respect.

Neither invited relaxation, so I didn't sit down. Instead, I shifted my weight from foot to foot while Scarlet dove right into business.

"A woman was murdered after leaving a shifter bar in Virginia last night," she informed me. "Wolf attack. You're on the case."

Chapter 5

My knees turned unaccountably weak and I had to grab onto the side of Scarlet's desk for stability. "Gate City? Full Moon Saloon?"

"Yes." My boss raised one eyebrow then proceeded to dish details I couldn't care less about. Where. When. Who found the body.

All I could think was—*Charlie.* Charlie had been in that bar last night. We'd taunted the wolves together then I'd left my human friend behind a flimsy door any shifter could break down. What had I been thinking?

"Our understanding with the human authorities holds," Scarlet continued. "But we need to deal with the issue fast. The victim's husband is a Marine and they'll want closure as quickly as possible."

"Husband? Marine?" Charlie hadn't told me she was married. And she would have during last night's gabfest.

I only realized I'd landed in the hard wooden chair everyone did their best to avoid when Scarlet came around to join me. Crouching down to eye level, she softened her tone. "What's going on, Kira?"

"I was in Gate City last night. At the Full Moon Saloon. I met a human friend there. I thought...."

"The woman who died was thirty-five. Name: Janet Allegra. Occupation: homemaker." Despite rattling off the information as tersely as usual, Scarlet's hand settled on my knee. Touch was shifter sympathy, which made her question warm me even though it was clipped. "Your friend?"

I shook my head, wordless, trying to pull myself back from the abyss I'd fallen into. Imagining Charlie dead made me realize how much I cared about her, never mind the six years we'd been incommunicado. Charlie was the single person outside the Fairwood pack I'd label a true friend.

And she was alive. Drawing in a deep breath that shuddered only slightly, I cleared my throat and remembered what I was here for. "You want me to figure out who's responsible for Janet Allegra's death."

To my surprise, Scarlet shook her head. "No. It's cut and dried. I simply need you to make the arrest."

Now I was confused. "Rupert's on duty this weekend."

"Rupert doesn't have what it takes to handle Gate City's unique environment. Humans mingling with shifters, the former unaware of the latter. We need to keep the innocent in the dark."

I nodded, stood. "I can be subtle."

"That's not what I meant."

Scarlet was exactly my height and not much older than me, but I found myself drawing back from the intensity of her stare anyway. Her eyes were dark pools above her slash of brilliant red lipstick. She lowered her voice, which was unnecessary given the soundproofing of the room.

"I expect you to use blood."

The office abruptly hummed with a new sort of tension. I'd disclosed my kitsune heritage on my application, but Scarlet had never mentioned my special skills previously. "You mean...." I rotated my wrist, summoning my star ball. The magic that differentiated me from werewolves glowed at my fingertips with an unearthly light.

My breath hitched as I displayed an ability I'd never shared outside the Fairwood pack. But Scarlet didn't step back or even lean away from something that must have been entirely outside her previous experience. Instead, she nodded. "I have complete faith in your ability to bring in an alpha under Gate City's constraints."

"An alpha?" A different sort of trepidation tap-danced down my spine now. "Who exactly is the murderer?"

"Thom Faris, owner of the Full Moon Saloon."

I walked out of Scarlet's office in a daze, the whiplash of emotions still wiggling their way out of my system. No wonder Rupert glanced up from his computer screen then barked out a cruel, snake-slither of laughter. "What's wrong with you? You look like something my cat vomited up."

Rupert, as I may have mentioned previously, was an asshole. He liked to change the good coffee in the break room out for cheap stuff so he could steal our quality caffeination for personal use. We'd taken to swapping out the double-ply toilet paper for single before the weekend so he wouldn't pull the same stunt there.

More personally, I'd returned to the office after my first weekend as a Lawkeeper to find a thousand-page binder of rules and regulations on my chair alongside a note informing me that pop quizzes would be administered without prior notice. So I wasn't surprised to find Rupert taking advantage of my current weakness to get a dig in now.

My first impulse was to dish disrespect right back at my tormentor. Here at work, though, I was trying to make it seem like kitsunes were no big problem. Mimicking a pack princess, I'd found, made me eminently overlookable.

So I rolled my eyes and donned my best Valley Girl impersonation. "Working on the weekend. Such a drag, right?"

Sure enough, Rupert changed gears into older, wiser bluster mode. He was still lecturing me about crime not taking vacations when I pushed outside mid-sentence and headed to my car.

Three hours and one to-go milkshake later, I'd relinquished my annoyance at Rupert along with my fear for Charlie. I'd also squished that wobbliness in my stomach that came from misjudging the bar's proprietor. Instead, as I rolled into the alley behind the Full Moon Saloon, I was ready to do my job and collar a murderer hard and fast.

Because being overlooked wasn't the only route to werewolf acceptance. In the long run, I wanted to be considered efficient, capable, a team player. Now was the time to achieve that goal.

Luckily, Scarlet had eyes on the ground feeding her information that she'd texted to me while I was in transit. Thom lived above the bar, had left for lunch, but was back home presently. This job would be simple, in and out.

I parked three doors down in the back alley, glanced around, then shifted right there in the front seat of my car. The tingle of magic made me sneeze once, then I was on the hunt.

Out the window, down the sidewalk. Disrespecting gravity, I leapt onto a planter box and from there to a wall ledge that was likely intended to be ornamental but was actually just the right size for dainty fox paws.

This ledge just happened to run along the level of Thom's second-floor living space, leading straight to an open window only twenty feet ahead. Werewolves and humans wouldn't have been able to use such a lofty entrance, so Thom wouldn't have his guard up. The element of surprise was always a plus.

As I scampered, I let my mind wander. The current gig, including drop-off, would be completed before dinner time. I'd thrill Grub when I showed up with the tale of my exploits, plus a gag gift I was already plotting involving rubber bands and peanut butter.

Only...words exploded, not from above but from below me. A voice that wasn't Thom's but did sound vaguely familiar. "I came in as ordered!"

I padded closer to ensure I caught the entirety of the exchange even as Thom replied, something dark simmering beneath his words' quiet restraint. "You did. And that's a point in your favor. But you know the rules. You broke the rules. You've lost the right to your paw."

My tail twitched with interest. Paw? Was Thom about to cut off someone's appendage? Apparently I'd been wrong and Scarlet had been right about his character....

I crept closer to the first-story vent that the words had seeped out of. Thom hadn't chosen to meet whoever this was in his living space. Instead, the two were in the area behind the bar—kitchen or office?

Didn't matter. I'd collect a little additional information, then I'd collar the culprit just as I'd planned.

To that end, I settled down to engage in some much-needed grooming. Meanwhile, the shifter being chastised burst out with a statement that told me exactly who he was.

"You would have done the exact same thing if some guy felt you up! He was getting ready to slobber all over my face!"

"There was nothing sexual about Eli's behavior." The warning in Thom's voice deepened. "Address your homophobia while you're gone, Smoke. I expect to see improvement before you reapply."

Reapply? I gave my tail one last lick then rose to my feet, trying to make sense of the sort of punishment Thom was doling out. If I bent down just right, maybe I could peer in through that vent....

And the ledge crumbled out from under me. Not just a few pebbles but a section as long as I was, cracking away from the wall.

I scrabbled for footing as chunks of mortar rained down beneath me. But there was no footing. Everything seemed to have turned slick and entirely without traction.

A larger chunk of stone let go. Then I was spinning as I fell, hoping for a patch of lawn to stifle the pain and noise of my fall.

No forgiving surface materialized. Just the pavement, which slammed into my paws at the same time Smoke turned belligerent. "You'll regret this! My brother is an alpha. You think you're safe here? Gate City is barely as big as our smallest hunting preserve. I'll...."

My feet stung, but at least the thud of my descent had been overshadowed by Smoke's bellow. I swiped my tongue across the bottom of one front foot then the other. There. All better. Now I was ready to deal with blustering males.

Only Thom dealt with Smoke first. "Don't want to reapply? Not my problem. Now, *go.*"

The alpha command sent ice down my spine, but it didn't force obedience from me the way it did from the less dominant werewolf. Smoke growled out threats but he stomped toward the back door anyway...the one I was parked directly in front of.

For my part, I really should have been preparing to slip into the bar as Smoke rushed out of it. As best I could tell, there was no one else present in the Full Moon Saloon and Smoke's crime appeared to be unrelated to the one I was investigating.

A pack wolf would have obeyed her temporary alpha and collared the perp Scarlet had earmarked. The look on Rupert's face if I returned before he clocked out would be priceless. It might even provoke a nod of appreciation from my tight-lipped boss.

But the story Scarlet had relayed didn't make sense any longer. Instead, my own first impression of Thom was supported by the way he'd punished the younger male with eviction rather than with physical punishment. The way he'd offered Smoke multiple opportunities to redeem himself.

Who was more likely to have killed a woman last night? A patient alpha who doled out second chances like full-size Snickers bars on Halloween? Or a hot-headed werewolf who'd had his initial target stolen by Charlie's and my Pied Piper impersonation?

So when Smoke slammed out into the parking lot, I ignored my orders. Instead, I pushed off hard with my back paws, leapt onto the surly werewolf's back, and dug my teeth into his neck.

Chapter 6

Here's why werewolves hate kitsunes—their blood grants us all kinds of fun power. My sister and I didn't imbibe often, so I'd forgotten the way a quick nip filled me with exhilaration greater than the most awesome sugar rush.

Wowee! My hair spiked out all around my body and I rose three inches off Smoke's shoulders without bothering to push off with my feet.

But this wasn't a game. I needed to use the energy I'd stolen to guide Smoke somewhere private before another werewolf noticed a kitsune was among them. Unfortunately, lack of practice meant I didn't really know what I was doing. Rather than Smoke toddling toward my car with my puffy tail curled around his neck the way I'd hoped he would, the shifter batted at me with one hand while trying to reopen the door behind his back with the other.

Speed, at least, was something I could manage even with my brain fizzing off in twenty different directions. I skittered up to the top of his head, clinging with my claws and preparing to leap if the knob turned.

Nope. The door, apparently, was locked.

And, finally, my brain cleared. Smoke's motion stuttered into stillness. Now to build upon that success by moving him in the car direction. One, two, three...*m ove.*

Hmm. That didn't work.

Instead, we lingered right out in the open where any passing werewolf could take offense at my existence. Or where a naive human could stumble upon us and get a clue she really shouldn't have about the supernatural.

"Nice fox," a girl observed from the other side of the parking lot. Her t-shirt was emblazoned with a sparkly unicorn while rainbows coated her backpack. Was she young enough to see beyond the ordinary and guess what Gate City hid?

"Humans mingling with shifters, the former unaware of the latter. We need to keep the innocent in the dark," Scarlet had warned. I was blowing this job just when I couldn't afford a misstep.

"Can I pet it?" the girl continued as I redoubled my efforts to control the werewolf beneath me.

No. This time, adrenaline tunneled my thoughts into a single command. And, sure enough, Smoke obeyed, albeit in his own less-than-delightful manner. His growled refusal included several choice four-letter words.

"Whatever," the girl rolled her eyes, muttering too quietly for a human to pick up on. "Didn't have to be a dick about it." Then she turned to wander off.

But Smoke and I both had shifter ears so we caught her sassing. His muscles tensed...and I redoubled my efforts to turn him in the opposite direction. Toward my car. Away from the girl.

He didn't move. Instead he grunted, feet shuffling as he struggled against me. A string of invective, low in volume yet sharp as thumbtacks, exploded out of his mouth.

Would the locked door be enough to keep Thom from hearing and rushing out to investigate? I didn't want to find out, and that was enough to prompt me to consider another dose from the oozing wound on the side of Smoke's neck.

The initial bite mark wasn't much worse than the result of rubbing up against an unfriendly rosebush. The punctures would scab over in a few minutes and disappear within a day.

Still, what I'd done and was about to do again made me distinctly queasy. How would I feel if this was one of my pack mates, forced to act against his will? What would Mai say if she could see me now?

But Scarlet had recommended I use my unique abilities to bring in the murderer. The key word being the last one. Smoke wasn't an innocent. He'd torn apart a human woman last night in wolf form...or at least I thought he had.

So I licked up another tongueful of blood, letting the hot, salty liquid rest in my mouth rather than swallowing this time. *Turn left*, I thought coldly, and Smoke obeyed without hesitation. *Open the car door. Get in.*

With Smoke's blood still salty on my tongue, I checked to make sure the alley was once again empty then I summoned my human body and pulled on my clothes. Beside me, the werewolf slouched in the passenger seat as immobile as a crash dummy. He did snap on his seat belt, though, when I murmured: "Click it or ticket."

After that, driving seemed safer than lingering in the alley. So I headed out to the highway, back in the direction from which I'd come. Traffic was light in the hour between schools letting out and jobs releasing adults, which meant it wasn't a stretch to rest one hand lightly on the steering wheel while scooping up a little more blood with the other to expedite the interrogation ahead.

This time, my conscience twinged only a little.

"Tell me about last night," I demanded. And the werewolf beside me opened his mouth to release a cascade of words.

"I already explained to the alpha-wannabe." Smoke's body language was combative, but the stolen blood kept his emoting fully verbal. "All I did was *push* somebody. That's not enough to take away my paw."

Okay, this wasn't the part of last night I should've been asking about. But my feet were tapping with energy from all of the blood I'd consumed, which made it hard to ignore fox curiosity. "What do you mean he took away your paw?"

Smoke answered just as easily as previously, no extra blood required this time. "Thom hands out a paw to shifters if we swear to abide by the rules in his city. He gives moons to humans we vouch for. Both are medallions, hunks of metal on a chain. Without one you can't enter the Moon Room. Have one then lose it and you're not welcome in town."

Well, that was…much nicer than what I'd been imagining. Smoke, apparently, didn't agree. Because, before I could toss out another question, his voice turned scathing.

"Thom likes to play alpha. But he's not. A real alpha wins his territory in battle. Thom *bought* this place. Like a gas lease. Or a politician's votes. He thinks he's so clever, but all it will take is one strong wolf and, *bam*, he's out! Guess who won't have a paw then?"

Smoke snickered into his chest and I drifted into the left lane to pass a truck hauling heavy equipment on its flatbed. "That's nice," I lied. "But I actually don't care about the twist in your tail. What I want to know is why you killed the human woman last night."

"Human woman?"

"Janet Allegra."

And now Smoke went silent. I glanced over, wondering if taking too much blood messed with a werewolf's cognitive abilities.

But Smoke appeared no less cogent than previously. If anything, he seemed to be blinking his way out of the blood daze. His right hand crept toward the passenger door…

…And, yet again, I swiped up blood, letting the red ooze across my tongue and teeth as I demanded. "Did you kill a woman last night? Yes or no."

Smoke's answer came fast and smelled like truth to me. "Of course not. What kind of creep do you think I am?"

Chapter 7

The jury was still out on Smoke's creepishness. But I dropped him off at a truck stop, swallowing a little extra blood to make sure he thought he'd chosen the spot under his own volition. Then I zipped back up the ramp onto the highway and floored it back toward the Full Moon Saloon.

Because I'd screwed up. I'd disregarded my boss's explicit orders and chosen wrong when presented with a two-man lineup. Now was the time to set my error right.

Speaking of errors, as I drove I succumbed to the urge to cleanse my soiled conscience. "Text Mai," I told my cell phone. Then: *"Do you think it's ever kosher to drink blood from random werewolves?"*

Her return text came fast, sounding only slightly odd in the phone's computer-generated voice. *"What happened? Where are you? We can help."*

"Unwrap the knot in your knickers," I had my phone reply. *"That was a hypothetical question only."*

"Like the time you hypothetically broke a $10,000 vase in the Raven twins' mansion?"

I grinned despite myself, remembering the antique I'd brushed up against and shattered during a game of hide and seek at Charlie and Jessie's house after school one year. I'd been so terrified at the idea of fessing up, knowing that Mai (there'd been no Gunner in the picture then) couldn't afford to pay for a replacement. My first impulse had been to literally sweep the shards under the rug.

But the rug—another antique—bulged like a sated boa constrictor. So I'd texted Mai and, at her insistence, told the twins' mom the truth.

To my surprise, Mrs. Raven had hugged me so hard the air whooshed out of my lungs. *"I hated that vase, but it's from my mother-in-law so it had to be on display constantly. I owe you one."*

I hoped the issue of Thom and blood drinking would have an equally happy ending. And…I was now pulling up in front of the Full Moon Saloon.

So—*"Gotta go,"* I texted Mai. *"More later."* Then I pulled into one of the diagonal parking spaces, looked around, and winced.

Because flashing neon lights above the front door meant the bar was now open. Which in turn meant I'd need a plan to get Thom alone before I could arrest him. The question was—where to do the deed and how to tempt a murderer into isolation now that there were far more people around?

For a moment, I considered heading for that tantalizing window around back the way I had the first time. But the ledge I'd been so proud to use an hour ago had crumbled beneath my feet halfway to the opening. Plus, I'd had enough of taking off-book risks today. It felt more kosher to talk my way through the public area.

Assuming I didn't go off half-cocked the way I had with Smoke, that is. To that end, I stayed put for a moment while visually scoping out the place.

The public part of the bar was sleepy this early in the day. Two fifty-something men in Carhartts and feed-store caps were parked at a table by the plate-glass window while a suited guy in his thirties hunched over a pint near an interior door. Each man's body language subtly marked him as human, and so did the posture of the woman who'd brought me and Charlie drinks last night and who now danced to music on her earbuds behind the bar.

She was the one I'd need to talk around if I wanted above-board access to the upstairs. Luckily, from the look of her skin-tight dress and carefully applied makeup, she'd be easy to bond with once I deployed the appropriate tools.

So I kicked out of my comfortable sneakers and turned my star ball into crazy high stilettos. Then, for the second time, strode in the front door of the Full Moon Saloon.

"Those shoes look like agony." Last night, Dixie Lee either hadn't donned her name tag or I hadn't noticed it. Today, I paid more attention to the woman who, although human, had been left in charge of a werewolf bar.

She was a scant decade older than me, with kind eyes and a soft southern accent that made me expect an offer of sweet tea. Instead, she went for the usual server question. "What can I get for you today?"

I donned my best smile as I leaned in closer, keeping my words truthful so the acrid scent of a lie wouldn't derail my efforts. Because that guy in a suit behind me? His body language had seemed human from outside but the scent of fur slipped into my nostrils the moment I strode past.

"This is really embarrassing," I told Dixie Lee. "But there's something upstairs I forgot earlier. Do you think I could pop around and get it now?"

Dixie Lee's eyes widened while a strangled sound emerged from the werewolf. Seemed like Charlie had been right. The Full Moon Saloon's proprietor didn't engage in hookups often, or maybe at all.

"You and Thom?" Dixie Lee sputtered. Then she seemed to remember she was a professional and shut down the surprise. "I'd like to help you out, honey, but Thom's not up there. He left half an hour ago."

While I was debriefing Smoke. Why hadn't Scarlet alerted me?

Most likely because she'd sent away her eyes on the ground as soon as my car pulled into the alley. To protect me if I had to utilize my kitsune nature on her command.

Which was thoughtful...but also meant my unwise choice of nabbing the wrong suspect was going to make this job much harder than it should have been. Still, I had confidence Dixie Lee could lead me to my target now.

Slipping my toes out of shoes that actually supported my feet perfectly, I reached down to rub at not-really-aching arches. Dixie Lee's face once again crinkled up in sympathy and I pushed a little harder for information. "Could you maybe give me his number?"

This time, the lone werewolf joined our conversation even though he didn't move from his spot by what I was guessing was the door to the Moon Room. "Thom doesn't take many days off," he observed. Like Dixie Lee, he had a noticeable accent, but his I didn't recognize. German? Russian? "If he didn't leave you a way to contact him," the werewolf continued, "well, maybe that was a hint."

"Bertrand." Dixie Lee frowned over my shoulder. "Be nice. I can at least call and check."

I hid my triumphant grin behind a hand as Dixie Lee dialed. Listened shamelessly to Thom's greeting after the third ring.

"I'm busy. What do you need?"

The words were terse. Even a human should have known better than to bait an annoyed werewolf.

Dixie Lee didn't know better. Instead, her voice turned teasing. "You left the bar early last night. What were you up to?"

A growl came through, then words. "None of your business."

Well, that was clear. No wonder Bertrand cleared his throat uncomfortably and Dixie Lee finally acted like the prey animal she was.

"I'm sorry to have bothered you. I'll let you go...."

I expected Thom to hang up. Instead, breath flared as if he'd sighed into the phone. His words softened. "You're not bothering me. Is there a problem at the bar?"

In the pause that followed, a strange noise emerged from the phone's speaker. One that resembled Grub's response while losing a tickle fight. One that made me rethink the earlier growl.

Because Gunner had always said his son sounded like a howling hyena. And, in southwest Virginia, the only place you found hyenas was in a zoo.

Tilting my head until I caught Dixie Lee's attention, I mouthed: "I can come back later."

Her relief was instantaneous. "No," she told her werewolf boss. "There's no problem." Then, after hanging up, she shrugged at me. "Sorry. It didn't seem like the right time."

Only it had been the right time. I'd gotten exactly what I'd come for. I knew where Thom was.

Chapter 8

My phone had exploded with texts while I was in the bar. All from Mai. All full of worry that I hadn't intended to instigate. All dancing around the same conclusion: no, she didn't think it was ever kosher to consume werewolf blood.

But she'd stopped texting several minutes ago, leaving Grub to twist my heart strings in her absence. Not in text form. Instead, Mai had sent a video clip of my nephew hugging his mother's knees while she filmed him from above.

"Tell Auntie Kira what you just told me," Mai suggested.

"I said Kira will come home if she gets into trouble. We'll take good care of her and she'll bring me gummy bears and caramel and chocolate and...."

The clip ended with Grub still reciting his favorite candies. And I couldn't decide whether to smile or to cry. Because none of those snacks were nearly as sweet as my nephew...while if I made the wrong move and sullied the Fairwood name, I might be forced to leave our pack rather than bring trouble back down on my sister's head.

Not that I intended to fail. I'd made one small misstep, letting Thom go while debriefing Smoke. But the real murderer was even now veering further than I had from the path of cleverness, allowing me plenty of time to catch back up.

Because the sounds caught over the phone—the feline growl, the hyena laugh—both suggested Thom had stepped into the stereotypical villain's downfall. He'd returned to the scene of the crime.

So I nosed my car east into the valley dipping out of town. And I headed toward the Creation Kingdom Zoo.

As best I could tell from the information my phone recited during the short drive over, this wasn't the type of city zoo I was used to. Instead, Creation Kingdom had been started as one family's passion project then grew as Gate City exploded in size over the last decade. Now, the organization was a mix between a petting zoo and a safari park.

The business was also closed, I saw as I pulled up in front.

Closed when it should have been open, presumably because of the dead body found in the lion pen not so many hours earlier. There was, however, a lone truck perfectly centered between two lines in the parking area, a pickup I vaguely remembered seeing behind the bar when I'd listened in on Smoke and Thom's conversation earlier in the day.

Yes, my target was here without obvious backup. I could make the surreptitious collar my boss had ordered and ensure my sister remained proud of me...assuming Thom didn't find me first.

Ignoring the knowledge that a wolf's teeth were three times as large as mine in fox form, I shed my clothes, shifted, then scampered along the outside of the fence seeking entrance. *There.* The scent of a heavier canine led me straight to a hole large enough to run through. Tufts of hair clinging to the edges promised that, for Thom, this wide avenue had been a tight squeeze.

I shivered, not sure why I was letting today's target get to me when I'd taken down several other werewolves over the past few weeks with very little hassle. Perhaps it was the dominance Thom had exuded when he'd sent Smoke packing. Or the strange attraction that hadn't entirely faded from my belly despite knowledge of the dark nature of the bartender's after-hours pursuits.

Or Scarlet's recommendation that I use blood to make the collar. Mai's quick negative response when I felt her out about the ethics of utilizing that kitsune power.

Whatever the reason, I'd committed to this job and I'd get it done before shivers turned into full-on stupidity. Unfortunately, the trail turned cold on the other side of the fence. Thom's aroma was lost amid tiger piss and camel spit, sweet corn and decaying venison.

So I'd hunt the way a fox did. Leaping from foothold to foothold, I was on top of the nearest shed within seconds, surveying the scene before my eyes.

Animal enclosures spread out in all directions. Most were large and all had barns to allow the inhabitants to get in out of the weather. Thom could be any-where, although the lion habitat would be the obvious location to start looking. I'd....

Movement sparked out of the corner of my eye. Closer than I'd thought and at my level.

I spun, only to find a giraffe tilting its head curiously as it considered me. Broad nostrils snuffled hot air in my face before the animal wandered away.

Okay, so hunting like a fox wasn't going to work after all. In a zoo, the inhab-itants were constantly moving, all catching my attention. I wouldn't find Thom by lingering on my safe little perch.

Instead, I descended back to ground level, never mind the sensation of predator eyes raising hairs on the back of my neck worse than ever. I tracked that particular sensation to the panther habitat, catching the glint of feline pupils following as I sidled past.

I was slowing my breathing and reminding myself that the predators were all in cages when I ran straight into an uncaged wolf.

Chapter 9

Thom was the biggest wolf I'd ever seen, with the possible exception of my brother-in-law. And bulky, as if he spent hours of every day running four-legged...which I guess wasn't so hard here in southwest Virginia where, outside city limits, trees outnumbered people thousands to one.

Size wasn't the only factor stacking the deck against me either. As Thom's icepick eyes met mine, something more than fear trickled down my spine.

This wolf was intriguing. Enticing. A danger to my purpose in joining the Lawkeepers.

Grub, I reminded myself. *My unborn niece.* Both were more important than animal magnetism. Even if both the animal and the magnet were pretty intense.

Swallowing down attraction, I abruptly understood why Scarlet had suggested I use the blood approach. I wasn't so sure I could bring Thom in with my sword alone. Blood would even the odds, but I'd find the liquid tough to acquire given our size differential and Thom's heavy fur quotient. There, though, my sword would come in handy. Not forcing Thom to surrender, but extending my reach so I could harvest that necessary tablespoonful of blood.

Before I could second-guess my orders another time, I blinked and magic suffused me. My perspective twisted as I rose to two-legged prominence. Now I was taller than any wolf, even Thom's. Plus, I had a magical blade in my hand.

Vision had fuzzed for a moment while I was between forms, but I slapped my eyelids back open before they were really ready and prepared to fight. Only...I wasn't gazing down on bared teeth the way I expected to be. Instead, I was considering furless skin, six-pack abs, and portions of the masculine anatomy that weren't really kosher to stare at even if you're a shifter and often wind up naked in mixed company.

"Oops." My cheeks reddened as my gaze resolutely lifted to Thom's neck level. And, to my surprise, he chuckled then let me off the hook.

"Easy mistake to make during a shift. I assume you're dropping by to check over the lion enclosure? It's been scrubbed clean by your people. But there might be something present I've missed."

He turned away and I was startled enough to fall into step as we wound back in the direction he'd come from. Was Thom really pretending that he'd entered the zoo to hunt the murderer just like I had?

Well, if he was willing to talk, then so was I. "You expected me?"

Thom's words turned slightly awkward in their carefulness. "It was clear a Lawkeeper would come given the military connection. I was hoping you'd be the one they sent."

Was Thom saying he'd killed a woman to tempt me back to Gate City? I shook my head to clear away the crazy and responded the way I would have to a non-murderer. "You knew I was a Lawkeeper. And you're not spooked by my fur form."

Were the tips of Thom's ears faintly red now, or was I merely wishing I hadn't been the only one to embarrass myself? His mutter suggested the former. "I may have looked you up."

"In the sixty minutes since you were informed of a murder in your territory?"

Yes, that really was redness blushing Thom's epidermis. A tantalizing, spicy aroma drifted off him—embarrassment combined with the sweetness of interest. He cleared his throat. "Before that. Last night."

And now we were outside the lion pen, currently devoid of big cats but clearly marked with an educational sign I didn't bother skimming. Damp beneath my feet suggested Thom was right about the deep cleaning, although I doubted Lawkeepers had been the ones responsible. The more likely culprit was standing by my side.

I needed to remember that. I had to trust Scarlet's legwork even if my instincts screamed that Thom wouldn't be stupid enough to revisit his body-stashing location the day after killing a woman. The man in front of me was the enemy, not some cute guy I'd met at a bar.

Even though I had met him at a bar. And he was cute, especially when a blush contrasted so adorably with his prominent nose and masculine chin.

I clenched my teeth, forcing focus. But, externally, I maintained my smile. No need to let Thom know his aw-shucks offensive had splatted against the hard wall of reality.

Instead, I leaned against the metal railing Thom had already chosen as his support, sidling closer until the air between us warmed from proximity of living skin. "About last night." I kept my voice light. "You left before we could trade numbers."

And...something about my statement must have come out wrong. Because for the first time since we'd stumbled upon each other outside the panther habitat, the brilliance of Thom's blue eyes clouded. "Trade numbers," he repeated.

My sword was still clenched in my right fist, so I lifted my left hand to trail a provocative line down his forearm as I elaborated. "So I could call you." Tilting my head, I peered up at Thom through my lashes. "Or so you could call me."

I kept my breath carefully even as I tried to reel him in...and the effort wasn't working. Thom's muscles were so tense beneath my finger that they might as well have been the iron railing. His scent had turned sharp and alert, the drowsy seduction I'd thought we both felt sloughing off faster than our shifts between animal fur and human skin.

When he opened his mouth, Thom's words were hard. "You're not investigating the murder, are you? You're investigating me."

"Who says I can't do both?" As I spoke, I twisted my star-ball sword into an entirely visible and tangible band of whip-like flexibility. Flinging the restraint around Thom's torso and pulling tight, he was caught just like that.

Which, come to think of it, would have been an easier solution than drawing his blood. Had Scarlet not realized I had other kitsune powers to call upon?

Tabling that issue, I tensed, waiting for the inevitable struggle. Only, it never came. Instead, Thom's icepick eyes merely watched as I grabbed his shoulders and pulled myself in closer.

I didn't need blood to restrain him right at this instant. But the drive to Roanoke took a few hours, during which time my focus might slip and my star-ball magic slip with it. I guessed I could see Scarlet's point.

Still, I hesitated as Mai's lips twisted in my memory the same way they had when I'd hidden my report card rather than admit that I'd failed sixth-grade science. Only, this wasn't anything like that, I reminded myself. My boss had okayed me using kitsune trump cards. And Thom was a *murderer*.

Plus, I wouldn't take much. One little nip, a modicum of blood, and physical restraints would no longer be required....

Only, it didn't quite work out that way.

Instead, the instant my lips touched Thom's neck, contact awoke an awareness more intense than the caress of his icepick eyes. His skin was salty but also succulent, tempting me to lick instead of bite. To sooth my fingers across those muscles until they loosened then flexed with pure pleasure....

Blinking myself back on track, I forced my teeth to sharpen. Tore more than I'd intended to. Blood poured out in a steady stream.

And the memory of Mai, once again, made me hesitate. Now her eyebrows were drawing together the same way they had this morning after Grub's impetuous invasion of my bedroom. My nephew's action had been harmless, but mine wasn't. The step I was about to take felt very wrong.

And, finally, Thom spoke, his voice rumbling through his body, across his skin, and into my belly. "You need to prove I'm innocent. I get that. Drink then ask whatever you want."

Thom hadn't been shocked into stillness, I now realized. Instead, he'd made a choice to let me do whatever I wanted.

Odd. But maybe he realized my star-ball magic outmatched his brute werewolf strength. Maybe this was just another way of messing with my mind and evading responsibility for his own actions.

Whatever the reason, his acquiescence thawed the cold ball of doubt Mai's memory had created. I dipped back down to that red glimmer and took a sip....

Thom's blood was nothing like Smoke's. Instead, it was invigorating but so much more than invigorating. Irresistibly sweet. Heady with a depth I'd expect from a top-shelf chardonnay.

After that, I stopped sipping and started gulping. I lost track of what I was drinking. I couldn't stop....

Only, I must have. Sometime. And my star-ball whip must have loosened and faded back into me in the process.

I must have lost my balance. Likely around the time when everything went black.

Because I came back to myself who knows how long afterwards with one of Thom's arms wrapped around my torso. I was curled up in his lap, my head tucked against the front of his bare shoulder. Thom hummed a soft melody, his free hand stroking my hair.

I was in the embrace of a murderer. And I didn't want the moment to end.

My breathing must have changed though because Thom observed: "You're awake." I started to pull back only to have his enfolding arm tighten. "Mud," he observed. "Allow me."

Then he was rising with me in his arms as easily as if I'd been a child. He was right. The spot where we'd wound up was a mucky mess...and Thom had been sitting right in it. His legs were smeared in the gunk, while I was pristine.

Which meant nothing. I told myself that as he set me down carefully, my bare feet coming to rest on a paved walkway that was damp but gunk-free. I swayed, strangely woozy. As if I'd lost blood rather than stealing far too much of it from the man who supported me now.

My gaze flew to the wound on Thom's neck, the wound that had stopped bleeding and started scabbing. He must have held me for quite a while. Sitting in the mud that—now that I no longer needed to scramble through it to get away from a presumed murderer—I could admit smelled more like manure than earth.

Finally, I cleared my throat and spoke. "Why are you still here?"

"You collapsed." Thom reached out, the back of his hand brushing against my forehead. "How are you feeling?"

I was feeling deeply confused. As relaxed as if I'd just woken in a warm bed on a lazy Sunday morning while also well aware that I had a daunting and unsavory job ahead.

The job won out. I straightened my spine and demanded: "Where did you go when you left the bar last night?"

Chapter 10

Thom's mouth flattened. "You'll want more blood to assure yourself I'm telling the truth on this one."

He lowered his head, exposing the scabbed wound. His scent pushed toward me even stronger, enfolding me in its embrace.

I wanted what he was offering. No, *want* wasn't the right word. I *needed* it. My mouth watered and I leaned forward, craving that blood with every iota of my being.

But I stopped just shy of his shoulder. I had no idea why I'd passed out and I didn't intend to do so again.

Instead, I forced myself backwards. Hardened my voice. "Just tell me. I'll smell a lie."

Thom cocked his head. "And you couldn't do that the first time?" When I remained silent, he shrugged and offered the most unlikely explanation imaginable. "Heartburn."

"You, who never take time off, left the Full Moon Saloon in the middle of a busy Friday night because you were suffering from heartburn?" I was tempted to change my mind and use the blood approach after all. But Thom shook his head, and this time his explanation made more sense.

"Dad had pains in his chest. I took him to the ER but it turned out to be a bad case of heartburn. I'd prefer not to spread his business around."

The scents that curled off Thom as he spoke were many and varied, but none had the acrid burn of mistruth. "Then why are you here?" I demanded.

"To find out what happened. A woman was killed in my territory." Thom seemed to grow taller with each word, his eyes turning from glacial ultramarine to spark-spitting fire. He was furious. "I understand this is a Lawkeeper case. But I don't intend to let the culprit become a repeat offender while I wait for the slow wheels of justice to turn."

This time, I believed him. I believed him even though the facts I'd been gathering no longer added up to anything coherent.

Which meant I needed more facts. I eyed the alpha in front of me, and this time he sighed and repeated his initial statement. "You want blood." Only he didn't stop there; he fixed the problem I hadn't mentioned aloud. "We'll go back to the parking lot and lock you in your car. Then you can use your kitsune magic while staying safe even if you pass out."

Our return journey to the vehicles was silent. Thom hadn't missed the fact I trailed behind, star-ball sword once again at the ready. He hadn't missed the fact that, when we came to the hole in the fence, I didn't shift to four legs until he was already on the other side.

No wonder he ditched fangs and claws the moment our toenails clicked on pavement. No wonder he strode away from me rather than hovering close.

"*Get in your car,*" he ordered once twenty feet of air separated us.

"Alpha compulsions don't work against kitsunes," I countered, standing my ground.

Thom's eyelids lowered halfway. He waited a beat, then added: "Please."

Only then did I obey him. Sliding into the front seat of my vehicle, I rolled down the window far enough to reach through.

But Thom didn't come closer. Instead, he shook his head. "That's too much room. I could grab you."

Never mind that he hadn't grabbed me when I was comatose outside the lion enclosure. Or, well, I guess he *had* grabbed me. But only to keep me out of the mud.

Still, Thom was as immovable as a brick wall. So I tapped the button until the air space between window and door frame was barely large enough for a finger to slide through. And, finally, Thom sidled closer, slow and careful as if he thought I might spook.

"Door locked?" he asked. I'd already flicked the relevant button, but I pressed it again so he could hear the gears engage. Only then did he nod. "Okay."

As he spoke, he picked at the thin scab on his neck with a broad thumbnail. Scooping up blood on his forefinger, he slid the single digit through the gap above my window glass.

And I couldn't help myself. I rose up on my knees to draw blood and fingertip into my mouth, holding the warmth in place with my lips. Licking.... Sucking....

Thom's eyelids lowered further and he growled. Or maybe he purred. Whatever the sound, it combined with his blood to hit me hard and low and wet.

I lost some time. Only a little. I didn't pass out, but I did fall into Thom's eyes.

They were no longer icepicks. More like moonbeams sparking through a gap in the clouds to lift me out of darkness. Like warm hands buoying me up.

I might have drifted in that daze forever if Thom hadn't mustered words. "You can't talk when you have"—his voice hitched—"my finger in your mouth."

He was right, but I curled my lips tighter around his skin anyway. I couldn't release him. I didn't want to.

"You have reasons for being here," Thom growled.

Reasons. Reluctantly, I remembered.

Justice for a dead innocent. A future for my unborn niece.

Thom's finger popped out of my mouth and words emerged along with it. "Did you kill Janet Allegra?"

Blue eyes that had been bright one moment earlier glazed over just a little. Enough to prove I had power over him. But Thom's answer was firm, simple. "No."

"Were you involved in her murder?"

"Not that I'm aware of."

"Do you know who killed her?"

"I don't."

Back inside the zoo, Thom's scent had said the same thing. So his answers shouldn't have come as a surprise now.

Still, I was floored. Glad to be kneeling on the front seat of my car because I wasn't sure I could have kept my feet if I'd been standing.

Smoke hadn't killed Janet Allegra and Thom hadn't either. So who was the murderer on the loose?

Chapter 11

"I don't know."

Thom's words proved that I'd muttered my question aloud. The lack of emotion in his response suggested he was still being forced to reply by the gift of his blood.

Which felt very, very wrong. Like I'd turned on stadium lights that totally washed away the poetry of moon shadows. Like I'd stolen mysteries that weren't mine to steal.

"You're released," I murmured and Thom sagged against the side of the vehicle. I swallowed, residual sweetness on my tongue souring at the sight of his strength shattered. I hesitated, then offered: "Do you need any help?"

Thom shook his head, tried to speak, then faltered. Even after clearing his throat and summoning words, his voice was hoarse. "Give me a minute. Please."

So I did. I gave him a minute while I grabbed onto the only thread I had available to tug on. I pulled out my phone and I called my boss.

Scarlet answered immediately. And this time I was grateful she wasn't a fan of small talk, because I didn't need to beat around the bush before asking: "Who did the legwork on this case?"

"Rupert. Is there a problem?"

Rupert. The office asshole. Was he enough of an asshole to kill a woman then implicate Thom in the murder?

I wasn't sure, but I would be. Soon.

As long as I was given time to investigate that is. "There might be a problem," I answered, keeping my tone light. "But I can handle it. It'll just take a little longer than expected to bring in the perp."

Scarlet sighed, the gust of air loud with disappointment but her subsequent words promising support anyway. "Rupert and I can be there in a few hours if you need backup."

"I have this covered."

"Don't be a martyr."

"Don't be a mother hen. I want to prove myself."

"You have twenty-four hours to collect the murderer or I'm coming down."

The tension in my neck unknotted. Twenty-four hours was good. In twenty-four hours, Rupert would be home reveling in his stolen coffee, leaving someone else to act as Scarlet's backup.

Assuming, that is, I hadn't cracked the case wide open and stuffed Rupert into a cell by that point. "Understood," I agreed before ending the call.

Then, flipping the lock on the door I pushed it open and gazed up at Thom. He'd found his footing while I was calling Scarlet. Now he was once again steady, strong, dependable.

Exactly the partner I needed to prove to everyone that a kitsune made an excellent Lawkeeper. "You and I," I observed, "have evidence to collect."

Rather than meeting my gaze, Thom peered over my shoulder at the road. But his question proved he'd been listening. "This Rupert. Who is he?"

"A coworker," I answered, seared by his eyes when they slid back to mine. Thom's gaze was resolutely polite, not dipping below my chin. Still, I shivered, averted my face, and babbled. "If you give me your number, I'll text over his photo. You can call your pack together and show it around while I dig into things back in Roanoke."

The icepick returned. I couldn't avoid it any longer. Only once I'd mustered the courage to look him in the face did Thom speak to me. "No."

"No to what?"

"No to all of that. But, mostly, no to splitting up. You haven't thought this through."

"I haven't?"

"You haven't." His voice was a low rumble. "What do you think the purpose might be for killing a woman while you were in town then sending you back to investigate?"

"I don't know what you mean." But, as soon as he said it, I did know. Thom thought *I* was the one being framed. "But I was sent to bring *you* in."

And yet...wasn't it odd that Charlie had contacted me out of the blue and asked me to meet her in Gate City? Odder still that she said I'd been the one to make contact in the first place.

"Do you mind?" I motioned at my phone and Thom shrugged.

"Be my guest."

He retreated a few steps, reaching into his truck for a towel then twisting to swipe at the mud coating the backs of his thighs. For a moment, I was unable to take my eyes off his rippling muscles. Then I remembered that Thom was giving me space to investigate, so I took the opening. Quickly, I typed out a text to my friend.

"What made you want to get together this week?"

Charlie's response was quick. Clearly, she wasn't engrossed in her Saturday evening entertainment. *"Your email, obviously. You said you were going to be in town."*

"I did? Could you forward it back to me?"

I flipped over to my personal email, found nothing. Tapped my fingernail against the phone screen as a car crunched past on the road fifty feet away from us. Either the internet was being unbelievably slow or something had happened to the email Charlie promised to forward.

Well, there was one other possibility. To cover my bases, I checked my work account.

And there it was. A quick, cheery note with the exact facts Charlie had just relayed. Words I knew I'd never typed out.

Only, when I went to my sent-messages folder and scrolled through it...there was the email. In an account I never used when contacting friends and family. One I often left my computer logged into at work.

A notification brought me back over to my texts. *"You weren't going to be in town last night?"*

"I came to Gate City to meet you. But I'm here now. Are you home and available?"

"Available but not at home. I'm on the Base, hanging with Eli." She included an address, information for picking up a visitor's badge at the main gate.

"On my way," I told her, then I looked up at Thom.

I expected him to be fidgeting at being ignored for so long. Or, given the patience that seemed to flow through him like ocean waves, simply waiting to be clued in.

Only Thom was doing neither. He hadn't even pulled on clothes, although he did appear to be manure-free now. Instead, his gaze was once again focused over my shoulder, intent upon something I couldn't see.

I was used to werewolves being easily distracted by passing birds and rabbits, but this felt different. Thom's back was a little too straight. His jaw muscles bulged with tension.

I let my phone drift back down to my side. "What's wrong?"

"That's the third time a blue Honda has driven past."

Chapter 12

Now that I paid attention, I could hear receding tires on gravel. Could hear what sounded like a car turning around just out of sight.

If so, we had mere seconds before the Honda would breach the trees again. My eyes turned just a little vulpine, brightening the evening dimness as I awoke to the hunt.

"I didn't recognize the driver, but you might." As he spoke, Thom took my hand and drew me out from behind the car and closer to the road.

"What, we're going to stand here and gawk? Naked? What if it's a human?"

The deep hum of a car engine was drawing closer. Soon the vehicle would pass out of the forest and into view.

"The window was down. I smelled fur."

"Okay, so it's a shifter. That's worse for me. If Rupert has an ally here, I can't look like I'm cozy with the murder suspect I'm supposed to be bringing in."

Our chatting time was fleeing fast, but Thom listened. He dropped my hand, dipped his head until our eyes were level. "We'll make it appear that you're otherwise occupied. I promise not to hurt you."

Not to *hurt* me?

Then the hand that had been so gentle one second earlier bit into my shoulder. The other lurched up even higher, clenching hard around the back of my neck.

Thom shook me with the same intensity he brought to everything. My teeth rattled like seeds in a dried gourd despite the fact he barely seemed to be exerting any effort.

And even though I knew this was an act, that Thom was pretending to attack me while using one broad palm at my neck to protect me from whiplash, adrenaline spiked. Except for that moment in the zoo, I'd never been scared of Thom's physical strength before. Sure, he was a big guy and an alpha werewolf. But he'd seemed careful, restrained.

Now, as the first stars in the darkening sky streaked into jittering confusion, it became painfully clear how wrong I'd been.

Fear suffused my mouth, salty and bitter. I struggled and made absolutely no headway. Tried for a head butt only to find myself being spun around until my back was to his front and the crook of his elbow pulled snug around my throat.

Thom wasn't choking me...yet. But the vertebrae of my neck felt painfully fragile. Breath wheezed in through a preemptively tightening windpipe.

Using my star ball was a last resort, yet I didn't even think. Just grabbed for my inherent magic, thrusting it between us in an amorphous ball of terror that wasn't a sword or any other shape that required mental focus. Just spikes and needles and get away, get away, get away!

Thom grunted but didn't release me. Instead, he did something I couldn't see, and my star ball was rolling off across the parking lot. In its physical form, the star ball was visible to both of us, but only I was aware of the results of being separated. I kicked out frantically, trying to hook my foot around my energy source even as distance weakened my muscles like spaghetti melting into boiling water.

No dice. It was too far away to touch.

Breath fuzzed against my ear. "Look now."

The words made no sense as I panted, unable to think of anything else to fight with. I tried to summon my star ball back toward me with sheer force of will. But strength was draining out through my bare feet. The sharp gravel on the ground grew painfully cold.

"*Look,*" Thom repeated, this time imbuing his words with alpha bite.

And I did look. At the blue car that had already rolled past us, at the driver who was craning his head to peer back at the battle I'd lost.

At long last, I remembered we were playacting. I wasn't in any danger. I was instead meant to be doing something. But what?

My vision was tunneling down toward darkness. My legs wouldn't have held me if Thom wasn't supporting my weight.

"Hang on for ten more seconds," Thom murmured. He was carrying me toward my star ball, as if I'd told him that was what I needed even though I knew I hadn't. Somehow, he managed to make it look like I was struggling even though I'd gone entirely limp.

Then the car was gone and my star ball was sliding up through my skin and restarting frozen lungs and I was digesting the fact that one of our field agents—not Rupert, no one whose name I knew—had just driven past what appeared to be my mauling without stopping to offer help.

My explanation came out as a gasping exhale. "That was a Lawkeeper. Nobody I've met personally. But I've seen him around."

I wavered a little, but managed to stay upright. Thom eyed me, his lips thinning as I imperceptibly flinched away from the hand he'd extended. "I hurt you."

I shook my head. He hadn't hurt me. But instinct had kicked in so much that the adrenaline in my blood now refused to listen to sense.

And none of that was relevant when there appeared to be two shifters arrayed against us rather than simply one. "The Honda will be back," I warned. "We need to focus."

Without acknowledging my words, Thom strode to my car. Only after picking up my phone from where I'd dropped it on the front seat did he speak. "Pictures?"

"Not of this guy. I've only seen him a couple of times in passing. I don't even know his name."

The phone spun between us. I was surprised when my lax fingers managed to grab it out of the air.

"The photo of your other coworker will do for now," Thom observed. "Text it to this number."

I paged through office snapshots, sending the only one I had—of Rupert glowering in a corner during a birthday party—to the digits Thom rattled off. Then I waited, expecting an alert to come from his truck. When nothing chimed, I guessed: "You're turning the issue over to your beta?"

"Beta?"

"You know. A pack leader's second."

Thom's brows drew together while he shook his head slowly. "Gate City doesn't host a pack."

And that issue wasn't exactly relevant. Not when the rumble of tires on gravel was once again approaching. Had the Lawkeeper changed his mind and decided to provide assistance? Or, more likely, was he just making another pass to see whether I'd survived a struggle that must have looked pretty bad from the road?

Thom's fingers settled over mine, and this time I didn't jerk away from him. He slipped my phone out of my hand, raising one eyebrow as he turned it over a couple of times.

"They could track this," he observed. "We can't take it with us. But we can't leave the evidence of your meeting with Charlie behind."

"How did you...?" Oh, my texts were right there in front of him. I wasn't quite as recovered as I'd thought I was, the aftermath of my separation from my star ball acted like molasses permeating my brain. "Yeah."

"Any personal mementos on here you'll miss?"

I had no clue what Thom was getting at, but headlights swept the road at the edge of the trees so I answered anyway. "No."

"Alright then." And just like that, Thom brought my phone down across his knee, cracking the plastic with a retort like a gunshot. He ripped out the guts as easily as if the phone had been a dinner roll before striding over to his truck, sending a quick text, then repeating the endeavor on his own device.

Only after the jumble of mangled electronics had been dropped in a puddle did he turn back to face me. "Go."

"Go?"

"I'm bait. They take me in and I'll see what I can figure out from the inside while you head to ground." Without waiting for an answer, he motioned back toward the zoo. "Run due east. You'll find a road on the other side of the ridge. Dad will pick you up there and take you somewhere off the radar."

Now, finally, cold air swept away the molasses. "No way." I stepped back up to Thom, wishing he had a collar I could grab onto and shake some sense into him. "You're the one who said we should stick together."

"I want you safe," Thom growled. "Me staying behind keeps you safe. *Go.*"

My muscles twitched with the urge to run, but not because of Thom's alpha order. The blue Honda's bumper had passed the tree line now. I could see the Lawkeeper and he could see me.

Still, I stood my ground. "Either we leave together or we stay together."

Thom's nostrils flared, eyes narrowing. Alphas didn't like to be disobeyed and I certainly couldn't physically overpower him the way he had me.

But...he pondered for one endless moment only. Then he was wolf and I was fox and we were running. Sprinting into the darkness, away from the organization I'd allied with for the good of my family and pack.

Chapter 13

For several long minutes, I lost track of where I was running to and from. All I noticed was the *with* part.

Because it had been months since I'd donned fur and let my muscles extend beside another shifter. Months based in Roanoke, going out on jobs then coming home to an empty apartment where, at most, I could shift indoors and stalk the occasional mouse.

"When do we hunt?" I'd asked Scarlet my second week of employment. Technically, she had an open-door policy, but she always seemed annoyed when anyone dared to walk all the way into her office without an engraved invitation. So I merely leaned against her door jamb now.

"Hunt?" Scarlet frowned as she glanced up from her laptop. The pen behind her ear had left a streak across one sharp cheekbone. Her tone of voice made it clear that she was busy and my question was frivolous at best.

Only it wasn't. Hunts were how werewolves blew off steam. Hunts were what kept us sane.

So I persevered. *"You know. Fur. Rocks. Crescent moon. Catching critters and building bonds."*

For a moment, my boss seemed even more confused than she'd been initially. Later, a coworker confided that Scarlet had been raised by a human mother who dropped her kid like a hot potato the first time she shifted. The Lawkeeper organization had given Scarlet a place to belong, but she had no clan to go home to. She might never have enjoyed a wild run through the forest alongside other shifters. No wonder the look on her face was blank for a good long while.

At the time, though, all I understood was the astringent scent that coated Scarlet's words as understanding dawned. *"You're talking pack."*

"Precisely."

She'd shrugged, her attention wandering toward her computer screen. Still, she graced me with an answer, if not the one I'd hoped for. *"Most people go home on the weekends. You could do the same, schedule permitting. Or you could run with Rupert. He's from the west coast, so he's usually around."*

I certainly didn't intend to run with Rupert. Unfortunately, as the most recent hire, my duties never seemed to provide two days off together. Not enough time to return to Mai's pack and mean it.

So I'd stayed human, save for frivolous rodent snatching and the seriousness of job targets. Until tonight.

Tonight, when a wolf's hot breath blew behind then beside me. A wolf who matched his pace to mine, despite his significantly longer legs.

The breeze seemed to waft us forward in tandem. An owl hooted in the distance. Leaves crunched beneath our paws.

We wouldn't catch much when every footfall sounded like bubble wrap popping. But, ahead, a log beckoned.

I leapt onto its mossy spine and ran straight and true down the length of the elevated highway. Not really hunting. Just reveling in the damp scent of crumbling wood and the sudden silence of my rapid footsteps.

Thom wasn't as quiet. He hadn't joined me atop the log, and now a wolf shoulder nudged my shoulder. Not enough to disrupt my balance, just enough to be companionable. To prove that we were currently of a height despite the disparate statures of wolf and fox.

His flank slid against my flank. A tremor of something warm and secretive thrilled through me. This was nothing like running with my pack mates. This was....

And I remembered what had slipped my pack-hungry vulpine brain. We weren't currently hunters but rather hunted. The danger lay behind rather than at the point of our teeth.

The danger, and also the hint of what we'd stumbled into. That Lawkeeper whose name I didn't know might harbor a clue about who the murderer was truly targeting—Thom or me or both of us. My coworker's reaction to our absence would be telling. We shouldn't flee without learning more.

I whirled, and Thom body blocked me. Or he tried to. I was well versed at evading wolves.

One leap and I was over his back, heading toward the parking lot we'd fled from. One step, two steps...and I came up short as teeth snapped shut around the brush of my tail.

He growled and I froze. Froze, then spun to face him, teeth bared.

Thom was a shadow against the night sky as I peered upward. My shoulders tried to hunch as my lack of height yawned between us.

But I didn't allow myself to cower. Didn't let the darkness press me down onto my belly.

Instead, I snarled right back. Spat out fury.

And...Thom released me. Released my tail one moment then caught up with me the next as we sprinted together back the way we'd come.

Of course, I didn't lead us straight out into the parking area. I wasn't an idiot. Instead, I curved around just within the edge of the forest. Found a tumbled tree lodged in the crook of another and used that diagonal to scamper up to the height of a giraffe's nose.

Thom growled again as I left him behind. Wolves weren't climbers and the scent of his frustration was strong enough to chase me upward. I ignored it as I peered out at where we'd left our vehicles.

Unfortunately, I didn't see much at first. The Lawkeeper's Honda blocked my view until I clambered just a little higher. Went out on a limb so thin it bent beneath my paws and provoked a whine from Thom.

But this wasn't an erratically crumbling ledge on the side of a building. This branch was resilient…and the view was, at last, perfect.

Perfect in that I could see my coworker. I just couldn't tell, in the fickle moonlight, what he was so intent upon.

All I knew was that he was leaning over the ground, his shoulders as hunched as mine hadn't been when facing Thom down. Was he ill maybe?

No. A flash of light. The simulated shutter snap of a digital camera. The Lawkeeper was stockpiling photos as if he'd stumbled across a crime scene. Photos of the mud. Of the puddle into which Thom had dropped my cell phone. And, yes, where he'd dropped his also.

The creamy dullness of latex gloves glinted as the Lawkeeper picked up each mangled hunk of plastic. He was acting like a human detective. Which made no sense. Why not simply use his nose?

While I pondered, each piece of evidence slid into its own ziplock. Only then did the Lawkeeper lift his chin and turn his head in a half circle. Toward the zoo then away.

Yes, this was a shifter. A shifter using his superhuman olfactory abilities. To smell…us?

The wind, I realized, had skittered around while I was busy climbing. Now it didn't blow toward the road. It blew from me and Thom toward the Lawkeeper, who had stopped his sniffing head-on facing us.

I tensed, preparing to pick my way down. The tree, which had seemed so clever as a vantage point moments earlier, now acted as a trap. There were sharp sticks between me and the ground, jagged rocks anywhere I might leap for a speedy exit. If the Lawkeeper gave chase, he'd reach me before I could escape.

And he would give chase. The evidence gathering. The way he'd let Thom manhandle me in front of the zoo. This Lawkeeper wasn't abiding by the rules of protecting our own.

My claws felt for traction beneath me only to slip on a patch of damp lichen. If I hurried, I'd regret it. If I didn't hurry…I'd likely regret it more.

But I'd forgotten Thom. No, not forgotten him. Just underestimated him. He took a step out from beneath the tree cover. Lifted his chin so the scent of alpha wafted down the hill toward the Lawkeeper.

I was behind Thom, but the overwhelming musk still made me shiver. So I wasn't surprised that the Lawkeeper flinched, even from this distance. Wasn't surprised when he yanked open the door of his Honda, dropped our plastic-swaddled cell phones into the passenger seat, then spun gravel beneath his tires in his haste to depart.

Chapter 14

The night hardened as Thom and I turned back in the direction we'd originally run in. Thom's body language matched his sharp scent of frustrated protectiveness. I didn't have it in me to be contrite.

Because, yes, maybe it hadn't been so wise to tree myself in the face of danger. But we'd come away with interesting information and made it out just fine.

So we were together but not together as I followed Thom across the ridge and down toward the headlights that first flickered then flared through dark stripes of trees in the distance. Thom's father was waiting, as promised. But when we stepped up onto the gravel and shed our fur, I frowned.

That wasn't a werewolf in the driver's seat. No, this was a seventy-something human complete with smile lines wrinkling his face.

A seventy-something human...who also appeared to be Thom's father. "Dad," Thom offered, his voice emotionless, "this is Kira. Kira, my father."

"I'm Thomas," the older man elaborated. Unlike his son's icepicks, his sky-blue eyes twinkled as he greeted me. Meanwhile, his lack of reaction to our nudity proved that he was well aware of the existence of shifters. "But everyone calls me Big T."

As he spoke, his eyebrows rose, cheeks rounding at the joke of his nickname. And I got it. After all, Thom towered head and shoulders above me while Big T was diminutive enough to be half hidden behind the steering wheel.

That wasn't where my mind went, however. If Big T was human and Thom was able to shift, that meant the latter's mother must have been a werewolf. "Your wife...?" I started.

And Big T's open smile shuttered. His hands clenched down around the steering wheel. "No wife."

"Mind your own business." Thom's words struck harder than the clothes he'd drawn out of the back seat of the bulky sedan and hurled toward me. I suspected it was no accident he aimed, not for my chest where the bundle would be easy to catch, but for my face.

"Look, I know you're upset," I answered, disentangling myself then pulling on the hoody—a tent—and scrunching up the waist of the sweatpants with the drawstring.

"That you're trying to get yourself killed? Why would I be?" Thom's icepick eyes evaded mine as he slipped into the back seat. Rather than drawing on clothes, he turned to face his father and barked out orders. "Drop us off at the Base then head to the bar. I don't want you alone until things are settled. Give Bertrand the photo to show around rather than doing it yourself."

Big T had as much reason to be upset at my words as Thom did, but he was already over me stepping in ancient history. Saluting ironically, he shifted the car back into gear as I settled into the front passenger seat. "Will do, son. But you're gonna need another set of clothes if you don't want the eggheads looking at you funny."

Only, Thom didn't need clothes because he was already lupine. Any questions I wanted answered about the sore spot that was his mother, I definitely couldn't ask them now.

"That's quite a dog." Despite clear appreciation for Thom's size, the uniformed gate guard didn't request permission before reaching down to pat the head of an alpha werewolf. I braced myself for a scene, knowing Thom's mood hadn't improved during the ride in his father's car.

But Thom merely whined, leaning away from the caress. And the guard, not realizing how close he'd come to disaster, asked: "What's the breed?"

"Half wolf."

"And half woolly mammoth?"

I forced a laugh, donning sparkle with an effort. "Something like that. Hey, you should have a visitor pass for me. From Charlie Raven? I'm Kira Fairwood." While he reentered the guard shack and started shuffling through papers, I succumbed to the itch to dig up further information. "I bet there are lots of huge dogs on Base. Soldiers like their manly breeds, don't they?"

The guard returned with a bright orange clip-on name tag that he handed over after checking my ID. "Naw, not really. I've seen a few German Shepards, but never anything quite like this."

As he spoke, he clunked a fist up against the side of Thom's temple, the gesture playful yet deeply inappropriate given the circumstances. I tensed again, and this time Thom cocked his head at me, tongue lolling out as if he really was a great big puppy. I could almost hear him laughing at my distress.

Well, okay then. Thom appeared to be over his snit at me placing myself in danger, and any fear of werewolf attack was clearly unfounded. So I moved on to consider the fact that this guard didn't appear to have seen another shifter in lupine form.

While not definitive, his reaction was a hint that the Base had nothing to do with the recent murder beyond the identity of the victim. The question became—was Charlie involved? And, if so, how and why?

Thanking the guard, I headed in the direction he'd indicated, keeping my eyes peeled for the proper street number. This part of the Base wasn't much different from any other pocket of suburbia, even if the houses did all look alike and the yards were on the sterile side. If there hadn't been a twelve-foot chain-link fence restricting entry, I would have thought I was in Gate City proper, albeit a much younger neighborhood than the historic downtown.

The Base was remarkably quiet for a Saturday evening though. Only a bare minimum of cars drove by, headlights splitting the darkness. Indoors, a child complained about the injustice of bedtime as we rounded a corner. But there was none of the life and excitement that hovered around the Full Moon Saloon.

Until, that is, Thom nudged me toward the house where Charlie was visiting. It was at the far edge of the Base, overlooking Gate City. But the view—only barely visible in moonlight—wasn't what caught my attention. The windows had been flung wide open and strange noises filled the air.

Static and mechanical screeches. Then Eli's voice. "I have it! Charlie, come quick." The register of his voice rose to a near-shriek. "It's the Gate City ghost!"

Chapter 15

There were major benefits to being four-legged. Thom leapt in the open window while I hesitated on the sidewalk eying both door and window. One promised easy entry at a distance. The other would be more difficult two-legged but led directly to the heart of whatever was going on.

A crash. A shout.

Screw it. I relinquished the idea of entering in a conventional manner and ran for the opening Thom had soared through.

Unfortunately, my less graceful human body meant I couldn't make a similar grand entrance. So I paused before heaving myself over the sill on my stomach and took a look first.

Good thing too. Because Charlie wielded a glowing lava lamp, apparently preventing a stiff-legged Thom from closing on a seated Eli. The overhead light seemed to flicker in sympathy as my friend waved the luminous object around.

For his part, the young man being protected held out part of an unwrapped granola bar as he crooned cute-animal noises. He certainly wasn't scared. And if you didn't count the wolf, there was no sign of danger. Definitely no visible ghost.

"Charlie?" I leaned on my crossed arms rather than rushing in, exuding nonchalance and aiming for emotional contagion.

My effort worked. The lava lamp drooped downward while Charlie blew a lock of hair out of her face.

"Let me guess," she muttered. "Your dog?"

Not really, but I could honestly say: "He's very well-behaved."

And even though Charlie shook her head slowly, her voice was now tinged with amusement. "You always were a bull in a china shop."

A pang of memory. I *used to be* a bull in a china shop. I'd grown up a lot since then. It had been years since my vase-breaking phase.

Years Charlie and I had spent apart.

Still, the moment of incipient violence appeared to have passed. So I shrugged off regret and offered an explanation. "We heard Eli and thought there might be trouble...."

"It was just something on the radio." As Charlie spoke, she replaced the lamp on Eli's desk then held out a hand, palm up, toward Thom.

Great. Part two of how not to treat an alpha werewolf, especially one who was already on his last nerve. From personal experience, I could promise that animal-form shifters had no particular affinity for human hand odor.

And yet...Thom politely sniffed Charlie's fingers in exactly the manner she appeared to be expecting. A single ear flick was his only indication that the gesture wasn't pure, instinctive dog.

Eli was the one who broke the awkward silence. "It wasn't just something on the radio. It was *the Gate City ghost.*" Dropping the granola bar, he turned a dial on what appeared to be a homemade device. The same odd noises emerged as before, but they didn't sound very ghostly to me.

More like static. No wonder Charlie's tone was squelching. "An urban legend."

Eli was too excited to be squelched. "The term 'urban legend' suggests a lack of veracity. But the Gate City ghost is a very real phenomenon. People have been hearing it for decades. My friend's grandmother picks up the voice in her head through a loose filling. Which made me think it might travel in the form of radio waves...."

Just like that, his attention became riveted on the device in front of him. It had gone silent, though. The ghost—or whatever it was—had finished its broadcast.

Which hadn't been words. At least none I understood.

No wonder Charlie dismissed Eli's hypothesis. As a scientist, she required proof of the inexplicable. "Let me know if you find it again," she said. Then, to me, "How about you come in through the front door?"

We settled in the kitchen with mugs of tea and tinned cookies. Or, rather, Charlie and I settled. Eli barely noticed when we left him to his radio. Then Thom scratched at the back door as if he was an ordinary dog asking to be let out.

"He'll be fine in the yard," Charlie offered. "It's fenced."

I glanced between wolf and woman, not quite sure what Thom was after. "I guess he'll be okay out there for fifteen minutes...." Then, when a wolf ear twitched four times in quick suggestion, I changed that to: "Or an hour?"

Subtle wolf nod, but I only had eyes for Charlie's grin. I'd forgotten how purely she expressed her pleasure. Me extending our time together was apparently all it took to summon delight.

Unfortunately, that grin also reminded me of the last time we'd hung out together in college. The day before Charlie and her sister had stopped replying to my texts and phone calls. The day before they dropped me with no explanation at all.

And it was as if Charlie was thinking the exact same thing. Because, as soon as Thom disappeared into the darkness and she closed the door behind him, she took a deep breath and dove right in.

"I'm grateful you came to town again. And I owe you an explanation. About what happened in college."

We should have been talking about the email. But...I couldn't lose this opportunity if Charlie was finally willing to speak about the past. My hand shook ever-so-slightly on my mug as I summoned an answer. "Shoot."

"It was Jessie," my friend started, her gaze no longer meeting mine. "You have to understand, the twin code means your sister comes before everyone else."

I did understand that. Charlie's parents were a piece of work, able to provide for their kids in all material ways but having a much harder time expressing love and affection. That hug I'd received after breaking her mother-in-law's vase was the only one I'd ever seen Mrs. Raven dole out.

When your pack consists of two people only, I could see why you'd do anything for your solitary pack mate. "I get it," I offered when Charlie didn't seem inclined to go on without some kind of reaction. "But I don't get what Jessie had against me."

After all, the three of us had been inseparable. I'd thought I was a member of their little pack.

Rather than answering, Charlie took a sip of the fancy herbal tea in her mug. Honey-doctored and pink, it suited her more than the spicy blend I'd selected for myself.

And I didn't want to think about tea. I wanted to finally air out the stink of our past. "Charlie?"

Another swallow, then her mug clinked down on the tabletop. "There was a guy."

This time, my laugh was honest. "With Jessie, there was always a guy."

Our eyes met at last, a shared understanding of her sister's dating habits overcoming the present awkwardness. "I know, right?" Charlie leaned in closer, conspiratorial. "This one, though, had some weird bee in his bonnet about you. He didn't want us hanging out together. And I went along because Jessie's boyfriends never lasted longer than a couple of weeks."

Charlie and I had joked about that all through high school and into college. Jessie inevitably fell hard, but her crushes were blessedly brief. We humored her, then cossetted her when it was all over. The frequent but short-lived relationships were, I suspected, Jessie's response to parents who'd doled out only conditional love.

"Your cousin," Charlie continued, and this time I couldn't prevent myself from interrupting.

"My cousin?" Because everything up until this point matched with my understanding. But I had no cousins. Well, not blood cousins. Gunner's pack was full of his distant relatives who had taken me into their hearts even though we shared no DNA.

I didn't think Charlie was talking about werewolf-style cousins. After all, she didn't know werewolves existed.

She cupped her mug, the fidget evidence I wasn't the only one who still felt tension thrumming between us. "I just assumed he was an unfriendly family member. Because of his obsession with staying away from you and...." Charlie released the warmth to wave one hand around her face.

"Because of mosquitoes?"

In response, Charlie huffed and pulled out her cell phone. Donning reading glasses she'd needed since we were kids, she flipped through several photos before angling the screen in my direction.

The image was of Jessie's wedding day, something I hadn't known about or been invited to. The bride's dress combined tradition with the kind of expensive fashion their mother insisted upon.

It looked uncomfortable but also deeply flattering. Still, the joy on Jessie's face was what drew the eye.

Only when Charlie's finger tapped the left side of the screen did I pay attention to the groom. He was a few years older than his new wife. On the short side, with straight dark hair and big eyes that angled downward.

No wonder Charlie thought we were related. We were at least the same ethnicity.

Which meant we might also share heritage linked to shifting into the form of a fox.

Chapter 16

"**I**to?" The name bubbled up out of distant memory. He'd been a member of another kitsune's honor guard, the term referring to a group of young men who powered star-ball magic with their devotion. The connection had always felt predatory on the kitsune's part. Mai and I had neither needed nor wanted such hangers-on.

Although, come to think of it, me drinking werewolf blood and forcing Smoke and Thom to do my bidding was considerably more predatory. Honor guard members, at least, willingly chose to be a kitsune's power source.

Charlie nodded, the reading glasses she was only now removing helping her miss my wince as I second-guessed past actions. "So you do know each other."

We did, very vaguely and from a very long time ago. Mai had dealt with the problematic kitsune who had been Ito's mistress, leaving him and the rest of the honor guard with plenty of cash and no obligation to any fox shifters. We'd parted on good terms, at least as far as the child me had been aware, and that was years before I enrolled in the same college as Charlie and Jessie.

So why would Ito have been opposed to seeing me then?

I half listened as Charlie rambled on about how good Ito had been for her two-sister pack. "He funded my first year of research, which likely helped me land this job right out of grad school."

A pause, into which I hummed. Charlie was talking faster than usual, which I knew from experience meant she wasn't entirely at ease. The only reason I could think of for her discomfort was the fact I hadn't absolved her for choosing her sister over me way back when.

The question became—was I ready to forgive Charlie for six years of cold shoulders? I wanted to say yes...but I wasn't quite there yet.

As I pondered, Charlie continued. "Of course, Ito wasn't being entirely selfless. It helps him out to have someone on the ground."

The instinct that ensured I didn't miss important facts when sleuthing sparked alert. Okay, and maybe part of it was that I didn't want to make a decision quite yet about whether to accept the implied apology of Charlie's long-winded explanation.

But personal drama wasn't why I was here. I was here to find a murderer. So I interjected. "Ito wants to have someone he trusts in Gate City?"

Charlie nodded. "Yeah, because of his brother. They moved him here to take advantage of the supposed healing properties of the valley. Did you know the cancer rates in Gate City are a tenth of what you see in the surrounding metro areas? I always figured it was air patterns blocking pollutants, but Ito is convinced his brother might wake up if he stays here long enough."

"Wake up?"

"From his coma."

Oh. My stomach clenched.

I hadn't realized some of the honor-guard members might be related to each other. Hadn't thought that those not chosen in my sister's desperate lottery might be nearly as deeply affected as the one who'd lost his consciousness to power a supervillain's demise.

Perhaps I didn't need to look any further to understand why Ito had such antipathy toward me after all.

Now I was the one cradling my mug as if it was a security blanket. The cinnamon wafting off the surface should have soothed me, but instead it burned my nostrils. I placed a hand over top to block the scent, ignoring the wet heat puddling against my palm.

Charlie reached across the table as if to offer a placating touch then aborted the gesture. "I said the wrong thing."

"Of course not." I smiled widely, trying not to let the moral ambiguity of my sister's past actions—and my own part in upping the chaos quotient twelve years earlier—derail us from the current task.

Only, Charlie wasn't done with ancient history. "It's not an excuse," she told me, her voice low, "but *this* is part of why I let Ito dictate my actions. Jessie and I told you all of our secrets. But you always seemed to be holding back from letting us in."

Silence yawned. Charlie was right. I hadn't been a good friend to her during our shared childhood. Couldn't be any better of a friend now, when it came right down to it. There were still secrets Charlie could never be privy to, not if I wanted her to remain safe.

Because a human who stumbled across the reality of werewolves painted a big, bloody target on her back. If she was vouched for by an alpha, she might be protected. Otherwise, innocents who discovered the supernatural were usually killed for the safety of the packs.

Put down, as the euphemism went, by Lawkeepers like me. Not that I'd ever been called upon to kill a human personally. The one time I'd been on a case where a partner had thought such an execution necessary I'd managed to wiggle the human out of danger with a Gryffindor scarf and a pinky swear.

But that, I admitted, had been a lucky circumstance. I couldn't count on it happening again, and I didn't want Charlie to get in over her head and end up on some Lawkeeper's shit list.

Fortunately, human knowledge of shifters wasn't relevant to the current discussion. Charlie could keep her science-tinted view of the world and I could hunt a murderer. No reason for those two worlds to collide.

That—not an unwillingness to delve further into the past—was why I cleared my throat and changed the subject. "I was really hoping you'd tell me more about the email I sent inviting you to meet up."

Only Charlie refused to be sidetracked. She'd always been able to read my emotions, even when I hid them beneath layers and layers of pleasantries. "You don't have to pretend not to be upset, and I'm not the only one who cares about you." She stood, but rather than walking around the table to provide the hug she would have six years ago, she headed for the exterior door. "Pets make everything better, or so I've been told."

Her hand was on the doorknob by the time my glance flew to the wall clock and subtracted minutes. Adrenaline seared all of the angst out of my chest. "No!"

"No?"

I shook my head, an abruptly crystal-clear mind racing through the timeline. Thom had requested an hour, of which he still had ten minutes. Chances were good he'd shifted and gone over the fence the moment the kitchen door closed behind him. He'd made it clear he needed a certain amount of time for whatever he wanted to ferret out here on Base property. There was zero chance he'd be waiting in the backyard like a well-behaved mutt if Charlie opened up that door now.

Which would mean Charlie and me searching the neighborhood. Derailing us both from the emotions that clogged the kitchen—possibly a good thing—and from the fact-finding mission I really needed to engage in—definitely bad.

And...I couldn't say any of that to Charlie. Instead, I spun the first lie that came into my head. "My dog. He's terrible with electronics."

"Scared of them?"

"Eats them. Laptops, cellphones, tablets. The GI blockages are pure yuck."

If there's one thing I'd learned in life, it was that talking about bowels had a way of turning the conversation. Sure enough, Charlie abandoned the door and returned to the table. Pushing her mug out of the way with a grimace, she opened a laptop that had been waiting in a shoulder bag. "What do you want to know about the email?"

I told her and, for the next ten minutes, she talked geek at me. Given the fact I didn't speak science, her explanation wasn't very informative. Still, the homeyness of sitting beside a Raven twin listening to words that went over my head was charmingly familiar. It settled my stomach. Reminded me that the past—both my sister's actions and Charlie's choices—had happened years ago. That, here and now, having Charlie in my life was something I didn't want to do without.

"You understand what I'm saying, right?" she asked at last, letting reading glasses slide down her nose as she looked up from the gobbledygook on her screen.

"Not a word." My cheeks, though, were sore from smiling. "Maybe try English."

"English." Charlie laugh-snorted, which almost but not quite covered up the scratch on the door. This time, I didn't stop her when she crossed the room to let Thom enter. I didn't explain to him, either, why my friend stood on tiptoe to slide her laptop on top of the fridge then pointed at her butt.

The look on his lupine face was priceless.

But he settled down at my feet as Charlie finished her explanation. "What I was trying to tell you is that the email originated in Roanoke. I can narrow it down to neighborhood." She pulled up a map on her phone, carefully elevated above wolf head level. "But no further. Does that help?"

It did help. The location—with the Lawkeeper's office dead center—confirmed that Rupert had set me up to be in Gate City at the time he was committing a murder.

Now, how were we going to disentangle the murderer's carefully woven knot?

Chapter 17

Charlie's hug goodbye made up for our six years separated. "I'm really sorry," she murmured into my hair. "Maybe next time you'll trust me enough to tell me about the guy."

I drew back, glancing down at Thom despite myself before returning my attention to Charlie. "Guy?"

This time it didn't take so long for me to understand my friend's elaborate hand gestures since they picked out the sag of my pants and the bag of my top. "Those clothes are absolutely not your style," she pointed out. "You didn't go home last night."

I *had* gone home last night…and these weren't my clothes. Charlie noticing the difference warmed me more than the tea had. So, even though I couldn't exactly tell her the truth, I laid down the first plank in a bridge between us. "Want to get together soon?" I offered. "To spar, maybe?"

This time when her words tumbled out fast, it was for a good reason. "Name the time and place and I'll clear my calendar."

On that note, we left her. I floated out of the base, buoyed up by the at-least-partial resumption of a friendship I'd thought was gone forever. Only after returning my visitor's badge and stepping out into the dimly lit street beyond the fence did I realize I had no idea where I was headed. And that I'd been awake for a really, really long time.

"We need someplace off the radar to spend the night."

I hadn't been talking to Thom, but his head found its way under my hand anyway. As if he really was just a dog, strengthening his person when the exhaustion of very little sleep landed on her head like a ton of unfinished responsibilities.

And I accepted the assistance. I followed his lead up the hill away from the town center until the sidewalk ended and the road narrowed. Further along, houselights gave way to dark forest. There, Thom left the pavement, leapt over a ditch, and guided me toward a towering tree.

I stumbled along in his wake, trying to make sense of his lupine lack of communication. The back side of the trunk he waited beside was hollowed out, making me remember tales of sycamores so big that European settlers had used them as cabins hundreds of years earlier.

This hollow, in contrast, was full of rot and far too small for comfort. I peered up at the sky and saw no stars. Chances were good it would rain tonight.

Still, my brain had succumbed to exhaustion and no other options presented themselves. So I just asked, "You want to sleep here?"

Thom was still in lupine form, so I didn't particularly expect him to answer. But he nosed into the hollow, drawing out what appeared to be a gallon-sized ziplock bag stuffed with...clothing?

"You want me to change?"

Thom shook his head, taking the hem of my pants in his teeth then tugging lightly. And I finally caught his drift.

This tree was a werewolf clothes repository. Thom didn't want me to borrow from it but rather to ditch the jogging pants and follow him four-legged deeper into the forest.

It felt easier to obey than to argue. So I slid out of the borrowed sweats, strangely disappointed when Thom turned to stare into the darkness rather than watching my strip tease. Then I stuffed both the ziplock and my own clothes back into the vegetative nook and summoned my fox.

Fur warmed me more than the clothes had. My whiskers twitched and the forest brightened, which was handy since we had a significant run ahead of us.

Running, though, was fine. Even with sleep begging to tug me under, it was a joy to pass through new territory on the heels of a wolf who knew all the animal trails. Thom led me up and up and up until we stepped out into a tiny clearing around what appeared to be an ancient farmhouse.

The walls were made of logs, but this wasn't a simple one-story structure. Instead, it loomed high above us, a chimney suggesting it dated from an era when wood was the primary heat source.

No sleeping in hollow sycamore trees then. There might be beds. Pillows. Toothpaste?

I looked again, noticing a complete lack of roads or power lines leading to the residence. Maybe I wouldn't set my heart on toothpaste.

Tom shifted upwards while I was still considering amenities. He didn't turn over rocks in search of a key, just twisted the knob and pushed open the door. "This place has been in my family for generations," he explained, looking back over his shoulder as I followed four-legged. I might have been watching the motion of his ass instead of his face, but tired eyes will do what tired eyes want.

"The county tax map considers the land unimproved," Thom continued, darkness keeping him oblivious to my objectification, "so we shouldn't be bothered. I'll...."

However he intended to finish that sentence, I had no idea. Because I'd slid past his knee just in time to see a dark shape rise off a futon in front of us. A dark shape that materialized into a bristling and growling wolf.

"Smoke." Thom's voice darkened, hardened. He stepped closer to the wall, and it took me a moment to realize he wasn't retreating but was rather moving himself out of the route to the door. "This territory remains off limits. I recommend you leave. Now."

Smoke didn't leave. Instead, he stalked stiff-legged around us, toward a cluster of shapes that gradually resolved into a dining set. Faster than my eyes could follow in the dimness of an unlit cabin, he leapt onto the closest chair. Wood clattered to the ground as he pushed off, aiming for the table top this time.

Now, the wolf's head and Thom's head were at the same level. The swift gain of height was an aggressive move I'd seen dozens of times among werewolves.

Preparation for an attack made more uneven due to Thom's current lack of weapons and claws.

The smart move would have been to shift. But Thom merely held up a human hand in the universal "stop" signal and tried to reason with the invader of this house he'd considered a safe haven. "Do you want to win back your paw? If so, this isn't the way to go about it. You...."

Smoke's muscles bunched...and he and I sprang at the exact same instant. Our goals, though, couldn't have been further apart.

Smoke was leading with an open mouth, aiming for Thom's throat. I was hoping to slam my shoulder against that snout, the only way a fox can muster sufficient force to impact a wolf's trajectory. Like harnessing a horse—turn the head and the body follows.

Only, Smoke wasn't a horse. His teeth were sharp and he'd seen me coming. I was midair when he slung his neck around to face me, lips curling back to reveal fangs not quite as sharp as mine but far more deadly. More able to crush a fox's skull.

Then Thom was wolf and streaking through the darkness also. Sleek fur separated me from Smoke before those fangs and I could make contact. I bounced off Thom's side as if I'd hit a brick wall.

Tumbling head over heels, all I heard was the intermittent scuff of claws on floorboards. Otherwise, the wolf fight was ominously silent.

And fast. By the time I'd caught my balance, halfway under the table and with even less visibility than previously, it was all over. One dark shape fled out the open door while the other padded in my direction. A massive wolf loomed between me and the window, blocking even that tiny shred of light.

Darkness made it impossible to tell who had won and who had lost. I must have flinched backwards because Thom was human a moment later. Human and far more furious than he'd seemed when Smoke disobeyed his direct command and attempted to attack him.

"What exactly," he growled—yes, the words really were a growl—"did you think you were doing just now?"

Chapter 18

I was on human feet an instant later, giving as good as I got. "What did *you* think you were doing? You don't rationalize with an angry werewolf."

Thom's arms crossed, muscles flexing. "And a fox doesn't leap into an angry werewolf's jaws."

"Just because someone's bigger, doesn't mean I should bow down and take whatever he dishes out to me."

"A fox would be wise to back off when faced with a larger predator."

"I would have backed off if my partner hadn't been standing there like an idiot while an enemy gained the elevation advantage." I paced closer, poking an angry finger at Thom's rock-solid chest. "Stop acting like an alpha who thinks he's Joe six pack."

My pointer finger was consumed by a tight fist while the owner of said fist leaned in to growl out his annoyance. "Says the fox who thinks she's a wolf."

We hovered there for a moment, frozen. Something zinged down that minimal connection of palm and finger. Something that made me realize I was gasping for air and so was Thom.

My toes pressed me upwards. His face was too far away and too hard to see in the darkness. If I reached his level....

Then Thom released my finger and spun away, his back to me as he inhaled with exaggerated slowness. Exhaled just as intentionally. "I apologize," Thom told the wall. "I was afraid for you. Perhaps next time, you could summon your magic sword rather than diving in four-legged."

I opened my mouth to spit out a furious rebuttal...then realized Thom was right. *Huh.* Perhaps my brain was more soggy with exhaustion than I'd thought.

As I considered Thom's analysis, he curved around so three feet of space grew between us. Darkened by distance, the shadow of Thom sniffed the air like the werewolf he sometimes seemed to forget he was.

"Charlie had a point last night," he observed after a moment. "You're starving."

"I'm not...." My hands flew to my stomach as it complained audibly. I *was* starving. Now that Thom mentioned it, the enormous cavern in my belly felt like it was creeping upward into my throat.

My legs wobbled, which had nothing to do with waves of emotion and everything to do with not having eaten since approximately the Jurassic Era. Still, Thom righted the chair Smoke had toppled with more force than was really necessary. *"Sit, "* he demanded.

I sat, but only because I wanted to. "That's what you should have used on Smoke," I informed Thom as he turned to rifle through cabinets.

Rather than answering immediately, he plunked a huge armload of canned goods down on the table between us then slid into the opposite seat. "A chair?"

"An alpha command. Far more efficient. And *safer.*"

Thom hummed what sounded like a question as he flicked a lighter. A candle flared to life, beating back the dark.

And, to my dismay, my nakedness was all I could think about. I'd shifted around werewolves for over a decade, none of us peering at personal bits. So why did my breasts feel like targets for heat-seeking missiles now?

Perhaps because my gaze had a hard time tearing itself away from Thom's pecs. Perhaps because the ripple of his muscles in candlelight mesmerized me.

I jerked my gaze up to Thom's face, only to discover he didn't appear to be suffering from a similar hang-up. His attention remained riveted on his task as he pulled the tab on a can of Vienna sausages. Spearing one oblong of meat on a wooden skewer, he passed it to me then jerked his chin toward the candle. "They're tastier roasted."

Since I was the only one suffering from unbearable attraction, now seemed like a good time to change the subject. "You don't know what an alpha command is, do you?" I asked as I spun the sausage over the mini fire.

Thom didn't evade this time. Instead, his head jerked from side to side while his answer, although brief, spoke volumes. "My dad raised me."

His human dad. The hint of vulnerability in Thom's voice helped me focus on something more important than naked bodies. "But you've used alpha commands. I overheard when you sent Smoke away back at the bar."

Thom's eyebrows rose, presumably at the fact I'd been listening in on a private conversation within a locked building. But he didn't remark upon it. Instead, he rumbled out: "Like this? *Eat something before you starve.*"

The Vienna sausage was hot between my fingers as I plucked it off the skewer. "Yeah. Except alpha commands don't work on kitsunes. They're only effective with werewolves less dominant than you. Why did you use an alpha command with Smoke if you didn't know what it was?"

Thom's pointer finger looped around in a repetitive circle. Once I started eating, he quirked his lips and explained.

"I deepen my voice when I want a dog to obey me. It seemed like the thing to do with someone losing his paw."

I laughed around the morsel of salty goodness. Of course Thom had stumbled onto alpha commands by treating underlings like misbehaving puppies.

Then I lost track of the thread of our conversation as my taste buds exploded. Thom had been right. The heat and slight charring on the exterior made the sausage so much more than canned mystery meat. I hummed my pleasure as I tried to make the tidbit last.

And Thom was the one who coughed out a strange strangled noise this time. I peered up from my feast, hoping for something....

Only, he was merely holding out another sausage, grilled while I was eating. And his voice was all business as he said, "We should talk about what we learned on the Base. Our plans for tomorrow."

So Thom grilled, I ate, and we talked. I explained how Charlie's geekiness had confirmed my invitation email originated from the Roanoke office. And Thom explained that he'd had a sudden wild thought that the Base and the Gate City ghost might be relevant to our case, which was why he'd gone hunting on his own in lupine form.

"What did you discover?" By this point, I'd eaten so many sausages my stomach was starting to groan for a different reason. So I waved away Thom's next offering, which he consumed in a single bite.

"Not much," he answered after swallowing. "The residential area is separated from the research facilities by another fence and gatehouse. I couldn't get through. But that doesn't appear to be relevant now." He steepled his hands and leaned on them. "How do you plan to collar Rupert?"

A full belly made me talkative. "Should be pretty simple. I'll head up to our office tomorrow and take a sip of his blood. Make him confess on camera then hold him there until my boss shows up."

And…that appeared to be the wrong answer. Thom's lips thinned. "What if you pass out like you did at Creation Kingdom?"

"I don't think that will happen."

"Don't *think* or *know*?"

The intensity of our conversation had made us both lean in closer. Only the tremulous flicker of candle flame separated our faces now.

Again, Thom was the one who drew back. "Let's table this until morning. There's a loft upstairs where I usually sleep when I bring newcomers up to be awarded their paws. You'll find clothes and clean sheets in a bin under the bed."

There was lots to argue about, but I didn't feel like arguing. Instead, I carried the candle in one hand as I clambered up the ladder buck naked, glancing back only once to see whether Thom was watching from below.

He wasn't. He'd rolled himself into a blanket in Smoke's vacated spot and appeared to be sound asleep already. So I shrugged and continued up.

Alone, I entered the den of this man who thought he wasn't an alpha werewolf yet often acted like one. Thom's musk embraced me the way the real man seemed to have no interest in doing. A tendril of air caressed my cheek.

I was tempted to slide between the sheets Thom had slept in and pretend he was there beside me. To revel in the brush of fabric against over-sensitized skin.

Instead, I stripped the bed and tucked in crisp, clean bedding. Flung open the window to clear away a scent that remained headily overwhelming.

I didn't think I'd sleep. But the warm sausages in my belly overcame the unrequited lust in lower portions of my anatomy. I was dreaming of running vulpine on Thom's wolf heels when I woke to a loud noise from below me.

It sounded like nothing so much as a gunshot.

Chapter 19

S moke was back. And Thom was in the line of fire. That certainty sent me tumbling out of bed without bothering to dig for borrowed clothing.

I did, however, spare a moment to summon my sword. Clenching the hilt in my left fist made it harder to ease my way down the ladder, but Thom's point last night had been well-taken. Steel trumped fox teeth when facing off against a wolf...especially one who carried a gun.

So I felt for the rungs with one bare foot after the other, balancing with my five spare fingers. Descending into pitch darkness, I stifled a gasp as a hand came out of nowhere to clench shut around my knee.

My sword swung wildly for one split second. Then the fingers loosened and I stilled just before my blade cut through flesh.

This was Thom. I somehow knew his identity without sniffing the air in search of alpha musk.

So the bullet hadn't hit its intended target. That was good, but there was still someone in the cabin alongside us. Moving air seethed against my skin, prompting me to turn my head away from Thom and peer to the right, the direction the motion seemed to come from.

Nothing. The cabin was even darker than it had been when we got here. The moon must have been completely covered by clouds.

I considered flaring my sword to star-ball brightness. But doing so would paint a target on me and Thom while we were helpfully clustered together. If the invader—Smoke? someone worse?—had a gun, we were better off keeping our location hidden.

Thom tapped my knee once and I continued descending. Heat confirmed his location. My free hand didn't falter as it used his shoulder to steady my last silent step down to the floor.

Before sleeping, we'd worked at cross purposes. But now an unvoiced understanding flowed between us. Cold metal pressed against my fingers and I pushed the offered knife back to its owner. To explain the rejection, I let the warmer blade of my star-ball sword lie flat for one split second against his skin.

A trickle of air against my cheek. This time, the motion could be traced to Thom nodding. I replied with a gentle push against his side.

Alright, we were ready. Without speaking, we split apart to slide along the inner walls of the cabin. Or at least I hoped that was what Thom was doing, that he was helping me form a pincer to snap shut around our prey.

Keeping my footsteps slow, I managed not to scuffle or bump against anything as I worked my way into place. Gently moving air continued wafting from the direction of the front door—the only door?—but complete darkness suggested that entrance wasn't open. Had Smoke stepped inside, fired once, and was now milling around seeking us in the dark?

I sniffed, reassured by a complete lack of wolf odor near me. Leading with my sword, I continued pacing closer and closer....

I was ten feet from the door when air slapped me. So strong, the gust couldn't have been provoked by a single wolf moving. It was a tsunami of night, something bigger and more powerful than could be created by a mere mortal.

Could this be the Gate City ghost?

Then a tremendous bang. Okay, enough of stealth.

"Thom, down!" I warned as I lifted my sword in front of me and flared the tip to life.

There was no one there. No one except Thom, shielding his eyes from the over-powering illumination while crouching with butcher knife extended toward the dark.

The heavy wooden door swung back closed then, banging hard against the frame. Open again, slamming into the log wall behind it. Then rain followed wind, and I guessed what had gone wrong.

"I opened my window last night. Change of air pressure. A storm blowing in." I didn't continue the explanation because Thom was nodding.

And now that I quenched my sword, I saw that there *was* light present when the door opened. The tiniest hint of impending dawn pressing through clouds and rain.

That was enough to send Thom striding out, his shadow now faintly visible. His nose lifted just as mine had done earlier, then he reentered along with rain-drops. "No one there. Looks like I need to fix the latch."

As he fiddled with the door, I started to sidle past him. But his arm came out straight, barring my exit.

"What are you doing?"

"Making sure you didn't miss anything."

"Alone?"

"Do you realize how much you sound like an alpha werewolf when you say that?"

Thom took one deep breath, then the scent of amusement flowed toward me on the exhale. "We'll both go out together to walk the perimeter once the rain clears. Until then, I have a suggestion. About Rupert."

I was interested, but I couldn't resist at least sticking my head out into the mael-strom of sideways water. Wind and scattered drops had turned into a downpour. I couldn't see anything. The combination quenched my urge to sleuth. I hoped it would send any intruder seeking cover as well.

I shivered as I retreated back into the protection of the cabin. Thom was right. Walking the perimeter could wait.

"Here." A blanket engulfed me. A blanket that smelled like alpha werewolf. I pulled it close and didn't interrupt as Thom finished his earlier thought. "If you're intent upon confronting Rupert within his place of power, please bring backup. You were sent to apprehend me, correct? Then do so. If you need assistance, I can muster an alpha command."

It was a good plan, but I had a better one. Especially in light of how we seemed to be working the kinks out of our partnership. After all, Thom hadn't stopped me from stalking out into the storm just now, and the blanket when I came back in was appreciated.

"Or," I countered, "I could pretend that I've captured you but am having trouble hauling you to Roanoke. I'll call for backup and we can deal with Rupert here on our own turf."

Well, on Thom's turf. A true alpha werewolf would have taken offense at my claiming of his territory. But Thom just nodded. Despite the storm, the sun had risen enough now so I could make out his mouth quirking ever so slightly upward. "A compromise. I like it."

Cuddling up in a blanket that still held Thom's body heat, I found I liked it too.

Chapter 20

F ive hours later, I tailed Thom as we ran four-legged back down the mountainside. Slick leaves underfoot gave way to pavement, trees opening up into neighborhoods. We dodged cars and pedestrian traffic, sticking to quiet suburban streets as much as possible on our way to the Full Moon Saloon.

Our plan was about to come to fruition, but I had a niggling suspicion I'd forgotten something important. So I let Thom take point while I considered the action steps we'd taken to get to this point.

Despite the backwoods nature of the cabin, Thom turned out to have an emergency-use burner phone stashed away behind more Vienna sausages and beanie weenies. He'd called Bertrand, the suited shifter from the bar who apparently acted as his unofficial second. Bertrand, in turn, promised to rope in several of the more dependable paws to hang out at the bar during our showdown, just in case both my kitsune abilities and Thom's alpha commands proved insufficient to deal with the threat.

After a nap and another meal, I'd used the same phone to call the Roanoke Lawkeepers' office, the main number that I knew would go directly to Rupert on a Sunday morning. Sure enough, his annoyed voice was the one to answer. "What?"

"Your phone etiquette could use some work," I informed him.

Rather than replying, Rupert slurped loudly. I had a feeling that if we'd been face to face, his scent would have been smug. "I found where you hid the good coffee," he told me after more smacking mouth noises. "Behind the copier paper? Really? You'll need to be sneakier than that."

Rupert had a way of spiking my blood pressure, but soon he wouldn't be sneaking anybody's coffee. That knowledge made it easier to don the poor, sweet girl impersonation that seemed to work so well on my least-favorite coworker.

"Look, I'm in a bit of a pickle. The guy I was supposed to bring in? He's really big. I don't think I can handle him solo."

A long-suffering sigh. Another slurp of the prime coffee that was only put on the shelf once per month, replaced by instant if we ran out. "Where are you?"

"Gate City. Full Moon Saloon. I have him restrained. I think. I mean, I *do*. It's just, if I try to take him outside and he makes a run for it, I might lose him. Again...."

The story of my failure outside Creation Kingdom must have filtered down to Rupert because he didn't press for details. Instead, he yawned. "It'd take me a few hours to get there. If I come, you're buying lunch."

I sniffled just the tiniest bit, imagining I'd been crying. Made my voice brave. "I promise. Anywhere. Most expensive place in town. I owe you one, Rupert."

"You do," he answered then hung up the phone.

So, yeah, the murderer was presumably on his way to a location that, due to Thom acting like a pack leader, would have plenty of backup in the wings if blood and alpha commands weren't sufficient to quell Rupert's protests. Meanwhile, if Rupert had tracked my call—likely given the tech savviness his hacking into my email suggested—he'd spin his wheels trying to locate the phone we'd left behind in Thom's cabin in the woods.

Soon enough, Rupert would be the one serving time while Thom's name was cleared. Scarlet would put a gold star on my file that would mark kitsunes as team players, then I could head home to Mai and Grub and Gunner and the weekend I'd missed.

So why was there a worried little knot in my gut?

Perhaps because the weekend I'd actually lived wasn't such a bad one. Thom and I shifted in unison behind a parked car just outside the back door of the Full Moon Saloon, his hand sliding to the small of my back to steady me when my soft human foot came down on a pointy pebble. The contact made my knees wobble and my breath come a little too fast.

The touch was fleeting though. Soon enough, Thom released me to reach under a planter box for a spare key then held the door open so I could enter first.

Inside, a large orange cat padded toward us down the length of what I gathered was the Moon Room. Long, mostly open, dim beneath industrial-style fluorescents due to lack of windows and age-darkened hardwood floors.

"Pumpkin," Thom greeted the cat, the words sounding so familiar on his tongue that I got the impression he used them daily. "We're home."

My stomach churned harder as that *we* caught at the knot and pulled it tighter. Or maybe I was instead fixating on the word *home*?

"Wait, don't step there." Thom's hand touched my hip ever so briefly as he guided me around what appeared to be water damage on the floorboards. "Toilet disaster two weeks ago. Here." He opened a huge wooden cabinet, the type that was often used in place of built-in closets. "Grab whatever you need."

Melancholy was replaced by stifled laughter as I peered into the space. "From the industrial-size box of condoms?"

The tips of Thom's ears reddened as he reached around me to grab a pair of jeans from the shelf below the prophylactics. Yanking them on without meeting my gaze, he muttered. "I meant the clothes. Condoms are part of the deal with being a paw. No shifter babies left behind with unwitting humans."

The cat—Pumpkin—butted against Thom's leg and he scooped the furball up to cuddle against his bare chest. An excuse not to meet my eyes? As if the mention of unwanted shifter babies hit too close to home.

And maybe it did after the way his father had refused to acknowledge the existence of his mother yesterday. Whatever the reason, Thom seemed intent upon scratching behind Pumpkin's ears now, murmuring apologies as he carried the cat to the far end of the long room. After shoving the pet through a small door-within-a-door into the display case out front, Thom snicked the entrance shut.

He still didn't turn around to meet my eyes.

"You don't have to talk about it," I told the clothes I was picking through. Huge jeans. Man-size button-down shirts. This was clearly going to be another baggy sweats day.

Only, it wasn't. Because the second door near Thom burst open and Dixie Lee plus the clatter of bar noises wafted inside. The latter dulled as the human bartender shoved the door shut with her hip. Her arms were full of what appeared to be a laptop plus a pile of black fabric and leather.

"Nothing in there is going to fit you," she told me while handing both clothes and electronics to Thom. "I brought something more appropriate."

My eyebrows rose. How had this human known I'd show up naked?

And, finally, Thom met my gaze again. "Moon," he murmured as he headed back past the row of arcade games that apparently provided the entertainment inside a top-secret werewolf lair.

Was that an explanation? Right, Smoke had mentioned the second type of person granted access to this windowless side of the bar. People who couldn't shift but who were still trusted allies of those of us who could. Those who were protected from Lawkeepers by Gate City's alpha, despite the fact Thom refused to grant himself that title.

And Dixie Lee, apparently, was one of those people. A moon. Which made sense if she was left in charge of a shifter bar while Thom was away.

"Thanks," I told both her and Thom as the latter offered me clothes before turning away to set up the laptop on the end of a folding table close to the parking-lot-side door. As we'd discussed, he pointed the webcam at the entrance then dragged over a chair to plunk down in front of it.

Dixie Lee shrugged, and I got the impression she wasn't entirely sure what to make of me. We'd bonded over the awfulness of high heels yesterday, so it seemed relevant that she'd included sneakers in today's bundle. But that momentary spark between us had been a party trick. Now that I was naked, our connection appeared to be lost.

Another odd ping in my stomach. I shook my head at the rollercoaster of emotions while unfolding my borrowed clothes. "These are great," I started.

Dixie Lee, though, had already returned her attention to Thom. "Nobody recognized the picture on your dad's phone. But the guy in the blue Honda was here for quite a while today. Nosing around, asking questions about both of you. He left about three hours ago."

Around the same time I'd placed the call to Rupert. So the pair were allies, just as I'd suspected. We'd have to deal with the nameless Lawkeeper after collaring the murderer, something else to add to my mental to-do list. First though....

Thom swiveled the computer around to face me, the video-chat screen requesting meeting and login info. My shoulders settled against the seams of clothes that actually fit, helping me shake off odd thoughts about friendships never to be made or lost.

While I typed, Thom jerked his chin toward the door Dixie Lee had come in through. "Any non-paws and moons out there?"

"Yeah," she answered, "but they won't hear anything on this side of the bar."

For the first time in hours, Thom's tone took on a dark edge. "You didn't."

And even though an alpha werewolf was verbally menacing her, Dixie Lee thudded her fists into her hips and glared at him. "Don't use that tone on me. Bertrand said I could do whatever I needed to do to keep the Moon Room under the radar this afternoon. It was what I needed to do."

Thom advanced a step, eyebrows lowering. "Dixie Lee. I told you. No karaoke."

"It's just for today," she said airily, heading back toward the door that led to the public side of the bar. Just before turning the knob though, she peered over her shoulder and added: "Unless people love it. In that case, we'll make karaoke a regular themed night."

Then she was gone, the deep thud of bass and the first notes of riotous singing seeping through the wall between us. My video-chat screen connected just as the rumble of an engine from the other direction suggested a vehicle was pulling up outside.

Rupert was right on time. "Lights, camera, action," I murmured.

"You forgot 'places.'" Thom sidled over to the wall beside the parking-lot door, where he wouldn't be seen immediately. I angled the computer screen to take in the view we'd decided on.

Then the game began.

Chapter 21

"**I** was starting to be concerned for you." Scarlet's face filled the computer screen, her lipstick perfect and her hair coiffed despite it being a lazy Sunday morning in her world. She didn't look particularly worried, but her eyes sparked wide and alert.

"Hold that thought," I said, leaving the laptop open and turning toward the door as a timid tap sounded. "Come in, Rupert."

My least favorite coworker led with his right cheek, as if expecting a blow. Fingers clutched the side of the door, which was still only halfway open, shielding him perfectly from Thom's presence. His gaze swept the Moon Room. "You're alone."

"Close the door," I suggested, forcing my toes not to bounce me up and down the way they wanted to. My star-ball sword was hidden beneath the jacket Dixie Lee had loaned me, something deeply flattering and dangerous-looking at the same time.

I was dressed for success and Rupert was here to face the music. Thom was present as backup and Scarlet was ready to serve as witness. All I needed was to block out looky-loos in the parking lot then we could continue to the grand reveal.

To that end, I raised my eyebrows and waited. Rupert's mouth pinched down, but he finally obeyed, if not without commentary.

"I appreciate caviar and fine wines," he observed as the exterior door snicked shut. "There are three places between here and Roanoke that are up to my standards. The first is...."

We didn't learn where the fine-dining establishments were located. Because Thom stepped out from behind the closing door, sliding so smoothly into Rupert's personal space that the Lawkeeper was left gaping. Broad hands closed around bony wrists. Rupert didn't even try to twist free until he was 100% caught.

Only then did Thom jerk his chin at me. As we'd agreed, I drew my sword, planning to take blood from a distance. But Rupert squeaked, the scent of urine biting my nostrils.

"It's only coffee!" Rupert's words fell over themselves in his haste to protect his skin from my weapon. "And toilet paper. And the paperclips are just nicer in the office!"

I paused. "You take paperclips also?"

"I'll replace them! I'll replace all of it! This isn't an appropriate punishment for a minor crime!"

Janet Allegra's death was far from minor, but there was no point in bringing that up until I'd sealed Rupert's cooperation. So I soothed him. "I only want a few drops of blood. A pinprick. The wound will heal in an hour."

"Then prick my finger! Not my neck! I only have one neck. I need it. Do you realize how useless heads are without necks to set them on? I've...."

Thom growled and Rupert fell silent. "If you're tempted to do anything stupid when I let go of your arm," Thom murmured, just barely loud enough for me to hear, "remember I'm right behind you."

"Nothing stupid. I swear. Not a thing. I'll just stick my finger out, slow and easy...."

Rupert didn't do anything stupid, but he did jerk the moment my sword connected. "Ow!" he yelped so loudly I was glad of the karaoke, and of the singer who chose that moment to engage in an almost lupine yodel.

But I wasn't really paying attention. I trusted Thom to restrain Rupert and I trusted Dixie Lee to keep the human patrons unaware of our existence. My job was to solicit a confession from a murderer.

To that end, I drew the blood back toward me on a receding sword blade. Rupert's eyes went wide as the magic made my kitsune nature clear, but his only complaint was a whimper. At the end, I took the blood onto my finger then raised it to my lips.

The morsel was warm on my tongue, not so heady as Thom's but still enough to add pep to my stride as I returned to the computer. "Sit here," I ordered Rupert, tapping the chair Thom had placed directly in front of the webcam.

Rupert sank down without complaint. Hands settled on knees until he'd donned the posture of a little boy in the principal's office. His gaze followed me as I paced two steps away then two steps back.

Thom watched also, far enough from Rupert so the murderer didn't lose further bladder control but close enough to keep him in hand if my kitsune control faltered. The alpha's presence lifted a weight off my shoulders, letting me focus on the questions I wanted to ask.

I only had one preliminary, actually, and that was for Scarlet's sake since I could smell the sweetness of obedience on the shifter before me. "Rupert, you will tell the truth. Do you understand me?"

"Yes."

After that, I cut straight to the heart of the matter. "Did you kill Janet Allegra?"

His answer this time came just as quickly. "No, I did not."

"What's this about?" Scarlet demanded, entering our conversation at last. My gaze flicked to the screen and I thought I saw something blink in the upper righthand corner before her voice wavered and returned my attention to her face. "You will let Rupert go immediately."

My boss sounded both tough and scared at the same time. Nothing like herself. I frowned, but obeyed. "Rupert, I release you. You are no longer under my control."

I tensed, expecting an attack. But Rupert just shook out his arms and cracked his knuckles, squinty eyes taking in the room a second time. "I was promised caviar," he muttered. "Caviar!"

While the other Lawkeeper regained his bearings, I exchanged a long look with Thom. I couldn't understand where my guesswork had run off the rails.

Then the fluorescent lights above us flickered, and the dimness seemed to shine a light directly to the heart of the matter. That change I'd noticed in the corner of the computer screen....

I ignored Rupert and leaned in closer, reading the word *recording* one moment before the red box disappeared.

Then Scarlet's entire posture tightened. Her voice hardened. "Yes, I taped your unfortunate choice of drawing blood from a Lawkeeper and using that blood in an attempt to compel him to confess to a crime for which he wasn't responsible. I also have physical evidence placing both you and Mr. Faris at the scene of Friday's crime."

Physical evidence? The knot in my stomach pulled tight again and I suddenly understood.

Our cell phones, swaddled in ziplocks to ensure scent remained on the items. That was Scarlet's evidence. And she'd drawn me here in the first place using an email that could have come from her computer as easily as from Rupert's.

This was a setup. It had all been a setup.

Not a setup on our part to collar Rupert, although that's what we'd thought we were taking part in. Instead, everything from my girls' night out with Charlie to the recorded video-chat session had been a setup in which the real murderer took both me and Thom down with one flick of her perfectly painted fingernail.

Because Scarlet had to be the murderer. She'd killed Janet Allegra, I now guessed, not through any particular antipathy toward military wives. Instead, her victim had just happened to be available when Scarlet needed a warm body to turn cold.

But why fixate on me and Thom?

The why was left to my imagination as Scarlet continued speaking, her voice just as firm and even as it had been in her office when she'd told me to use blood to apprehend Janet Allegra's murderer. "Turn yourself in," she ordered. "You and Mr. Faris will both be dealt with according to inter-pack law. Rupert, restrain them."

This, when it came right down to it, was the only flaw in Scarlet's plan. The puny man who stole our coffee, our toilet paper, and our paperclips, rose to his full height...which put the crown of his head at approximately my eye level. "Well," he started. "I guess I can *try*."

He could try and we could beat him back...while Scarlet once again recorded our actions? The slightest movement from Thom drew my attention. He raised one eyebrow and I nodded. Yes, I understood the mess I'd led us into.

Unfortunately, as best I could tell, there was no easy way out again. Or so I thought. Thom disagreed.

"Alright," he said, holding out his wrists as if he expected human-style hand-cuffs to materialize in Rupert's pockets. "I confess. Take me in. But the blood consumption today wasn't Kira's idea or fault. I forced that issue just like I masterminded the rest."

He did *what* exactly?

Before I could object to Thom's lie, the door to the parking lot slammed open to reveal blue Honda guy...and his gun.

Chapter 22

"Excellent timing, Nathaniel," Scarlet greeted him, the webcam acting against us now as it provided a clear view of the door. "Mr. Faris has confessed to a murder and Kira has used her kitsune abilities in an attempt to turn a law-abiding werewolf off the proper path. They will need to be disabled before being transported. A shot to each knee should suffice. Please proceed."

The *please* was the most chilling part of Scarlet's monologue. Chilling and effective. Because blue Honda guy—Nathaniel—didn't ask any questions. Instead, he raised his handgun, its barrel a tunnel to darkness.

And I dove.

Toward the gun. Yes, a nutty move. But I was the closest and the most likely to survive if Nathaniel went for a more mortal wound than Scarlet had suggested.

After all, I wasn't exactly defenseless. The star-ball magic that had sat in sword form at my back for the last few minutes was already hardening around the most at-risk portions of my anatomy. A magical tank top plus knee pads would stop a bullet.

Or at least so I hoped.

Thom didn't appear to agree with my reasoning. He shouted something wordless and full of fury as my knees thudded hard against floorboards. Splinters pricked through jeans into my shins—maybe I should have protected those also?—as I slid toward my goal.

In front of me, Nathaniel had braced himself to obey our employer. The gun cupped in his hands was steady. Which would travel faster? Me, in my effort to topple Nathaniel, or the bullet he would inevitably unleash once I got too close?

The sound of thunder crashing over us was so profound that at first I thought Nathaniel had pulled the trigger. Then I realized that was Thom's voice, if you could call the roll of crackling power a voice.

"Drop it."

Something hard and heavy struck my left shoulder. Then I was barreling into Nathaniel, tilting him off balance.

My enemy flailed, not quite falling. And I took a breath, slapping one hand against a body part that ached like the dickens.

No blood. Whatever hit me, it hadn't been a bullet. Instead, a glint of silver sparked up from the floor beside me. The painful projectile had been the gun itself.

I swiped up the weapon, cold metal on the barrel becoming warm where Nathaniel had clutched the grip. The revolver felt as dangerous in my hands as it had pointed in my direction. I vastly preferred my sword.

Still, I aimed the action end at Nathaniel. Not that I needed to. Thom continued spitting out alpha commands so hardcore they made even my muscles quiver.

"Nathaniel. Rupert. Leave this bar. Leave Gate City. Don't set foot in my territory ever again."

With jerky steps, Nathaniel turned and walked out the door into the parking lot. He resembled nothing so much as a marionette being manipulated by an inexperienced handler.

Inexperienced yet crazy powerful. I'd never felt an alpha command so serious it fizzed in my body like swallowed werewolf blood. I braced myself against the compulsion to *obey, obey, obey* for one long moment, then I sucked in a wheezing breath and worked my way up to my feet.

The laptop was shut, presumably by Thom in an effort to prevent Scarlet from recording anything even more incriminating. Rupert, though, still hovered by the chair I'd led him to. He tapped his index finger against the back of his opposite hand over and over, muttering a nursery rhyme under his breath.

"Is this usual?" Thom asked, stalking in a circle around the immobile Lawkeeper. With each step, his nostrils flared as he sniffed.

"No." I set the gun down on an arcade-game seat. Then, glancing at Rupert, I changed my mind and picked it up again before addressing Thom. "I'm gonna head outside and make sure Nathaniel is really gone."

Thom was beside me in two strides. The firearm that had felt so wrong between my fingers turned into a simple tool as he popped the clip then removed one last bullet from somewhere within the gun itself. "Let's go," he agreed.

Time slowed by the gun's presence sped back up as we stepped outside. The blue Honda was just reaching the far edge of the lot. And even though Nathaniel was leaving, as ordered, I focused on his license plate anyway. Memorized the string of numbers and letters just in case. *MHX....*

A harsh burst of expletive from Thom shifted my attention. I'd never heard him use even a single four-letter word, and this was sailor caliber. Scanning the lot furiously, though, nothing problematic jumped out at me.

Nothing, that is, until I checked over the blue Honda more thoroughly as it turned right into the alley in response to Thom's Moon Room command.

The Lawkeeper driving wasn't the only one inside, I realized. A woman slumped in the passenger seat, her cheek pressed up against the window as if she was napping.

Only she wasn't napping. Charlie wouldn't be napping inside the car of an unknown werewolf.

I broke into a run as the blue Honda completed its turn and sped off.

Chapter 23

“**T**he license plate!” I shouted as I ran. “MHX 6587.”

I expected Thom to pluck the information I'd tossed his way and utilize it just as deftly as he'd supported me previously. But he didn't. Instead, footfalls pounded behind mine and Thom's long legs caught up as I reached the first cross street.

A block away, the blue Honda swerved left onto Gate City's main drag. From there, Nathaniel could head for the highway, toward Creation Kingdom, or just melt back into the city proper. I needed to follow if I had any hope of discovering where Charlie was being taken.

But Thom hadn't pulled out a cell phone or returned to the bar to summon assistance. So I spat out the license-plate number a second time. “Give that to your sentries,” I finished, stating what I believed to be the obvious.

“No sentries.”

I opened my mouth to argue, then closed it again. Of course Thom had no sentries. He wasn't an alpha. Didn't, apparently, believe in patrolling the boundaries of his territory to make sure unfriendly shifters stayed out.

Which meant I was on a fool's errand. There was no point in following the blue Honda on foot if no motorized backup waited to take that information and run with it. I might as well spit into the wind that even now whipped hair around my face.

Still, I couldn't stop myself from sprinting after Charlie. Thud, right foot. Memory of us as children when proximity to me and Mai had gotten Jessie Raven kidnapped by a wannabe alpha. Thud, left foot. Charlie and me on a bus, ditching adults and saving her twin while I maintained the secrecy of shifters by juggling lies. Thud, right foot. The past was the best indicator of the future. Thud, left foot. I'd find a way to get Charlie out of her current mess.

I shot across Main Street without regard for honking drivers who didn't understand that Charlie's life depended on my jaywalking. Was that the taillights of the blue Honda turning down Kane Street toward the highway? I wasn't sure. Nathaniel was so far ahead of me now that my chances of catching up were zilch.

Breath wheezed through my nostrils at the same speed self-recrimination whooshed through my neurons. Was this why Ito had wanted Jessie and Charlie to steer clear of me? Because he knew being friends with shifters was bad for his wife and sister-in-law's health?

A car honked and I shot it the middle finger. I wasn't even in the road now. So what if I'd snarled up traffic earlier. I wanted to snarl more than traffic. I wanted to....

The car had stopped, the rear passenger-side door swinging open to reveal an empty back seat. From the front, Thom suggested: "Perhaps you should get in."

My breast brushed Thom's hand as I flung myself inside, and his arm retreated so fast I got the distinct impression he found the contact distasteful. Ignoring the weirdness, I barked out an order—"Turn right on Kane Street"—while trying to make sense of the fact that Rupert appeared to be the one behind the wheel.

Rupert, who we'd left in the Moon Room reciting nursery rhymes. Who had been poised, before that, to apprehend me and Thom for crimes we hadn't committed.

Well, I'd committed my crime. If drinking werewolf blood under orders from Scarlet really was a crime.

"Nice of you to ask how I'm faring after that traumatic incident," the Lawkeeper in question groused as he followed my instructions. He didn't, however, pick up speed after taking the turn. Instead, he slowed and I must have huffed in disbelief because he admonished, "Can't you see the squirrel? It's not ethical to kill animals you don't intend to eat."

"At this pace, the squirrel might kill us rather than vice versa," I countered. But Rupert was the only game in town at this instant, so I literally sat on my hands as he toodled along at the pace of a nonagenarian. At least we were headed in the right direction, toward the highway.

By the time we reached the dual on-ramps, there was no sign of the blue Honda. So we were left guessing on direction. "Go south," Thom suggested. "It's the fastest way out of my territory."

A good assumption if Nathaniel was obeying Thom's alpha command at an instinctive level. Speaking of which, "Why aren't you fleeing mindlessly, Rupert?"

Maybe if we talked, Rupert would drive a little faster. The distance between me and Charlie felt like a rubber band, stretching tighter and tighter. How soon would it snap?

Rupert was the one who snapped. "Oh, no apology? No explanation of your unsavory heritage?"

I was too worried about Charlie to answer, but Thom growled. Which had the entirely wrong effect on Rupert's gas pedal. He'd been veering onto the highway, but now he slowed down rather than speeding up, allowing a string of cars to race past.

I closed my eyes while Rupert nattered on as if we weren't blowing our one chance to get Charlie back. "I'm afraid your pet alpha isn't very good at what he does."

I expected another growl from Thom at this point. But he and I both held our silence as Rupert slowly came up to the official speed limit.

Not highway speed, of course. We weren't getting any closer to Nathaniel. We were almost certainly falling further behind.

"It was a powerful command," Rupert acknowledged. "I *still* have static on my sweater. But it wasn't very targeted. And you're asking the wrong questions. You should be asking why I'm helping you now."

I grabbed the door handle as our car rocked with the gale-force wind of a tractor trailer passing far too close for comfort. "I assumed there was another alpha command involved," I observed between gritted teeth. *Go faster,* I begged him silently.

Rupert made a rude noise with his lips, his speed unwavering. "Ha. You wish. No. I'm merely doing my job. The Roanoke office has been rotten for years, which is why I transferred into it. I wasn't certain where the origin of the rot lay. I'm nearly certain now."

And, for the first time since Scarlet recorded me drinking Rupert's blood, I relaxed just a little. "You're with some sort of internal affairs division."

The existence of an overseeing arm wouldn't help Charlie immediately. But if Rupert had other Lawkeepers—more effective Lawkeepers—to turn the issue over to, they might apprehend Scarlet before she was able to harm my friend.

Which was when I admitted the truth. We weren't going to catch up to Nathaniel at this snail's pace. I closed my eyes and accepted reality. "Pull over and call your superiors."

"Bossy, aren't you?" And yet, Rupert obeyed. He cut across northbound traffic at an official intersection, finding a spot to park where a smaller highway intersected 23. "Here's where you get out."

"Wait. What?"

Rupert straightened to his full five foot zero inches, even shorter when seated. "Nathaniel's gone and I don't intend to be seen with you. It will be hard enough prying a human out of his grip without backup. I assume the victim isn't aware of our existence?"

Victim sounded harsh...and true. I swallowed. "Charlie? No. But what do you mean about 'without backup'?"

Rupert didn't even look sorrowful as he squashed the hopes I'd nurtured just a few seconds earlier. "I'm the only straight arrow I know of within the department," he observed, fingers tapping against the steering wheel. "I'd hoped to recruit you. But you're worse than useless to me now. If I think of something you can do to help without causing more damage to the situation, I'll be in touch."

Chapter 24

"You'll be in *touch*?" My fists clenched around a sword that had materialized without conscious thought. "We don't have time for you to spend *months* drinking fancy coffee while pretending to do research. Charlie is in danger. Charlie..."

"Will be just fine," Rupert interrupted. "She was clearly taken to ensure your good behavior. Scarlet would have mentioned her shortly if your pet alpha hadn't taken matters into his own hands."

The repeated use of the term *pet alpha* would have set most werewolves off. But Thom's tone was even as he ignored Rupert and addressed me.

"We can return to plan B. I closed the laptop, so your superior won't know what happened after Nathaniel left. It's believable that Rupert apprehended me and brought me in."

I couldn't help it. I winced.

Because Thom knew nothing about werewolves. On the one hand, there was Rupert with his combover that only made the tremendous balding patch at the center of his pate more obvious. In stark contrast, Thom's virility filled the car with alpha musk. The chance of the former overcoming the latter was midway between zero and way-the-hell-no.

Thom gave me time to think before providing a verbal nudge. "What do you think?"

I took a deep breath and said what I never wanted to say. "I think Rupert's right."

"Ha!" My coworker pumped his fist in the air, doing a funny sort of dance there in the driver's seat. In the process, his elbow struck the horn, which blared out a noise vaguely resembling a fart.

"Been meaning to get that fixed," Rupert muttered.

Ignoring our driver's antics, Thom focused his blue eyes on me. "Are you certain?" he asked, his gaze saying much more than the three words he actually uttered.

The cold hole in my gut warmed. Thom was willing to back me up in any way I considered necessary. Unfortunately, the necessary thing right now was unfolding myself out of Rupert's car and accepting the fact I was leaving Charlie's safety in the hands of the office dunderhead.

I closed my eyes, which didn't actually make the admission any easier. "I'm certain," I said.

Thom must have grabbed a cell phone from that overfull closet along with his clothes because he called for pickup as Rupert disappeared down the highway. The air of passing vehicles buffeted us despite the depth of the pull-off, and I had to raise my voice to speak once Thom finished his call.

"Do you mind if I use that for a minute?" I gestured at the phone.

"Be my guest."

All of my contacts' numbers were lost back in that puddle at Creation Kingdom. But the digits I had to dial now, I knew by heart.

My sister answered on the fifth ring, just before I was shunted over to voice mail. "Hello?"

Her tone of voice suggested she was about to hang up on me. This was, after all, an unfamiliar number. So I fumbled through a greeting I didn't usually bother with.

"Mai. It's me. Kira."

"My favorite chaos bringer." A smile warmed her words. "Of course I recognize you, little sister. And I'm glad you called. I've been thinking about where we left our conversation yesterday."

Our conversation? Right. I'd asked if it was ever kosher to drink werewolf blood. Mai had knee-jerked negative...then I'd consumed the blood anyway. "That's not really important...."

"It *is* important," she countered, "or you wouldn't have asked. No, I don't think drinking werewolf blood is the right thing to do outside life-or-death situations. Ethically, it's dicey. And werewolves aren't likely to think highly of you after the fact."

Now that she mentioned it, I vividly remembered Mai fighting battle after battle to make a place for us in Gunner's pack when I was a kid. And, yes, things had gotten worse for a good long while after the blood-drinking episode. I'd somehow let the joy of present pack happiness block out the distant past.

"But," my sister continued, her voice softening the same way it had when she brushed hair off my forehead before offering bedtime kisses, "we all make mistakes and I'm here to help you if you stumble. You're important to me, Kira. I want to back you up."

My throat tightened. She was offering to fall on her sword for me, the same way she always had. "You're important to me too," I managed.

And so was my niece, who would suffer just as much as her mother from that video of me compelling Rupert after consuming werewolf blood. They'd both suffer due to my faulty moral compass and failure to think through the consequences of my actions. The only way I could have downgraded kitsune-werewolf relations further was if I'd killed Janet Allegra myself.

And now, if I hoped to protect my niece, I had to do the unthinkable. Divorce my family from my decisions until I dealt with Scarlet. Keep Mai and Grub and my niecelet safe within their pack bubble while hoping any awfulness Scarlet unleashed stayed focused on me.

"Anyway," I continued, speaking around the lump in my throat, "that's not why I called. I just wanted to say—if you hear weird things about me, keep your distance. Don't dive in and try to fix it. Just tell them I'm an adult and make my own choices. I have nothing to do with the Fairwood pack."

A silence so extensive I thought we'd been disconnected. I removed the phone from my ear and peered at the screen.

Nope. Still active.

Then, finally, Mai got her words together. "Kira, your job isn't to protect me. Where are you?"

I didn't answer her question. Instead, I told the truth. "Your job isn't to protect me either, Mai. Not anymore. Your job is to protect my niece."

Mai chuckled. "I'm pretty sure she's my daughter first."

"We can argue over custody later." Or never. The thought of missing my niece's birth speared me like the bullet Nathaniel hadn't quite managed to fire.

But such an extended separation from family wouldn't be necessary. Mai had a few months left before her due date. This awfulness with Scarlet would be long over by then, one way or another.

I raised my eyes to the cars barreling past then to Thom, who'd ambled several feet away to give my conversation privacy. Finally, I swallowed and repeated my request. "For now, Mai, I want your promise. If any Lawkeepers contact you, tell them you haven't heard from me. That I'm a loose cannon. I do my own thing."

"You're not a...." Mai's voice trailed off and I think she was trying to cover the speaker because what I heard next was muffled. "Grub, sweetie, talk to your Auntie Kira while I find your father, okay?"

Then little-boy breath huffed into the speaker. "Keeeeeeraaaaaa! Have you ever heard of worms on a string? They're really cool. Like fluffy dragons you run between your fingers. They wiggle! Do you think you can find me one? I really, really want it."

Meanwhile, in the background, Gunner's gruff voice murmured, "Of course we'll pull Kira out. Just keep her on the line until I can pin down her location."

I had no idea how easy it was to track cell phones, but Gunner had a way of snapping his fingers and making things happen. So I hung up on my nephew. Hung up on the pack I'd do anything for.

Hung up and spent the next few minutes before our ride arrived browsing internet stores. Grub's worm on a string would be delivered tomorrow. I hoped the toy would tide my nephew over until I could see him again.

Chapter 25

I'd sunk down behind the guard rail and was pressing the buy button when Bertrand pulled up in a mini-SUV. Just like the suits that Thom's unofficial second always selected, this vehicle screamed human instead of werewolf. Because it wasn't extra-large or even average, both typical size choices for shifters swimming in hefty helpings of testosterone. Instead, Bertrand appeared to have picked the smallest version off the lot.

Now, he brought the vehicle to a gentle halt and rolled down the window. I was hidden by the guard rail, so I wasn't surprised he neither addressed nor seemed to notice me. "Thom, I want to talk to you about...."

"Not in front of the lady."

Lady? All consideration for Bertrand's choice of self-representation fled as niggling suspicions about Thom's motivations curdled into a hard lump in my gut.

After all, I knew from Southern classmates that this term—derided by feminists—was a sign of respect in the Gate City area. Thom calling me a lady suggested he was shielding the ears of a member of the weaker sex.

Which sounded okay on the surface. But...were my ears all he'd been shielding? More clues aligned no matter how hard I tried to ignore them. My short stature, which meant I was often treated like a child. Thom's upbringing as a human, which might make looking out for women an ingrained obligation.

Each time Thom had touched me, his impulse could be traced back to mere chivalry. Keeping my bare butt out of the mud? Check. Preventing me from stumbling on saggy floorboards? Also, unfortunately, check.

Add to that the recent episode in Rupert's car when he'd jerked away from intimate contact. My face heated as I realized I'd been lusting after a brick wall.

As I pondered, Bertrand's mouth snapped shut over whatever words he'd planned. And, as if reading from a textbook of Southern manners, Thom sped his footsteps so he could open the front passenger-side door and hold it ready for me.

"Thanks," I offered, not meaning the gratitude in the least. I didn't want to be cossetted and protected. I wanted to be considered a woman, not a piece of precious porcelain to be covered in bubble wrap and put away in a box.

Thom didn't seem to notice my distress. Instead, he gently snicked my door shut before folding his longer limbs into the back.

Bertrand was the one who shot a questioning glance in my direction. Only once though, then he pulled back out onto the highway and proceeded to point out landmarks in a clear effort to dissolve whatever unhappiness seasoned my scent.

"That's Hillcrest Heights," he observed, his faint accent adding a hint of exoticism to the ordinary as he pointed to the mountain above Gate City. "Used to be, just a few rich families lived there. Then the Base moved in."

Now, the hillside was peppered with mansions. I murmured mostly feigned interest, my hand settling over the ache in my belly, as Bertrand transitioned to telling me about the ferris wheel in Grogan Park and the bullet train to Kingsport. None of the emotions queasily roiling around in my gut would get the current job done.

Which meant it was time to forget hanging up on my family. Time to forget unprofessional thoughts about my current investigative partner. Instead, my focus had to stay firmly fixed to taking Scarlet down and getting Charlie back.

Then we were pulling into the one open spot in front of the Full Moon Saloon. Neon lights were dark now, the plastic sign on the door flipped around to apologize for being closed. Karaoke afternoon had ended quite abruptly.

As I sat there in a daze, Thom hopped out and opened my door before I could beat him to it. "Go on in," he suggested, his deep voice still vibrating certain portions of my anatomy even though I now realized our attraction was one-sided. "We'll be right behind you."

I fixed the image of Charlie's face in my mind and left the men to their private conversation. Inside, the bar was empty except for half-filled beer mugs. Muffled voices, though, carried through the wall from the Moon Room.

I turned in that direction and realized I'd been wrong. The main part of the bar wasn't empty. I'd overlooked a child, twelve-ish, who stepped into my path while clutching a thick library book to her chest.

"Moon or paw?" she asked, her eyes on the ground. "You need one to go in."

She was coltishly tall but not the sort of sentry I would have chosen to maintain the privacy of werewolves. Only, the air patterns changed then and I smelled her.

Shifter. Not run-of-the-mill wolf shifter either. This girl would one day turn into a fox.

"Perhaps you shouldn't be sniffing my daughter." Dixie Lee emerged from the kitchen drying her hands on a dish towel. Dropping the cloth on the edge of the bar, she headed toward us slowly enough not to be menacing but fast enough to suggest her words were meant to be obeyed.

Rule of the wild: never get between a mama bear and her cub. I lifted both hands, taking one long step away from the other kitsune. "I'm sorry. I didn't realize...."

"Ava, honey, maybe you should go on in?"

Into the Moon Room, which I knew from overhearing Thom's phone call would be full of high-alert werewolves. "That's not the best idea," I started, the adrenaline that was beginning to fade after chasing the blue Honda coming back full force.

But Ava had already opened the door and slipped through. All I could do was shoot one more glance at her mother—blond curls, as American as apple pie—before rushing after the kid who must have been a half-breed.

Half-breed or not, Ava was old enough to be considered a threat by werewol ves...and possibly also a prize. Her face, from the glimpse I'd gotten, was well on its way to stunning, especially when framed by honey-colored curls.

Unfortunately, the girl was also too young to shift or to magic up a star ball. Good thing I had plenty of oomph to protect us both.

I grabbed the door knob before it could click shut. "Kira," Dixie Lee started. She was reaching for me. But despite the scent on her daughter, she was only human. Not much of an asset in a room full of charged-up werewolves.

So I ignored her and slid inside, placing myself between Ava and what appeared to be dozens of people packed into far too small a space. All were focused on our little corner. They didn't pounce, but the momentum of inconspicuous movements seemed to be drawing the crowd closer. I'd never seen so many pointy teeth in grinning human mouths.

"I can't see," Ava said at my back, but I ignored her. If she couldn't see, that was good. Every prey animal knew to hunker down and hide their eyes when faced with insurmountable danger.

I, however, wasn't a prey animal. Instead, I openly surveyed the shifters crowd-ing into my personal space.

There weren't any other women present. Unsurprising, I supposed, given the lone-wolf nature of the shifters who gravitated toward Thom's not-quite-pack. A few reminded me of Bertrand—solid, well-dressed, possibly dependable. But most were more like Smoke.

This more numerous type of shifter was rough around the edges. Half feral. Bringing to mind strays who'd been invited in off the street but hadn't left their wild heritage behind.

Not all of the werewolves were two-legged either. Fully a quarter stalked lupine through the crowd, jockeying for position with ruffs raised.

The Moon Room was no place for a child, let alone a kitsune child.

But Ava was here and a sword would only go so far in this situation. It was time to turn on the charm.

Chapter 26

The knowledge of predator eyes tingled against the nape of my neck as I turned to debrief the child behind me. "Any big events in your recent past? Kindergarten graduation? New job?"

As I'd hoped, the preposterous suggestions summoned a smile and Ava actually managed to meet my gaze for the first time. "My birthday is next week...."

"Perfect." I looped one arm around the girl's shoulder and carried her with me as I twirled us back around. Her library book was now our only shield against the werewolves who had drawn even closer during the seconds my attention had been focused elsewhere. Her mother, I noted, had entered behind us and now leaned against the wall ten feet away.

Dixie Lee didn't seem particularly concerned about the way werewolf breath heated a room that had been chilly when I'd entered it naked with Thom on my heels an hour earlier. A cascade of murmurs broke over us, individual words incomprehensible but their intensity unmistakable. I was glad the cat had been locked away.

Ava wasn't locked away however. So I grinned at the crowd as if their presence wasn't making my muscles twitch. As if I didn't feel like a snow hare trying to hide on a sprawling, open expanse of blacktop. "You're all upset. It's understandable." I tapped the girl on top of her head, twisting my mouth in teasing disappointment. "Ava, dear, I *told* you it was better to send out invitations on time rather than hand letter them and risk being late."

"Huh?" Ava's confusion was covered up by a snort from the back of the room. Someone thought my humor was funny. Even Dixie Lee's mouth curved up into a smile.

"Yes," I told the crowd as a whole. "Each of you is invited to the birthday party. Gifts are required, however. No gift, no cake. Don't be a freeloader."

Gazes were still intent upon me and Ava, but they felt softer now. Gentler. Which wasn't surprising. Everyone loved a good birthday party.

Everyone except, apparently, two of the grungiest werewolves off to one side. Their hair was shaggy, their clothes rumpled. In a different city, I would have thought they were homeless humans reduced to sleeping on the street.

Here, though, the sharp glint of canines said otherwise. The blond shook his head and the one with a scar cutting through his left eyebrow rebutted. "She *is*. I saw her."

"You're high."

"Not lately. She's a fox."

The word shivered down my spine. *Fox.* No one else seemed to have noticed, though. Well, no one except Dixie Lee, whose smile was fading fast.

If I'd been on top of my game, I would have come up with another distraction. But my mind blanked and the room went quiet at the same moment Scar Eyebrow tossed out the word that was anathema to werewolves. "She's a kitsune."

Sure enough, the ease imbuing the room's inhabitants fell away. Danger rebounded.

I clenched down hard on Ava's shoulders, shoving her behind my back again. Star ball gleamed into sword form in my right hand, proving my own identity. But right now, the presence of a weapon was more important than trying to talk my way out of being what I was.

"So what if Ava is a kitsune?" I raised my voice. "The ability to turn into a fox doesn't mean anything. Judge us by what we do not by what we shift into."

Dixie Lee glared at me so hotly I expected blisters to pop up like zits on my forehead. Then she yanked out her phone and muttered furiously into the microphone.

"Thom. We need you in the Moon Room."

Good idea calling in backup, but Thom wouldn't arrive fast enough. The walls pushed in closer as the sea of werewolves regained their predatory intensity. I wasn't sure exactly what I'd said wrong, but I'd clearly shoved my foot halfway down my throat.

"Head for the door," I murmured, hoping Ava would hear me. But her warm weight behind my back didn't move. She'd frozen like a deer in the headlights.

No, the girl hadn't frozen. She was merely preparing to give me instructions. "Show them your medallion."

"Medallion?" I didn't have a medallion.

Ava was faster on her feet than I would have expected...but that was me forgetting she was a fox. Of course the girl was able to slip out from behind my back, tucking the library book under one arm while she fumbled for a necklace hidden beneath her hoody. "Like this."

The crescent moon she pulled out was three inches across, gleaming silver.

Wait, why did the kid have a moon, not a paw?

I blinked as the past rewrote itself. When I'd walked in, had all those eyes been focused on Ava...or on me? Had their predatory attention been based on knowledge that we two were kitsunes or on the simple fact that I was the only adult female shifter in the room?

Too late, I remembered the obvious. Werewolves couldn't smell the subtle distinction between wolf and fox while we were two-legged. Otherwise, how could I have been incognito on the job for months? The guy who'd outed me must have seen me shift and known nothing about Ava.

I'd just...forgotten. Shaken up by recent events, I'd made a world-class blunder.

No wonder Dixie Lee had glared so hard. The girl beside me probably didn't even understand what was happening.

Which would make Ava that much harder to protect.

The wolves closed in further. Teeth first wasn't exactly how I'd hoped to meet Thom's pack.

Speak of the devil. I looked up and Thom was there, his bulk closer than seemed possible when I was certain I'd had no backup a moment earlier. I wasn't sure how someone so large had made it through the door without any of us noticing, but he'd managed the trick.

And now, when he wanted to be apparent, every eye trained on him. If I hadn't just screwed up so badly, the notion that Thom wasn't an alpha would have made me laugh out loud.

Instead, I hunched my shoulders to make myself smaller as Thom drew every werewolf's attention away from me and the girl I shielded. "Ava is a moon. You won't bother her." His voice wasn't quite an alpha command but it veered into that territory. Deep and so quiet we wouldn't have caught the words if anyone else had been speaking at the same time.

No one else dared to open their mouths though. The shaggy guys who'd set the mess into motion dipped their heads in submission. The room was so quiet I could hear the toilet tank gurgling full.

Only after three throat clearings did someone in the crowd manage a complaint. "But if she's a fox...."

"Right now, the child is a moon. Ava, go with Bertrand."

The shifter who'd picked me and Thom up beside the highway was curling protectively around Dixie Lee's much smaller body. I got the distinct impression she was what he'd wanted to talk to Thom about. That Bertrand had been angling for the role of bodyguard. The warmth in his eyes suggested Ava's kitsune heritage didn't faze him in the least.

So the problem I'd created would be resolved once Ava got to the door. I didn't particularly want her walking there unprotected though. As the girl moved out from behind me, I grabbed for her arm...and Thom's scowl turned so intense it made me miss the easy catch.

If I'd thought Dixie Lee's glare was searing, Thom's was like sticking my head into a fire. I winced and Ava padded away from me. The crowd, released by Thom's changed focus, shuffled their feet and murmured among themselves.

They didn't surge forward to confront Ava, however, as she sidled along the wall toward her mother. Instead, a new voice piped up. "And the woman?"

Me. He meant me.

My shoulders hunched further. The fact I was a fox in a roomful of wolves, the latter led by someone who wasn't particularly pleased by my behavior, was unmistakable. Gunner's reasoning for keeping me and Mai in the heart of his pack for the last decade had never been so clear.

Still, I forced myself to straighten. My star-ball sword flared as I thinned the blade to extend my protective buffer. I could fight my way out of here if I had to. I could....

A handful of metal shot through the air between me and Thom even as a surprised cough came from elsewhere. I shot a glance toward the sound—Big T, entering via the door Dixie Lee, Ava, and Bertrand had just left through—just as instinct sent my free hand up to catch whatever Thom had flung at me. The expression on the older man's face was strange, his attention riveted on my hand.

I looked down, considering the item I'd captured. A stone on a gold chain, the former sparkling amethyst. It was lovely...but nothing like Ava's medallion.

"Temporary immunity," Thom growled.

The necklace wasn't a paw or a moon but its mere existence eased the tension in the Moon Room. Eyes turned away from me. The hunger quotient lessened. I could breathe at last.

Could breathe...and notice motion as the parking-lot door opened slowly and jerkily. The process was laborious, the person working his way through entirely unexpected.

Eli and his walker filled the opening after one endless minute. "Did you realize," he told the roomful of shifters, "that there are wolves coming down the mountain into our town?"

Chapter 27

olves. The word reminded me of why I was here and what I was up against.

Scarlet. Nathaniel. *Charlie.*

If my boss had chosen to raise the stakes by siccing more Lawkeepers on us, did that mean my human friend was no longer on the table as a pawn to be turned over at Thom's and my surrender?

I tried to push my way toward the other end of the room where Thom's laptop might still have a video call with Scarlet waiting beneath its lid. But the crowd had turned impenetrable. And Thom's attention was fixated on the young human who'd brought us word. "Wolves?"

"*Canis lupus,*" Eli confirmed. "I saw them through my scope." A pause as he wobbled and tried to catch his breath, still holding the heavy door open with his walker. "I was watching for elk. Did you know the Kentucky herd sometimes makes its way down here? Or maybe they come over from Grundy. Either way, I've seen *Cervus canadensis* on Hillcrest five times."

"Good eating once you gnaw through the fur," someone muttered, hopefully quietly enough for Eli to miss the commentary. I tensed, considering changing direction from my snail's pace flight toward the laptop.

Did that muttering shifter have no concept how dangerous it was for a human to be introduced to the world of werewolves? Most mundanes didn't take the news lightly. Most had to be dealt with by Lawkeepers like me.

Was that what was happening to Charlie at this very minute? Had she been shown a shifter's fur and was now being dealt with?

Luckily, the mutterer went silent, allowing me to turn back toward my original quest. The laptop was only twenty feet away now, but the distance might as well have been measured in miles. I had absolutely no luck pushing myself between the solid wall of shifters, so I hunched over and tried to burrow through a gap.

No dice.

By the time my head popped back up, only about three feet closer to my destination, a shifter was dragging a chair out of the shadows then helping with both the door and walker so Eli could sit down. The process took long enough for Thom to stride effortlessly through the crowd to join the young human.

"How many were there?" The intensity of Thom's question heightened the alert level in the room. I wasn't the only one who thought strange shifters had no right to be in Gate City territory. But Eli appeared to be oblivious to the subtext.

"I'm not sure." The young man's face scrunched up in remembered confusion. "I thought I saw twelve wolves plus a bunch of people. Then I definitely counted eighteen wolves. What's going on? Can you take me up there? I've never seen *Canis lupus* in real life."

Eighteen invaders? That was more Lawkeepers than worked in the entire Roanoke office. Did Scarlet have the backing of the alphas who fed employees into our organization? If they believed whatever lies she spun as she summoned reinforcements, would they accept her conclusions about me, Thom, and Charlie just as easily?

My fingers twitched as if they were already tapping laptop keys. But I paused. Because Eli was on the cusp of understanding, a revelation hovering around him like a particularly odiferous fart.

I wasn't the only one who saw it. Four-legged shifters did their best to melt behind human legs without moving quickly enough to catch the young man's attention. But they were still wolves, still jockeying for territory. Someone stepped on someone else's toes quite literally, and the latter snarled. Eli's eyes grew wider than they had when he'd regaled me with his theories about the Gate City ghost.

"*Canis lupus,*" he repeated under his breath, his voice awed. The fluorescents flickered worse than usual and the return of brightness afterwards seemed to clear the last shred of resistance out of Eli's mind. "They're not though, are they? That's why I thought there were more people than wolves at first, then more wolves than people later."

"Eli," Thom started. "Don't jump to conclusions."

But Eli was already jumping. Jumping right off the cliff of knowledge that threatened his skin.

After all, there was a reason Lawkeepers were sent into problematic packs, and it wasn't really to prevent murders. Our primary purpose was simple. Keep unwitting humans from realizing shifters existed, even if that meant putting those humans to death.

The issue of Scarlet and Charlie would have to keep for one more minute. "Don't go there," I called toward the young man who was adult in posture but childlike in innocence.

Unfortunately, I was too far back in the crowd for my words to carry. The gem that lay cold against my collarbone made the werewolves around me willing to begrudge my existence, but they had no interest in assisting my forward progress.

No wonder my renewed efforts to press between werewolves—this time heading toward Eli—made no more headway than previously. No wonder Eli spoke before I could sidetrack his brain.

"They're werewolves." Eli's voice rose with excitement until it rang through the Moon Room. "You're all werewolves."

"Well, not precisely," someone in the crowd answered. He pointed in my direction. "*She's* a fox."

I winced, and not because I'd been singled out either. I liked Eli. Charlie liked Eli. But I still considered myself a Lawkeeper, which meant the young man had just become a liability and a target.

Unless, of course, I could find this situation's equivalent of a Gryffindor scarf. Something to prove to the Lawkeepers at large—and to my own conscience—that

Eli would never share shifters' existence with the wider world no matter the temptation.

The trouble being: this young man in stature was a kid in mentality. You couldn't expect kids to keep secrets. Not unless, like Ava, the kid lived with a parent in the know and had a very personal reason to toe the line.

Possibilities buzzed through my brain, none particularly palatable. I swallowed. There had to be a way out of this, but workarounds eluded my searching like a fish swimming through my fingers.

Thom was the one who captured the elusive solution. "Dad, grab a moon medallion. Eli, you wanted permission to enter this room? You've got it as long as you agree to two rules."

I held my breath, waiting for the outburst that would require me to step in and do something I found deeply distasteful. Well, *try* to do something deeply distasteful. I wasn't so sure how far I'd get in this room full of wolves.

But Eli didn't babble, didn't fight against the impossible. Instead, he accepted the wonder of werewolves, clinging to his walker as he struggled back to his feet. "I will!" he declared, his eyes shining with hero worship.

Thom nodded. "You've already proven you can abide by the first rule. If there's a problem, bring it to me. The other is equally simple: everything you learn here is top secret. No sharing with anyone who doesn't have a medallion like this or this."

Thom snapped his fingers and a young werewolf stepped forward displaying a paw medallion. At the same moment, Big T reappeared with a moon like the one Ava wore.

"Wow." Eli accepted the moon-shaped medallion as if it was a magical artifact. And it was by my standards. The moon medallion meant that Thom really might have control over this human, even though he said Gate City wasn't a pack and he wasn't an alpha. It meant I might not have to step in and apply brute force.

But only if Eli took the responsibility seriously. I watched intently as the young man tried to pull the chain over his head one-handed. His fingers shook, his other hand bracing against the walker's handlebars.

Then Thom was gripping his arm, removing the medallion while keeping Eli upright. "Allow me."

The flannel-clad shifter looked, in that moment, like a medieval king knighting one of his squires. And Eli glowed like a squire who wished for nothing more than knighthood, a squire who would give his life before revealing secrets he'd been tasked with keeping to himself.

It was working. I could honestly tell anyone who asked that Eli would obey Thom like a pack wolf obeyed his alpha. Even if Thom refused the honorific, even if he wasn't going about this the way a normal pack leader might.

At long last, I released my pent-up breath.

Then Thom snapped his fingers and the space exploded into action. A cabinet I hadn't paid attention to previously was flung open to reveal an arsenal of swords and handguns. Two shifters began doling out weapons while Thom spoke to the room at large.

"If you have people you care about who can't protect themselves, bring them to the bar now. They can camp out here or upstairs until this is over. You'll be on guard duty to ensure nothing goes wrong while the rest of us head up to Hillcrest."

Thom intended to *fight* an army of Lawkeepers? Okay, yes, he'd dealt with Eli quite efficiently. But going up against a multi-pack force of professionals was suicide. Especially since Lawkeepers from other districts would pile on later if today was a success.

I tried again to insert myself into his inner circle. Instead, I found myself being pushed closer to the outskirts by the second.

I wasn't entirely ignored, however. Someone did come up to my elbow and offer a sword.

I took it reflexively, testing a weight that was ungainly and awkward. Still, any blade would be better than no blade if I needed to hide my star ball. I nodded my thanks while strapping the associated belt around my waist.

"Dad," Thom continued, "call the police chief. Make up a reason why he should ignore wolves running through the city for the next few hours."

"On it," Big T promised before slipping out to the bar area. As with his son, the crowd parted easily to let him through.

The Moon Room was growing lighter on bodies by the minute as shifters left to do Thom's bidding. Which meant I could finally work my way closer to the laptop, and to Thom who appeared to be ignoring many things including one not-so-minor point. "The police chief will accept an excuse just like that?" I asked.

Thom didn't acknowledge I'd spoken. Instead, the same shifter who'd offered me the sword answered.

"Of course," he said, as if my question was nonsensical. "Farises have been in this valley longer than Gate City has existed."

Which I guess also explained why Eli had seen wolves and rushed over to share the news with a mere bartender. But Thom's deep roots in a human town would mean nothing to Scarlet. They'd mean nothing to Lawkeepers intent upon obeying werewolf strictures much older than these city streets.

On the other hand, I'd finally settled within arm's length of the laptop we'd used to communicate with Scarlet previously. I shoved through the last of the thinning crowd, slamming open the laptop lid.

If Scarlet was still there, waiting, then maybe I could talk her around. Save Charlie. Prevent what was bound to be a bloodbath on Hillcrest in mere minutes.

But the video chat had ended. The screen was blank.

Chapter 28

"Are we going or staying?"

"What?" I looked up from the computer, noticing as I did so that the Moon Room was now empty save for me and the cowboy-hat-wearing shifter who'd handed me the sword earlier. Well, us plus Eli, who was being ushered out into the bar by another werewolf I'd never met before.

Meanwhile, the door to the parking lot was drifting shut behind the last to leave. The roar of engines sprang to life in the back lot.

"Well?" Cowboy Hat nudged, eyebrows raised.

Ah, this shifter wanted to know if I intended to hide away with the women and children. The answer to that was a big fat no.

Rather than replying, I raced to the unlocked cabinet, the one full of clothes and condoms. As I'd hoped, there were also cell phones stacked on the bottom. Grabbing one and powering it up, I was out the door, one foot on the bumper of a half-filled pickup truck, by the time Cowboy Hat caught up.

"I'll let down the tailgate," he offered, proving my guess right. He'd been left behind to manage me.

But I didn't need management. I'd already vaulted up and over, landing fox silent on the metal bed. The closest wheel well was occupied...then it wasn't. I thanked the shifter who'd slid off, even if his return gesture had more in common with grade-school boys yelling about cooties than it did with Southern manners.

Then the whole bed sagged under Cowboy Hat's weight one second before the pickup eased out of the lot and sped up toward Hillcrest. Here in the open, it was easier to ignore the sidelong glances of the werewolves. Especially when I had a murderous employer to track down.

Because if I could get in touch with Scarlet, I could avert the upcoming battle between Thom's not-quite-pack and my coworkers. I could talk her around to releasing Charlie. I could....

The truck hit a bump and the phone nearly flew out of my fingers. Okay, so in order to do any of that, I had to make contact first.

Thankfully, the endless startup sequence was over, so I was able to start poking for contact points. Nothing in my personal inbox from Scarlet. Just an ever-increasing deluge of messages from my barely literate nephew....

I meant to ignore them, but the subject lines were frantic. *"Help!" "O no!" "I need U!" "BLOOD!"*

There was no time to waste, but I opened the last one anyway.

Skimming as fast as I could over misspelled ramblings about a knife and his finger, I came to an attached image file at the bottom. If Grub had injured himself....

I tapped the icon, but a photo didn't open. Instead, some sort of program sprang to life.

Shit. Gunner was wily. The truck swerved and I fumbled, requiring two tries to uninstall both the virus and the email program.

Whatever Gunner was up to, though, was currently irrelevant. Based on our gain of elevation, we were less than five minutes from the wolves Eli had seen and I'd yet to find a way to contact Scarlet. Work email it was.

Switching over to the other app, I found that inbox ominously empty. Which made no sense. Wouldn't Scarlet have at least tried to slap me with an ultimatum? What was the point of kidnapping Charlie if she wasn't going to use my friend to demand action on my part?

I needed to call Scarlet and hash things out. But the broken cell phone Nathaniel had collected at Creation Kingdom was the only place where I'd saved my boss's direct number. Which meant slow and uncertain email was my best bet.

The effort was probably pointless, but still I thumb typed as quickly as possible. *"Tell me what you want in exchange for Charlie. For calling off this invasion."*

I added on the number of the burner phone I was using so my boss could get through to me without delay.

There, that was clear enough. And my time was up.

Because the truck had slowed so much the scent of riled werewolf washed up my nostrils. Now the driver slammed on his brakes more abruptly than was really smart with unseatbelted people filling the bed.

A swearing werewolf jumble imploded around me. But, on my wheel well, I was above the fray.

Then I was higher above it. Popping to my feet, I peered over the roof of the cab to see what was ahead of us.

We'd reached the end of the road. Had gone beyond it, actually. Eli must have given Thom more specific instructions while I wasn't listening, because we'd pulled into the driveway of a seemingly empty mansion, driving past the house and into the backyard.

And the person waiting for us there wasn't Scarlet or anyone else I recognized. Instead, it was a stranger who I could tell from a distance boasted an alpha mantle. The power hung heavy around his rather slender shoulders, buzzed like heated air around his scruffed jaw.

By his side, stood a wolf who was strikingly familiar. Young, gangly, lacking in the alpha's power but full of reason to hate us.

Smoke.

This invasion had nothing to do with Scarlet? I evaded Cowboy Hat's attempt to assist or restrain me, scrambling out of the truck and striding over to join Thom.

He didn't seem surprised by the invader's identity. Instead, the owner of the Full Moon Saloon stopped ten feet from the other alpha. "You're trespassing."

The alpha smiled humorlessly, revealing teeth that were even now sharpening. "I hear that's what you told my brother. Unneighborly if you ask me."

At the alpha's knee, Smoke curled back his lips, and I put two and two together. This mess could be traced back to little brother getting the snot knocked out of him at Thom's cabin yesterday. Smoke had run home and tattled, perhaps pointing out Gate City's weaknesses in the process. The result was a run-of-the-mill alpha altercation, nothing to do with our deeper mess.

Still, something felt wrong about the current standoff. Something raised hairs on the back of my neck and tugged at my fox senses. So, while Thom and the other alpha traded barbs, I peered around, considering the scene.

A scent of fur seethed through the backyard, and it didn't just come from Thom's allies who were working their way out of vehicles. The mowed lawn was obviously empty, which meant the trees above us must host Smoke's contingent. I tilted my neck back, staring upwards. Yes, there was the glint of an eyeball. My straining ears caught the rustle of paws on leaves.

Still, Eli had reported nearly two dozen invaders. So why was Smoke the only one who stood by his alpha out in the open? Smoke, who despite his earlier snarl now had his belly pressed to the earth in the face of Thom's dominance?

The submissive younger sibling wasn't the backup most alphas would have chosen. And even Smoke's big brother appeared to be outmatched at the moment. Thom towered above the other alpha by several inches, muscular where his opponent was stringy. Confident in his home-turf advantage.

Smoke's brother, on the other hand, knew how to use his alpha powers. He puffed out a wordless breath and the Gate City shifters who'd been ambling over to join us froze in their tracks.

So maybe that explained it. These invaders were banking on Thom's not-quite-alpha status to win them the war.

For his part, Thom either didn't notice what had happened to his allies or he didn't care. "What exactly do you want?" he asked, as if the alpha in front of him was a salesman who'd knocked on his door and interrupted family dinner.

I twitched. Thom hadn't even tried freezing Smoke's contingent in retaliation. He hadn't used his height to tower over the enemy, despite the fact that alpha posturing was an important part of any werewolf confrontation. No wonder the other alpha's smile widened into a smirk.

"Your territory is so small. A pocket only. I hadn't considered it worth my while to seize, but Smoke informed me otherwise."

As he spoke, the enemy shaded his eyes, peering west across a small valley to the sister ridge that housed the military base. From here, the newness of its construction was deeply evident. Concrete had barely faded; metal gleamed rather than dulling with rust. Beyond the perimeter fence, new houses dotted the countryside. Gate City really had grown in the last decade, sprawling out to fill several miles of former farmland.

It made sense that riches sprang from a revitalized city, perhaps enough to attract a neighboring alpha. Still, something continued to make my fox instincts twitch.

I couldn't figure out what was bothering me, but I was a Lawkeeper. As such, I had authority no one else here possessed.

"Is this an official challenge?" I demanded, inserting myself into the conversation. I kept one hand on the butt of my sword but didn't raise it...yet.

The other alpha's eyes had flicked across me when I raced up to join Thom, but he affected astonishment at my presence now. "Little girl." He peered down, our difference in height much greater than the inches that separated him from Thom. "I don't believe this is any of your business."

Slurs of this sort were so familiar I didn't even acknowledge them. "As a Lawkeeper," I countered, "this is no one's business so much as mine."

Because I'd read that handbook Rupert left on my desk when I was first hired. It hadn't been so long ago that I couldn't pluck out relevant passages to paraphrase now. "Were you aware," I continued, "that challenges between alphas must be filed with the local Lawkeeper's office in advance?"

It was a rule I was pretty sure nobody followed. Something like the unofficial custom that prevented state troopers from pulling over speeders who were merely traveling the speed of the road.

No wonder the alpha snickered, turning away from me to address Thom again. "I'll accept your total surrender," he said, as if he was offering a great boon to someone much weaker than he was. "In exchange...."

He broke off as a phone rang. For half a second, I thought the chime came from the burner phone I'd grabbed from the cabinet. That Scarlet was calling to make a deal for Charlie's release.

My heart leapt, then plummeted as the screen of the device I removed from my pocket remained blank and silent. The enemy alpha huffed amusement at my mistake while pulling out his own phone to answer the call. "Yes?"

A female voice emerged from the speaker. Scarlet's voice? I frowned, not understanding.

"We're in place," my boss told the invading alpha. "You can fall back."

Chapter 29

Smoke's brother closed his eyes for one split second, and I could almost feel him tugging on pack bonds. Ordering his troops...to do what exactly?

We could have tried to restrain him and find out. But Thom's allies were frozen in their tracks and it didn't seem wise to waste time when Scarlet had made an end run around us. Instead, Thom let the brothers go while consolidating his own forces. It took three attempts to release his friends from the other alpha's compulsion. And by that time, his phone had rung.

"Good news," Bertrand said without preamble. His voice was loud enough to be heard by everyone with shifter ears, which meant all of us and possibly also Smoke and whatever small force had been padding through the forest and making themselves appear more numerous than they actually were.

But Thom didn't shush him and Bertrand continued. "We got everyone inside. Bad news is: there are non-paw shifters staging down the block. I recognized the man whose picture you passed around yesterday plus the one who was asking questions in the bar this morning."

Rupert and Nathaniel. Likely they were there with Scarlet and perhaps some of Smoke's brother's pack mates.

And other Lawkeepers? It was hard to say.

I opened my mouth then snapped it shut. I didn't want to discuss strategy out here in the open.

And it was almost as if Thom heard my thoughts. Because even though he'd ridden up here in the front seat of a minivan, he strode toward the pickup. Opened the passenger side door and nodded at me. "Kira."

Werewolves scurried around us, finding spots in the pickup bed and the mini-van seats. Our little pocket of air, however, was still and quiet. No, more than that, it sparked with awareness, the same awareness that had surrounded us in the cabin last night.

I cocked my head. Had I been wrong about Thom's Southern gentleman chivalry? And did his reason for offering me the front seat now really matter when every wasted moment endangered the lives of innocents like Charlie?

I slid in, ignoring the haze of alpha musk that tried to embrace me. And I didn't protest when Thom cut off that tendril of connection by closing my door.

With the windows rolled up, alpha musk grew twice as strong inside as it had been outside by the time Thom turned the ignition key. I slid a glance in his direction, the rumble of the engine making the silence between us even more pronounced.

Thom had barely met my eyes since I revealed Ava's heritage back in the Moon Room, our shattered partnership prickly in the enclosed space now. And, unlike everything else, I could do something about that problem. Fixing my own mistakes was something I'd learned the hard way, my tendency to break things giving me ample opportunity to practice repairs.

I cleared my throat. "I went off half-cocked."

Thom made some sound deep and low in his throat that could have been "Please go on" or "Would you shut up?"

His gaze remained riveted on the road—which was largely empty and didn't require such profound attention. Still, I tucked one knee under me and swiveled to face him anyway.

Then I babbled. Verbal diarrhea round two. Words, words, words.

They coalesced around an apology. For outing Ava. For instigating Smoke's backstabbing. For thinking I understood Thom's world better than he did.

Finally, Thom lifted one hand off the steering wheel and raised it in the universal stop signal. Was that the barest hint of a smile tugging at the edge of his lips?

"Not your fault," he rumbled. "And not why we're here. The engine will cover up our voices. I thought you wanted to toss around ideas about dealing with Scarlet without being overheard?"

Oh. *Oh!* That's why we were in the cab of this pickup together?

I ignored a twinge of disappointment, letting the rekindling of our partnership ease me back onto track. "Scarlet likes trickery," I started, thinking as I talked. "That's twice now she's led us to believe one thing while doing another."

Thom hummed agreement, so I continued. "My gut says she likes hostages also. She hasn't even used Charlie. I think she snagged my friend on instinct, sensing a weakness. If so, she might do the same with everyone in the Full Moon Saloon. We either get them out fast or we use them to keep her focus on the bar while planning an emergency exit route."

"Agreed." Under Thom's strong hands, the pickup didn't bump and buck over rough road the way it had on the way up. Instead, we rolled smoothly down the mountainside. "Good thing there's a tunnel under the bar."

"A tunnel?"

Thom glanced at me side-eyed, his gaze resting for one moment on the chain of the necklace he'd provided back in the Moon Room. Then he nodded. "Under the carpet in the main-floor pantry. It leads beneath the alley and into Dad's basement."

Despite time running out as houses came closer together, I couldn't help noting: "That sounds more fox than wolf."

Thom's cheek twitched, which was when I remembered the bar hadn't been owned by werewolves until the present generation. Thom had inherited his fur from his mother, and she was a sticky topic neither he nor his father wanted broached.

Foot meet mouth. *Again.*

I winced, but all Thom said was, "I always assumed there was a speakeasy in the basement back during Prohibition."

Well, yes. If the owners of the Full Moon Saloon had continued selling alcohol when doing so was illegal, they would definitely have the same urge as foxes. The instinct to plan a back door for situations like this one now made sense.

Before I could wiggle through a verbal back door of my own, Thom cleared his throat and continued. "The tunnel is a family secret. No one inside is aware of it, and if Scarlet has found a way to tap into phone calls...."

"You're right. We have to do this in person. Someone will need to go in."

"Someone I trust." Thom's voice lowered, roughened. "You were right about the alpha thing. I've treated visitors to Gate City like exactly that—visitors. All of these men"—he jerked his head toward the full pickup bed—"were willing to come up on Hillcrest to fight with me because werewolves like fighting. But I can count on one hand the number of people I trust with the lives of innocents."

"Bertrand," I guessed. "Dixie Lee?"

Thom nodded then provided the third name that was already on the tip of my tongue. "And Dad. He's at home now."

Something about his tone suggested there'd been an argument I'd missed. One Thom had lost.

I opened my mouth, but Thom had more to say. "I don't want Dad crawling through tight spaces." His hands clenched around the wheel. "Friday, the pain was just heartburn. But three years ago it was a heart attack."

The scent in the air deepened into the bitterness of over brewed coffee. I wanted to reach over and pat Thom's shoulder. Among wolves, the gesture would have been ordinary empathy.

But Thom had been raised among humans and he'd jerked away from contact when I'd fallen into the car with him and Rupert. So I used my words. "I like small spaces," I said honestly. "If you trust me...."

We were turning into the alley now. The building across the street—Big T's house, I assumed—was small and not particularly noticeable. Sure enough, the vehicle Thom and I had been picked up in last night was parked outside the front door.

I took all of that in with one glance then turned my attention elsewhere. Hopefully Scarlet hadn't dug deep enough to know Big T was Thom's Achilles heel just like Charlie was mine. Even if she had, I was certain Thom would have werewolves patrolling around his dad's residence.

"Of course I trust you," Thom rumbled. "That's why you're here."

Nine words were enough to expand my lungs to twice their former capacity. I felt like I'd just lapped up werewolf blood, even though I hadn't.

"I'll be glad to do it," I assured him. "You draw Scarlet's attention to the front of the bar, then I can go in through the tunnel and...."

"No."

"No?"

Thom shook his head. We were parking now. Our time was up, but the werewolf beside me simply sat there, his words streaming out fast while his eyes swallowed me up.

"I'd rather you be inside the bar from the beginning. No chance of anyone seeing you go in Dad's house. I'll have him close the curtains on the window facing the bar once Scarlet is committed elsewhere and we have an exit plan. Until then, just sit tight."

That made sense. Except....

"Scarlet knows I don't hide from confrontation. She'll think something's fishy if I retreat into the bar and don't come out."

Werewolves were rocking the cab as they jumped out of the pickup bed now, but Thom didn't turn off the engine. Instead, he left that noise in place to mask the tail end of our conversation.

"I've got that covered." He glanced out at the waiting shifters, some of whom were close enough to the window that they would likely overhear us now. Pursing his lips as if he'd intended to say more, he instead shook his head. "If I have your permission to touch you?"

Ah, I was about to be manhandled again. I nodded and waited as Thom removed the keys and strode around the front of the cab to open my door.

Cold air rushed in as he reached for me. And I couldn't help it. Muscles tensed. My star ball materialized into a sword.

But Thom didn't shake me this time. Instead, his fingers were gentle on my shoulders as he turned me ninety degrees to face him.

My legs hung halfway out of the truck now even though my butt was still firmly planted on the cushion. And Thom stepped between my thighs. Into my space. This close, his alpha musk turned from burnt coffee to rich chocolate cheesecake.

"What?" I started.

Then he kissed me. Hard and long and so intense the world shattered into shards of sparkling light.

Chapter 30

Toes curled inside my borrowed sneakers. My fingers crept up to Thom's nape and tugged him closer until our mouths weren't the only body parts touching.

I hummed. Or we hummed. Likely, we both hummed. The vibration bubbled through my veins until I levitated off the seat cushion.

No, I wasn't levitating. Thom had lifted me, swirling us through air that smelled like crisp autumn leaves and warm, strong werewolf. I opened my eyes to find his gaze piercing me. Intense, but not glacial. Instead, Thom's irises were the blue of the hottest part of a fire. The molten core that could burn me forever and I wouldn't mind.

"Be careful today." He drew back to speak, and I barely registered the words. Instead, I watched his lips move, feeling mine curl upward. Remembering pleasure. Anticipating a repeat.

"Mmm," I hummed, tugging once more at the hair on the back of his head.

But our bodies parted rather than coming back together. The broad, strong hands that had held me up until now released. Pavement tapped my sneakers. Thom's gaze pierced me one last time, then rose to peer over my shoulder. "Keep her inside where it's safe."

Again, hands fell on my shoulders, but not Thom's hands this time. My brain had turned as soggy as a cookie dipped in hot chocolate but I vaguely recalled agreeing to be touched by Thom. I hadn't agreed to be touched by whoever this was.

Instinct took over. I grabbed my star-ball sword—such a better fit than the non-magical one at my hip—and raised it as I spun.

Or tried to spin. Thom's huge hand closed over my smaller one, squeezing my fingers until pain made me drop my weapon. My star ball.

It clattered onto the pavement, bouncing away. The distance between me and my magic sapped my energy instantly. Just like it had done at Creation Kingdom, when Thom had become privy to my kitsune weakness.

A weakness he now used against me. Bertrand drew me away from my sword, into the Moon Room, and I had no will to struggle. Not with the distance between me and my star ball expanding. Lassitude cupped me as Thom told us both, "Don't call me. I'll call you."

One moment before the door closed between us, he kicked my sword after me into the room.

The blade melted into star-ball magic the instant it touched my flesh, pins and needles of returning life seeping back into my calf then my entire body. Still, I leaned against the wall inside the Moon Room for one long moment, catching my breath.

Thom's display had been deeply believable. *I* would have thought he'd forced his lover inside for her own protection if I hadn't known better. I only hoped Scarlet had been close enough to enjoy the show.

Unfortunately, the subterfuge had done its work all too well on Bertrand. He stood between me and the parking-lot door as if he expected me to dash back out and fling myself at Thom. His voice, when he spoke, was gentle and concerned. "Do you need anything? A chair? Food?"

My stomach growled and I ignored it. Bertrand's overprotective attitude was something I'd need to squelch if I wanted to lead everyone to safety. I shook my head, then changed my mind. "Where are the stairs?"

"In the kitchen." He led me through a door I hadn't noticed, one not far from the rotten floorboards. An empty industrial kitchen gleamed with stainless steel and glass. All this and the bar served only microwave pizzas?

Ignoring the entrepreneurial oddity, I watched as Bertrand opened yet another door. It led out of the kitchen into an enclosed stairwell leading upward. I cocked my head, considering.

There should have been voices from above. Scents at least. I hadn't noticed how many werewolves had left to gather dependents and how many had come with us to Hillcrest. But, at the least, Eli, Dixie Lee, and her daughter should be hiding up there.

But the staircase was dark and silent. It smelled of dust and cedar and Thom.

No one else had walked through here recently. And the voices that bubbled up into the silence came from behind me rather than above me.

I turned, noticing two other doors on the other side of the kitchen. One must lead to the pantry, the other to the bar.

The second door was where the voices originated. From the area that might as well have been a plate-glass fish bowl, the most dangerous spot to gather during a siege.

The last residual haze of kiss-happy fog burned out of my brain in an instant. "You can go up if you want," Bertrand observed, misinterpreting my body's jolt.

Rather than answering, I stalked past him so I could push out into the Full Moon Saloon's public space. The windows were just as huge from this side of the bar, turning the bartender's station into the perfect hunter's vantage point. Despite the danger, I took a moment to assess the view.

Multiple blocks of Jackson Street were visible out front. On my left, a figure—Nathaniel?—placed a traffic cone under the stop light. Wolves sidled past, taking advantage of the late afternoon shadows to act less than human. A woman who clearly lacked a fur form tapped her way down the sidewalk until someone shoved into her path with shaking head and wide gesticulations. Eventually, the woman shrugged and turned around.

I shivered. Scarlet's allies were blocking off the main street of Gate City, turning away human spectators. She was preparing for battle, and all of Thom's weakest pack mates were right here on full display.

Because no one had gone upstairs or stayed in the Moon Room the way Thom had mandated. Instead, they lollygagged around the bar as if this was any other day and they were waiting for a party to get started.

Eli and a boy who—I sniffed to confirm—happened to be a werewolf played darts in one corner. Ava hunched over her library book, mother beside her. Two adult male werewolves anchored the corners while an old woman with jet black hair focused on her knitting at one end of the bar.

The scene was homey, enticing. Or it would have been if I hadn't known that the windows making this such a good hunter's station also worked quite admirably in the other direction.

My brain raced. Big T had called off the police chief, so no one would show up to discover why the main street was being closed to traffic. Soon, the last non-shifter spectators would disperse, their ability to quench werewolf warfare dispersing along with them.

Not that it would require outright warfare to pick off these innocents. Once the street was clear, how hard would it be to grab a rifle and shoot straight through the window into the pack's heart?

Chapter 31

"**T**ime to move to the kitchen!" I kept my voice cheerful, not wanting to alarm Ava and the boy I'd yet to be introduced to.

Unfortunately, cheerful flew like one of Eli's darts right over everyone's heads. The old woman glanced up at me before returning to her knitting, but no one else even bothered to acknowledge the fact that I'd spoken.

So I'd make my words more than a suggestion. I wasn't an alpha, but I knew how to imbue my voice with the bite of dominance. Lowering my register, I inhaled deeply then tried again. "Grab whatever you need and take it with you."

No one moved. No, that wasn't right. One of the adult werewolves yawned.

Okay, so I'd reason with them. Once everyone understood what Thom had asked me to do, surely they'd be willing.

But...doubt twinged. I'd lose my one shot at persuasion if I led this crowd to the final unopened door in the kitchen and it turned out to be something other than a pantry. Or if we all crowded into the pantry and there was no subterranean bolthole to be found.

Perhaps it would be smarter to do a little reconnaissance first. I turned away from people who weren't interested in me...and slammed into Bertrand's suited bulk.

"Going somewhere?" Then, over my shoulder, he jerked his chin at the same werewolf who'd yawned a moment earlier. "Watch the back door, would you?"

As if I was a prisoner here rather than the one tasked with preventing all of these people from turning into hostages or victims. My teeth tried to sharpen, but I clenched one hand and pressed my fingernails into my palm instead. I knew how to manage werewolves who thought they were stronger and smarter than I was. It had gone so well with Rupert after all.

Well, maybe not so well. But, after a moment of silent staring on both our parts, Bertrand moved out of my path. His eyes and no one else's followed as I retreated to the kitchen. Alone, I padded across clean tiles, opening the final unexplored door.

A pantry, just as I'd suspected. The shelves were full of cans as large as my head along with big bags of flour. Someone, it seemed, was gearing up to turn the Full Moon Saloon into more than a frozen-pizza destination.

And...guessing the future of the bar wasn't what I was here for. I scuffed at the floor, where a ratty square of carpet was tacked down beneath the door with a thin metal runner. Under the shelves, though, the floor covering wasn't attached. I dug my fingernails into the fluff and yanked.

The carpet rolled across me as if it had been waiting to release its secrets. I fell back onto my heels, knocked off balance by the weight.

Still, I grinned. There was a square crack in the floor in front of me. The trapdoor existed.

"You *are* up to something." Dixie Lee glowered above me, hands on her hips.

My first impulse was to fling the carpet over the trapdoor. Which made no sense. I intended to lead Dixie Lee and everyone else down this hole as soon as Thom sounded the all clear with a yank of Big T's curtains.

Still, I was a fox. When startled, we hid our secrets. The carpet crumpled up on itself as it slid back over the floor.

But Dixie Lee had already seen everything. Almost as agile as a shifter, she leapt across the carpet hills and valleys to tap one foot against the still-exposed corner of the trapdoor. It rang hollow and her eyebrows shot up.

She didn't remark upon the find however. Instead, she glared down at me. "You think I don't know about kitsunes, but I learned quite a lot from Ava's father before he dumped me. You're dangerous for werewolves. You drink their blood then force them to do whatever you want." She seemed to grow taller as she told me: "I saw the marks on Thom's neck."

I opened my mouth, but Dixie Lee didn't allow time for me to either confirm or deny. Instead, she stomped closer, her hard-soled shoes landing inches from my fingers.

"You manipulate everyone. You manipulated me yesterday. Those high heels. Did you put them on for the sake of female bonding?" Her tone falsettoed. "Us downtrodden women and our poor aching feet."

I flushed. In retrospect, that piece of cleverness hadn't been particularly kind.

Dixie Lee wasn't a shifter, but her final words came out as a snarl. "What are you doing here?"

I itched to rise to my full height. Crouching beneath a furious opponent went against every instinct, and it also felt a bit like manipulation now that she brought that up. Here I was, small and defenseless, hunching my shoulders as if I expected a blow. Pity me. Be kind to me.

So I straightened my back, but I stayed submissively lower. Dixie Lee had lived among wolves for quite a while now. Surely she'd understand this posture was an apology, not an attempt to hoodwink.

"You're right," I told the ground. "I bit Thom yesterday. I was sent here to arrest him for murder."

"Murder?" Dixie Lee caught one of the shelves to steady herself. Then her voice hardened. "You're lying."

"No, my boss was lying. And now she's lying in wait on the street with her cronies, plotting how to harm everyone in this bar. They're sitting ducks out front. They *need* to *move* to the *kitchen*."

I only realized I was on my feet punctuating my words by pounding one fist into the other when Dixie Lee barked out a short huff of laughter. "Now you're finally telling the truth. While we're on a roll, what are you hiding here?"

"The way out. But we can't use it until Thom clears the other end."

Her arms crossed, a barrier between us. "Let's see then."

"You'll have to get off first."

Dixie Lee's laugh this time was a little longer, a little truer. She not only retreated to the doorway, she pulled the carpet along with her. Then she waited with arms crossed. "Be my guest."

There was a metal loop in place of a handle, one that had been laid flat into a recess in the wood so it wouldn't be felt by those walking over top. The loop was pitted with age, rough bits catching on my fingers as I slipped them underneath.

I braced myself, expecting the trapdoor hinge to be rusted shut. But it opened as easily as if it had been waiting for me. Revealed....

Blackness. Nothing but the damp mildew of the distant ground.

"We'll need flashlights," I realized. "Some sort of sling to get Eli down there. It won't be easy."

For a moment, the air sweetened as if Dixie Lee was running through the same sort of mental checklist I was. But then she glared at me.

"I still don't trust you," she said as she turned on her heel.

<h1 style="text-align:center">Chapter 32</h1>

Dixie Lee didn't trust me, but she must have seen my point about the dangers of hanging out in front of the plate-glass windows. Because werewolves and humans began filtering into the kitchen moments later. At Dixie Lee's order, food emerged from the refrigerator and pantry shelves. Soon, everyone was busy chopping and stirring, nibbling on cheese and crackers while waiting on a vegetable soup.

I hadn't been given a job, so I just wandered around trying to look helpful. Finally, I made my way to the heart of the flurry, peering into the vat of mellowing tomatoes, beans, and corn. "It looks like enough to drown an army."

Dixie Lee slammed a lid over the stew, her eyes narrowing. "Everyone will be starving when this is over."

Suggesting she intended to stay here until after Thom and the other werewolves dealt with Scarlet. No escaping through the tunnel for her.

From the eyes that had flitted in our direction then away again, I could safely assume that if Dixie Lee stayed, Ava and Bertrand stayed. Likely also the old woman and all the werewolves.

Eli was the only one who met my gaze, his smile as wide as ever. Yes, he'd willingly crawl through a dark hole with me...if he was physically able to crawl.

I sighed, assessing Dixie Lee's stance, so solid she might as well have grown roots here in the Full Moon Saloon's kitchen. There was nothing I could do to bring her around at the moment.

So I didn't try. Instead, I shrugged and changed gears.

I'd yet to find a vantage point through which I could surreptitiously check on the state of Big T's curtains, both the back of the kitchen and the Moon Room being windowless. The obvious solution was to head up to the window-heavy second story. But when I opened the relevant door and stepped through it, prickles on the back of my neck suggested I hadn't left the hubbub in the center of the kitchen on my own.

"Bertrand." I turned to face my minder just as he closed the door behind him. Despite his suits, in the near darkness his bulk screamed *wolf.*

Worse, the stairwell smelled so deeply of Thom that each breath grew increasingly overwhelming. How could Bertrand miss the obvious absence of my own scent? A scent that should have been there based on the conclusions I'd let him and Dixie Lee draw yesterday.

Still, he merely gestured upward. So I climbed, wishing Bertrand was in front of me rather than behind me. Walking away from the werewolf, I couldn't smell his mood. Couldn't tell how close he was either. Was Bertrand following at a polite distance, staying behind at the bottom, or nearly treading on my heels?

At the top, I pushed open a door and strode a little faster than I'd really meant to into a midsize living room. There, the sensation that I'd invaded Thom's enigmatic privacy halted me in my tracks.

Because this space revealed more about the bartender's character than he'd let slip during our entire day together. There were plants on the windowsills. Books on shelves. The only clothing on display was a padded flannel shirt hanging from a hook inside the door.

I itched to run my fingers across spines and read every title. To lie down on the sofa and see if the cushions smelled the same as Thom had in the pickup cab or whether his musk mellowed when he was relaxing at home.

Instead I padded across the room to peer out the nearest window. There was no sign of closed curtains at Big T's house. Thom wasn't ready for us yet.

Only when I turned back around did I see that Bertrand was inside along with me. His clenched jaw suggested he'd noticed my intense perusal of Thom's living room.

"You've never been here before, have you?" Bertrand surmised.

My explanation this time around went a little better than it had with Dixie Lee. A little, not a lot. Bertrand listened without interruption, but he didn't smile or hum agreement. Instead, he waited for me to finish while donning the male version of resting bitch face.

For my part, each admission made my skin chafe more under the intensity of Bertrand's disapproval. I slid one finger under the chain around my neck, relieving its pressure for one split second. And, to my surprise, Bertrand nodded at last.

"He wouldn't have given you his mother's necklace if he didn't want us to follow you."

Thom's mother's necklace? I itched to pull the gem out from under my shirt and peer at it more closely. I'd thought the absence of a moon or paw signified Thom's lack of trust in me, but again I appeared to have jumped to unwarranted conclusions.

Rather than exploring my borrowed jewelry, however, I seized the unexpected advantage. If Bertrand thought the necklace gave him a reason to listen, I'd provide something for him to listen to.

So I dug deeper, debriefing this werewolf Thom trusted on everything from Scarlet to the tunnel and my own copious mistakes. Bertrand's scent softened from reserved to indecisive. He was coming around to my point of view...perhaps. Unless I said something wrong and tipped him back the other way.

For the first time around a werewolf, I wished our heritages were reversed so I could offer blood as proof of my veracity. But that wasn't possible, and I was swearing off blood drinking anyway. Instead, I chose my words carefully, staying close enough to Bertrand's glowering presence so he could smell the truth on my breath.

And it worked. His shoulders loosened. His stance opened. He nodded. "I'll talk Dixie Lee around." The tiniest twitch of a smile. "Or try to."

Without me even asking, he also offered to hunt down supplies for our evacuation. Then Bertrand left me alone in Thom's space, a space that felt far too personal to be invaded by someone he hadn't known three days ago.

I fingered the chain a second time, then I followed Bertrand down the stairs.

Time yawned. Soup ingredients melded into perfection and we ladled out the result hungrily. Flashlights materialized and a sling was created out of an armful of knotted sheets.

My phone remained resolutely silent, no word from Scarlet about Charlie. Interspersed with futile email checks, I repeatedly padded up the stairs to Thom's space and checked Big T's windows. They remained uncovered, darkening even before sunset. The house across the way appeared empty.

The streets were not.

At first, only an occasional werewolf slunk through the alley. But by the time the first streetlight flickered on, I counted at least a dozen animal-form shifters lingering in the space behind the bar. These weren't Thom's allies; I was 99% sure of that.

Then a flash of light I only caught from the corner of one eye. A pop as every streetlight blinked out in unison.

A change in the timbre of the voices beneath me drew my attention away from the window. Which was when I realized it wasn't just the streetlights that had fallen dark.

The hum of Thom's fridge had stopped also. I flicked the switch on the wall—the bulb in the ceiling light stayed quiescent.

Someone had knocked out the power. To the whole block?

My phone rang. I grabbed it and answered, hoping the caller was Thom even though he hadn't implemented our all-clear symbol.

Instead, Scarlet's voice greeted me. "Time's up."

Chapter 33

"For Charlie?" I was playing right into my boss's hands, but I couldn't help it. The words popped out without my permission. "Is she safe?"

"Check your texts."

My texts? I took the phone away from my ear and found one message waiting. A photograph of Charlie that was ten times worse than the vision of her comatose and boneless in Nathaniel's car.

In the photo, my friend was wide awake and staring into the camera through glasses that were never allowed to get so smudged in her ordinary life. "She's terrified," I snarled. If Scarlet had been in front of me, I would have led with my sword, never mind the consequences.

Scarlet appeared to find my rage amusing. "Wouldn't it be a shame," she purred into my ear, "if your little human friend saw something she shouldn't? Wouldn't it be a shame if someone shifted in front of her—accidentally, of course—and she had to be put to death?"

Stillness was impossible. My feet carried me away from the window and back again as I answered. "I already told you I'll do anything in exchange for Charlie's safety. The question is, what do you want?"

"I want Gate City."

Now I was the one who spat out a bark of disbelief. "Gate City? It's not exactly a strategic location. Maybe aim higher. LA. New York."

"This place is too important to be run by an upstart bartender." For the first time, Scarlet's amusement faded into solemnity and I got the impression she was, at long last, telling the truth about why I'd been sent on this job. "Its secrets can't fall into the hands of the human military. With your help, we'll put a true alpha in charge and lock down those secrets. If the human's fate means nothing to you, you should do this for the greater good."

Scarlet wasn't the kind of boss who cajoled or explained her reasoning. Her stalling suggested....

I leaned against the side of the windowsill, scanning the darkness out of the corner of my right eye. I hoped anyone watching would think I was just trying to digest Scarlet's deluge of information. Instead, I was seeking something fox instincts swore would be out there.

Trouble. Danger.

There it was. The faintest glint of metal halfway down the block, almost swallowed up by hungry darkness. Wolves had been patrolling the alley earlier, wolves who could see better at night than humans did. So why were Scarlet's allies now turning two-legged and armed?

Unfortunately, my perusal of the scene hadn't gone unnoticed. "If you're looking for Mr. Faris," Scarlet purred into my ear, "you'll be disappointed. I'm afraid he left Gate City hours ago. I don't expect him back anytime soon."

She was lying. She had to be lying.

Still, I drew away from the window and spoke while speed walking toward the door. "You don't just want access to the Gate City ghost, if such a thing exists. That might explain setting Thom up to take the fall for a murder, but you worked hard to discredit me as well."

I bit out the last words, then I pressed my palm hard against the microphone as I plummeted down the stairs. Bursting into a homey scene of second supper by flashlight, humans and werewolves alike looked up from blowing on soup.

"We have to go. Now," I demanded, only half-listening to Scarlet as she berated me through the cell phone. Apparently, my boss hadn't been keen on the idea of a kitsune in the ranks. But she'd changed her mind, or so she promised.

"You made mistakes." Scarlet's voice turned condescending. "But I'll help you clear your record. You'll relinquish the bar and I'll make sure our superiors understand your loyalty. I'll tell them you've had a change of heart."

Dixie Lee and Bertrand were whispering furiously but I stamped my foot and held up a finger to quiet them. Only once the room had gone dead silent did I take my hand off the microphone.

"That's it? You want to be let into the Full Moon Saloon? It will still belong to Thom."

"As I said, he isn't there to claim it," Scarlet answered easily. "And possession is nine tenths of the law." Her voice hardened as she continued. "I'd hate for innocents to be injured in the crossfire. When my men knock, you'll let them in if you want your human friend and all those pretty little hostages to remain safe."

Scarlet hung up on me, which was just as well. Because the shockwave of Dixie Lee's anger was too intense to keep silent. Her daughter had been threatened and I was, finally, the lesser of two evils.

"You." She poked her index finger into the chest of one of the adult werewolves whose name hadn't yet been uttered in my presence. "Go through now and scout the other end of the tunnel. We'll be getting Eli situated." She shot the young human a questioning look. "Assuming you can handle it? This will be difficult."

Eli didn't hesitate. Instead, I could feel the memory of Thom's trust in him buoying up his spirits as he nodded. "I'm game."

Dixie Lee didn't acknowledge Eli's courage, just continued barking orders at all and sundry. "Turn off the stove. Clean up the table so it won't be obvious we were here. Ava, you'll need to leave that book behind."

Everyone jumped to obey, well everyone except Bertrand. His stillness was a rock in the turbulent stream as he observed, "We should contact Thom."

"We can't," I answered. Scarlet's voice had rung with truth when she said Thom had left town, but what was to stop him from sneaking back in behind her forces? He wouldn't abandon us and I refused to mess up whatever he was planning. "If our call is overheard, Scarlet would be on the other end of that tunnel long before we got through it."

I glanced at Ava, the shifter boy, the old woman, and Eli. None of them would last a minute in a pitched battle with wolves.

None of them...and not Charlie either. I was grateful for Bertrand's slow nod and Dixie Lee's drill-sergeant tendencies since their leadership let me slip away into the public side of the bar.

Without lights, the hunter's post had turned even more claustrophobic. When I pulled my phone back out, its glow seemed to paint a target on my chest.

Still, I forced myself to ignore the danger and focus on Charlie's photograph. I wouldn't put it past Scarlet to execute my friend out of spite whether or not I did her bidding, especially if our bid to move everyone in the kitchen to safety proved a success.

I had to figure out where my friend was being held and go get her. Unfortunately, the picture was zoomed in too close to give me any clue of Charlie's surroundings. She was somewhere partially lit, which ruled out the closest block or two. Other than that, she could have been anywhere.

No, wait. I scanned back over Charlie's face. Over her *glasses.*

Charlie only needed spectacles when she was reading, so why had she put them on in a hostage situation? I pinched the screen with thumb and forefinger, expanding the image and hoping for a clue.

Only, the smudged surfaces didn't reflect Charlie's location as I'd hoped. Instead, they provided an image of the werewolf in charge of holding her there.

Rupert. The weedy little Lawkeeper who was, hopefully, on our side.

The only way I had to contact him was email, which was slow and unhelpful. But I tried anyway. *"You have to get Charlie out of there. She's in immediate danger."*

To my surprise, my coworker's answer came before my tapping feet forced me back into motion. *"That would be stupid. I'd blow my cover."*

"Is your cover more important than a life?"

No answer. Given that Rupert had dismissed Charlie as a victim, he likely didn't consider her life worth saving.

And…something problematic had broken loose in the kitchen. No longer did feet pad obediently to the tune of Dixie Lee's orders. Instead, her daughter's voice rose high enough to carry past me out to the street. "No!"

The room I burst back into was nearly empty. Eli must have been lowered down into the tunnel and most of the rest had joined him. Only Ava, her mother, and Bertrand hovered above the gaping hole that filled most of the pantry floor.

The trio was lit by the gentle glow of a flashlight. And for one split second, their huddle resembled the family grouping I'd driven away from so easily yesterday morning, assuming I'd be back among my loved ones before memory had time to fade.

"What's the problem?" I asked, squashing any tremor of distress out of my voice.

Ava turned teary eyes on me. "We can't leave without Pumpkin!"

"Pumpkin?"

"The cat," Dixie Lee snapped.

The cat who Thom had carefully locked away to protect from his assemblage of werewolves. The cat who would be an easy object lesson for invaders likely to tap on the back door demanding entrance any second now.

The cat who Ava clearly wanted to hug to her chest in place of her absent library book. Her mother's gaze met mine and, for the first time, fear dilated her pupils.

Delay could mean death for a girl with kitsune heritage.

I nodded. "I'll get him. You go on ahead."

Chapter 34

I waited until all three disappeared into the tunnel before dealing with the factor Dixie Lee's human sensibilities had overlooked. Yes, the kitchen appeared spic and span, at least by the glow of my cell phone. But the air hummed with the scent of humans and werewolves who'd huddled inside moments earlier. The aroma of fresh soup and sharp cheddar hugged me close.

Scarlet's forces couldn't be allowed inside, not until the scents had been given time to dissipate. Which meant I couldn't grab the cat and hurry after Thom's escaping pack mates. Instead, I'd free Pumpkin, then I'd make a stand.

To that end, I eased the trapdoor back into place, smoothing the carpet over it. Next, I hunted locks on the pantry door and the door leading to the Moon Room, found none, and improvised.

The refrigerator overbalanced as I shoved it in front of the shortcut between Moon Room and kitchen. The tall rectangle teetered in the darkness and I held my breath, trying to stabilize an object that weighed considerably more than I did.

Please don't topple. Steady, steady.

In that pause, I heard the first scratch.

The noise came from the back of the Moon Room, just where Scarlet had told me her allies would knock to gain entry. But it wasn't a knock. Instead, the intrusion sounded like fingernails gouging into rough metal. Or like wolf claws raking through a door hinge.

The refrigerator blocked my own easy path into the Moon Room, so I strode away from the scratching rather than toward it. Into the bar, where dull moonlight filtered through plate-glass windows, then through the door Ava had tried to block my entrance to what felt like an eternity ago.

Scritch. Scritch. Hairs rose on the back of my neck as I eased into the Moon Room, closing the door behind me. Even fox eyes couldn't make out shapes in pitch darkness, so I pulled out my cell phone, tilting it toward Pumpkin's side of the room.

An email from Rupert flashed across the screen. *"Okay. You win. I'll drop her off at the front of the bar in five minutes. Be ready."*

The message had been sent four minutes ago.

"No! Take Charlie out of Gate City!" I tapped in my response as I rushed toward the cat area. Opening the door, I found Pumpkin cowering in the corner closest to the street. He wasn't an idiot. He could hear predators scratching, trying to claw their way inside to us.

I half expected the feline to flee from my unfamiliar shadow, but instead he arched into my touch as I reached for him. He was warm and purring the moment I curled him into the crook of one arm.

The cat was the only warm thing present however. Because ice formed in the pit of my stomach as I glanced once more at the cell phone.

"Too late," Rupert had answered. *"I'm here. Take her or leave her. I've done my part."*

Panting had joined scratching by the time I reentered the Moon Room. That plus snuffling, the sound of a predator seeking the entrance to a smaller animal's lair.

Turning my back on the danger was physically painful, but if Charlie was at the front door.... I rushed too fast, stubbing one foot hard against the door jamb. Even in sneakers, my big toe throbbed.

And now Pumpkin started to struggle. His claws sank into my bicep and I clutched him harder, easing through the bar and opening the front door as quietly as I could.

I'd half expected a trap. But no, this was Rupert with Charlie, just as he'd promised. My friend was blindfolded, her hands bound behind her. Her breathing was heavy. The scent of fear slapped me in the face.

I itched to reassure her. But it was better if Charlie didn't know I was present. She couldn't get drawn into what was about to occur.

So I pitched my voice shifter low, a mere whisper of sound. "You have to take her somewhere safe." As I spoke, I peered into the darkness behind Rupert, expecting to find sentries. Scarlet might be massing her forces at the back, but she wouldn't leave the front entirely unguarded.

No one appeared to be present, however. Which was a good thing since Rupert sucked at caution. His whisper reminded me of Grub's when we'd gotten up early last Christmas to hunt for our stockings, a whisper Mai later told me was loud enough to pull her out of a dead sleep.

"I told you, I'm not blowing my cover for this. I've already punched myself in the eye as proof she fought free of me." Rupert pushed closer into my personal space, thumb and forefinger stretching apart what might have been a slight smudge on his cheek. "*Look* at this. I'll need plastic surgery."

And Pumpkin, who had purred for me, took offense at the proximity of this particular werewolf. Squawking and wriggling, he leapt out of my arms, onto Rupert's shoulder, then to the ground far faster than a cat of his size should have been able to move.

"Shit! It clawed me!" Rupert released his hold on Charlie so he could clap both hands against what couldn't have been more than a minor scratch. And Charlie took advantage of his lack of focus to swirl, still blindfolded, and kick her captor hard in the knee.

Well, she was aiming for the knee. My friend couldn't see, so it was no wonder she connected with air instead.

Unchecked momentum sent her tumbling. Tumbling toward the hard corner marking the outside of Pumpkin's display-case home.

I relinquished concern for the cat, catching my friend one second before she cracked her head open. She flailed against my arms, but I managed to grab the blindfold and drag it off. "Shh," I soothed. "You're okay."

Charlie was no longer wearing glasses and I was well within reading distance. But she must have recognized me anyway because she went still. "Kira."

"In the flesh. I need you to go with...."

I turned toward Rupert. Or rather, toward where Rupert had been.

But he'd fled already. He and the cat, faded into darkness.

And, at the opposite end of the Full Moon Saloon, something slammed down with the intensity of a whale beaching itself. If I didn't miss my guess, the back door had just been kicked in.

Chapter 35

"I know you've just been through a significant trauma, but I need you to run...." I stopped talking, and not because Charlie was shaking her head furiously. The street in front of the bar was no longer empty. Instead, human-shaped shadows blocked both ends.

I couldn't make out individuals' identities but Rupert's thready voice spiraled upward from my right. "No, let me go! I'm on your side!"

From the sound of it, they didn't believe him. But I didn't stay to find out what would happen. Rupert was adept at slithering out from under problems, and I had more important matters on my plate.

"Change of plans," I decided, dragging Charlie inside with me. The door banged shut behind us and I could only hope the noise outside and the bark of voices emanating from the Moon Room overwhelmed it. Flipping the lock, I dropped to my knees so I could work at the knots around my friend's wrists.

"You have two choices," I said as I pried at what appeared to be a necktie. "They're both bad but I recommend this one. Go straight behind the bar into the kitchen and you'll see a door on your right. Open it, head up the stairs, and find someplace to hide. If I can, I'll come and get you when everything's over. If I don't, wait for silence then hightail it to the Base and forget anything you see on the way."

The knots released at last and I sprang back to my feet to face Charlie. I expected obedience, fear, *something* helpful. Instead, she huffed, her thumb rising as if to push glasses that didn't exist up on her nose. "Not likely. Option two?"

I took a deep breath and accepted the inevitable. Our relationship had plummeted, in part, because I hadn't trusted Charlie with my secrets when we were both in college. It was time to have some faith in her ability to adapt.

"Option two is coming into the Moon Room with me and fighting werewolves."

"Werewolves?" The word emerged as a hiccup. Charlie's hand patted at her pocket, where a notebook was usually hiding.

"You can't be a scientist right now," I warned her. "And you can't tell anyone what you learn either. Remember our self-defense classes, when you weren't paying attention and Mai would come up behind you and whack you so hard on the cheek that it left a bruise?"

"Yeah."

"This time, it'll be blood not bruises. My first offer is still the best."

A crash emerged from the Moon Room. Not the parking-lot door coming down, since the invaders had already entered. Something else large and destructive. Please, not the fridge....

The image of innocents slowly crawling away beneath the alley almost sent my feet moving without waiting for an answer. But Charlie had to be given time to make this decision. So I forced myself to breathe slowly, waiting her out.

Finally, she shook her head. "I'm not hiding."

"Okay." I closed my eyes against the memory of Charlie as a hostage. Opened them back up to take in Charlie as a smart, strong woman who had my back. "You'll need a sword. Here." I passed over the weapon I'd snatched from Big T's arsenal, holding it carefully by the blade so she could capture the hilt.

In my hand, the borrowed sword had been ungainly, weighted subtly incorrectly. In Charlie's hand...it fit.

She met my gaze. "What will you use?"

Well, if I was dishing out secrets, I might as well ladle them generously. "This," I told Charlie, materializing my star ball in a blaze of magical light.

The Moon Room was no longer pitch black when we eased the door open and peered inside it. Invaders had bound glow sticks around their biceps, resulting in flashes of illumination from every corner. There were so many. More than Charlie and I could handle...unless we focused our energies on guarding this one very important door.

Because the fridge hadn't toppled. Several shifters clustered around the shortcut to the kitchen, trying and failing to shove the door open. Everyone else milled around, tearing apart furniture seemingly for the sake of good, old-fashioned fun.

Our entrance hadn't been noticed amid the barely lit mayhem. But Scarlet's forces were close and would likely be on us in minutes.

Without the need for discussion, Charlie and I lifted our blades, our backs drawing together as if they were magnetized. After our test run in the bar Friday, we were entirely in tune.

"Goal?" Charlie murmured. "I assume we're waiting for the arrival of the cavalry?"

I swallowed, imagining Eli making his laborious way toward the precarious safety of Big T's basement. Layered on top of those stakes, the remembered certainty in Scarlet's voice when she swore Thom had left the city made me wince.

"I'm afraid," I admitted, "the cavalry is us."

I expected at least a little fear. After all, I'd just introduced Charlie to a world she'd never imagined existed. I certainly didn't feel good about our chances of survival.

Rather than blubbering in terror, though, my friend whinnied out a burst of horse-snort laughter. Which, at last, drew the attention of the werewolves.

Three shadows turned toward us, a familiar scent wafting off them. Not the aromas of coworkers the way I'd expected. Instead, this was the musk I'd become intimately familiar with after spending so much time around Thom.

They were alphas, all three of them. After a moment of frantic squinting, I picked out Smoke's brother in the near darkness. But the other two pack leaders were strangers to me.

My sword faltered for only one millisecond before I tightened my hold on it. I'd assumed Scarlet was running this game on the side, drawing in a few coworkers she could bribe or manipulate then offering Gate City to one particular alpha in exchange for his assistance. If she'd officially gone up the chain of command and drawn in all the pack leaders who channeled shifters into the Roanoke Lawkeepers...well then, win, lose, or draw, we were pretty much screwed.

At least I didn't have much time to think about it. The attack came quickly, although not in the form of a sword stroke or wolf lunge. *"Surrender."*

The alpha's word crept like ice up my spine, but it didn't coerce obedience. "Know your audience," I chided, hoping to startle him with my ability to shrug off the compulsion.

He wasn't startled. "Ah yes," he murmured. "You're the fox. Such a shame we'll have to do this the hard way."

His sword snicked out of its scabbard, the blade gleaming a reflected orange light.

"Ready," Charlie said behind me. I braced my feet and felt her back muscles stiffen behind my shoulders.

Then we fought.

There was an easy way out, I realized the first time my blade sliced through alpha flesh. The wound was only a scratch, one my opponent shook off with a growl. But werewolf blood would strengthen me and at the same time allow me to command the shifter I'd stolen life fluid from. All it would take was a sip from each alpha and I'd own this room.

But...was that ethical? Outside our circle of swords, werewolves continued to demolish the building Thom was so deeply committed to. Beneath our feet, those unable to defend themselves retreated at what I had to assume was the pace of a drowsy snail.

Still, no one was currently being harmed. Well, no one other than me and Charlie, who grunted out a pained expletive as an alpha's sword bit into her skin.

"Alright?" I called over my shoulder, speeding up my own attacks to give her time to recover.

"Fine."

She wasn't fine. I knew that tone, spoken through gritted teeth.

But Charlie's sword glinted in my peripheral vision. She was still fighting. Still holding her own. No, I couldn't end this by lapping up blood from the three worst possible victims—pack leaders. I couldn't expose my family to the danger that would result, at least not yet.

Still, I squinted at my sword, willing it to form a tiny channel down its center leading to a hollow vial. I'd collect blood as I fought. If I needed a saving grace later...well, it would be there waiting for my beck and call.

Unfortunately, my focus on tweaking my weapon let Smoke's brother, the alpha who'd been least aggressive, sneak up on my right. He came in hard and fast, driving me back into Charlie who responded by retreating down the side of the Moon Room.

Away from the door. The space wasn't quite unguarded yet, but it would be soon if we kept going in this direction.

I sped up my blows, trying to force the alpha in front of me to retreat so we could regain lost ground. My star-ball sword spat sparks as I attacked with a vengeance. But he just planted his feet and laughed in my face.

Meanwhile, Smoke's brother proved that he wasn't less aggressive, just more cunning. He waited until my main opponent doubled down, then he swooped in low, stacking their attack.

Two against one was more than I could handle when both of the alphas seemed to have picked up swords in the cradle. They beat their way in closer, tag-teaming me breathless.

One hard whack nearly knocked my sword out of my hand. Would have if I hadn't curled the star-ball magic into a locking manacle around my wrist.

Still, the blow reverberated through my bones, shuddering sense out of my fingers. I needed time to recover. I needed....

"About face!" I yelled, curling around Charlie. Thankfully, she followed my lead without delay, remembering our ace in the hole when we were outmatched.

Because Smoke's brother and the other alpha had already learned my favorite jabs and parries. But they didn't know Charlie's, not yet. By switching positions, we shook up our opponents. Made them relearn their opponent's weaknesses. Won precious time for Eli to crawl a little further down that tunnel beneath the bar.

Unfortunately, we lost ground while rotating one-eighty. The alphas surged against Charlie, forcing her to retreat and me also. I couldn't see the door into the bar from this angle, but I suspected it gaped unguarded. Hopefully no one would think to walk through it....

A crash of glass bottles burst in the near distance. From the bar proper. Sounded like we'd run out of luck.

Because from the bar the invaders had easy access to the kitchen. And Eli? Had he crawled all the way to safety? Had the scents of human dinner had time to recede enough not to give away his and others' retreat?

I had no way of knowing, which meant perhaps it was time to grasp at straws.

Unfortunately, I'd gathered blood from only two alphas. The third, who'd been fighting Charlie at first and who was now my primary opponent, proved more elusive. He seemed to dissolve into the darkness each time I jabbed in his direction, evading my sword as easily as I might slip fox-footed through the forest on midnight hunts.

I tried again, only to be sidetracked by a flicker of movement out of the corner of my eye. Was that more werewolves piling into battle against Charlie?

"Dude, pants," she complained. She was breathless, but her spirits didn't seem to be sagging despite the additional opponents. "Wear them or I'll aim lower."

Someone squawked and the alpha in front of me hesitated. Pack bonds flowed strong between alpha and underling, so he might really have felt the pain if Charlie sliced her new opponent in a very intimate spot.

This was my opening, and I took it even though Smoke's brother had turned on me the instant Charlie addressed the naked werewolf. Lunging, I accepted the fact that I was failing to defend my side while I pressed forward. Smoke's brother would attack, but it would be worth a few cuts to harvest blood from the final alpha....

A sword whistled past my ear, just missing. But red tinged the blade of my own weapon and I grinned triumphant.

Grinned for one split second until my foot struck floor that crunched and collapsed out from under me. *Rotten floorboards. Right.* I'd forgotten.

I tumbled into darkness as Charlie shrieked above me. A deep rumble of werewolf laughter promised she'd been caught.

Chapter 36

The hole was far too deep to be a crawl space. Or so I guessed in the second before my knees came down so hard that landing knocked my breath away. Which meant...I'd somehow managed to collapse the roof of the same tunnel Charlie and I were trying to draw the alpha's attention away from. Supremely bad luck.

To make matters worse, Gate City's municipal workers must have been pulling overtime. Because ceiling lights flared back into operation even as I blinked tears of pain out of stinging eyes. The room above and also the pit I'd fallen into settled into focus as a head crested the edge of the splintered floorboards.

"Are you coming up?" Scarlet demanded. Her hair was unruffled as if she'd let everyone else fight then stepped in to claim victory afterwards. "Or will someone have to drag you out?"

I certainly couldn't afford that. If a shifter jumped down from above, they'd smell the same faint whiffs of human and werewolf that were currently drifting out of the dark area off to my left. I tried to struggle to my feet...and failed.

"I'm coming," I promised, buying time while feeling blindly for a handhold. Then I yelped as my fingers touched what felt like a live electric wire.

Scarlet was uninterested in the cause of my pain. Her voice turned into a snarl. "I don't have all day."

Despite her warning, I risked flaring the faintest flicker through my star-ball sword to illuminate the surrounding area. There wasn't an exposed wire present. Just rock, rock, and more rock.

Or, no, make that limestone formations. I'd assumed from Thom's description that this was a dirt-lined tunnel, but it appeared that his ancestors had actually tapped into a natural cave.

A natural cave with damp stone flowing around something smoother and paler. The lights above me flickered and its identity clicked into focus.

A skull. A *fox* skull.

The implications were many...and I had no time to consider them now. Because Scarlet's limited patience had faded. Her head was no longer visible at the edge of my pit as she barked. "Bring me the human."

I could guess what she was about to do. To Charlie. To hurry me out of the pit.

Grabbing onto another rock flow, I expected a shock but got none this time. *Good.* That made it easier to unfold a leg that screamed with every movement. Ignoring its warnings, I found a toehold and launched myself up.

My landing was wobbly but vertical. And I was armed, although my weapon was a vial of blood rather than a sword. The time had come to use every resource at my disposal.

Only...no one was looking at me as I teetered on the edge of broken floorboards. Instead, heads had turned to face the doorway they'd all come in through. The doorway full of Thom and Gunner and my very pregnant sister Mai.

So this was what Thom had been up to for the last many hours. Why he'd left Gate City rather than pulling the curtains on his father's house as promised. He'd been gathering backup.

And maybe also engaging in a crash course in alpha behavior? Because he didn't offer a mild rebuke the way he had with Smoke. Instead, he addressed the crowd at large as he growled out a command that was even more powerful for its low volume. *"Demolition time is over. Get out."*

Less dominant wolves stampeded for various exits only to be stopped in their tracks as one of the invading alphas countered Thom's order. *"Halt."*

Shifters froze, stuck between dueling compulsions. By the look of the few at the edges who were still inching toward the exit, Thom's order seemed to be slightly stronger. But there were two more alpha invaders ready to chime in versus only Gunner backing Thom up.

Two alphas and three excellent swordswomen on our side—assuming I could break Charlie free of the werewolf who held her arms twisted behind her back—against dozens of enemies. We couldn't win through brute force alone.

We couldn't win. And the stakes had risen the moment I'd been shocked while fumbling for a handhold down beneath the floor of the Moon Room.

Because Scarlet was convinced Gate City hid a rather hefty power source. She wanted this bar as a result, had sent in alphas and their lackeys to break apart walls hunting something.

And I'd just stumbled upon a fox skull cemented beneath the floor.

It couldn't be a coincidence. Not when my vague understanding of kitsune history involved the knowledge that our bones in animal form harbored some sort of inherent power.

A power that might flicker lights and send words into dental fillings? A power that these invading alphas might be able to twist to an unsavory end?

I didn't know, but I couldn't risk it. Not when Mai was right in front of me, a visual reminder of who would be most harmed by the aftermath of kitsune magic gone haywire. The vial of blood I clutched burned hot in my hand.

My ace in the hole. The fox's way out of a battle against stronger opponents. Only it had many of the same negative consequences as giving Scarlet this bar.

I glanced toward Mai, who was making frantic hand gestures as if she expected me to scurry over and hide behind her pregnant belly. What I was about to do would go against my entire purpose over the last few months, even if it was meant to save my sister from worse blowback further down the line. I'd drink the alphas' blood then, since I couldn't stomach the idea of killing every one of our enemies afterwards, they'd eventually come to their senses and label me a kitsune rogue.

Once the story got out, life would be much worse for my unborn niece. Gunner would have to barricade his borders to keep out angry alphas. The small fragments of freedom Mai had enjoyed within her own territory would dissipate in a puff of smoke.

No, I couldn't let the action I was about to take hurt my sister and her family. So I dealt with Mai before I took my first sip of alpha blood.

"What are you doing here?" I demanded, stalking toward Gunner and Mai as if no one else was present. "I told you—I left. I make my own choices. I'm sick of your stupid rules."

Stupid rules like not using werewolf blood to manipulate. I hoped the alphas would remember my rant later. Would consider what I was about to do a personal failing rather than a danger presented by all kitsunes large and very small.

Mai's head cocked. She didn't believe me. She was trying to figure out my angle so she could play along with it.

That wasn't going to work. These alphas needed to smell her pain. Smell the reality of the split between me and the Fairwoods.

And the solution presented itself in a flicker of lights and a burst of understanding. *The pack bond.* The connection I'd been offered over a decade ago and wrapped around myself with such a sense of perfect belonging that even weeks outside the pack's proximity didn't weaken the invisible tether one bit.

If I broke that bond, every alpha in the Moon Room would smell the singed-hair reek of shattered connection. They'd know I meant business, that I wasn't playacting this separation from my only blood kin.

Assuming, that is, I could force myself to dismiss the very best part of my life.

My throat clenched, refusing to let me swallow. Losing Mai and Gunner and Grub was inconceivable.

But Thom was right. I wasn't a wolf, obsessed with pack bonds. I was a fox, ready and willing to act alone to protect those I loved.

So I broke the bond. Not with my hands, but with words that shattered my sister's composure the same way they shattered our immaterial connection.

"The Fairwood pack is mine no longer. I don't want it. I don't need it. I'm out."

Chapter 37

Mai splintered, her warrior nature shedding like a snake skin as she folded inward to sob on her mate's shoulder. For his part, Gunner growled something fierce and furious, aimed most likely at me.

And Thom...I got the distinct impression he understood what I was doing. Because those blue eyes pierced me, not with ice or fire this time but with the gentle uplift of a cloudless horizon. "Kira," he ordered, taking the fall for what I'd chosen to do already, "drink the blood."

I drank. Alpha ichor, already starting to congeal inside the magical vial I'd hidden in my fist. The clots were lumpy as cottage cheese on my tongue and I'd always detested cottage cheese.

It wasn't just the texture that was wrong either. When I'd drunk werewolf blood previously, it bubbled energy beneath my skin. This time, all I felt was faintly nauseous. Like putting this blood in my mouth was deeply wrong.

Still, I didn't hurry to swallow. Instead, I let the awfulness sit on my tongue while I used words to tug at the alphas' muscles. "Release every prisoner you've seized in Gate City. Then take your lackeys with you and go."

They tried to fight, but a kitsune's blood power isn't like alpha dominance. Their inherent strength couldn't counter my ability to control werewolves. Within minutes, I knew, they'd cave.

Still, my injured leg was threatening to give out under me. Tears bit at the backs of my eyelids every time I caught a whiff of my sister's agony. It was best these alphas left quickly. Left *now*.

"There's no shortage of blood," I warned them, holding up the vial and turning the outside translucent so they could see that it still contained several additional doses. Then I tipped it up to wet my tongue a second time in an effort to hurry things along.

This time, they didn't even try to fight me. Instead, they swiveled as a unit toward the parking-lot door, all three alphas plus the glow-stick-labelled werewolves who'd demolished the Moon Room. Two released Charlie before padding after the others. Then several more filtered in from the bar-side door before striding past us. A rumble of engines heralded their exit from the parking lot.

Thom was the only one who moved in the opposite direction. "That was more effective than I expected," he observed as he came up beside me. His broad chest was close enough I could have sagged against it, but as much as I craved the support I didn't take it. Because a woman I hadn't realized was still present stepped out of the shadows and into the dust-sparkling light.

"Pack bonds," Scarlet observed, brushing bits of wall plaster off her shoulder. "More trouble than they're worth."

I'd forgotten that Scarlet wasn't a member of any pack. That the Lawkeepers were her only loyalty. So none of the alphas would have ordered her to retreat with them. And I had no way of coercing her now.

"You've lost," I gritted out, hoping to end this without bloodshed.

She laughed. "Maybe. But there are loose ends to tie up."

My gaze flew to Charlie, who lingered dangerously close to Scarlet's elbow. My friend's sword dangled unnoticed from lax fingers. She swayed as adrenaline faded, her precarious humanity on full display.

Her humanity...and the reason for her current weakness. Charlie had been exposed to secrets werewolves couldn't afford to allow into the hands of non-pack-mates. Her knowledge threatened her continued existence by werewolf law.

I'd assumed when I opened Charlie's eyes to the supernatural that I'd be able to whisk her away before anyone official noticed the lack of fur scent about her. After all, I trusted Charlie to keep my secrets. I trusted her the same way she'd trusted me.

Unfortunately, whisking hadn't happened. I could only hope to distract Scarlet from my friend's humanity so she wouldn't draw well-founded conclusions. "What sort of loose ends?" I asked, keeping my feet still with an effort. They wanted to carry me to Charlie. Wanted to put my body between my friend and danger.

But it was already too late. "Loose ends like the power source in Gate City that should be managed by shifters instead of human jarheads." Scarlet knocked Charlie's sword away with one fast blow then seized my friend's wrist with her free arm. "And like this."

I tried to say something, but only a wordless wheeze emerged from my mouth. Scarlet had no such problem with a tied tongue.

"This human is a danger to pack," she continued. "If you don't want to see her put down, I recommend you turn your backs now."

"Put down?" Thom murmured behind me.

"Killed," I managed, unable to take my eyes off Charlie. She was frozen, the gumption she'd shown earlier fading like fog at the dawn.

This couldn't be happening. I took a step forward. I wouldn't let it.

Options tumbled all over themselves in my brain. Thom and I could overpower Scarlet between us, I knew, even if we kept Gunner and Mai out of it. But cut down one Lawkeeper and a dozen more would be sent in to squelch the problem. Gate City would end up in an even more precarious position than it was in now.

My left foot froze rather than following my right foot. Scarlet pursed her lips. "Final warning. I wouldn't want to scar your little fox brain."

"Kira." Thom brushed past me then stopped, his neck bending to bring his face closer to my level. His eyes held questions. What were the rules? How could we wiggle under or over them? How could we save Charlie's life?

We couldn't...or could we? At long last, the obvious solution bubbled up. Trouble was, success depended upon Thom accepting a role he'd roundly refused the last time I mentioned it.

Still, I had to try. *We* had to try.

"Alpha," I started, expecting a wince at the form of address and not seeing one. Just those icepick eyes boring into me, expecting magic. "Only you can vouch for a human."

Instead of recoiling, Thom dimpled. As if he was amused this was all saving Charlie would require. "Of course." His voice reverberated with command. "Charlie falls under my protection."

It wasn't quite enough. Scarlet's eyebrows rose. "Is that so? You're vouching for *this*"—she shook Charlie, not at all gently—"not to unveil mysteries humanity isn't ready for?"

Thom growled, the perfect alpha response. Then he extending one fist, fingers popping open in a demand that Charlie be handed over. "Precisely what I said. Must I repeat myself?"

I could imagine his arctic eyes boring into Scarlet. Saw her darker irises flashing anger in reply.

Scarlet wasn't convinced, but she was outclassed and that might be enough for now. She held Thom's glare for one long moment...then her gaze dropped. Shoving Charlie at Thom as if knocking aside an inanimate object, she muttered, "On your head be it if she breaks."

Thom caught my friend much more gently than she'd been thrown at him. And he didn't deign to reply to that veiled threat. Instead, he removed my ex-boss's other reason to trespass in Gate City in the future.

"Your job here is done. I personally promise this town's magic won't fall into the hands of the human military. You have no further reason to murder our citizens."

The last came out in a throaty growl. Thom wasn't pretending any longer. This was his true self, warning away a danger to his pack mates.

And maybe that's why Scarlet acceded. Or maybe she just knew when to retreat with grace.

After all, there were other Gate City wolves filtering in the door now. Shifters who might not make up an official pack but who bristled with aggression as they took in the destruction of the Moon Room. One tapped his fist against a shattered video-game console then turned to face Scarlet with pointy teeth bared.

Despite being outnumbered, my ex-boss didn't acknowledge the implied threat of stiff body language and subvocal growls. Instead, she stalked past everyone, stopping only long enough to toss one last threat in Thom's direction.

"There are other pack leaders who will listen just as easily as todays' did," she warned us. "A rogue kitsune will capture their attention when you fail."

Chapter 38

The Moon Room was packed with jostling bodies within seconds. Thom's allies, it seemed, had been out tracking down Lawkeepers. And as each street came up empty of danger, they drifted back to the bar...along with Rupert, who had apparently been released at my command.

"You've ruined everything," my least favorite ex-coworker groused as he half-trotted toward me. I suspected he intended to look imposing, but his hair stood on end and his usually perfect suit was torn in three places. He also smelled like the insides of a well-used dumpster. "Scarlet will never receive justice for committing cold-blooded murder. And look at *me*! What am I supposed to do now?"

I shook my head. I didn't have energy to deal with Rupert, not when my sister was still sagging against Gunner.

So I was grateful when Thom stepped between us, angling Rupert further away from me. "We'll find you a room. A job."

Rupert's rejoinder was loud enough to carry after me as I limped in the opposite direction. "Do I look like I want to live in this hick town?"

"You look tired."

Weren't we all?

Exhaustion nearly took me down when I came within scent range of my sister. The singed-hair broken pack scent was so strong here that it choked me. Worse, though, were the tendrils of seeking that tried to reconnect with each step I took.

I stopped, batting away sisterly efforts to rebuild our pack bond. "Mai, you can't."

Gunner opened his mouth and I expected him to bark at me the way he had that one time I dared Grub to climb a very dangerous tree that resulted in little-boy tears and a wrenched ankle. Instead, my brother-in-law's voice was kind and aimed at my sister. "She's right, Mai. If Kira wants to fly, you have to let her go."

"No." Mai's single word was enough to snap Gunner's gaze in the other direction, his eyes if not his body giving us space even in the midst of an increasingly crowded room.

"Kira," My sister's voice softened as she reached out as if to take my hands then stopped herself. But her words continued the effort to connect. "Of course I can recreate what you've broken. I'm your sister. What does that mean other than pack?"

I had no answer. Or, no, I could remember, just barely, life before werewolves. When it was just the two of us surviving by the skin of our teeth.

I managed five broken words. "Love doesn't require pack bonds."

It did require proximity, however. At least when children were involved.

I swallowed against the knowledge that Grub's young memory of me might not last more than a year or two. That I wouldn't hold my niece when she was born, wouldn't count her tiny fingers and toes.

Both Mai and I were actively crying now, and I wasn't so sure my sister could take in what I was about to ask. So I sidestepped until I was in Gunner's sight line. "Teach Grub some of my stupid pranks now and then, will you? I don't want him to forget...."

I thought my brother-in-law might not acknowledge me. After all, despite our connection, Mai was his number one priority.

And I'd broken my sister. There weren't just tears on her face now. There was snot and goo and all kinds of crumpled features she wasn't even trying to cover up.

Gunner reached out one arm and drew his mate back in against himself, shielding her misery. Then he nodded a promise just as air brushed against the back of my neck.

Someone had crept up to join us. I turned, expecting Thom. But it was Charlie. Charlie, who held out a single-serving shot bottle full of clear alcohol. She'd likely found it behind the bar.

I swiped at my face, drying pesky liquid. "You want me to drink away the pain?"

"No, this is for the blood. And, about that." Charlie jerked her chin at Mai, who had been like a big sister to her for years during our shared childhood. "I get that Kira can't let magical trouble land in your laps. But hasn't anyone here ever heard of anonymous video calls?"

Charlie's solution wasn't perfect, but it was just barely enough to give me strength to turn away from my sister without hugging her. It was enough to keep me from running after Mai and Gunner as they limped like the walking wounded out the door.

And this time, when air currents warned of someone's proximity, it really was Thom. Thom plus Dixie Lee and her daughter, the latter of whom had Pumpkin cradled in her arms.

"He was in the alley," the girl whispered into the cat's fur. "He looked scared."

"He'll bounce right back in the morning," Dixie Lee answered, smoothing the hair out of her daughter's eyes. "It's past his bedtime."

Thom cleared his throat and took the opening. "Past all of our bedtimes. I was hoping you might offer Kira your guest room."

Dixie Lee's eyes flashed onto me then away again as she shook her head in fiery refusal. She kept her tone light, though, for the sake of her daughter. "Bertrand already claimed it." It was clear she wasn't interested in being friends.

"I can stay with Charlie," I started.

But when I swiveled to look for my human friend, she turned out to be absent. Someone had likely walked her home already. After the day she'd had, Charlie didn't need me pounding on her door restarting her adrenaline the moment she collapsed, exhausted, into her bed.

The Moon Room, I noted, was emptying out again. Everyone had been reassured of friends' safety, then they'd headed out into the night to their own homes.

Well. I could shift into my fur and find a corner to curl up in. A fox was never without a blanket when she had her tail.

Thom had other ideas. "There's a bed and a couch in my apartment. May I?"

Somehow, I found myself being carried up stairs that would have been too much for my sore leg to navigate solo. Somehow, I found myself being settled onto the softness of a mattress that smelled like Thom.

He growled something under his breath and started to pick me back up again. "I should have changed the sheets."

"No. Leave them." Just for tonight, I needed to be not entirely alone.

Sliding under the covers, I watched Thom turn off the light and head out into his living room. Listened until I heard water running. Only then did I release the last shreds of my self-control.

Fear for Charlie and Eli and Ava crested against the pain of losing the bond with my sister. Like one wave trying to slide back off the beach colliding with another wave relentlessly forcing its way forward. The reverberation racked me from head to toe.

Tears were no release. I thrust my fist against my mouth, trying to stifle sobs that I knew would carry to shifter ears, shower notwithstanding.

Then Thom was back. Damp yet warm arms enclosed me. "Shh. Dixie Lee was right. Everything will look brighter in the morning."

This thing between us, it wasn't a pack bond. But it was real. It was hot enough to burn away the ice in my belly.

And despite the darkness, I could tell Thom was naked. Hard muscles pressed up against me. A different sensation slicked my skin.

"Kiss me," I demanded.

He did, but not in the way I yearned for. Instead, warm lips brushed across my forehead. "You have a place here as long as you need it," Thom promised.

And, somehow, I fell asleep.

Chapter 39

I t wasn't brighter in the morning. Instead, I woke to gray rain pouring across the window and a nearly unbearable urge to clamber down the outside of the Full Moon Saloon in fur form and flee into the forest to lick my wounds.

It was either that or deal with the fox skull I'd uncovered yesterday. The fox skull that might make everything even worse for my kind.

Back home, I would have passed the buck, trusting Gunner to deal with a magical artifact cemented into his basement. But here in Gate City, I was leery of the loose affiliation between unfamiliar shifters that didn't quite add up to a pack.

Perhaps it would be better not to mention what I'd seen, to let the hole be covered up and the skull be hidden for another century. Assuming, that is, it hadn't been noticed yet.

Thunder crashed as I eased onto a leg that was now only barely sore. No, that hadn't been thunder. The sound had come from below rather than above and now the buzz of an electric saw joined in the cacophony.

Curiosity drew me out of my head, down the stairs, and through an empty kitchen. Out front, the bar was full, but not with patrons. Instead, increasingly familiar shifters repaired furniture, cleaned up graffiti, and swept away broken glass.

In the midst of the activity, Thom spoke to a human in a dark uniform. "You can't really blame kids for releasing party balloons, even if they did shut down the lights on half the downtown."

The police officer's eyebrows rose. "I don't believe the cause of the outage made the news this morning."

"This city runs on gossip. You know that."

"I know this city depends on good relations with the Base. Their liaison wasn't happy. This bar seems to have been the center of last night's trouble. If you know something...."

"I promise you. What happened here had nothing to do with the Base."

The two men stood, eyes locked, for one long moment. Then the officer shrugged. Relatives were asked after. Backs were slapped.

Thom turned away from the exiting human and addressed everyone in the bar. "I appreciate you all coming in this morning." He met eye after eye, waiting for the policeman to retreat out of earshot before speaking more plainly. "So you should be the first to know there will be changes in Gate City. Such as a signup sheet for boundary patrols."

His gaze found mine and the faintest hint of a smile tugged his lips upward before he continued. "Community meals will be mandatory. In fact, I'd like a few volunteers to start breakfast now."

A voice grumped from my left. "Are you saying we have to act like a pack?"

Feet shuffled. Harsh whispers erupted. This was a major change in policy and a risk on Thom's part, especially when he'd drawn all of these wanderers in by providing a town with very few rules.

A human would have mitigated his demands. But Thom merely shrugged. "I am. There's no shame if you choose to leave now."

They didn't though. Of course they didn't. Because, like it or not, Thom had been an alpha already. His words this morning just made that reality clear.

No wonder two shifters headed into the kitchen while the rest picked back up their tools. No wonder I padded over to Thom's side.

"Sleep okay?" he asked.

I nodded, my decision resolving itself. "There's something I need to show you."

Together, we headed for the skull.

There were shifters in the Moon Room, sawing away rotten floorboards and repairing the kicked-in door. But they looked up when we entered. At some wordless signal from Thom, each one dropped what they were doing and exited into the bar.

Then we were alone.

"You'll have to get down in the hole to see it," I offered. My injured knee only protested a little as I hopped into the same pit I'd ended up in yesterday.

Thom landed beside me, his larger boots settling beside my sneakers with the same near-soundless shifter agility. He considered the dim space and I flared my star ball to make the skull more obvious.

"This?" he asked, reaching out to touch it.

"Don't...."

I hadn't spoken fast enough and his finger grazed the surface. But he didn't jerk away. And when I tapped the skull after he did, the electric jolt from last night failed to materialize.

"It shocked me yesterday."

My explanation came out uncertain, but Thom just nodded. "What is it?"

"A fox skull." I cleared my throat then corrected myself. "A kitsune skull."

"And its purpose?"

I shook my head. "I'm not sure. But it seems likely the skull is what Scarlet was so concerned about. It would help to know how it got here. Could you have Japanese ancestors?"

"I don't know." The pit wasn't large, so it was no wonder Thom's scent curled like fingers tugging me toward him. His subsequent words drew me in closer yet. "I wanted to explain," he rumbled. "About my mother. About us."

The polite thing to do would have been to stop him. After all, Thom didn't owe me any secrets.

But I wanted to hear him out. And not just because I was curious. A shared secret felt like a pack bond, and last night's icy pit in my stomach hadn't entirely thawed.

So I listened as the scent of toasting bread carried from the kitchen and Thom told me about what he called the Faris family curse. Single parents going back at least three generations. His father the result of a one-night stand.

For his part, Big T had enjoyed a summer fling he thought was serious...until his lover left him for the husband she'd forgotten to mention when they first hooked up. "A woman Dad had never seen before showed up with me in her arms nine months later," Thom told the ground between us. "She had a cock-and-bull story about werewolves and her sister hoping her mate would accept me until I came out smelling like Dad. He wouldn't have believed a word of it, but the woman offered him the same necklace his lover had worn."

The necklace that now hung around my neck. My hand closed around the chain, preparing to remove it. I didn't deserve Thom's only link to his mother.

But Thom shook his head and I offered words instead. "Must have been a shock when you shifted the first time."

"Yeah." His voice was rough. "And a wakeup call. That's when I decided to break the family curse."

The distance Thom had always kept between us made more sense now. Still—"There are prophylactics."

Which Thom well knew. The contents of the huge box of condoms were scattered across the Moon Room floor.

He nodded. "I counted on modern science at first. Then came prom night, my girlfriend, a condom plus an IUD." The toe of his boot nudged at the bottom of a rock flow. "Her period didn't come two weeks later. I asked her to marry me. She laughed in my face."

My banged-up knee tried to collapse and I grabbed onto the rock to steady myself. "You have a kid."

"Miscarriage." The smile Thom tried on fit about as well as the clothes he'd lent me two days earlier. "And this is way too much information when we haven't gone on a single date."

"It isn't." I swallowed. "I get it. You're telling me it's not me, it's you."

"No." Thom's refusal came out so fierce the chatter of voices from the bar stilled for one split second. In the kitchen, a tremendous crash suggested the cooks had been startled enough to drop something large.

Thom waited until bustle restarted itself before speaking again. His voice had returned to its normal register.

"No. I'm telling you that I"—he cleared his throat—"need a committed relationship before I'm willing to be intimate."

The tips of Thom's ears flamed red. I opened my mouth...and nothing came out.

Because, after last night, I didn't trust myself not to latch onto Thom for all the wrong reasons. Didn't trust myself not to seize upon any available bond to thaw the ice floe in my gut.

And, at the same time, my skin wanted his skin. My arms craved his arms.

Silence yawned and Thom's icepick gaze dropped to the ground. "I'm well aware that we haven't known each other long enough for you to decide anything," he muttered. "We...."

Then fast footsteps clattered across the floor toward us. Charlie's head poked over the edge of the hole.

"He's gone!" she blurted out, the phone that had likely provided some sort of bad news still clasped in one hand.

I glanced at Thom then accepted the fact that this conversation—so important, so loaded, so impossible for me to take part in at the present moment—needed to be tabled. His mouth quirked upward in acceptance and he created a stirrup out of his hands to help boost me out of the hole.

At floor level, I grasped Charlie's shaking shoulders. "Who's gone?"

"My brother-in-law." She shook her head. "Not Jessie's husband. Ito's brother. Is that my brother-in-law? Maybe not. Maybe he's no relation to me at all."

She didn't mean that last bit. I could smell the reek of family-in-danger pouring off her. Charlie, with only her twin to rely on, had bonded to Jessie's in-laws with an intensity that spoke of pack.

And if they were her pack, they were mine now also.

"The one in a coma here in Gate City?" I clarified, sliding my grasp down the length of her arms until I could still her hands' shaking.

"Yes." My friend swallowed, seemingly unable to give more than that one word answer.

After a pause, I drew her out. "But Ito's his legal guardian? How could his brother be taken by anyone else?"

Charlie nodded more times than she really needed to for simple confirmation. "He is. He was. But, last night, Kaito woke up and refused further treatment. He walked out and no one knows where he went."

No one knew where he went...and could it really be a coincidence that this person so important to Charlie disappeared the day after a werewolf showdown? The day after Scarlet was stopped from murdering Charlie on this very spot?

A sensation very much like an ice cube trickled down my spine, promising there was no such thing as coincidence when it came to werewolves. I'd drawn Charlie into my world, and it was already biting back at her.

No, my world wasn't biting back at her. It was biting back at *us*.

Up until this point, Thom had given us privacy. But now he heaved himself up out of the hole and straightened to stand beside me. His attention was on Charlie but his words were meant for me.

"We'll find him."

Despite the awfulness of the occasion, I couldn't help turning away from my friend to face this not-quite-alpha who refused to kiss me unless I made impossible promises. "We?"

Thom cleared his throat but his gaze on mine was steady. "I meant what I said last night about finding a place for you here if you decide you have reason to spend time in Gate City."

"You'll find a place for me like you did for Rupert?"

Thom's eyes crinkled. "Not exactly."

As he spoke, his hand inched toward my hand. Our fingers brushed, sparking a different sort of electric shock than last night's magical discovery.

And in my stomach, fire flared. Ice thawed. I realized I hadn't been breathing properly all morning long.

Until now, when my lungs finally inflated to their fullest extent.

"You don't have to worry," I told Charlie, smiling more widely than I should have in the face of a missing family member. "Shifter noses. We'll track him down in an eye blink."

Then I focused on Thom while ensuring my little finger didn't lose contact with his little finger. And I made the only promise I was currently capable of.

"For now, for a while, I'll stay."

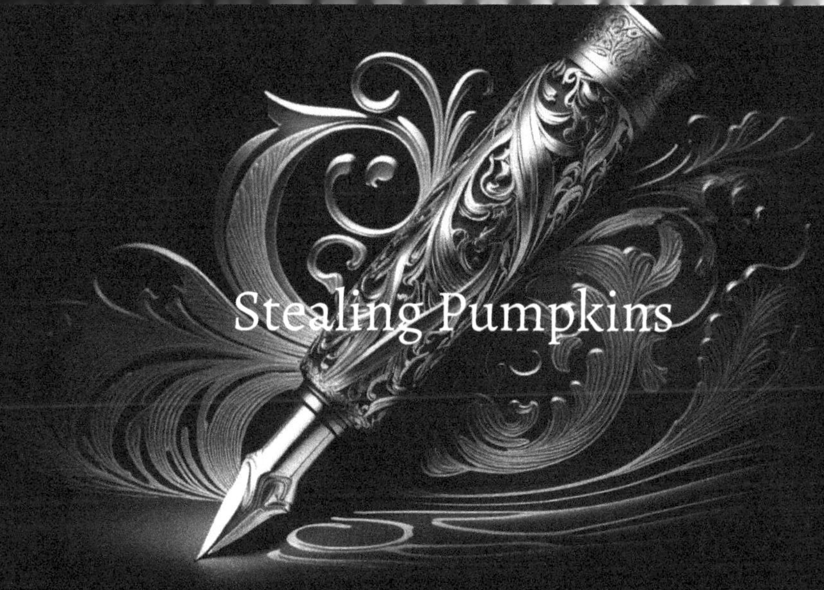

Stealing Pumpkins

A note from the author...

The authorial rule of thumb is never to steal a character whole cloth. If you're basing the villain on your elementary school principal, be sure to change the gender and the fact he always wore green suits.

I broke this rule.

You see, my current hometown hosts a celebrity who was too good not to insert directly into Kira's world. The real Pumpkin is a big orange tomcat who lives in the Athens, Ohio, election office. He likes to sit in the window so his adoring fans can snap selfies with him. He goes on vacation only twice a year—during elections—since he disapproves of the heavy traffic and would rather board with a local vet at that time.

Okay, so I didn't steal every bit of Pumpkin's lifestyle. In my fictional world, he's a bar cat who turns into a bit of a traveler as the series progresses. But I kept his name and he looks pretty much exactly like his namesake.

Here's hoping the real Pumpkin doesn't figure out how to lawyer up!

The Real Gate City

Gate City is a very real town near the southwestern tip of Virginia, but my version is a little different. A military base set up operations next door in Kira's world, and that one change ballooned a real-life community of just under 2,000 people into a mid-sized city. What follows are photos from my scouting trip to the existing town.

Main Street (actually called Jackson Street) in the real world.

Gate City got its name because it's a low spot where European settlers could make it through the mountains without climbing over huge ridges.

*My mom in front of the building that
became the Full Moon Saloon.*

*The back parking lot of what I turned into
the Full Moon Saloon. Thom, of course,
keeps this area far more spick and span.*

ROGUE MOON
KIRA FAIRWOOD: BOOK 2
USA TODAY BESTSELLING AUTHOR
AIMEE EASTERLING

Rogue Moon

Chapter 1

The tug of the full moon slapped me in the face with all the finesse of a stinky locker-room towel. Bar-interior dimness brightened as my pupils dilated. Hubbub faded as my attention laser-focused on the man serving pints half a room away.

Not just any man. If Thom ever wanted a break from his current gig as bar owner, he could make a go of it as a pinup model. After all, the muscles of his forearms were dreamily displayed by rolled-up flannel shirt sleeves. The rest of him was equally super-sized, but bulk didn't equate to slowness. Instead, Thom crossed the room with all the speed and agility of what he also was—an alpha werewolf.

I hummed, fingers settling on the medallion between my breasts as I licked my lips. And—

"*Out.*" Thom shoved the man on the neighboring bar stool away from me. The guy—a human—uttered only one complaining syllable before he took a look at Thom's face, changed his mind, and yanked out his wallet with shaking fingers instead.

Smart man. Obey the alpha werewolf. Give him space so he could wrap himself around my skin and....

I snorted displeasure as an annoyingly familiar human woman joined our threesome. Subsided as she did what her role as pack hanger-on mandated—she moved the non-pack male along.

"On the house. Here, let me get you a doggy bag for the road. Do you like burgers? Fries? How about pie? We have lemon meringue and cherry."

I didn't bother watching Thom's employee soothe the evicted human as she drew him away from us. Because Thom was in my personal space now, finally and fully. He'd settled onto the vacated bar stool, jeans-clad thighs splaying wide as he encompassed me in his alpha musk.

"Kira. Look at me."

I hummed again. Thom didn't have to ask for my attention. In fact, I thought it might be time for us to do more than look.

Would his stubbled jaw feel as roughly enticing as it appeared from a distance? If I reached out to test the terrain, would he open his lips and take my finger into his mouth?

My hand didn't complete its journey, unfortunately. Instead, a hot fist manacled my wrist as Thom barked. "Bertrand. Get over here."

A suited shadow blocked the light. "I can't see why you two don't just seal the deal. You're into her. She's into you. I'm sick of playing chaperone."

"You think this is ordinary behavior?" Thom's voice was so deep it vibrated his hand and my arm along with it. I leaned in closer, or tried to. His muscles flexed as he fended off my advance.

"I guess not," the other man said after a moment. He cocked his head, snapping his fingers in front of my face then jerking them away as I clicked my teeth together irritably. "Kira. Focus."

I hissed. Suit dude wasn't the man I wanted. If I shifted, my needle-sharp teeth would make him think again about addressing me while I was busy.

I craved the alpha. I *needed....*

"Hey, hey, hey, hey. Not here." The unwanted man had his hands on my shoulders now. And Thom was gone, moving so fast I'd missed his exit. Dimly, in the distance, I heard the deep rumble of his voice:

"Bar's closing. Family emergency."

Feet shuffled toward the exit, which was irrelevant. What was relevant was Thom's distance from my aching center. I could barely smell him. The loss hollowed out my core.

I yanked against my jailer's grip, but it was as firm as his alpha's had been. My voice rose into a yodel as I flung myself from side to side.

"She's going to hurt herself."

That was the woman. The woman who'd crept closer to Thom than I was. How *dared* she?

I lashed out, fingernails turning into claws as fur rose on a dwindling body. Soon I was smaller than all of them, approximately the size of a well-fed tomcat.

I wasn't a tomcat, though. I was a fox. And that grip on my shoulders after one fast wriggle? Gone. Their ability to catch me as I slipped through grasping fingers? A joke.

Now it was my turn to take control. First order of business: the woman was going down.

Except I wasn't the only four-legger in the bar. I skidded to a halt in front of a wolf who'd planted himself between me and the woman. A tie dangled from his neck and suit pants slid off his rump.

Which should have been humorous, but the wolf's size wasn't funny. His raised ruff radiated menace. The shadows beneath his legs were large enough to swallow me up.

Not that I intended to hide myself. Not between *his* legs. I'd gotten turned away from my target, but now I realigned myself. *The alpha.* He was still in human form, which was good. Shortly, I'd be human again, and naked. It wouldn't take much effort to rip his clothes off as well.

Well, the belt might present a challenge since my brain was oddly muzzy. He could take care of that part. I took a step...

...and something soft and warm dropped over my nose and back. Enveloped me just like I wanted Thom's arms to do.

But this wasn't arms and it didn't smell like alpha.

I spat and hissed, but the bindings just pulled tighter. Then the woman—I could smell her—scooped me up. The swaddling fabric that stunk of her man resisted the tearing of my claws.

"Give her to me."

For a moment, cool air pressed through cloth bindings, then the warmth of body contact rekindled. I was no longer restrained by the woman. Instead, I'd found the arms of the alpha, my goal from the start.

"What's going on?" This was suit dude, returned from wolf form to question his alpha.

I growled. You didn't *question* an alpha. You obeyed him. Lay beneath him. Let him pet you until you shattered from pure pleasure and delight.

Like I wanted to. Hadn't yet but would soon, unless....

A distant memory of Thom's months-old explanation filtered through the moon craze. *"The Faris curse,"* he'd confided. *"Single parents going back at least three generations. I"*—he'd cleared his throat—*"need a committed relationship before I'm willing to be intimate."*

Now I was the one who shook my head, whipping irrelevant human words away and fragments of the past along with them. I wanted Thom and I'd smelled how much the alpha wanted me. It was time for us both to take.

"I don't know what's going on," Thom answered suit dude, his voice slightly choked. Could he smell my arousal the same way I smelled his presence? If so, he knew I craved his skin slicking my skin. He knew....

Thom took a step backwards, his voice hardening as he shared our private business with those irrelevant to us. "Two months ago, it started with flirtation. Last full moon, Kira wasn't herself, but she held it together. Tonight...."

"I thought moon phases didn't impact werewolves." This was the woman. Why was she still so close to my alpha?

I struggled and Thom's hand settled on my nape, caressing me through the fabric. My muscles eased.

Yes, he'd take me to bed shortly. I could wait a moment while he addressed annoying pack members, sent them away and won privacy for our tryst.

"Moon phases *are* irrelevant to us," Thom confirmed, his rumble like a rocking boat lulling my senses into somnolence. "Shouldn't impact kitsunes either. Something's wrong, and I intend to stop it."

The other male snorted then muttered, "Good luck with that."

Chapter 2

I woke to a pounding head, Pumpkin on my chest, and Charlie's face inches from my eyeballs. "Rise and shine!"

For several seconds, I blinked confusion. Had the craziness of last night merely been a stress dream? The evidence seemed to suggest as much. Because here I was with my entirely human housemate along with Thom's cat who slipped in to sleep with me every night before wandering back to the bar to be fed by his real owner. Meanwhile, the light—or lack thereof—pointed to this being just another ordinary January morning.

So why did my fingertips throb as if I'd used them in an attempt to rip away bindings? Why, as I sat up from a couch that released me reluctantly, did a quilt crumple to the floor and cold air slap my naked stomach and thighs?

Because that stress dream had been reality, despite the fact I had no explanation for my out-of-character behavior. It had been reality that faded into darkness after Bertrand and Dixie Lee left me and Thom alone in the Full Moon Saloon.

Well, alone except for my moon-crazed refusal to abide by Thom's relationship line in the sand. My head fell into my hands. "Oh shit."

Before I could indulge in full-on hysterics, a fried-egg sandwich nudged its way into my view field. The offering wiggled as Charlie misunderstood the reason for my distress.

"Yes, you overslept, and on the lumpy couch instead of in your bed. We all drink too much sometimes. Or were you feeling foxy? Whatever. Eat and you'll feel better."

My lips quirked at Charlie's mothering, humor cradling me for one split second until my hand rose to the empty spot where Thom's medallion should have hung at my throat. The jewelry was missing, just like my clothes. Missing...along with the bond it implied?

Eating abruptly felt impossible. I drew the discarded quilt up over me instead, an action Charlie's keen eye didn't miss. "Hey, you don't have to cover up on my account. Casual nudity. Shifters. I get it."

"You've come a long way since last fall," I murmured, hugging the quilt a little tighter and hoping it would warm the cold hole in my belly.

"Shifters. Magic." Charlie shrugged. "Once I accepted that the majority of the human body is made up of empty spaces between electrons, everything else was a breeze. Now *eat.*"

The trouble was, the cut egg yolk oozing out of my half of the sandwich was precisely the texture of semen. I had an abrupt urge to hit the bathroom and peer at my thighs in search of crusted substances. Because if Thom and I had broken our friends-only agreement...well, he might never forgive me.

"Kira. Food. I mean it."

Charlie wasn't going to let the matter slide. So I forced myself to pick up her gift, allowing the awfulness to drip onto the plate while I contemplated bringing it to my lips.

A bite was beyond me, but a word wasn't. "Sure."

And, apparently that was enough for Charlie because she took a deep breath then spoke a little too fast. "So...Jessie's coming to visit this weekend. She's bringing the whole family. You good with that?"

My eyebrows shot up, the question marks of last night fading for one split second. I hadn't seen Charlie's twin since college. Hadn't seen Jessie's husband either, which was very understandable since Ito was the reason the Raven girls and I had lost touch.

"Is Ito willing to see me?"

"He's not *un*willing," Charlie prevaricated, polishing off the last of her sandwich then licking crumbs off her fingers. A dab of yolk on the corner of her mouth made my gorge rise. "He doesn't blame you for not being able to find his brother, you know. You and Thom pulled out all the stops, uncovered everything there was to uncover. The trail is simply cold."

While true, my recent failure to track down Charlie's sister's husband's brother—and, yes, I knew how convoluted that sounded—only layered on top of Ito's and my ancient history. History that culminated with my sister using his brother to fuel a spell that locked Kaito in a coma for over a decade. No wonder Kaito had fled after waking up three months ago, completely disappearing off the face of the earth.

Whatever Charlie said, given the fact that all my efforts to track down Kaito turned up goose eggs, I didn't expect Ito to be keen on seeing me tomorrow.

"Maybe I should make myself scarce," I offered, letting my half of the breakfast sandwich drift back down to the plate.

"No." Charlie was halfway across the room now, pulling on her coat, hat, and gloves. "I want you here. It'll be fine. Oh, and Thom asked me to give you this."

My cell phone tumbled through the air between us. The phone...but no medallion.

I must have winced because Charlie breezed back over to pat me on the head the same way she used to when I was the younger tagalong to her two-sister posse. "Don't worry about my brother-in-law. Ito is a teddy bear. Once you two spend a little time together, you'll be BFFs."

I'd actually forgotten about Ito already. And about the fact that Charlie's sister's visit wasn't the only thing my housemate had wanted to discuss with me. I forced my voice to brighten. "You said we had two things to talk about?"

Charlie considered me for a moment, then she shook her head. "Later. Don't want to make us both late for work."

Chapter 3

I wasn't late for work, but only because I lacked a permanent job. I did have a login to an app from a temp agency, though, one that offered the best gigs to the earliest applicants to rise.

It was already half an hour past my usual check-in time, but I headed for my personal messages first. And there, at the top of my notifications, was a text from Thom.

"Nothing happened."

My breath whooshed out in what was only half relief. Nothing happened...because Thom had stood firm against my wild advances? Because he'd brought me home and, what, sedated me?

And if nothing had happened, why hadn't his mother's medallion been sent back to me along with my phone?

Just like Charlie's aborted conversation, Thom and I would need to talk at some point. But, right now, retreating ice beneath my skin turned that drippy egg yolk back into food I was ravenous for. I wolfed it down while opening up the temping app.

The best jobs went to the early birds and I'd overslept. Which is how, three hours later, I came to be standing on a cold street corner dressed like a slice of pizza while twirling a saucer of fabric that was supposed to look like dough over my head.

"Delicious pizza! Get your slice here!"

A couple of teenage boys walked past, snickering into their fists. "I'd like a slice of that," one said just loudly enough that even a human would have overheard him.

I ignored the commentary and focused on the lines I'd been given. "Hot and ready! Deep dish!"

The next laugh was feminine, familiar...and behind me where no one should have been.

I spun on feet that weren't as fleet as usual when bogged down by the non-bending crust of the pizza costume. My star ball—the magic that let me turn into a fox or materialize pointy as well as non-pointy objects—tingled at my fingertips, but I didn't dare pull a weapon out of thin air at the moment. Not here among humans. Not in front of someone who had been known to put non-shifters to death for seeing things they shouldn't see.

Instead, I greeted the woman who used to employ me with her name only. "Scarlet."

When I'd seen her last, my ex-boss had been vanquished but not downtrodden. She'd tossed warnings back over her shoulder at me and Thom. Warnings that had teeth as sharp as any werewolf's. Specifically, she'd sworn to gather more alphas to defeat us if we didn't keep the magic of Gate City under wraps.

But the fox skull in the Full Moon Saloon's crawl space was locked away beneath a newly formed trapdoor only Thom and I were aware of. The drama of a werewolf battle on city streets had faded as those not in the know accepted Thom's reimagining of events.

Noses were clean. Scarlet had no reason to track me down. So I twirled my pizza with only a small twinge of trepidation while demanding: "What do you want?"

My ex-boss graced me with a smile that didn't reach her eyes. "I'm here about your darling niece."

The dough splatted onto the sidewalk. "Chipmunk? What's wrong with her?"

"Sniffles. A cough. I hear she cries half the night."

And now my star ball was a stiletto. A knife small and thin enough not to be obvious to passersby, but wickedly sharp anyway as it dug into the skin above

Scarlet's left kidney. Rather than threatening with words, I released a vulpine growl.

Scarlet merely laughed. "Relax. I saw the baby when I asked your sister for a favor. She turned me down, so I've come to you."

I snorted. If Mai didn't want to assist Scarlet, I didn't either.

Still, the fastest way to get rid of Scarlet likely involved hearing her out. "I'm listening."

Of course, she didn't tell me what she wanted immediately. Instead, she tried to reel me in first. "I'm in a bind that requires a kitsune and you have a hankering to meet your sister's newborn. Make a deal with me and we can both get what we want."

The knife sagged for one split second. I wanted that. I wanted that badly.

But it wasn't happening. Pressing the weapon back into place, I shook my head. "Let me guess. You're asking me to drink a werewolf's blood on video and turn into a pariah while nearly bringing my family down with me. Oh, wait, that happened already. What else do you have planned?"

"You take things so personally. Last fall was only business."

I dropped my voice as I let the knife dig in deeper. "Murdering an innocent was only business?"

"She was meat. Irrelevant." Rather than taking evasive action against my very tangible threat, Scarlet flicked a speck of invisible dust off the sleeve of her silk blouse. "Do you want to be back in the packs' good graces or don't you? This is your path home."

And I did want that, darn Scarlet anyway. I wanted to be able to see my niece in the flesh, rather than through a phone screen. I wanted to be able to smell her and hold her and have her understand I was present in a way she couldn't via video chat.

I wanted all that...and at the same time I wanted to make sure my sister's family remained safe. That my mistakes in the past didn't color Chipmunk's future. That angry werewolves didn't invade the Fairwood territory to take out what many considered to be a threat.

Kitsunes. Our reputation for danger had doubled after I drank the blood of three alphas and forced them to do my bidding. *Oops.*

I stood by my decisions last fall, especially the one where I'd broken off official ties with my sister so my actions wouldn't blow back on her. It was why I hadn't been present for the birth of her daughter. It was why I was trying to make a place for myself in Gate City, even though half the werewolves there didn't trust me and their alpha now likely considered me a loose cannon with a lit fuse.

Despite the awkwardness of last night, the thought of Thom settled me. What would he say in the face of Scarlet's insidious offer?

Words that tasted like Thom rolled off my tongue easily. "I'd need assurances this time. That I'm acting in an official Lawkeeper capacity. That what I do is entirely aboveboard."

Because that was the clincher. Scarlet had tricked me twice already. A third attempt at trickery was—as Charlie would have said—a statistical likelihood. I'd be an idiot to ignore that fact.

Sure enough, my ex-boss's lips pursed. "Well, that's the trouble. It won't be aboveboard. You'll be hunting on the land of one of the alphas whose blood you drank and who has no wish to see you living."

Her words wound around me like slithering snakes as she continued. "But if you catch the fox who's wreaking havoc, I give you my word I will do everything in my power to polish your reputation so you can safely go home to your sister."

Her words reeked of truth.

Chapter 4

I was going to do it, or at least I was going to stick my nose into the problem and hope to come out better than I'd started. I knew that even as I snapped back at Scarlet. "I'm surprised you don't think Mai and I are responsible for whatever's happened." We were, after all, the only known kitsunes in the United States who weren't currently stuck in the form of a fox.

And even though my tone had been as sharp-edged as the blade I still pressed into her side, Scarlet's scent sweetened. She knew she had me. "Well, I would have made that assumption if the fox had been female."

Curiosity tugged words from my lips before I could edit them. "That makes no sense. Kitsunes are always female."

I didn't bother to expand on the information, to tell Scarlet what became of the sons and cousins of fox shifters. Traditionally, male relatives were turned over to a different kitsune mistress to form her honor guard, boosting her magic with their mindless devotion. So, yes, in their own way, males were powerful. But they didn't shift into fox form.

Of course, mentioning that semi-parasitic relationship to Scarlet was bound to turn me into even more of a dangerous outsider. I winced and Scarlet noticed because her eyes glinted.

She stuck to the point, however, when she answered. "That was my understanding also. But this fox? He was male."

Male and, as I learned when Scarlet added more details, performing some sort of ritual in the Reed pack's territory. Once a month, on the night of the full moon.

My breath must have caught at that point because Scarlet's eyes narrowed again. "You know something about this already."

"No." I didn't *know* anything. But I was drawing conclusions about the strange obsession that had come over me at the exact same time this male fox trespassed. And, perhaps, about Kaito, woken from his coma then disappearing off the radar a short time before the first tug at my libido that just happened to coincide with the November full moon.

If the fox in question was Kaito…. Well, any information Scarlet had would help me figure out how to approach the problem.

"You say he's male," I pressed, "so you've seen this fox. Why didn't you deal with him already?"

For the first time, Scarlet showed signs of agitation. Her foot tapped. Her muscles stiffened. She wasn't lying, just unhappy with what she was about to say.

"We didn't see him," she admitted after a pause. "We smelled him. The Reed alpha found his trail after the first incursion, patrolled and prepared then somehow ended up running in circles during the second full moon."

"So they called in the Lawkeepers," I guessed.

Scarlet nodded, a sharp jerk of her chin. "Last night, I was ready for anything. I had two wolves with me as backup. And all three of us ended up falling asleep in the forest, waking to the scent of an absent fox."

Inhaling deeply, I let my knife seep back into my fingers. The danger from Scarlet was no less, but it wasn't imminent. Instead, peril hung on the fine line I intended to walk.

Because I wasn't about to turn Charlie against me. My human friend loved her brother-in-law and that brother-in-law loved Kaito.

But if Kaito was manipulating my emotions, I needed to stop him. To help him find another way to achieve whatever desperate end he was working toward.

Teaming up with Scarlet, however temporarily, might achieve that effect.

A shout from behind us interrupted my thought processes. "Hey!" My boss for the day, a plump woman with a drill sergeant's voice, had burst out of her restaurant's door and stood with her hands on her hips, glaring. "More tossing, less gabbing!"

And it turned out I didn't need to make my case because Scarlet's smile was almost feline. "You have twenty-eight days to find this fox," she told me. "He needs to be caught before the next full moon. Miss this window and my offer is void."

I could have gone hunting alone in an enemy werewolf's territory, or I could have left my shift early and headed to Gate City to ask Thom for help in person. Instead, I took the middle road and texted him my plans.

Thom's reply was quick and helpful. He wasn't keen on the idea, but if I was going he was going. He was willing to strategize and even offered a GPS address at the edge of his territory, one that appeared to represent a place where we could park cars on Gate City turf and keep our trespassing to the bare minimum.

What he didn't mention was anything more about yesterday. Nor did he clue me in that he planned to invite the entire pack.

Which is why I slammed on my brakes as I drove down the isolated forest-service road expecting Thom's truck to be the only one in the pull-off and found a dozen vehicles crammed along the verge instead. Men of all ages were stripping, breath pluming in front of headlights but shivers irrelevant since fur was quickly forthcoming. Half were four-footed already, chasing each other through the trees in werewolf joy at running wild. The rest were well on their way to lupine form.

Except me, Thom, and the shifter who'd apparently left his only family member behind in Gate City.

"What part of all hands on deck sounded optional to you?" Thom demanded, his voice both firm and commanding. Raised by a human father, Thom had been a reluctant alpha. Now, though, his newfound combination of power and control drew me in closer. It wasn't the moon this time that made my eyes soak up his form as if he was water in the desert. It wasn't the moon, so I managed to keep my thoughts to myself.

Still I advanced. And as I did, I noted the moment my scent invaded Thom's nostrils. Saw his eyes flick toward me then away again.

He didn't spare me any words however. Not even a carefully weighted admonition like the one he'd lowered on his underling. I flinched. Clearly, even though he said nothing had happened, Thom wasn't over last night.

The urge to clear the air with words was nearly overwhelming, but this was very much not the time or place. Especially since the shifter Thom had addressed was muttering a half-hearted explanation. "Kid wasn't feeling good."

With an effort, I transferred my gaze from Thom to Hank, taking in as much of the latter as I could with his ever-present cowboy hat blocking moonlight from his features. Even without a view of the shifter's face, I could sense his recalcitrance. Saw it in the way his square chin turned away from his alpha. Smelled it in the acrid scent that lingered in the air.

That resistance to Thom's orders was odd coming from a shifter who acted as a dependable protector to his decade-younger brother. By lone wolf standards and despite being only in his early twenties, Hank was a solid family man.

"I understand that you want to protect him," Thom answered, his thoughts likely following a similar path to mine. "But your brother is old enough to shift and he's part of this pack. I want him here."

The proper response would have been an apology or at least an explanation. Instead, Hank shrugged. "Too late now. Kid's in bed."

He punctuated his statement by spitting on the ground in a mild act of insolence. The stream of fluid, I noted, was aimed well clear of his alpha.

Unfortunately, Hank hadn't counted on my proximity. Perhaps hadn't smelled me the way Thom had.

Whatever the reason, liquid splattered against the boots I'd drawn back on after shedding my pizza costume. Thom's scent turned dark and dangerous as his fists clenched.

Chapter 5

U p until the spit hit my boots, it had appeared that all other werewolves were busy kicking up their heels and reveling in their fur forms. But every action in the pack revolved around Thom. Even the most hardcore frolickers kept one eye tuned to their alpha as they played.

No wonder silence and stillness settled on the gathering like dust after an explosion. The only sound came from a single werewolf caught midshift who seemed to be afraid to move backward to humanity or forward to fur form. The stuck shifter's pain nipped at my nostrils while his lupine hind legs scratched uncontrollably against the earth.

Despite being able to smell the issue as well as I could, Thom did nothing. Well, nothing other than loom and glower like the alpha he'd become over the last three months.

No wonder Hank's cowboy hat bowed down in apology. "Forgive me, Chief Faris."

Thom didn't absolve him, but he didn't attack either. Instead, he made a sound in the back of his throat that could have been acceptance if that's what you were listening for, then he turned away to strip alongside the rest of his pack.

And I stripped too. Stripped and shifted, not to wolf but to fox form.

Fox with a magical backpack created out of my star ball. Because I wasn't about to trespass without tools.

In this case, I chose to bring along my cell phone plus a vial of stolen werewolf blood that would hopefully keep the Reed alpha in line if we came face to face with him. I'd used the blood once before, last fall, to force invaders out of Thom's territory. If I had to, I'd drink another sip and force Chief Reed to let our pack go today.

Even though my entire purpose in materializing the backpack was to protect us, Thom's wolves still shied away from the luminous evidence of my difference. Teeth bared, they put space between themselves and the glowing star-ball magic. Their larger size was daunting in moonlight.

But there was no time to be daunted. Not when Thom was drawing us all into the darkness of tree cover. The pack avoided me at first, then accepted matters and enfolded me. Behind us, one by one, shifters left in charge of idling vehicles winked their headlights out.

I once read that wild wolf territories contain unused spaces running the length of boundaries, the no man's land meant to prevent bloody battles. But werewolves are half-human with the two-legger urge to mark the exact edges of their property. No wonder I smelled piss on both sides as we leapt one by one over the line that separated Thom's land from the domain of the Reed pack.

Now we were trespassing, silent save for frost crunching beneath our paws as we pressed deeper into Reed territory. In our planning texts, the ones where Thom had neglected to mention he was bringing along the entire pack plus a bad attitude, I'd suggested that he howl and draw the patrols away so I could sleuth solo. But he'd rejected that plan, wanting any discovery of our presence to appear organic. Now, we slowed our footfalls and spread out into a looser wedge, the better to be stumbled across.

Then I smelled it. The first hint of fox scent suggesting Scarlet hadn't been playing with me. Scent not just vulpine but also undeniably *male*.

And now that I'd had time to digest Scarlet's bombshell, maybe the presumed impossibility made sense after all. Yes, it was true that, unlike werewolves, kitsunes were always female while male relatives donated their latent magic to a mistress. They had no ability to form a star ball or to shift, but wouldn't those males still smell a little foxy? Especially if they were performing a magical ritual, one that might or might not have forced me to make a fool of myself last night.

Whatever the reason, I smelled a male fox now. I couldn't tell if this was Kaito, but I intended to follow that scent trail and discover what lay at the end of it regardless. Veering away from Thom and his pack mates, I leapt onto a fallen tree and used it to bypass a tangle of thorns and brush.

The fox scent beneath my feet was fresher than the wolf urine at the boundary, suggesting whoever I smelled was actively walking through the forest right at this moment. Which was a good thing. Maybe we could nab Kaito and be back at the cars before our presence was noted. Perhaps it would be simple to talk him out of whatever he was doing, simple enough that I could set Scarlet's mind at ease without handing Kaito over to the Lawkeepers.

A howl rose from behind me. Another, then a sharp bark of warning.

No such luck.

Chapter 6

When Thom and I had planned out this maneuver, I'd asked if he was willing to draw the patrols away so I could nose out evidence. His answer, I now realized, had been evasive. *"I'll make sure you have time and space to work."* He hadn't actually said he'd lead the wild-goose chase himself.

So I shouldn't have been surprised when the wedge of wolves peeled away from me...and their alpha didn't peel along with them. Instead, Thom's musk crept up behind me. His bulk blocked the light from the just-past-full moon.

A shiver of something—fear? Desire?—skittered down my spine, but I shook it off and kept running. Even with the entire Gate City pack on the job of distracting Reed sentries, I couldn't extend this trespassing session indefinitely. Not if we wanted our neighbors to think the chase had merely been a testosterone-laden lark.

So I ran, nostrils flaring, as the scent of fox grew stronger. And there, just where Scarlet had said it would be, was the beaten down circle of leaf litter. The puddle of candle wax. The tingle of residual magic seeping up through my paw pads when I slowed to examine the space.

Scarlet's scent was nearly as strong here as the fox's, hers and two of my ex-coworkers. All three had sniffed around this little clearing just like I was doing, but they hadn't followed the fox's path where he left the area. Why the heck not?

Probably because wolf noses weren't as adept at catching hints of fox on two-leggers as I was. I traced the path Kaito—if it had been Kaito—followed away from the clearing. Up, up, up, until the hill crested in front of a jumble of house-sized boulders. The moon hid behind the geological feature, shadowed rocks looming far over my head.

The space between boulders wasn't impenetrable, however. Cracks large enough to walk through turned the space into a maze which night made into a blind labyrinth. No wonder Thom tried to push in front of me before I could enter that pitch darkness in search of an unidentified male fox.

Well, Thom started to push in front of me, then his shoulders stiffened. His head turned to peer back in the direction from which we'd come.

I froze, expecting to hear or smell some sign of danger. But there was nothing close. Even the scent of fox was fading, as if the magic clinging to Kaito's hide had seeped away the further he distanced himself from the scene of the ritual. He might have merely used this rock maze to confuse followers, although my gut said otherwise. My gut said he was inside somewhere, holed up deep within the jumble of boulders waiting for wolves to abandon the hunt.

We needed to enter and find him, but as I tried to slip around Thom he side-stepped to stop me. I hopped right; he countered. I growled; he waited impassively for me to give up.

So I shifted up to two legs, and as soon as I did, my skin prickled. Kaito was close, I somehow knew that. Not fleeing but lingering, intrigued by our presence. Was he close enough to hear me? Interested enough to come out of hiding if I called him by name?

"Kaito." As I spoke, Thom whined so softly I almost missed the sound over my own breathing. He thought this was a mistake. But what had Kaito done to make us distrust him? If anything, he should be the one distrusting us.

"You don't know me," I continued, "but my friend Charlie is your brother's sister-in-law. This isn't a safe place for you. The wolf who owns this territory hates kitsunes. Come out now and I'll bring you to Ito. We'll deal with whatever has been going on together. We'll get you out of this mess."

A rustle of feet on leaves, soft enough that it might have been made by a mouse hiding from owls. But it hadn't been. That sound was Kaito, inching closer.

Then a different noise erupted from the direction of the clearing. Snarls. Yelps. The wild-goose chase was turning into battle. Our time was nearly up.

A flare of heat on my skin warned one second before Thom rose two-legged beside me. I caught my breath, shocked for one split second by his naked beauty, saturated by moonlight. His words—deep and rough—caressed me with their cadence. It took longer than it should have to realize what words the sounds represented.

"We have to go," he'd murmured. "The pack is outnumbered. I gave them the order to retreat."

Within the rock maze, the rustle of feet on leaves skittered away far faster than it had advanced. Kaito must have thought I was alone to be so spooked by Thom's words now.

I was spooked also, but for a different reason. I hadn't realized Thom's alpha abilities had advanced to the stage where he could communicate with his underlings mind-to-mind.

Cold bit at the tips of my ears and the end of my nose. Unlike the werewolves who were now drawing the Reed sentries back toward where we'd parked, I hadn't heard Thom speaking. Clear evidence I wasn't part of his pack.

And wasn't that a good thing? Didn't I need to leave that void in my belly open so my sister could refill it?

For one split second, twenty-year-old memories consumed me. My entirely human and very American father, setting me on his knee after I'd melted down about the fact that Mai's extra decade made her perpetually bigger and faster. *"I hate her!"* I'd whined.

"No you don't," he answered. *"You're disappointed that Mai is older, but she'll always be older the same way you'll always be sisters. Don't let one thing tarnish the other."*

And I hadn't. Not because I'd been smart enough to accept my father's wisdom, but because Mai had put my good above all else. Her only slip in the guardian department—a single week when she couldn't pay the rent—was presented to me as a fur-form camping trip in which we slept beneath the willow where we'd scattered our father's ashes. Mai, I later realized, had been terrified that we'd lapse into permanent homelessness. But she'd kept my spirits up so skillfully that I still smiled every time I thought of waking up with those slender yellow leaves dotting my fur.

Which was why everything I did now had to be aimed at reuniting with my sister. Still, knowing Thom could speak to his pack but not to me settled like frost in my belly. That plus the missing medallion raised a storm of contradictory feelings that I shook off like so many fallen willow leaves.

Pack bonds and sister bonds were currently irrelevant. Dismissing the past and future in favor of the present, I sprinted into the gap in the rocks after Kaito.

Or, rather, I tried to.

Because Thom was in my way again, our skin almost but not quite touching. "Let him go." His eyes flared dark and wild. "There are a hundred ways out of these boulders. We'll never catch him. Not before the Reed pack shows up."

If Kaito was close enough to hear, Thom's choice of words would have the exact opposite effect of what I'd been going for. We should have discussed my plan in more depth before starting our hunt, I realized. But I'd intended to do this part alone.

"We're not trying to *catch* him," I corrected.

"Doesn't matter. Shift."

Then Thom was lupine beside me. His shoulder pressed against my hip, guiding me away from the rock maze. I stumbled but he shoved harder, forcing me further away from my chosen path.

Behind us, snarls erupted into howls. Then, worse, the wind picked up, carrying with it the scent of wolves far closer than those battling in the distance.

Of course. The Reed clan had split in two, some chasing Thom's pack mates and some following our scent trail. The latter were too close for comfort, especially if I didn't want them finding Kaito.

This time when Thom shoulder-bumped me, I accepted the inevitable. I suffused my skin with star-ball magic and was trotting the moment my forefeet struck the ground.

Chapter 7

Making it back to the vehicles was impossible. There was no point trying when a wall of wolves hunted between us and the rest of Thom's pack.

So I wasn't surprised when Thom turned west instead of south. We'd reach Gate City territory just as quickly heading in that direction. And, if we were lucky, Thom's ability to communicate via the pack bond meant someone would bring a car around to pick us up the moment we crossed the line.

The plan sounded good in theory...until my shorter vulpine legs let our pursuers gain on us. Their panting breaths grew closer, proving that evasive actions weren't working. We'd have to turn and fight.

Or perhaps I'd have to use the vial I'd brought along for emergencies. The stolen blood should work...assuming the Reed alpha was close enough to hear my command, assuming he'd chosen to follow us instead of the larger group of Gate City wolves.

Assuming slapping the Reed alpha in the face with my kitsune abilities a second time wasn't worse than drawing a sword and hacking at his underlings. Assuming three-month-old werewolf blood even had power still embedded inside.

It would be better not to test any of those assumptions. So I pushed the barest hint of extra length into my stride, my lungs screaming at the effort. I couldn't keep this up much longer and even at my fastest I wasn't outpacing any wolves....

But we did have one other tool at our disposal. Between us, Thom and I had overcome the impossible more than once. We might again if we were able to communicate without stopping and shifting.

But I was a fox and he was a wolf and I wasn't a true member of his pack.

Or was I? As if created by my wish, words materialized in my head, words in Thom's deep baritone. *"...Through the hole and down...expecting us at the farmh ouse...pickup in the morning."*

I should have been thrilled; I knew that. But my paws faltered on the frosty leaves while something deep inside me twisted. A shifter can only bond with one pack at a time. If I was linked to Thom, then the not-quite-material wound where I'd torn out my sister's tether three months earlier must be fully cauterized at last.

My thoughts slammed into a stone wall just as I literally ran into one. Thom had slowed to guard my back, leaving me in the lead...and I'd clearly taken a wrong turn somewhere. Because the path we'd been following had turned into a trap, ending at a sheer cliff face even I couldn't climb with clever vulpine feet.

This shortcut to Gate City territory wasn't a shortcut after all. We'd been herded into a blind canyon.

No, that wasn't true. The moon came out from behind a cloud just in time to shine on the forest floor around us. The forest floor here...and on the other side of the cliff, visible through a fox-sized hole.

"Kira, go!"

Thom's voice in my head was a roar that hit me like a blow then quenched like a flaming brand falling into ice water. But I heard him and I understood.

He wanted me to slide through this gap only I could fit through, giving his longer legs leave to escape the Reeds via speed alone. The plan made sense and I had confidence he could outrun our pursuers. As long as my hesitation didn't slow him down.

So I obeyed. I shot through the gap in the rock and out the other side, pausing only long enough to make sure Thom hadn't been trapped behind me. But no sounds of battle followed. Just snuffling at the hole. A whine. A bark.

Then the Reed wolves were gone and I was alone in Gate City territory. Alone...and not lost either. This patch of forest was faintly familiar, especially when I turned to face south.

The pack had run here two months ago, I realized, introducing me to this tricky little pocket accessible by road only on the Reed side but on foot from our usual stomping grounds. On our side of the border was a human-inhabited farmhouse, one I suspected Thom wanted me to head for. Was it a B&B maybe? I'd gotten an image along with Thom's splutter of truncated words, an image of a soft bed in a well-lit room rather than a shivering night in a scratchy hayloft. Of pack mates driving down that long, twisty road through Reed territory in daylight, safe due to their visibility the way they wouldn't be at night.

Still, my fur stood on end, the sensation of danger hugging me like a too-tight sweater. I was nearly out of the woods, both literally and metaphorically, but was Thom? Had he outrun the Reed wolves as easily as he'd hoped?

I could wait and worry...or I could contact him down the pack bond. Check in. Ask if he needed any help.

Despite my qualms about replacing the connection to my sister, I whispered a question into the darkness of my own body. Waited as the moon beat down like frozen sunlight. My paws shuffled uncomfortably atop harsh ice crystals but no answer came back.

So plan A it was. Down the hill, through a grove of pines so dense their needles blocked the moonlight and made ambush a likelihood. I slunk from tree trunk to tree trunk, keeping my footfalls silent while stopping to sniff every third step for signs of danger.

Fox instinct warned me one second before something struck the back of my head. I was turning into the blow, teeth bared, when I realized my enemy wasn't an enemy. It was a fallen branch, clinging to a patch of greenbriar then knocked loose by my passage. I was biting at a stick like a not-very-bright dog.

And still I jumped at nothing three more times before I reached my destination. Finally, though, I saw it. The welcome vision of humanity, a two-story farmhouse with windows gleaming yellow. Safety where I could let down my guard...just as soon as I passed through the intervening spotlight-like glow illuminating the cover-free lawn.

Shifting to two legs here felt like dropping my pants in public. The air was even colder than it had been earlier, frosty breezes gliding across skin damp from exertion. My toes slammed into stones I hadn't noticed in fox form. But I ignored the pain because instinct warned there was something behind me. I spun....

In the pine forest, my senses had played tricks on me. But not here. Here, I'd been right. A wolf stood just beyond the play of porch lights, silhouetted against the forest. He took a step forward and I breathed again.

It wasn't just any wolf. It was Thom.

Chapter 8

My star ball stretched large enough to encompass me in a paper-thin trench coat, the magical fabric shielding me from view but doing little to block the icy wind that gusted down the hillside. Without similar magic, Thom stayed lupine as we paced together onto the well-lit porch.

Turning once, I peered back in the direction of the rock maze. If wolves were watching, I couldn't see them. Couldn't smell them, either, over the scents of humanity oozing out cracks in the clapboard farmhouse. Whoever ran this place liked scented candles and air fresheners, fabric softener and the type of cleaning product that left a haze of perfume behind.

Then a bird-thin woman redolent with old-lady perfume was opening the door and bustling us into her aromatic haven. "Shall I take your coat?"

I couldn't help it. My hand clutched closed a neckline that wasn't even really an opening. "No, I'll keep it."

"You can leave your shoes here." While her voice was kind, the words were clearly an order. Especially when she added: "The rugs are antiques."

Together, we peered down at my bare toes. This wasn't going to work. Even if Thom's pack had made a reservation at this B&B, I didn't have luggage. Didn't have a car. Didn't have *shoes.*

Well, I *could* have shoes. If the woman in front of me was as farsighted as her age suggested, maybe she wouldn't notice a little magical flimflammery.

I clenched my jaw and it was almost as if Thom read my intentions. He wagged his tail and pressed closer to the woman as if begging for a biscuit. Taking advantage of the distraction, I drew a shred of trench coat away from my back, sliding it down my calves until the energy could materialize into flesh-colored slippers

Kicking the footwear off then snagging the fragment of magic in one hand, I smiled at our hostess just as Thom circled back to join me. "I'm really tired. Maybe you could point me to my room?"

"Yes, of course." She pulled out a sheaf of papers, which she handed over in lieu of a key. It was rules, I saw as I skimmed over the words. Everything in this house, apparently, was an antique. Luggage was to be carried, not rolled. Food wasn't allowed outside the dining room.

Plus—"I'll need your cell phone." Her wrinkled hand shook slightly as it hovered between us. This old woman was crazy. What kind of guest turned over her cell phone at check-in?

Then words jumped out at me from the top of the first page. Domestic Abuse Shelter. This wasn't a B&B at all.

And my cell phone was the least of the items I'd hoped to bring up to my room as I huddled away from Reed wolves until morning. "My dog..." I started.

"Will be well taken care of. We have a kennel out back."

For the first time since stepping inside, Thom's body language stiffened. The woman appeared not to notice as she pressed her point, cutting me off from all potential avenues for help. "Please power your phone off for the safety of all our residents and place it in here."

She punctuated her words by holding out a wooden box and this time Thom growled. He didn't like the idea any more than I did.

But we had no choice, other than making a mad dash over a mountain with Reed wolves behind us. My short fox legs were meant for climbing and hiding not racing. It wasn't really a choice.

So my hand settled on Thom's ruff, soothing him just as he'd soothed me during last night's moon craze. To our hostess, I asked: "You lock the doors at night?"

Within her wrinkles, kind eyes twinkled. "Of course. You're safe here. I promise."

I gave the old woman my cell phone and watched as she snapped a collar around Thom's furry neck.

My room was on the second story with two windows overlooking the porch roof and its view of pitch blackness. Stepping around the old-fashioned—or was that antique?—steam radiator, I opened one pane and leaned out into the cold.

Howls filtered down from the rock maze. Howls of hunters who'd found a different sort of prey after Thom and I eluded them? I shivered, hoping Kaito was as elusive as his fox blood suggested.

Then Thom was there, biceps bulging as he pulled himself up onto the porch roof. I stepped back so he could swing his legs through the window and unfold himself inside.

By the faint illumination of the moon, his nakedness had been intriguing. Here, under electric lights that were brighter than average, I had a hard time thinking of anything else.

Well, anything other than current eye candy...and my off-the-wall reaction yesterday. "About last night," I started.

I intended to continue that thought. To ask what had happened when my mind and body weren't obeying rational mandates. To ask if I'd broken the agreement Thom and I had sealed with a handshake three months before.

Then I wimped out. Words refused to come.

Well, not those words. Instead, I retreated into the familiar safety of skin-level perkiness. Turning up the wattage of my smile, I shrugged off the past with an eye bat and a chuckle. "My bad."

Thom's brows thudded down, his scent turning sharp. He thought I was dismissing the fact that I'd broken my word. Was dismissing the moon craze as irrelevant.

Despite the smallness of the room, distance yawned between us. I'd created that distance, and I didn't know how to walk it back again.

Instead, I turned toward the bed, hoping for a mint on the pillow to settle whatever was going on in my stomach. No such luck. Of course—our hostess forbade food around her beloved antiques.

In the silence that followed, I half expected Thom to climb back out the window and leave me there. Instead, after a long moment, he spoke.

"Hey." His tone was softer than I'd expected. He waited until I turned to face him, then cocked his head in question. "You don't remember?"

The kindness in his voice said he'd seen through my charade, that he accepted both my strength and my weakness. Being understood so thoroughly clenched my throat just a little. Clenched it...but also gave me the courage to swallow and let a few honest words creep out.

"After turning fox? Not much."

Nothing really. Only the sensation of Thom's broad hand on my nape, the warmth of being pressed against his chest and relaxing into known safety.

Waking up naked without his mother's medallion....

"I took you home." Thom's rumble felt like he was handing over a coat off his own back to warm and protect me. "Charlie wasn't there and you'd gone furry, so I figured it might help to"—he cleared his throat—"give you a bath."

"A bath?"

He shrugged. "A random idea that popped into my head. It worked though. There was something oily in your fur. It washed out and you fell asleep." His eyes flicked sideways as he added: "I didn't feel comfortable going into your bedroom without permission, so I left you there on the couch."

Facts realigned, mortification sloughing off me. Yes, Thom had been involved in my couch nakedness, but I'd been furry the entire time he was present. I must have shifted in my sleep the way I sometimes had a tendency to do. There'd been no funny business lost in that memory void.

Which should have been obvious from the beginning. Thom was an eternal gentleman, incapable of preying on those unable to consent. And yet...perhaps I didn't want him to remain a gentleman. Not tonight.

Because he was naked and I was the next thing to it and we were stuck until morning in this one small room.

Only, his gaze was resolutely focused out the window, even though I knew for a fact he couldn't see anything in the darkness. I took a step sideways until I was back in Thom's sight line, my skin tingling as his eyes made contact with the exposed curve of my neck.

"The moon isn't full today," I murmured. "My brain is as clear as it's ever been and you don't have any pack business to be concerned with." One step closer, until his breath warmed the air between us. "Perhaps we should get to know each other better."

My trench coat seeped back into my body, leaving me shivering from more than cold.

Chapter 9

"Kira." Thom kept his eyes averted as he strode around me. Picking the quilt up off the bed—both antiques—he twirled the fabric around my shoulders. "I thought we had an agreement."

Rejection brought a fox snap to my retort. "An agreement to get to know each other better before indulging in the physical. But it's been *three months*, Thom. I know you. You know me. Even the Amish allow bundling before marriage."

"If you want to talk Amish, the more relevant tradition is the rumspringa," Thom countered, settling himself onto the hard metal ridges of the radiator rather than sinking into the bed that took up most of the room. "The way I see it, you're enjoying your running-around time. After you explore, you'll go home to your family and nothing you did here will leave a mark on anyone other than me."

"That's a self-fulfilling prophecy if you won't touch me." My feet refused to stay still, so I paced as I argued my point. "I'm not interested in a purely platonic relationship."

Rather than answering immediately, Thom's gaze returned to the darkness outside the window. When he spoke, his words weren't harsh the way mine had been. Instead, they were even and just the faintest bit bittersweet. "You haven't put down a single root all winter, Kira. You haven't signed so much as a month-to-month lease."

That wasn't fair. "Charlie's my friend. She and I enjoy spending time together. Why shouldn't I live in her spare room as long as I pay rent?"

"Charlie is a reminder of your shared childhood. Of the home that was once yours and will be yours again." When I started to growl out a negation, Thom changed gears. "What about jobs?"

"I have a job." My words came out more defensive than I meant them to.

"You choose a new employer every day. I hear Eli's father offered you a permanent spot in his lab but you refused it."

Thom was referring to the young human, master at darts and scientific facts but emotionally more akin to a child, who'd become an honorary member of the pack last fall. I liked Eli a lot and his father seemed nice enough, but the latter was employed by the government base that was nosing into local oddities. No wonder I stared at Thom. "You really think I'd pass a government background check? You want shifters on the Base's radar now?"

Thom breathed out through his nose just a little harder than was truly necessary. But he did look at me finally, those ice-pick eyes boring through my skin and seemingly under it. "Okay, how about this: Now that Dixie Lee is turning the Full Moon Saloon into a meal-serving establishment, I could use another hand at the bar. No background check required. Flexible hours. Good wages and full benefits. What do you say?"

I couldn't say anything. I stood there, frozen, one hand settling on the spot where Mai's tether used to flow into me, the other feeling for a missing medallion around my neck.

"You can't agree, can you?" Thom's voice was both sad and kind at the same time. "Just like you couldn't accept our pack bond tonight. I yelled so loud to get your attention that some of the guys' ears bled."

I winced. That flicker of sound, almost inaudible, had been Thom yelling? I'd never heard him raise his voice.

My stomach took advantage of our thorny silence to complain loudly about interpersonal tension, about lost pack bonds, about the distant memory of pizza for dinner. And Thom opened a clenched fist to reveal a granola bar he must have filched from the animal-housing area. "Here."

The plastic crinkled between my fingers as I caught it. "We can share this...."

Thom shook his head. "Eat in the bathroom so you don't leave crumbs on the antiques. And when you're ready to commit to us, to Gate City, to *something*, let me know and I'll return your necklace."

The last words were still hanging in the air as he turned lupine. No wonder I fled into the tiny tiled haven away from Thom's presence, chewing through sweetened oats that tasted like cardboard in my mouth.

Dixie Lee, her daughter Ava, and Thom's second Bertrand showed up to collect us the next morning, Dixie Lee with clothes for me while Bertrand tagged along in wolf form to keep the all-female residents of the shelter at ease. Thom hadn't shifted back to two legs in my presence, although he did slip out the window and return to the kennel at first light. Later, he rode in the back seat with Bertrand and Ava, both wolves sticking their heads out their respective windows to warn away Reed shifters while Ava, in the middle, laughed at them both.

"You guys just like feeling the wind against your cheeks, don't you?" Her ever-present library book lay abandoned on her lap.

"Reminds me of the man who bought a self-driving car so his dog could ride around with the window down," I agreed. And, to my delight, the usually shy thirteen-year-old pushed her torso up between the two front seats to engage me further.

"Is that true?" she asked. Then, changing gears without waiting for an answer: "And can you tell me more about kitsunes? I want to know if...."

"Ava, seat belt." Dixie Lee put her foot down on both the gas pedal and on our conversation. Then, after one seething glance in my direction, she turned up the radio to squelch any further contact between me and her daughter.

Which wasn't exactly surprising. Dixie Lee and I had suffered from a subpar first impression and I'd yet to find a way back into her good graces. I'm sure me trying to claw her eyes out in fox form two nights ago hadn't helped matters either. Still, it was a shame to do nothing as Ava disappeared back into her library book. A shame to ride in silence all the way to Gate City.

Dixie Lee's words, when she finally addressed me, were sandpapery. "Where to?"

"Home, if it's not out of your way."

My unwilling driver shrugged. "I'm on the clock."

Then we were pulling up in front of Charlie's house, which should have decreased the awkwardness quotient. Except...there was another vehicle unloading in my friend's driveway. A minivan with two dark-haired girls peering out the back windows, their mom and dad just emerging from the front seats.

I'd forgotten Charlie's sister was coming to visit today. Her sister, her nieces.. .and her brother-in-law.

Ito and I hadn't seen each other since I was a child, so he really shouldn't have recognized me. But his dark-eyed gaze locked with mine over the top of the minivan. Something electric and painful shook me while Ito's slender body jolted as if he'd suffered a similar shock.

Then mundanity intruded. "A little help here would be appreciated," his wife complained as she wrestled one of the little girls out of a car seat. Although biologically identical to Charlie, the woman Jessie had grown into couldn't have been more different than her sister. Jessie gave off a motherly vibe without being matronly. Her clothes, I was pretty sure, cost more than my car.

And Ito was the perfect match for her. I hadn't noticed until he looked away from me how well his turtleneck showed off his lithe muscles. Hadn't noticed that his hair was not only cut in a timely manner but also styled and gelled.

Plus, he maintained his cool in the face of his wife's annoyance. "My apologies," he murmured, unlatching the intricate straps surrounding the closest daughter without applying any snark in the face of Jessie's demand.

But the instant his task was completed, Ito's eyes returned to mine. As the girl he'd released scampered across the vehicle toward her mother, the intensity of his gaze turned up from simmer to flame.

Behind me, a lupine growl emerged, dark and dangerous. Thom had noticed Ito's interest and he wasn't pleased by it.

I wasn't particularly thrilled either, but an angry alpha wolf wasn't going to help this already awkward reunion. Instead of waiting for Thom to finish lining himself so he could fit his bulk out the open window, I disembarked quickly, slamming the door behind me. "Thanks for the lift. You can go now."

I thought for a moment that Dixie Lee wouldn't take the hint. But that was the good thing about her antipathy—she had no problem leaving me to fend for myself in the face of trouble. The car's back windows rolled up as she shot back out into traffic. Now two gazes pricked the back of my neck—Thom's intense focus receding while Ito's fixation remained far too close for comfort.

Ignoring both of them, I turned toward the woman I'd last seen avoiding my gaze at her college graduation.

"Jessie. Long time, no see."

Chapter 10

"Kira, sweetie! Charlie told me you guys were housemates." Back when we'd been friends, Jessie was the softer of the two twins, the one Charlie and I had spent years protecting. But she'd grown into herself in the time since I'd last seen her. With a toddler on one hip and a youngster clinging to the opposite belt loop, Jessie radiated a calm she'd never possessed previously. A calm...and a wry humor I didn't expect. "I'd hug you, but first I'd have to detach this limpet."

"No need for snail surgery," I assured her. I would have left it there, but she didn't let me.

"There *is* a need, though. Ito was an idiot to tell me to stay away from you back in college and I was an idiot to listen to him. I'm sorry. Neither of us will be so stupid again."

The older girl's eyes had gone wide at the use of what, I guessed, passed for strong language in their household. But Jessie's free hand rumpled the kid's hair and she relaxed just as Ito entered our conversation.

"I apologize also, Kira-san." Despite the honorific attached to my name, his gaze was no less electric than it had been previously. "Perhaps you could spare a moment of your time?" He paused, then added: "Alone."

"Ito?" This time, Jessie's voice quavered, and I finally saw the girl she used to be hovering beneath the woman she'd become. The girl who never kept a boyfriend long, in large part because she never trusted any of them to remain faithful.

Back then, Charlie and I had done everything we could to keep Jessie's insecurities from eroding her tranquility. After all, every shifter knows that you shield your pack mates' weaknesses. So I opened my mouth to reassure her...

...Then snapped it shut again. Because Ito was tied to my current investigation by more than DNA. Back when Kaito woke up from his coma and went missing, Ito had been the one who called me off the hunt via his sister-in-law. At the time, I'd assumed old feelings were rearing their ugly head, that Ito was slapping me down in the only way he knew how to slap me.

But now...the intensity of his gaze plus that old data point made me wonder whether Ito might know exactly where his brother was hiding. And, more importantly, what Kaito was trying to accomplish with his trespassing and candlelit ceremonies.

Which meant a moment alone with Ito was exactly what I needed. "We'll be back shortly," I promised Jessie. And I was glad when Charlie chose that moment to open the front door and wave her sister inside.

"The backyard will be more private," I said the moment the door closed behind Jessie and her daughters. The older girl had peered back at us the entire time she was walking away from her father, her eyes growing wider and wider and making me feel like the worst sort of homewrecker. A sensation that was exacerbated by the way Ito backpedaled the instant I headed in his general direction.

I'd merely been aiming for the gate, but apparently my proximity was distasteful. So I swung wide and was glad to see that Ito followed. Followed...and had a sword in his hand by the time I turned to face him in the seclusion of the backyard.

"I would be more comfortable sparring as we speak, Kira-san." He observed, dancing lightly around me.

I let him dance. I was here for conversation, not fighting. "What if I don't have a sword?"

"A kitsune always has a sword," the ex-honor-guard member countered. "Even when she doesn't."

Which was true. My star ball coalesced into a blade as Ito's sword thrust toward me. The clang of metal on metal stilled bird song but set a squirrel chittering in the tree above our heads.

Rather than discussing the pent-up aggression evident in Ito's attack, I tossed out a verbal parry. "You've been in touch with your brother."

Unlike Ito's attack, mine evaded his guard. Ito faltered, and if I'd been serious about this match I could have locked our blades and ripped his sword out of his hands. Instead, I tapped lightly, offering time for him to hunt down words.

Instead of words, Ito found his will to fight. One moment I was in control of our match, the next I wasn't. His blade flashed so quickly a human wouldn't have been able to follow the motion, would have been cut down where she stood.

I wasn't human however. My breath came faster, but my sword blocked blow after blow easily.

Blocked, then twisted beneath my opponent's guard just like my words had done. My sword tip pricked the skin of Ito's throat and we stood there panting, an electric charge racing up the length of my star-ball sword and into my fingers. They tingled as badly as when I'd put my hand on the fox skull beneath the Full Moon Saloon last October. It took an effort not to flinch.

"What are you doing to me?" I demanded.

In response, Ito laughed, a sound that had no humor in it. "What am *I* doing? You're the kitsune."

"You're going to have to use more words than that." Despite my admonition, when the silence lengthened I was the one who broke it. "Okay, let me tell you what I know. I know your brother is working some sort of magic every full moon and that it's affecting me. I know he's trespassing on werewolf territory and has Lawkeepers after him with blood in their eyes. I know I want to help Kaito find a safe haven, but I won't be able to if I can't talk to him. You know where he is."

For another moment, silence hovered around us. My fingers shook despite my effort to ignore the electric current streaming through them. Above us, a bird decided we were done with our battle and warbled out its own mood music.

And, finally, Ito shook his head minutely, the skin puckering beneath my blade as he did so. "I don't know where my brother is. But I can put the two of you in touch if you swear an oath first."

An oath? I shivered. In lieu of the typical talk about STDs and the dangers of drug use, Mai had sat me down when I turned thirteen and warned about the pitfalls of being a kitsune. She'd explained how separation from our star balls made us weak as kittens. How an oath could force us to change our behavior in ways we might not anticipate when we made what seemed to be a light-hearted promise.

I didn't like the idea of willingly indulging in that sort of binding, but Ito was the only lead I had pointing me toward his brother. Scarlet aside, I needed to stop the craziness that cascaded over me once a month if I didn't want to do more damage to Thom's and my tenuous connection.

Plus, I felt responsible for Kaito. Which, perhaps, was an example of yet another kitsune weakness—how deeply we reacted to being in anybody's debt.

Despite these points, I wasn't about to swear an oath without more information. I'd read fairy tales. I knew the pitfalls. "What sort of oath?" I demanded.

Ito's answer came out just as harsh. "My brother seeks a mistress. If you take him on, you'll be kind to him."

A mistress. A kitsune who built a harem around her, called it an honor guard, and turned sentient beings into lap dogs who had no will to even snap at the hand that stole their lives.

I recoiled. "I'm not a parasite, to suck power out of the unwilling." After all, that was part of why Mai had frozen our grandmother in fox form. To free the members of her honor guard, releasing them from a custom that seemed dangerously close to slavery.

Ito disagreed with my assessment. "But Kaito isn't unwilling, is he? Not if he's been calling you at each full moon."

Then light spun off his blade as he knocked my sword away so adeptly he didn't shed a single drop of blood in the process. Ito had been toying with me, I realized. Letting me think I had him pinned until he was ready to defend himself.

This time, our flurry of blows ended with Ito's sword at my throat. This time, the connection between us hit me differently.

A throbbing below my chin made it hard to swallow. Sun glaring off Ito's blade made me squint and tear up.

Then someone was behind me. Warmth against my back overcame the sun's watery radiation. A very familiar hand lashed out and grabbed Ito's sword arm.

"I wouldn't do that if I were you," growled Thom.

Chapter 11

"Dogs, they understand nothing."

Ito's comment was in Japanese, something I halfway understood due to two semesters in college spent reconnecting with my roots. Thom likely lacked the ability to translate word for word, but he didn't need to. The sardonic tilt of Ito's lips got his message across.

No wonder Thom's muscles flexed as his grip tightened. The sword inched away from my skin, one finger's breadth, two fingers' breadth. Ito's cheek twitched, our only warning before he released the hilt with a harsh oath.

We all leapt away from the sharpness spinning uncontrollably between us. And when we resettled, Ito had somehow ended up closer to me than he'd started. Ignoring Thom, his gaze latched back onto my face.

It was that same unpleasant stare he'd greeted me with across the minivan. Here, up close, I could smell the emotions that fueled it. Resentment and anger, just as I'd expected, but the most dominant scent was a deeply hungry greed.

The resulting reek wasn't even remotely pleasant, but our tussle had given me breathing room to make my decision. So I swore an oath...though not the exact one Ito had requested. "If you put me in touch with your brother, I swear to hold his best interests at the forefront of my decision-making."

I included no mention of becoming Kaito's mistress. That wasn't the type of kitsune I intended to become.

But the promise I made was apparently enough for Ito. He nodded, reaching in his pocket and drawing out a key chain. Somehow, his feet wriggled four inches closer to my feet while he worked a key off the loop.

"Here." Our hands didn't need to touch for Ito to relinquish the clue to his brother's location but they did anyway. Heat scalded my palm where his fingertips made contact. I had to fight the urge to stick the injured area into my mouth.

Instead, I turned the key over. *USPS* was engraved on one side along with a warning of dire consequences if it was duplicated. "A P.O. box?"

"It was the mistress's," Ito confirmed. "But Kaito and I were the only ones who checked it. I thought perhaps he might go there after he woke, so I left him a note, some money. The next time I opened the box, both were gone."

Up until this point, Thom had been silent. But now he pointed out the gaping hole in Ito's story. "I'm sure you provided your own contact information. And yet, you say you don't know where your brother is. What makes you think he'll share with Kira that he didn't share with you?"

"She's a kitsune," Ito rebutted, as if that explained everything. He hadn't bothered to look at Thom while speaking. Instead, he sidled closer to me until our toe tips touched, then he reminded me of my promise. "Your oath binds you, Kira-san. That means you won't stake out the post office. You won't install cameras or tracking devices to force Kaito's compliance. You will leave my brother a note just as I did and let him decide whether or not to come to you."

Ito barely had time to tell us a town and a box number before Charlie's back door slammed open. And since Ito's gaze held me captive, I heard, rather than saw, what happened next.

"Shiny!" his older daughter shrieked, her increasing volume suggesting she was making a beeline for the discarded weapon we'd all forgotten about. The weapon that could cut a little girl's hand open...or worse.

"Penny, no!" That was Jessie, had to be with the maternal sob underneath a whip-crack command. If I had to guess, her grip on the smaller child made her incapable of running after the one currently rushing into danger.

"No blades until you're at least double digits!" Charlie added, her voice muffled as if she was still in the house and too far away to provide physical backup.

With an effort, I twisted around to see Penny ignoring both mother and aunt, scampering toward us so quickly they were unlikely to catch up. Ito's sword gleamed in the brown grass at my feet, easy for me to scoop up. Or I could have grabbed the child. Penny was only six, after all, and unlikely to put up much of a fight.

But my feet were ice blocks. Ito's also, I gathered from the way his upper body strained away from mine while his legs refused to lose contact with my sneakers. We were locked in some sort of toe-touch dance that made us absolutely useless in the face of a kid about to do serious harm to herself.

Thom was the one who tackled the girl as if she was a football. Thom was the one who twirled her up onto his shoulders and whinnied like a horse. "Which way, my lady?"

She could have wriggled free. Children, I knew from babysitting Grub, were slippery even when dry.

But Penny grabbed Thom's ears and twisted the left one. "That way! Giddy-up!"

Obediently, Thom giddy-upped all the way around the backyard, neighing and snorting. The tantalizing sword was forgotten by Penny, but not by Thom. He veered toward Penny's mother and away from the blade. After reassuring Jessie that her child wasn't in danger, he obeyed ear tugs and cavorted off again in a funny sort of dance.

The scene was so sweetly adorable, it was no wonder the ice blocks around my feet melted. Ito snatched up his sword, sheathing it as I turned to face Jessie.

Now that she knew Penny was safe, my former friend appeared to have developed heartburn. Her features twisted the same way they had out front. Her gaze slid back and forth between me and Ito as she measured my proximity to her husband.

This time, though, I didn't need to leave her hanging. Not when I had visual proof of my lack of romantic designs on Ito. "Jessie," I said, "I'd like you to meet Thom. My significant other."

I gestured in Thom's direction as he cantered back toward us, both of Penny's fists embedded in his hair now. "Hang on, my lady," warned the alpha of Gate City. Then he bowed with one foot extended, just like a circus steed. After rising, he addressed Jessie. "It's an honor to meet any friend of Kira's."

While he spoke, his piercing blue eyes found mine, something warm and heady passing between us. Was that the first time I'd labeled Thom my significant other? I guessed it was. And I had absolutely no urge to take the words back.

Just like her sister, Jessie had no problem recognizing true attraction. No wonder her face brightened.

"We're available," she said, grabbing Charlie's arm as her sister came up behind her. Then she proceeded to weave a castle in the air the way she always used to when we were younger. "As bridesmaids, I mean. A matched pair is classy. And the kids can be flower girls."

Most single men would have spooked at talk of marriage before we'd even had an official first date, but Thom didn't waver. Instead, his gaze still on me, he nodded. "We won't get a better offer than that."

Chapter 12

The rest of the day was a prime example of negativity bias, a psychological concept I always remember as explained in my favorite professor's Irish bur. "Close your eyes," he'd told the crowded lecture hall, "and imagine you're walking through an orchard on a sunny autumn day. The trees are loaded with fruit and you reach up to pick the most perfect apple. The skin is red and shiny; when you take the first bite, the flesh is crisp between your teeth. The flavor is out of this world amazing, sweet and tart with just the right amount of something extra. You eat and eat and just before you hit the core"—he paused, his gaze sliding across the rapt students—"a worm!"

"Ew!" The cascade of disgust rippled across the rows until it reached me. For my part, I grinned behind my laptop. Foxes are big fans of grasshoppers, an excellent source of omega-3s. Worms were an acceptable substitute in a pinch.

Still, I got the prof's point when he intoned: "The only thing you're going to remember about that day is the worm." Whipping an apple out of his jacket pocket, he offered it around to students who shrank away as expected. Then he shrugged and tossed the glossy fruit into the closest trash bin.

"In fact," he continued, "you might never want to eat an apple again. Not that I'm speaking from personal experience or anything." He waited for the titters of laughter to fade before adding: "That's negativity bias."

So, given the worm at the core of that Saturday, I have a hard time focusing on what happened after Thom and I left Charlie's house. Still, I *do* remember some of the sweetness. I remember the buzz of adrenaline as I accelerated my twelve-year-old Corolla into race-car speeds in order to evade Reed wolves during our drive up to that little West Virginia post office. Glancing over at Thom after the danger had passed, I expected to find him clinging to the oh-shit handle. Instead, our eyes connected and he burst out in the deepest belly laugh I'd ever heard, one that carried me along with it until my eyes grew so mirth-filled watery I could barely see the road.

Later, walking down a root-heaved sidewalk toward the post office, I couldn't resist hopping up on top of a retaining wall. Beside me, Thom cleared his throat, a reminder—I thought—that full-grown human women didn't cavort like children. But when I glanced his way, he merely reached up one hand, his fingers curving through mine as soon as they made contact.

I raised my eyebrows. "You're not ashamed to be seen with me?"

"Shame," Thom answered, "is the furthest thing from my mind."

I remember the pack dinner in Gate City we made it back just in time for. A long table overloaded with steaming dishes filled up the entire Moon Room while Pumpkin pranced down the length of the table, accepting tidbits from both doting and not-so-doting werewolves. Reluctant pack mate Rupert sat at the absolutely opposite end from me so I didn't have to hear him complain the food wasn't up to his standards. Hank and his kid brother made up for their lapse the previous evening by charming the socks off everyone before excusing themselves to get started on the dishes.

Most of our human pack mates were there also—Dixie Lee, Eli, and Thom's father, although Charlie regretfully informed us of a previous engagement. Dixie Lee's daughter Ava was treated to the same courtesy Pumpkin merited even though she smelled like fox.

And, okay, so the shifter on my left sometimes tried to pass dishes around me rather than to me, until Thom cleared his throat meaningfully, that is. And, sure, Dixie Lee griped that Hank's younger brother smelled like locker room as the kid walked by, which made the boy's cheeks flame and his brother growl. A conversation I wasn't privy to ended with a shoving match and someone punching a hole in the wall...which was pretty much par for the course among werewolves.

So, yes, the mood was festive. It felt like a pack gathering, like home, like family. The sweetness around me soaked into every pore.

I remember all of that, but it's not vivid. What's vivid is what came later, after Kaito's text.

"He answered." I looked up from my phone, not quite believing that my note in the P.O. box had born fruit so quickly. At the time, I didn't realize there was a worm in the center of the apple being dangled in front of me. All I saw was its crisp, white flesh.

One moment earlier, Thom had been engaging his wolves like the best sort of alpha. He knew how everyone's week had gone, who craved encouragement and who deserved a quick kick in the rear. Now, though, his focus was 100% on me as he asked, "Kaito?"

I nodded. "He wants to meet."

I tilted the screen so Thom could see the address. It was in Virginia just like we were, which might make the location easy to get to. Or, alternatively, might not. Gate City was near the southwestern tip of a long state that contained lots of werewolf packs. Reaching the diagonally opposite corner would either take my best evasive driving tactics or Thom's best diplomacy or, more likely, a combination of both.

Turned out, neither was required. "That's close," Thom rumbled. "In my territory. We can go tonight."

"*I* can go," I corrected, thumb typing an answer. When did Kaito want to meet me?

"How about now?"

My blood fizzed but I kept my fingers steady as I answered: *"How about in an hour?"* Thom's territory was small enough that I knew I could reach the furthest limits in less time than that.

Before I could tap the send button, though, Thom's grip settled over the phone. His palm was almost as big as my entire hand including the fingers, but he wasn't forcing me to stop typing. He was merely requesting a pause to discuss.

"You're right," he agreed. "We won't spook him. You'll go in solo, but the pack will be nearby. Backup."

I nodded. It was an obvious solution, fully acceptable. Again, I tilted the phone, this time to display the unsent message. "Timeline good?"

Thom nodded. The message went out. Dinner wrapped up quicker than anticipated. Only the humans and the cleanup crew were left behind.

And while Thom managed his wolves, I drove down windy roads, singing along to the radio. What I hadn't realized about a freely given oath was how *good* it felt to do as I'd promised. The tingle in my fingers zinged up into my throat then through my thoughts until they bubbled like champagne.

I'd meet Kaito and help him get out of whatever mess had sent him into hiding. I'd prove to Scarlet that Kaito was no longer a problem. Even if she didn't keep her word and go to bat for me afterwards, I'd be no worse off than I'd been two days before.

And Kaito would be safe. Kaito would be happy. Kaito would be....

My phone's mapping software reminded me to turn right. I was way out in the boonies now, the last farmhouse having receded in my rearview mirror five minutes ago.

Then a light flickered through the trees on my left just as my phone warned of an upcoming turn. A mailbox sported the number Kaito had texted. Bubbles in my brain turned into ping-pong balls of happiness as I turned into a gravel driveway...and came face-to-face with that metaphorical worm.

The first warning was smoke. Just a tendril, drifting out of the heater vents. A glow on the other side of the hill that seemed too intense for porch lights. I steered around the curve and slammed on my brakes.

The house—the only house for miles, the one Kaito must be inside—rose before me. It was easily visible in the night because what might once have been a two-level porch in front of a tall, imposing residence had been replaced by a raging mass of flames.

Chapter 13

"Kira! Help!"

The male voice—Kaito's voice—came from a window on the fourth and final story. He was a shadow in the single dark patch that hadn't yet caught fire, but I recognized him easily when the ping-pong balls turned to buckshot in my stomach. I sprinted forward, leaving the car door gaping open behind my back.

The Corolla dinged complaint, but I ignored it. "Kaito!" I called, depending on my words to travel faster than my feet. "Shut the window! Stuff something under the door!"

I hoped he understood what I was saying. Because he was too high up to jump, especially with a brick patio stretched out below his window. Meanwhile, the air space he stood in front of was an invitation for flames to gush into the one small pocket of safety he'd retreated to.

I barely heard the window slam above the pounding of my own blood. Spinning, I surveyed a yard that was dark, or would have been if it wasn't for the fire that gushed out the house's front door like a dragon's exhale. That glow seared away my night vision, making it impossible to hunt for a way up.

I blinked frantically, squeezing my eyes shut then reopening them. Open, shut, open, shut. *There.*

A ladder, neatly stowed on two hooks along the outside of a shed just far enough from the house that it hadn't yet caught fire. It was an extension ladder, long enough to reach the fourth story if I was lucky.

Unfortunately, the hooks had been installed by someone considerably taller than I was. My fingers touched the metal but only barely. Even leaping upward, I failed to bump the ladder loose.

Behind me, something crumpled. The flames roared out their laughter. I couldn't afford to waste a second, but I turned to peer back over my shoulder anyway and saw light where Kaito had been standing. Light instead of darkness. The fire had invaded the unburned fourth floor.

Then Thom was there. Thom was lifting the ladder down from the wall as easily as if it was a beer on the shelf behind the bar. "Where to?"

I pointed, words eluding me. We ran, him with the ladder on his shoulder and me by his side. Together, we ratcheted up the extension until it thudded against the side of the house. Thom only fought me for a moment when I put my foot on the first rung.

"I might need to carry him out," Thom rumbled.

"He might not trust you," I answered.

Then I was climbing so fast I might as well have been vulpine. Up to the window from which Kaito had yelled my name. It was old, with a wooden frame that gave my fingers easy purchase.

I dug in. Pushed. Grunted with effort and pushed yet harder.

But the window wouldn't budge. It was stuck.

My first impulse was to break the glass and wriggle through on my belly. But there was so much smoke inside and I couldn't see where Kaito had gone. He must have crumpled onto the floor, beneath the haze of gray. It would take time to find him, time during which, given extra oxygen, that smoke might burst into flames....

"Need help?" Thom's voice from below settled me. I shook my head, letting the oath bubbles speed my thought processes.

A vent halfway down the length of the house was barely visible in darkness. It was a way in, further from the fire and thus safer to open. If I shifted....

Thought became motion. My paws pushed off the ladder as my clothes drifted toward the ground beneath me. Thom shouted something. But I ignored him, scampering across shingles that were warm but not hot here. There was no time to explain.

The vent was loose. Loose enough to dig free with my claws and my teeth without having to shift back and use thumb and fingers. Then I was inside a space so narrow a human wouldn't have fit through it, some sort of ductwork likely meant to cool and dehumidify the top of the house. Or so I gathered when a breeze washed over me, a distant fan humming as it pushed smoky air into my face.

Breathing as shallowly as possible, I scrambled forward into the darkness until the path split. Kaito was to my left, so I turned that way. But the path split again, and again. Whoever had built this house hadn't planned for fox travel. Shouldn't that sort of consideration have been in the engineering drawings? Glowing signposts for four-legged rescuers. Instructions on how to reach each room.

The notion made me laugh, or maybe the smoke mixing with oath bubbles was turning me loopy. Whatever the reason, I inhaled too deeply and reality struck as my lungs screamed out a seemingly endless cascade of coughs.

I couldn't force my lungs to stop convulsing. Couldn't breathe. Couldn't....

I thrust my nose into the long hairs of my tail. They weren't much of a filter, but fur was just enough to give my aching ribs a break from coughing. Enough to let me focus when I cautiously unfolded and peered back around again.

The metal beneath my paws was hotter than it had been. And it wasn't really dark inside, not any longer. Instead, light seeped in through hair-thin gaps in the ductwork, gaps that were letting smoke through as well.

Which might mean I was closer to Kaito? It certainly meant I was closer to danger.

Then the hum of the exhaust fan went silent. If the fire had dug deep enough into the structure of the house to burn out the electricity, I needed to find Kaito *now.*

But I couldn't. I'd had my nose out of my tail for too long and this time it wasn't humor that shook me. Ahead, the path split in two yet again and I had no clue which way to turn to reach Kaito.

In fact, my mind was turning muzzy and fuzzy. The warmth was seductive, tempting me to curl up and bask in it. Perhaps what I needed was one small nap....

Chapter 14

"Kira!" Thom's voice echoed down the ductwork, joining with the rumble of the fire. "This way!"

I let my mouth loll open, fox-smiling in my half-sleep. Thom must have caved and chosen to spend the night with me. Wasn't that lovely? Maybe we'd shower together later. I could think up all sorts of games to keep us busy. We'd start with….

Another deep voice, not Thom's this time. "Sir, the house is coming down. You need to retreat to a safe distance."

"I'm not leaving without her."

"No pet is worth losing your life for."

Thom's voice grew gruffer than I'd ever heard it. "This one is."

There were other words then. Threats of law-enforcement carrying Thom out whether or not he was willing, but warmth cocooned me in cotton and I relaxed into my pillow. Thom would get rid of whoever that was and lie back down beside me. He'd be the big spoon and I'd be the little spoon and we'd snuggle closer until it was impossible to tell where he stopped and I began.

"Kira." Thom's voice intruded upon my daydream. "I need you to get up and come this way. *Now*."

I wanted to tell him that I was a fox and alpha commands didn't work on me. But a yawn overcame me. A yawn followed by a cough.

Not just one cough. Or, well, I guess it was one cough since it never stopped. The shaking racked my body, too solidly of-this-world to be handled.

And I didn't have to handle it. Instead, I retreated back into myself, letting dream-Thom enfold me. He'd stroke my nape just like he had in the bar at the full moon. He'd stroke my nape, then continue down the length of my body. I'd shift and....

Something slapped me in the face. Something strangely solid even though instinct told me it wasn't tangible. Something warm in a different way than my dream was warm.

"You don't have to accept the bond." Thom's voice sounded strangely desperate. As if he was in trouble. I fought the undertow of sleep, rising up enough to let the rest of his words roll over me. "Just grab it with your teeth. I'll pull you out. It will work." He muttered an addendum: "I think."

I arched my neck, retreating from the strangeness in front of me. Why would I want to be yanked out of my dream? Here, Thom didn't abide by crazy, self-imposed rules that kept us separate. Here, I didn't have a family I wasn't allowed to be with but couldn't bear replacing either.

"Sir, this is your last chance to come willingly. You are risking our lives and your own."

"Kira! Please!" Thom's voice was no longer a rumble. It rose in pitch until he almost sounded like a woman.

Like my sister that time I'd clambered out onto the railing of a third-story balcony to pirouette on tiptoe. Wind had whistled past my ears and there'd been tears beneath her pleading. Tears and terror and...

...The dream left me. Faded away until I found myself alone in a metal cage so hot it roasted my paw pads. I couldn't breathe. Could only hack against smoke so thick I could no longer see even the glare of flames through cracks in the ducts.

There was no way out. I might as well let the dream continue.

Then that thing slapped me a second time. A thing that was familiar even though I'd lacked anything like it for three long months.

A pack bond. Invisible yet real in every way that mattered.

"Alright, sir, you're forcing our hands."

They were going to take Thom away. I couldn't let that happen.

I lunged forward...and the pack bond retreated like a snake escaping a mongoose. My muscles quivered as I forced myself back up onto feet that screamed in agony. This time when I struck, it was more of a controlled fall than anything more elegant.

But the effort paid off. My nosedive ended with me on top of the pack bond. I had just enough presence of mind to snap my teeth together.

After that, everything went black.

"*This* is what we were waiting for? Is that thing a *fox*?"

Despite the stranger's words, it was Thom's arms that cradled me. Thom's arms that carefully exposed my scorched pads to the icy air while smothering the rest of me. Contact helped ease the shudders of aching muscles bombarding throbbing skin.

"I appreciate all of your help." Thom's words were a clear dismissal, but the other man kept talking.

"Are you the owner of this property?"

"No."

"Renter?"

"No."

We were moving fast. Cold air brushed across my paws and I whimpered.

"Sir, I need information on what you're doing here."

Thom spun so fast my stomach lurched. "And I need to get her help. You can talk to Bertrand."

"Bertrand's the property owner?"

"I don't have time for this."

Then my body was jostling up and down as Thom raced away from the human. Away from the roar of flames. "Ssh," he soothed me. "It won't be so bad after you shift. But you can't do that here. Your car is close."

Then we were inside. A key clicked but no engine revved. Faintly, I recalled leaving the door open. Hearing the electronic dings of warning. The Corolla's battery was likely dead.

Thom didn't know any of that, but he must have come to the same conclusion based on his swearing. He only allowed himself one string of expletives, though, then his voice turned solid again. "Okay, this is okay. We can work with this."

His warm hands lifted me higher. Grunting and rustling promised he was maneuvering us both through a tight space—into the back seat?—but nothing other than his arms touched my hyper-sensitive skin.

Then I was being settled onto a semi-soft surface. Thom's retreating touch made me whimper while darkness threatened to consume me.

"Listen to me, Kira." His voice pulled me back to the present. "Shifting should deal with the burns, might even heal your lungs. If not, we'll take you to the hospital. You just need to shift. Please, Kira. Do this one thing for me."

I tried; I really did. But just thinking about the heat of my star ball invading my skin started me coughing. The coughing set off cascades of torment. I couldn't do this. It was too much.

I collapsed back against the surface that didn't feel soft any longer. Every inch of my body howled with pain and I flinched away from it. Ignoring Thom's voice, I retreated into the dream of his arms and his bed and his scent cuddling me up....

Then it wasn't Thom speaking. It was someone I'd known much longer. Someone who didn't sound at all pleased with my behavior.

"Young lady, you listen to me."

My sister's voice forced my eyes open. There was a screen in front of my nose. A cell phone. I couldn't quite focus on the moving blobs, but Mai refused to let me drift away again.

"I swear to you, Kira, if you don't shift right this instant, I'm going to put the kids in the car and drive to the closest Lawkeeper's office. I'm going to tell them that I was personally responsible for what happened last October. I'm going to let them punish me and the *children*. Do you hear me, Kira? I mean it!"

She was crying and yelling and I knew from experience that Mai didn't raise her voice if she wasn't prepared to back up threats with action.

Grub. Chipmunk. My mistakes couldn't be allowed to harm them. I'd promised.

I didn't want to but I had to. I grabbed onto my star ball, ignoring the searing pain as magical energy combined with third-degree burns to ooze agony across parts of my body I hadn't known existed. I screamed...

...then Thom was holding my human body up against his human body. He smelled of smoke but also, beneath that, of himself. Of alpha and bartender and solid dependability.

"You"—my throat was so sore I could barely speak, but I managed—"fight dirty. No fair bringing in Mai to threaten the kids."

Chapter 15

Thom's rumbled laughter surged through me. On the phone screen, my sister grinned, then her image blurred as she strode out of the light and into a dim hallway. "How about I make it up to you by letting you see the monsters in their lair?"

My throat was so sore I could barely swallow and my lungs felt full of gunk rather than oxygen. But I forgot all of that when the camera tilted to display a lump in a bed plus a much smaller lump in a crib, both illuminated by the glow of Grub's wolf-shaped night light.

Then Grub himself was bounding up and pushing his face into the camera. "Auntie Kira! Mommy says I can't call my sister Chipmunk. But that's her name, isn't it?"

"Of course it is," I answered, forcing scratchiness out of my voice with an effort. "Just like your name is Grub."

"Yes!" Unable to stand still for even a moment, he made a beeline for his bed and started jumping, caroling the nickname Mai had not yet accepted for her newborn at the top of his lungs.

Which, of course, woke Chipmunk. She chirruped rather than cried, the same sort of sound that had suggested her name to me in the first place. Well, that plus her fat little cheeks that looked ready to be filled to bursting with stockpiled nuts.

Then Mai turned the phone back in her own direction. "Now look what you've done." She tried to sound exasperated, but her eyes were smiling. Mayhem after bedtime was nothing new in her household. "Punishment all around. Grub is going back to sleep, I'll hold the baby, and you'll talk to Gunner."

A groan from my favorite nephew. Another chirrup from Chipmunk. Then—

"One moment while I exit the disaster zone," my brother-in-law said, his dry voice not quite as comforting as the water bottle Thom pressed into my hand. I took a sip while Gunner retreated back down the hallway, and the liquid made me human enough to realize I was video-chatting with my brother-in-law while stark naked.

Then I wasn't. Thom's warmth receded before drawing close again, warmth that felt even better now that my skin no longer exuded its own heat. His shoulder pressed against my shoulder as he draped a blanket across my lap and wrapped a jacket around my shoulders, but he stayed silent. Just held the phone and let me have this moment I needed with my far-flung family.

My darned astute far-flung family. "You look terrible," Gunner observed as he sank into his favorite armchair and picked up a glass. "Half dead. What happened?"

I didn't know where to start, so when Thom raised his eyebrows I waved for him to take over. And I was glad I did since the story Thom told wasn't the same as what I'd thought I was experiencing.

"Wait, what?" I stopped him mid-report. "You smelled gasoline?"

"I came in from a slightly different angle," Thom confirmed, "and the place reeked of it."

Gunner was the one who spoke what I was trying not to imagine. "Someone set the fire. Kaito?"

"I doubt it," Thom answered. "As best we can tell, he never made it out."

The image of Kaito standing in that window, the bottom stories already blazing, fixed itself in my memory. Still, I fought against the obvious. "He might have gotten free. It's possible he ran out the back while we were manhandling the ladder."

The tone of Thom's voice said *no* even as he offered: "Maybe." A pause, then—"The pack is scouring the woods now. Smoke makes it impossible to track by scent, so Kaito could have left before they arrived. But the timeline would have been tight and he wouldn't be in any better shape than you are. If he's alive, they'll find him soon."

They'd find him crumpled atop cold leaves, lungs overcome by smoke inhalation and skin charred. Unlike me, Kaito wouldn't be able to shift and heal skin-level damage. Unlike me, he wouldn't have had fur to buffer the smoke.

And who would want to harm him so badly? If the fire had been set intentionally....

While I tried to work through a slew of maybes, Thom and Gunner proceeded to plan around me. "Kira can recover here," my brother-in-law was saying. "I know she hasn't wanted to visit because of Mai and the baby, but I'm confident we can sneak her in under the Lawkeepers' noses. The alpha to our west—Randolph—has been wanting to search our territory ever since he misplaced a pack princess. I stonewalled because if a young woman flees she usually has a good reason. Telling Randolph no keeps the focus on us."

My brother-in-law drummed on the arm of a chair that had perennial finger marks from previous thinking sessions. Then he lowered his voice to a growl. "But if we let his pack in, he'll do us a favor. You can drop Kira at the border and they'll bring her along when they enter. The Lawkeepers will be none the wiser about where she's ended up."

Thom nodded. "The Lawkeepers and whoever set the fire. We can be there by morning. I'll..."

Mention of the Lawkeepers jogged my fuzzy brain back into motion. Of course. There was one Lawkeeper who was both interested in Kaito and had proven her willingness to kill in the past.

"Scratch that," I told both alphas. "I'm not running home with my tail between my legs."

"I want that tail, those legs, and every other part of you safe," Gunner rebutted. Then he ruined it with a muttered, "You know you're a unique sort of trouble magnet."

By my side, Thom growled very softly. But I didn't need him to stick up for me around my brother-in-law, who just happened to be right about my tendency to attract trouble. Instead, I poked at the issue I knew would refocus Gunner's attention on something other than me. "My gut says Kaito's death has to do with kitsunes," I observed. "And if that's true...you have your own dangers to deal with."

"Mai." My sister's name on my brother-in-law's lips sounded both sweet and threat-like at the same time. "They wouldn't dare."

"I hope not. But I'd feel better if you kept her close...."

"She will be protected."

"Excellent. Then this call is over. I have an arsonist to catch."

The call was over, but I wasn't done with the phone. After all, when Gunner tracked me using my cell last autumn, I'd demanded that he hand over similar tools by way of apology. I had high hopes the software he'd hooked me up with would pin down Scarlet's location now. The tricky part would be keeping her on the line long enough for technology to do its work.

Unfortunately, my ex-boss didn't answer when I called her. And why should she when she'd been busy torching a house moments before?

"Tell the pack to keep an eye out for Scarlet," I suggested to Thom. Then I turned to the only other avenue I could think of. I dialed the Roanoke Lawkeepers' main number.

The voice that answered was male and unfamiliar. "Emergency?" he asked.

If I didn't recognize the shifter on duty, I could only hope he wouldn't recognize me either. Wouldn't recognize me...and wouldn't know I was persona non grata around the office.

"Yes." I kept my tone clipped, squashing any bubbles of charm that might give away my identity. "I need to get in touch with Scarlet immediately. Do you know how I can reach her?"

I expected this Lawkeeper, whoever he was, to take a message. Or to tell me to call back Monday. Instead, he murmured, "One moment." Then, without asking my name, he texted over a link for a video chat.

It seemed far too easy, but I clicked the link anyway. An app opened. *Connecting*, it reported in a flashing, italic font.

Then Scarlet was there on the screen, but a very different Scarlet than the one I was used to. In the past, she'd always been buttoned up both literally and metaphorically. Now, sweat-streaked hair clung to cheeks nearly as red as her hair was. Her eyes flitted back and forth wildly. Her shirt gaped open at the neck.

Still, she greeted me. "Kira, just the woman I was hoping for. Did you find him?"

"You have to ask?" My fist clenched around the phone, hitting the power button and darkening the screen. By the time I corrected my error, someone else had joined Scarlet. Someone I'd seen only once back when I was still a Lawkeeper.

This man—thirtyish, tall, terrifying—had strode into our office building four months ago clad all in black, a sword at his hip despite our location in the middle of a human-dominated city. The toughest Lawkeepers I knew cringed out of his path and I'd whispered to the co-worker beside me. "Who's that?"

"Executioner," she'd mouthed in reply.

The Executioner couldn't have heard her, but his head turned toward us anyway. I peered into eyes that were eerily empty and I understood why all of my coworkers had abruptly decided they needed to be somewhere else.

Then Scarlet had emerged from her office. "You're spooking the mice," she'd told him. "Come in before they all quit in terror."

Scarlet laughed, but her statement hadn't really been a joke. The moment the Executioner's back was turned, every single person, me included, decided to take an extra long lunch break to avoid the unnamed shifter's glowering presence. When we finally forced ourselves back to the office, the source of our terror was gone and unflappable Scarlet appeared a trifle flapped.

Now, the Executioner stared into the camera with that same emptiness in his expression. An emptiness that suggested he didn't care whether I lived or died. He raised one eyebrow but didn't bother speaking.

Scarlet didn't speak either, but not through boredom. I could still see her behind the Executioner, strapped down in what I hoped was just a chair rather than some sort of torture apparatus. There was blood dripping from both of her arms.

In the silence that followed, the bloodletter followed my gaze and smiled. A blade was in his hand, I saw now. Something small but unbearably sharp. He pressed the sharp side against the skin of Scarlet's forearm like an artist choosing his next brushstroke. A thin thread of red rose up in the blade's wake.

The cut must have been painful, but it was fear more than pain that impacted Scarlet. Her throat worked but no sound came out. Her chest heaved faster. The Executioner's cut was no worse than a briar scratch she might get running four-footed, yet she was ready to wet her pants.

Scarlet and I were enemies, but I hated this. And I was also curious. So I interrupted the torture with words. "How did you know Scarlet killed Kaito? The fire just happened."

I'd never heard the Executioner speak before, so I wasn't ready for a quiet rasp as rough as a saw blade. "If this Kaito was killed within the last twelve hours," he murmured, "you've found the wrong murderer. Now, if you'll excuse me, I have a stray fox to track down."

He turned back to Scarlet and she broke. Slamming her body back and forth, she fought against unyielding bindings. "No more! Please! Kaito is the stray fox! Kira took care of him! You heard her! He's *dead!*"

"Perhaps." The Executioner placed his used blade on a silver tray and picked up something long and sharp and hooked at the end, something I didn't want to look at too closely. "But you lied to your superiors. You disrupted the peace within Reed territory. Their alpha requested remuneration and you have nothing but your blood to pay with. You and I are not done."

They might not be done, but our video call apparently was. The app went dark, the connection lost.

Chapter 16

For five more minutes, my brain fired on all cylinders. There was nothing I could do about Scarlet and I wasn't entirely sure I wanted to given the fact she was a cold-blooded murderer. But Kaito....

At my recommendation, Thom redialed the main Lawkeeper's number to report the fire. That way, human officials would be drawn away from the investigative aftermath, leaving it in shifter hands.

In *our* hands.

I pushed myself up on shaky arms so I could peer out the window at the house in question, or what was left of it. Flames had been quenched but the structure tilted precariously, burnt-over studs jutting out like broken bones. Smoke obscured the roof line I'd crawled beneath, but what I could see was as crooked as a snapped backbone. Without Thom, I never would have made it out alive.

And Kaito? I wasn't ready to admit the truth, but I could see Thom's point now.

Which meant, if I couldn't save my grandmother's ex-honor-guard member, my oath to his brother required a different sort of focus. Finding the party responsible. Making sure a similar murder never happened again.

"The Reeds might have tracked down Kaito before we did," I murmured.

Thom's jaw clenched as he followed my gaze. "Maybe."

Before he could elaborate on the source of the doubt in his voice, Bertrand's car was pulling up beside ours and the sugar high of star-ball energy was fading from my flesh as quickly as it had consumed me. Thom had been right about shifting—the effort had dealt with both my burns and lung damage. But healing always came with a price tag. Exhaustion grabbed me hard and yanked me under, my head drifting down to rest against Thom's broad chest even as Bertrand stalked over to the window closest to Thom.

"Orders?"

Thom's reply vibrated through my skin. "Jump the car and take her home."

I tried to rise and speak, but my body was having none of it. Neither was Thom. His arm rose to drape across my shoulders, and I accepted the invitation to snuggle in closer. Was half asleep when Bertrand replied.

"You don't want to drive her yourself?"

A subtle jolting of my pillow suggested Thom was shaking his head in negation. "I need to pin down alibis."

Bertrand asked the question I wanted an answer to. "Alibis?"

"Our pack knew where Kaito was tonight."

Our pack? My eyebrows drew together just a little, the motion all I could tease out of my somnolent body. Surely Thom didn't think any of the wolves who'd acted so much like family around the dinner table tonight could have murdered Kaito?

I wanted to argue. Wanted to tell Thom to search in a different direction. But by the time I blinked my eyes back open, I was alone in the back seat of my car, the rumble of tires on pavement suggesting we were halfway back to Gate City already.

I could deal with Thom's suspicions tomorrow. Healing slumber drew me into its welcoming embrace.

I woke to lungs that didn't ache and a body that felt as good as new. I stunk, however. Stretching, the scents of sweat and smoke swirled around my head.

Yuck. Definitely time for a shower. No wonder Pumpkin had chosen to nap at my feet rather than on top of my head.

But when I padded out of my room, Charlie was nursing a mug of tea at the dining-room table. Charlie, who didn't believe in lazy Sunday mornings. Maybe I hadn't slept as long as I'd thought I had.

Nope, the light outside the window was so bright it had to be nearly lunchtime. And Charlie's mug wasn't steaming, suggesting she'd been sitting there for quite a while. So much for that shower.

I took my usual chair and addressed my housemate. "What's up?"

Bracing myself, I expected her to mention Kaito. I'd wanted to break the news to her gently once we had proof that he'd either died or escaped the fire. But I'd fallen asleep before discussing that plan with Thom last night. Maybe he'd decided Charlie deserved to be kept in the loop.

She considered me over the top of her mug for one long moment. Then she shook her head. "You look like you had a really bad night. This isn't the right time to talk, is it?"

To talk? Charlie had mentioned having something to discuss days ago...and I'd forgotten. Given the hard conversation she and I were going to have about Kaito in the very near future, chances were good that I'd forget again.

So I focused on my friend, forcing all other concerns to fade into the background. "There may never be a right time," I told her. "Spit it out."

Rather than accepting my invitation, Charlie closed her eyes and inhaled deeply. When she finally spoke, she did so with her eyes on her mug. "We need to talk about when you're moving out."

I jolted. "Moving out?"

Maybe I wasn't fully awake yet, but Charlie's words didn't make sense. After all, for the last three months we'd gotten along like gangbusters. We talked half the night sometimes, gave each other space other times. And even though we'd never formalized our rental agreement, I handed over cash in a timely manner, did extra chores before Charlie mentioned them, and thought we were even. If we weren't....

"I didn't mean to impose." Springing back to my feet, I found them oddly wobbly. Maybe sleep hadn't fixed me up as much as I'd thought it had.

Either that or Thom was right. I was clinging to Charlie as a link to home.

Wincing, I headed for my room. It wouldn't take long to pack since I'd stocked up on the bare minimum to get me through. It wasn't like I could just drop by the cabin down the road from Mai's house and retrieve my possessions, not with the Lawkeepers considering me a loose cannon poisoning everything I touched.

Just like I'd, apparently, poisoned my friendship with Charlie.

"Kira." Charlie followed me, or so I assumed even though I didn't turn around to face her. "You're going silent on me. I don't like it when you go silent."

With an effort, I pasted on a smile and forced myself to meet her gaze at last. "Hey, no big deal. I get it. House guests and fish both stink after three days, right? It's been a lot longer than that for me." And—I raised one arm to confirm what I'd already gotten a whiff of—I really did stink.

"Kira, stop it." Charlie bent sideways to invade my sight line, which had drifted back to the floor when I wasn't paying attention. "You have the wrong idea. I love being your housemate. But you shift into a fox. Run through the house furry...."

That was the problem? I'd thought Charlie accepted who I was after learning my true nature last autumn. The fact my fur form was what had come between us made this whole thing ten times worse.

"I can't really help shifting when I'm sleeping," I muttered, stuffing clothes into a backpack that wasn't going to be large enough to hold all of them. Maybe I'd grab a trash bag from the kitchen cabinet for the rest, or just leave behind whatever I couldn't cram in.

My skin itched for me to be outside, to be gone from this space where I was no longer welcome. And Charlie snarled out a growl that would have done a shifter credit.

"This isn't going at all the way I expected it to," she muttered. Then, louder, "The thing is, I met somebody recently. I was going to wait to tell you until we were more serious. But she's into me and I'm into her and I want to be able to take her back here...and she's seriously allergic to fur."

Chapter 17

"**S**he?" The backpack I'd been stuffing overturned and spilled my belongings back over the unmade bed.

"She," Charlie confirmed, her voice quavering only a little. When I turned around to face her, I found her arms crossed defensively in front of her chest.

And my fox exuberance took over. I lunged at my friend, grabbing her shoulders and spinning her around while caroling my excitement. "Charlie has a girlfriend! Charlie has a girlfriend!"

My friend was usually willing to jump and squee with the best of them. But, this time, her muscles stayed stiff under my fingers, her tone cautious. "Well, maybe. I mean, it's very new. And I told you completely the wrong way. It's not that I don't want to share a house any longer...."

"...It's just that you need some space. And I really can't promise not to shed on the furniture, even if I was able to keep Pumpkin from inviting himself in every night. I get it."

I did get it. Got so many things that hadn't made sense in the past.

Like the way Charlie had never dated all through college, at least not where I could see her. I'd assumed she was just being thoughtful toward her sister, who tended toward irrational jealousy. Had thought Charlie might be as cautious around romantic relationships as she was around platonic ones. If that wasn't the issue—

"Did you really think I'd judge you for who you're attracted to?" I shook my friend not entirely gently. "Have you been refusing to bring women home to meet the family because you were afraid of what we'd say?"

Only after my demand came out did I realize how it sounded. I wasn't part of Charlie's family, not really. The two of us had spent three months rekindling a friendship that had previously lain dormant for nearly as long as we'd initially hung out together. Calling myself family was unbelievably bold.

Or maybe not. Because Charlie's muscles loosened beneath my grip at long last. "I haven't been hiding," she promised. "There was never anyone special before this. I'm not even sure there is now. I just…"

The fizz of joy returned, strumming through my body as I finished her sentence. "You want to find out."

"I do." And now her words came a little too fast. "And, about what I said earlier…. I didn't mean you need to move out *today*, Kira. Take a few weeks. Find a place within walking distance that won't blow your budget. There's no big hurry."

There it was. The nervous backpedaling I'd expected from the moment Charlie brought up a significant other. We certainly couldn't have her derailing her first foray into dating while using me as the excuse.

So I shook my head, glad Charlie wasn't a shifter able to smell mistruth. Then I lied through my teeth. "I've got multiple places to choose from. You can have your girlfriend over tonight."

Whether or not Charlie would have seen through my fib given enough time, she wasn't offered that opportunity. Because someone pounded on the front door before our conversation could progress any further. And when we ambled over to open it, Thom stood on the doorstep with a long skinny object I couldn't quite make out clenched in his right hand.

Something was up, but he didn't tell us what immediately. Instead, his blue eyes met mine, the faintest hint of a smile warming his entire face and my face by reflection. "You're better."

"Completely recovered," I answered, considering the fact that Thom wasn't. He hadn't slept, that much was clear from his tangled hair and the beard stubble that had gone from a flattering shadow to slightly unkempt. Meanwhile, something about the set of his shoulders said more than lack of sleep was bothering him now.

Which is when I remembered what had slipped my mind while talking to Charlie this morning. Thom was convinced someone in our pack had lit that house fire. He'd intended to check alibis after sending me away with Bertrand. Surely he hadn't found rot close to home?

"Did someone we know...?" I started.

Thom shook his head. "Inconclusive but unlikely."

Charlie looked back and forth between the two of us. "What's going on?" she demanded. Then, to me, "You shouldn't have let me ramble if there was a problem."

Thom's blue eyes slid away from mine, taking their heat with them. "Ramble?"

This was Charlie's opportunity to share her news with someone we both trusted implicitly. But when I raised my eyebrows, my friend shook her head minutely. "Just girl stuff," she answered, which was literally the truth.

And that was enough for Thom. Because he brushed past us, coming in without being invited. Silently, he led the way to the kitchen, filled the kettle and set it on the stove.

Only then did he pull out a chair for me and one for Charlie. "Have a seat," he murmured, his words the furthest thing from a command.

Charlie looked at me, toward Thom, then over at me again. "You're scaring me," she said, remaining standing.

I was the one who sat. I was the one who nudged Charlie's chair a little further in her direction.

Because if Thom was here, heating water for tea in Charlie's kitchen.... Well, that meant he'd likely found something in the smoldering remnants of last night's house fire that proved his guess about Kaito's lack of survival.

Sure enough, once Charlie sank down to perch on the edge of the chair we'd both offered her, Thom slid the object he'd been grasping across the table. It was about six inches long, sooty yet shiny in patches. Like a metal object that had been scuffed and dirtied.

Or like a metal object that had gone through a fire.

"Kaito was in a house that burned down last night," Thom said gently. "The flames were hot and there was very little left afterwards. Just this, which I'm told is the type of pin used to mend a badly fractured bone. Do you happen to know whether Kaito…?"

And Charlie's face crumpled. She didn't have to speak. Couldn't, I suspected, or she would have started sobbing.

But her face said it all. Kaito had perished in that fire.

Chapter 18

Reality struck and the remnants of my oath squirmed like bad fish in my stomach. I'd failed Kaito. Couldn't even hunt for his murderer, not really, since the most likely suspects were within a very unfriendly alpha's territory.

All I could do was contact his brother. Let Ito down gently. But Charlie shook her head when I suggested being the one to break the news.

"No, I'll do it. I need to talk to Jessie anyway." Her eyes flicked to Thom as he set a fresh mug of tea in front of her then her attention returned to me. "You know how she gets her feelings hurt if she's not in the know."

And Jessie would inevitably discover that her twin had come out to me before her. Or she would unless the timeline was so tight that the difference of minutes could be swept under the rug.

"Of course," I answered. "I can vacuum fox hair while you're talking. Even shifter ears can't hear over that roar." That way I could give my friend space while providing moral support if she needed me. When she needed me. Because Charlie's eyes were still watery even if she hadn't shed more than a few tears.

But my friend was shaking her head while ushering me and Thom toward the front door. "We'll have a cleaning party later. Not right now. Please?"

What could we do? It was Charlie's house.

So Thom and I left her alone with her phone and her news—one piece terrible and one piece joyous yet potentially incendiary. Thom accepted his eviction immediately while I slipped into my bedroom, restuffing my backpack with what came easily to hand while leaving behind everything not within arm's reach. This time, I wasn't concerned about the abandoned items. I could come back for them later, a good excuse to check up on Charlie and provide any necessary pep talks.

Speaking of which.... Even though I knew it would make her grumble, I set my house key on the kitchen table along with a scrawled note. *"In case you have someone you want to give this to."* Then I left the cozy cottage that had been home for the last three months.

Thom was waiting outside, just as I'd suspected he would be. His piercing eyes took in my bulging backpack and he raised one eyebrow. At my shrug, he vocalized the question. "Is there anything you or Charlie need help with?"

"Are you asking as an alpha?" The squirm in my stomach turned into something else as I crossed the space between us without fully intending to. This wasn't the tug of the full moon, just our usual magnetic attraction.

Magnetic attraction that went against Thom's rule—no displays of affection when unchaperoned. I forced my feet to stop at what Thom had, in the past, considered an appropriate distance. But he reached out to interlace our fingers, tugging me closer and settling our joined hands against his chest.

"I'm asking," he rumbled, "as a friend."

Unfortunately, even friendship wasn't simple between Thom and me. If I told him I'd lost my place to sleep, he'd pull strings within the pack and find me a bed in a heartbeat. Or he'd offer up the third story of the Full Moon Saloon, the one above his personal quarters that was currently devoted to storage of his father's excess possessions. Either choice came with its own pitfalls and its own seductive appeal.

It wasn't fair to lead Thom on when I couldn't provide the requested commitment. So I shook my head. "No. I've got it covered."

"I can't tell if you really mean that. I'm so tired I'm not thinking straight."

His breath kissed my forehead, proving that Thom really was fog-brained. Usually, by now, he would have pushed me away, creating buffer space between our bodies.

And, much as I wanted to, I couldn't take advantage of his exhaustion any more than he had taken advantage of my moon craze. So I slipped out of his hold, which was becoming more like an embrace by the moment. And I considered the way

Thom was swaying, barely upright. "Do you want me to call someone to help you back to the bar?"

"It's just a few blocks. I can manage."

Still, he didn't turn away from me. Instead, he stood and watched as I gathered up every bit of self control I could muster. In the end, I was the one who spun on my heel and strode off down the sidewalk away from everything that felt like home.

I had no idea where I was going, but I did know what I needed to do this afternoon. Eventually, I'd hunt for Kaito's murderer, but I currently lacked re-searchable leads. Instead, I had a more pressing puzzle—finding a place to stay now that the gray sky had opened up into an icy rain.

Well, finding a place to stay and reassuring my sister. Mai had texted to demand proof of life, and as I hunkered down on a cafe stool I winced at the selfie I'd just snapped. The rain had at least washed away the stink of smoke, but I looked more like a drowned rat than a fox.

Still, I shrugged and hit send, and thankfully the photo did the trick. My phone didn't ring with a demand that I take Gunner up on his convoluted plan of sneaking me into Fairwood territory via the pack-princess-hunting Randolphs. Instead, my sister reciprocated with a photo of Grub and Chipmunk napping, their pile of intertwined limbs tugging at my heart strings.

I replied with a stern admonition that she keep both children on pack land and within her sight line for the foreseeable future. *"There might be someone hunting those of us with kitsune blood,"* I warned.

"You're in a lot more danger than they are if that's the case," Mai answered. *"Take care of yourself or I'll never forgive you."*

"Yes ma'am."

The emoji she sent back made me grin.

So that was good. But finding an apartment didn't go so well. I sipped hot chocolate while working my phone so hard the screen should have sizzled, but I kept slamming into dead ends.

Which is how I ended up backtracking to Charlie's to collect my car then parking in the back lot of the Full Moon Saloon. The interior lights were off, unsurprising since the bar closed on most Sundays and Thom had looked tired enough to fall asleep the moment he climbed the stairs to his apartment. But there was a shower in the Moon Room that was always accessible and no one would hassle me after that if I curled up in the back seat of my car.

The moment I flipped on the single tier of industrial fluorescents, however, the flicker of overhead lights led me not toward the bathroom but deeper into the dim gathering space. I stopped near a spot where, three months ago, rotten floorboards had dropped me into a pit housing a cemented-in-place kitsune skull. At my request, Thom had hidden the artifact beneath a trap door then a wardrobe that appeared crazy heavy while actually rolling easily on hidden wheels.

When I pushed aside the wardrobe and lifted the door now, the pit exhaled musty darkness. A scritch of claws prompted me to flare my nostrils and I caught the sharp hint of rat.

Rodents, of course, weren't a problem for a shifter. So I dropped down into darkness, landing fox-light even though I was currently two-legged. Sinking to my knees, I felt around in search of the skull.

My emotions were stretched taut, yearning for people I wanted near me but couldn't afford to allow there. My sister. My niece and nephew. Thom.

Something told me this inert and silent skull held the answers. Assuming I could find it....

My eyes finished adjusting to the darkness, revealing the pale gleam of bone off to my right. I reached forward, only to jerk my hand away at a hint of movement from the direction of the bar entrance. The angle was bad from down in my hole, so I could only see the very top of the door swinging open, not the person who had pushed through it.

Whoever had entered, they were in a hurry. As quickly as the door had opened it now slammed very loudly shut.

Chapter 19

I froze, trying to guess who was there. Trying not to remember Thom's doubts about his pack mates.

Yesterday, with our raucous dinner fresh on my mind, the idea that a Gate City wolf could have killed Kaito had seemed ludicrous. But how well did I know all of those wolves, really? Most had been loners, showing up on Thom's doorstep with no past they cared to admit to. Could one have a history with kitsunes? A bone to pick that led to murder?

It did seem more likely than a random stranger killing Kaito. Mai's suggestion that I was at greater risk than her family suddenly made sense.

Still, I found myself more concerned for the fox skull than for my own skin. Limestone had cemented the artifact into place, so I couldn't move it somewhere less public. And I'd made the mistake of rolling aside the wardrobe. I could only hope the gaping hole in the floor would be overlooked....

Then my concerns were derailed as a young, female voice burst out with a single word: "Meanie!" The second syllable strangled upon itself as the speaker burst into sobs.

I unfolded myself from around the artifact I'd been instinctively trying to protect with my body. Not a hunting wolf but an upset child. In that case....

The smart thing to do would have been to hide in my hole until the girl headed back to the bar proper. But I wasn't about to let a kid cry alone.

Instead, I straightened, my head still too low to broach floor level. "Ava?"

Feet pattered toward me, then Dixie Lee's daughter was leaning over the edge of the hole. The bit of her body I could see was backlit against the fluorescents. For one split second, she looked like a fox with a long fluffy tail.

But, no, that was just her hair tied up in a scrunchy. The plump vulpine body I'd thought I'd seen was just a child's head. "Can I come down?" Ava asked, voice far too tentative to emerge from any sort of shifter.

And even though I should have said no, I instead pressed myself against the slick rock wall to make room for her. "Sure."

She landed as lightly as I had in the bottom of the pit, bringing the musky scent of fox along with her. And her eyes latched onto the skull even more quickly than mine had. Reaching out to run one finger across the domed crown, she jerked backwards with a yelped "Ow!"

My eyebrows shot up. The skull had shocked me too the first time I touched it. There'd been no electricity on subsequent contact, though, and Thom had seemed immune.

Then I lost track of that data point as Ava turned to face me. It was almost as if the skull had given her backbone because her statement came out like a demand. "Mom says I can't ask, but I want you to teach me to be a fox!"

Back when I was Ava's age, shifting came as second nature. Unlike most kitsunes, I'd had a star ball from birth, a gift from my dead mother. But that wasn't the ordinary turn of events.

In contrast, my older sister told me she'd woken on her thirteenth birthday to a warm glow above her pillow. Mai had learned to use her star ball at the same time she was wrapping her head around puberty, which, frankly, seemed like a terrible combination. Still, it was the more usual path for a kitsune and was better than the alternative.

The alternative which I suspected the girl beside me suffered from. Ava might smell foxy, but she was entirely human. Human and sensitive enough that she often found it hard to face the world's ugliness, instead disappearing behind books.

I hated to be the one to break the news, but the truth would have to be faced eventually. So—"Do you have a star ball?" I asked.

"Star ball?"

Rather than explaining in words, I drew my magic into its purest form, letting the luminous orb bounce lightly up and down above my fingertips. "This."

Ava's face, lit by the glow of my star ball, turned ethereal. She shook her head, glossy curls bouncing within their ponytail. "No."

"And you're thirteen already?"

Ava's voice took on the tone of a teen being asked a question the adult already knew the answer to. "You came to my party. You saw the candles."

Which meant she lacked what it took to be a full kitsune. Still, I found myself hedging instead of answering outright. "What does your mom say about shifting?"

"She *says* I shouldn't want to."

A clatter of pots from the other side of the wall suggested the mother in question was close enough to catch us at this forbidden conversation if we weren't careful. In response, Ava lowered her voice back to our former conversational murmur.

"She says kitsunes are trouble and my father was a mistake that led to a wonderful daughter." Ava's nose wrinkled up as she repeated words I suspect she'd heard many, many times. "But you're not trouble. You're a *hero*."

"I'm pretty sure I *am* trouble." I mean, I was talking to a kid whose mother clearly didn't want me in her vicinity. But if I was going to sneak around behind Dixie Lee's back, the least I could do was prevent Ava from running off to cry alone in the dark again.

The pit suddenly felt too small for the two of us, so I hoisted myself out and offered Ava a hand up. She barely needed it.

Unfortunately, the leap to floor level didn't manage to knock her off the scent of her preferred topic. "Well?" she demanded. "Will you help me learn to shift?"

There it was—I'd either have to tell the truth or lie to her face. "I don't think you can," I admitted. Then, as Ava's face started to crumple: "But shifting has no bearing on being a hero. Being a hero means sticking up for the underdog. Which, yes, can mean fox teeth or swords, but it can also mean cleverness. Sometimes a well-timed laugh is all it takes to turn the tables."

Ava was still digesting my assertion when her mom called through the wall. "Ava! You ready?"

The girl was halfway to the door when I remembered the fox skull she'd been shocked by. The one that Thom and I had so carefully kept hidden for the past season.

"You can't..."

"...Tell anyone about the skull. I get it. We kitsune keep our secrets."

"And be careful," I demanded.

Ava shrugged, a thread of fox scent hovering in the air behind her as she scampered toward the public side of the bar.

Then I was alone in the Moon Room. Well, alone for a few more minutes until I retreated to my car, pulled on my warmest winter clothes, and settled down in the backseat. Eventually, Pumpkin found me and provided a much-needed lump of warmth near my belly.

I'd finally stopped shivering and started drifting off when a fist pounded on the glass above my head.

Chapter 20

I jolted upright so quickly my head banged against the side of the car. And for one long moment, I couldn't focus on the face pressed close to the glass.

"Well, are you going to open this door or aren't you?"

I recognized Dixie Lee's voice before I managed to blink the tears out of my vision. Recognized her complete lack of patience when she didn't wait for me to obey and instead yanked the door open, letting out all of my hard-won warmth.

"You can't sleep here," she continued, as if we were taking part in a conversation rather than a monologue. "You'll freeze to death, which would be bad publicity for the bar. I have a spare room available. And a shower, which you clearly, badly need."

I blinked. Maybe this was some sort of nightmare? Dixie Lee would morph into a monster who bit my head off at midnight, crunching up my bones with long, sharp teeth. Or she'd lead me to her house only to laugh in my face and lock me out in the cold afterwards.

Still, the human woman who'd taken a dislike to me months ago appeared very corporeal as she tapped her foot, waiting for me to say something. Eventually, I obliged her.

"Last I heard, Bertrand was staying in your spare room."

The other woman's lips pursed, the elbows of her crossed arms jutting out aggressively. "You clearly haven't been paying attention. Bertrand slept there for a couple of days last fall to keep Ava safe. That's everything going on between us."

"Are you sure? He doesn't seem to think that's everything."

"Well, we may be dating occasionally. But we're certainly not moving in together. I have a child."

"Taking things slow, eh?"

"Pot meet kettle."

We glared at each other for one long moment, then Dixie Lee circled back around to her point. "Do you want the bed or not?"

I did. The honest truth was that I'd been wiggling my chilled toes ever since I woke up, hoping to work some feeling back into them. And Pumpkin, my backup foot warmer, had fled toward the bar as soon as Dixie Lee opened the car door.

But—"You don't like me. Why are you offering?"

"Because you're desperate."

I waited, knowing there was more to it. And, finally, Dixie Lee rolled her eyes. "Plus, I have an infestation. I don't want Ava exposed to pesticides and I can't handle the bugs in my house any longer. You seemed like the lesser of two evils."

Which is how I came to spend the rest of the week snapping up stink bugs, which were even more vile tasting that the name suggested.

Stink bugs weren't all I hunted that week either. I hunted Kaito's killer as best I could, visiting the burned-down hulk of the house he'd died inside and sniffing around the exterior. Unfortunately, the villain hadn't handily dropped a business card with a name and address on it. And when I got Ito's number from Charlie and tried to call him to press for more information about his brother, he hung up at the sound of my voice.

Which left the pack to investigate. Something that Thom accidentally made easier.

I wasn't thinking about investigations, though, when we ran into each other on the street that first Monday. "I have a proposal," Thom said, drawing me out of the flow of pedestrians.

"Yes?" The word emerged breathier than I meant it to. My back straightened, my chin yearning upward. I had a sinking suspicion my posture was just as adoring as Ava's had been an hour earlier when I gave her tips on midair splits.

I half expected Thom to step away. To at least put emotional distance between us. Instead, he leaned in closer, dropping his voice to a deep rumble.

"The pack bond. It feels strange to you because you haven't spent unstructured time around any of us. How would you feel about hanging out before my shift begins?"

My reluctance to commit to Gate City and its alpha didn't stem from unfamiliarity with the pack bond, but I would take whatever time Thom was offering. "Alone?" I asked, expecting him to shake his head and mutter about family curses.

Instead, blue eyes pierced mine, Thom's smile warming my insides. "Alone," he confirmed, before adding: "In fur."

And, yes, four-legged we couldn't get up to any hanky-panky. The first day, we spent the entire time watching an action flick, Thom's huge wolf tongue licking invisible dirt out my erect fox ears while I struggled not to yawn at the total lack of character development on the screen. The whole time, his pack bond curled around me like a curious puppy and I neither avoided nor accepted its advances.

When Thom's work beckoned, he shifted in the bathroom, waiting longer than I needed before coming back out to join me. But his question then was as warm as the stolen heat that lingered within my body. "Tomorrow? Same time, same place?"

I nodded. Boring movie or no boring movie, I was definitely up for more of the same.

But the next day, Thom didn't just put on something he thought I'd like. He considered me while scrolling past streaming options then paused when he came to my favorite show. Raising one eyebrow, he asked, "More your style?"

I hesitated. Family drama wasn't the sort of thing tough swordfighters watched during their downtime. Plus, "How'd you know that's my secret indulgence?"

"I'm a bartender. I pay attention."

And I paid attention, half an hour later, when the lights went briefly dark and Thom shifted back to two legs to fix the technology. This wasn't a date and Thom was trying hard to keep sex off the table, so I did my level best not to stare at his butt.

I tried so hard that I experienced a minor epiphany in the process.

The Gate City pack bond that had once again danced around me all evening might not be something I was comfortable accepting now, or maybe ever. But it was a tool worth utilizing, a way to find out whether the local werewolves had anything to do with Kaito's demise.

Because I could feel hints of emotions coursing down the bond as connections flowed toward Thom and past me. Tidbits of surface thoughts. Nothing incriminating or Thom would have noticed. But I was a fox; I could recognize when a thread was shielded by subterfuge.

So I grabbed a particularly skittish tendril after shifting back to human form at the end of our non-date. I ran my hand along the length of the pack bond until it split then split then split again. Each time, I kept myself attuned to the one darkened thread, not that I could physically see it. In fact, outside Thom's presence, I wouldn't have even known pack bonds existed if I hadn't already wrapped this one around my wrist.

I was starting to think the sneakiness I'd scented was all in my imagination...until I trotted up a street toward a house like Charlie's—paint bright, no dangling trim, carefully mulched flower beds. A woman's silhouette was visible through one curtained window while a human man, briefcase in hand, strode out the front.

At the same moment, a shifter I knew in passing slipped in through the back.

I crept closer, materializing my star ball into a sword as I waited for the shatter of breaking objects. A scream maybe.

Instead, a woman's throaty voice murmured, "Perfect timing." Through the lacy curtain, the pair recreated Klimt's *Kiss*.

So, yes, that particular shifter was up to something illicit. But his subterfuge was consensual and far from a danger to the pack.

Despite striking out on Tuesday, I continued pack-bond hunting for the rest of the week. I learned that Hank's kid brother skipped school to run in the forest—although when I caught him with only his first shoe off, his face turned beet red and he suddenly decided education was a better bet. On Thursday, the shifter I tracked down was shoplifting—that one I tattled about to his alpha. And on Friday the best I could come up with was a very healthy werewolf calling in sick to work.

The trouble with my plan, and likely the reason Thom hadn't taken a similar approach, was that pack bonds only presented a tiny sliver of each shifter's thoughts and actions. And Kaito's death was fading from all of our realities quickly. Even the roiling in my stomach had begun to ease up.

But a sworn oath wasn't the only reason to do right by Kaito. He was Charlie's pack mate. He had links to Gate City. Somewhere back in his history, he bore kitsune blood.

Plus, there was always the possibility, no matter how minor, that his murderer could come after my sister and her children. So I took on the task willingly, dead ends notwithstanding.

I was still trying to think up a new avenue of exploration when an opportunity to sleuth arose in the form of a Friday afternoon attack.

Chapter 21

"**I**nvasion!" Hank sprinted into the bar with his cowboy hat nearly falling off his head and no concern for the wide-eyed humans who immediately started muttering questions.

Dixie Lee was the one who saved our bacon. "The British Invasion? Yes, I do think it's time for some Beatles." She cranked up the volume on the sound system, shimmied her hips, and soon half the barflies were singing along to *Sgt Pepper's Lonely Heart's Club Band.*

Focus diverted, the shifters present subtly melted away into the Moon Room's human-free interior. From there, after very little discussion, we piled into vehicles and raced for the invasion point while Thom debriefed Hank.

The latter had been on patrol east of the city when he stumbled across a fresh scent trail. He'd stalked closer, seen at least a dozen human-form shifters hiking into Gate City territory, and had figured retrieving backup was smarter than engaging in direct attack.

"Agreed," Thom said, deftly steering the minivan he'd commandeered in the indicated direction. "But, perhaps, next time you could tell me in private? Where humans aren't listening?"

In the front passenger seat, Hank's cowboy hat sunk lower as his chin tilted downward. "Yes, Chief Faris. Although I don't understand why you cater to meat."

Thom—who I suspected had never before heard that term for non-shifters—was silent for a moment too long. So I inserted myself into the conversation, pushing my words up between the seats in front of me. "We don't use slurs like *meat* here."

Hank snorted very softly and this time when Thom came to a turn in the road, he wrenched the wheel more aggressively than was really necessary. "Kira speaks the truth," he growled. "You may have come from an old-fashioned pack, but things are done differently here."

Hank's scent instantly grew submissive. "Yes, Chief Faris. I won't use the word again."

There was no time for further discussion, because we'd reached our destination. Doors slammed as shifters hopped out, some two-legged and some already in wolf form. The forest encroached on the city here, a park giving way to private woodlots then to national forest. It was an easy access point for invaders, although I would have thought they'd travel on lupine paws.

The reason for their choice became clear as men stepped out of long tree shadows. They'd circled around so they came from the direction of the sun, but that wasn't the biggest danger. The danger lay in the grace with which each shifter moved and the sword clenched in each man's fist.

Of course. Most traditional packs trained in swordsmanship.

Unfortunately, ours didn't. There were a few weapons in our vehicles, or so I assumed when mutterings and rustlings suggested Gate City shifters were retreating in search of blades. But I'd seen these guys fight. Most used the hack-and-hope technique.

It wouldn't be nearly enough.

What would have shut things down immediately was my vial of alpha blood, the one that sat in the bottom of my backpack in Dixie Lee's spare bedroom. I squinted into the lowering sun, trying to count invaders silhouetted against the blazing light. How could we turn the tables on these shifters so the battle didn't come down to a contest of swordsmanship?

While I was still grasping at mental straws, Thom strode forward. Hands empty, his voice held just the right amount of alpha command. "You look lost, neighbor. Perhaps you didn't realize Gate City territory began three miles that way."

He jerked his chin in the proper direction, but the Reed alpha didn't pay the gesture any attention. Instead, Chief Reed raised what appeared to be a monocle to his right eye, head swinging slowly from side to side.

The gesture was clearly theater—I mean, who used monocles in the twenty-first century? Still, if our enemy was assessing us then I could take the time to do the same.

He was a fit man on the upper end of middle age. A sword that appeared almost too ornamental to be functional dangled from what I knew from experience was a deceptively relaxed en-garde position. That plus his playacting suggested our enemy would toy with his prey, perhaps long enough for....

Just as an idea struck, Chief Reed's gaze landed on me. I knew, not because I could see his eyes with his whole body backlit, but because I could *feel* them. Gauging me. Weighing me.

I shivered. This alpha might enjoy the limelight, but he wasn't empty-brained or a lightweight. Not nearly.

Then, with the faintest shift of his posture, the intensity of his focus returned to Thom. "You're a new alpha," Chief Reed murmured. "But surely even you understand tit for tat?"

His words hung heavy in the chilling air as he lunged forward, his sword aimed at Thom's unprotected chest.

Thom, as far as I knew, had even less experience with swords than his underlings did. I'd certainly never known him to spar. Saw at a glance that he bore no weapon now.

So I sprinted toward the narrowing space between the two pack leaders, my star-ball sword extending my reach not quite enough to make any difference. Still I tried, pushing every hint of vulpine speed into my stride even though I knew the effort wasn't going to work.

Thom's name hung in my throat, but I didn't voice it. Didn't want to distract him from the imminent danger slicing toward his skin.

I almost didn't see the blade spiraling through the air above us all. A sword functional instead of ornamental. It glinted with sunlight, blinding me for one split second.

It didn't blind Thom. Without being warned, without turning, Thom lifted his hand and the hilt thudded perfectly into his grip.

And it turned out I was wrong about something else also. Thom had skill. His blade sliced through the air as if it wasn't made of steel but rather of magic. He countered the Reed alpha's blow and thrust forward with an attack of his own.

After that, there was no time for further posturing, verbal or otherwise. Enemy swordsmen surged forward out of the sun-drenched west and those of us with weapons countered. In terms of overall numbers, the two sides were evenly matched. But Gate City shifters in lupine form were soon beaten back to the safety of our vehicles. Teeth and claws were no match for long, sharp blades.

That left our side outnumbered, but the Reed shifters didn't band together to overcome the weaponed few remaining. Instead, the enemies I tried to engage shunted me sideways then forward, forcing me through the maelstrom of battle and closer to their alpha.

An alpha who had subtly turned Thom over to two of his pack mates and waited, grinning, for me to approach. He had something in mind that required a kitsune. Or maybe he intended to use me against Thom.

Well, that was fine. I was glad to deal with Chief Reed directly. After all, my aborted hunt within Thom's pack had turned up no leads. The man before me was now my top suspect in Kaito's murder. He and I had a lot to discuss.

The Reed alpha would make his confession at the point of a weapon, I decided. But his underlings were likely to turn protective if I appeared too proficient. So I mimicked Ava and shrank in on myself. I allowed my blade to slip a few times, allowed swords to nearly—but not quite—cut through my guard as I was herded where they and I both wanted me to go.

Then, at last, I stood in front of the Reed alpha. My heart rate was elevated just enough to get my blood pumping but not enough to slow my reflexes. My opponent's breath, in contrast, wheezed in and out like a winded race horse.

He was older than I'd thought, I decided, considering the nearly invisible wrinkles lining his forehead. Older and, I hoped, as cocky as most alpha werewolves tended to be around small-statured women.

I lined myself up for the attack that would lay him out flat...then I tripped. Feet flew out from under me. My sword slapped the ground one second before knees and hands followed.

Chief Reed's elbow was around my throat before I could rebalance myself.

Chapter 22

Thom must have communicated a stark command via the pack bond. Because he didn't speak, but every Gate City shifter instantly fell still and silent. The only sound was the wheeze of the Reed alpha's breathing as he knelt behind me. That plus my own blood pounding in my ears.

Then the tendril of pack bond that had bounced enthusiastically around my shoulders during Thom's and my fur-form mornings slid through my fingers like a cat's tail. Questing, begging for entrance. All I had to do was accept the connection, then the two of us could speak mind to mind, collaborate, get me out of this gnarly mess....

I didn't accept. Couldn't. Still, perhaps the tendril could be used to prevent Thom from doing anything rash?

To that end, as the Reed alpha pulled my back up against his chest, I wiggled my fingers. Stroked the pack bond, soothing it. Promising this wasn't as bad as it looked.

I could only hope I was right.

I wasn't given time to learn whether I'd gotten my point across. Instead, I was being spun around to face Chief Reed, who might be past his prime but was definitely no weakling. So quickly I couldn't break free, he'd shifted his grip on my neck from an elbow to the opposite hand, fingers clenched tight enough to partially restrict my breathing. The sword he'd dropped when he initially pinned me was now back in his dominant hand. The tip eased forward like a stalking rattlesnake, turning me a trifle cross-eyed as it halted too close for comfort to my face.

This I hadn't counted on. I relaxed my muscles with an effort. "Perhaps we could talk about this," I started.

"The only thing we have to discuss," Chief Reed growled, "is an eye for an eye." Then the blade struck.

I had only one millisecond to think that, perhaps, I'd misjudged the Reed alpha. A millisecond to realize that changing to fox form and back wouldn't replace an eyeball gouged out. And if the sword tip continued into my brain...well, then I was toast.

Searing pain followed. I yelped and Thom snarled something that wasn't words yet was clearly a threat to exact gross bodily damage. Hot blood slid down my cheek.

But I seized onto the pack tendril and shook it. *No,* I thought as hard as I could, even though I knew Thom wouldn't hear me. The cut was painful but it wasn't maiming. Chief Reed's reference to eyes had been metaphorical. He'd merely sliced open my skin.

And, somehow, Thom must have understood. Because there was no eruption of renewed battle. Just the distant gurgle of a stream and the faint shuffle of feet on leaves.

I blinked hard and Chief Reed's face came back into focus. His cheekbone, I now noted, boasted a relatively fresh scar. One I'd likely made last fall while harvesting blood to twist him and his pack around my little finger. One that mirrored the cut now seeping bodily fluids onto my own face.

So I wasn't surprised when the alpha jerked his head and a pack mate strode forward to take the sword out of his hand. We both watched as my blood was scraped down into a small glass jar. The viscous liquid lay in the bottom, bright red and, as far as I knew, completely useless.

After all, I was a kitsune. Chief Reed was not.

But he had taken from me what I'd taken from him. Had taken what he wanted and—swiping up dirt from beside us and scrubbing it into my wound while holding my head steady with that harsh hand at my neck—had ensured I'd bear a scar to match his own.

Obsessed with appearances. Yes, I'd judged him correctly. I could only hope he would continue to act to type.

I bided my time as Chief Reed settled back on his heels, not releasing me but waiting out the tears that blocked my vision in response to the wound abrasion. Only once I'd blinked my sight clear again did he intone: "Now we're even."

I was the one who shook my head, well as much as I could with his fist still half-choking me. I was the one who swallowed hard then managed words. "Nowhere near."

My opponent raised a single eyebrow. "No? You tested our boundaries and we tested yours. You took my blood and I took yours."

"And Kaito?" Despite my intention to keep this conversation light, my heart started racing. This was the moment I'd been waiting for. The point of this farce. "Do you think he'd call this even?"

Chief Reed's brow wrinkled further. The hand around my throat loosened. "I have no idea who you're referring to."

This close to the Reed alpha, I could smell the truth on his breath. Not that it meant anything. He likely had never bothered to learn the name of the man he'd murdered.

And it was time for me to turn the tables. Because I hadn't tripped accidentally. I'd fallen entirely on purpose, morphing my star ball from sword to skinny dagger when I landed on top of it. The hand that hadn't been stroking the pack bond a moment earlier had secreted the weapon in the hidden spot between my bent leg's thigh and calf.

Now, I whipped my dagger out of its concealment. One sharp edge landed a millimeter above Chief Reed's left eye before he knew what was happening. A murmur from behind us went still as I halved the already minute distance between blade and flesh.

Only when our conversation was once again the only sound did I make my demand. "You will admit to the murder." I let my dagger just barely skim across his blinking eyelashes before I added: "*Now.*"

To his credit, Chief Reed didn't release my throat and scramble backwards. He didn't signal to his pack to begin fighting either. Instead, he laughed, the deep rumble similar to Thom's in timbre but lacking familiar warmth at the bottom.

This alpha would make a bad opponent. I shivered, knowing he already was our enemy, and that I was making him more of one with every second I held a blade above his eye.

Just as second thoughts started spiraling to epic proportions, Chief Reed agreed. "I'll gladly admit to murder. But which one in particular?"

The oath I'd sworn twisted in my gut. Kaito had been killed by a man who didn't even find the act memorable.

And that was enough to make me forget how reckless I was being. Instead, I took my time, my words a tribute to Charlie's fallen pack mate.

"Do you remember the fox-scented male who visited your territory during three successive full moons? He died in a house fire a week ago. His name was Kaito. He was a good man with a loving family and he will be missed."

Chief Reed considered me for one long moment. Then he shook his head just the faintest fraction, even though my dagger skimmed his lashes each time he moved. "Your Kaito is not one of the notches on my war belt," he promised. "You, little fox, are barking up the wrong tree."

Chapter 23

The alpha's words smelled like truth, which didn't mean no one in his pack had killed Kaito. Still, there was a limit to how long I could keep a pack leader pinned without bringing further repercussions down upon Gate City. So I eased my dagger back inch by inch as Chief Reed released his grip on my throat at the same snail's pace. Finally, skin prickling, I turned my back on danger and strode to Thom's side.

"Remember this," Chief Reed called after me. "Tit for tat."

I turned to find that the sun had fallen below the horizon, lack of glare making it easy to see Gate City and Reed pack mates separating into two lines. The battle was apparently over. Sure enough, with a jerk of his chin, both Chief Reed and his underlings faded into the trees, not heading west toward Gate City this time but traveling east toward his own land.

For his part, Thom's white-knuckled fists suggested his patience had run thin. Keeping his attention on my face, he growled an order over my shoulder: "Bertrand, Hank, escort our uninvited guests to the border."

"Yes, alpha."

Receding footsteps proved they'd obeyed him, but the reek of barely repressed fury continued roiling off the man in front of me. I understood why when one of his fists eased open and he reached up to almost, but not quite, touch my wound.

"I'm fine," I reassured him. "I'll shift and it'll fade to almost nothing."

"Then we can celebrate." A werewolf who'd always given me the cold shoulder in the past strode up to clap me on the back. "Meet up at the bar?"

Jubilation was already breaking out among Thom's pack mates. We hadn't precisely won, but my sneak attack had apparently given them a reason to howl and frolic. Not that, with werewolves, it took much to reach that point.

Their alpha, however, wasn't ready to embrace the relief of a battle ended with no major injuries. "First-aid kit," he demanded and someone handed over a red box with a white cross on top. "Water bottle?" Half a dozen shifters offered what he'd requested.

So I knew what was coming before Thom warned: "This will sting."

Water slapped my wound, cold and painful. It made sense to irrigate out as much dirt as possible, but I still yelped despite myself.

And Thom swore, flinging the borrowed water bottle at a tree trunk where it struck with a rather unsatisfying crackle. Despite the complete lack of damage to anything other than disposable plastic, I winced. Rage was out of character for this man who usually took gentleness to extremes.

"Thom," I started. But his body had turned away from me, toward Reed territory. His alpha scent had turned dark and dangerous.

Tit for tat. Anything Thom did now would blow back on the pack later.

"Thom," I repeated, grabbing his wrist. "Cool it."

Around us, the sounds of celebration ceased. But I ignored watchful eyes, focusing only on the man in front of me. The man who was still facing a forest darkening by the second, just like our future if he gave in to simmering rage.

"This is what it means to be a werewolf," I reminded him, keeping my voice as low as possible. "Blood and wounds but also pack and responsibilities."

It wasn't wise to school an alpha in public, but I didn't think Thom would care. Still, he didn't answer for one long moment. Didn't turn back to face me for far too long.

Then, finally, he did. His breath teased the hair off my forehead as he murmured so low only the closest few shifters could hear him. "You're not, though, are you? Not a werewolf. Not pack."

So that's what this was about. Not just my wound but the fact I hadn't accepted the pack bond even when I appeared to be in mortal danger.

A wind picked up, blowing through the trees with all the ice of January. "No," I admitted. "No, I'm not."

I hadn't wanted to lie, but I fully expected my words to make matters worse. They didn't. Instead, Thom's shoulders relaxed as he opened the first-aid kit. "Can you handle an alcohol pad?" he asked.

I nodded. Then his huge left hand was cupping my face, thumb beneath my chin and warm fingers sliding up into my hairline. I shivered, but not from pain this time. I had a crazy urge to lean into this single point of contact, as if a hand on my cheek could hold my entire body up.

It couldn't, of course, and I didn't ask it to. But I did focus on seizing every bit of pleasure while Thom ripped open a sterile packet then dabbed unbearably gently at the wound on the side of my face. The disinfection hurt, but not enough to overcome the warmth suffusing me. Not enough to make me jerk away from his skin touching my skin.

"All done." Despite his words, Thom didn't release me. True night was falling and I could no longer make out the blue of his eyes. Instead, they'd turned dark and deep, pits I could fall into and lose all sense of reality. I wanted nothing more than to fall.

"Shift," he murmured, thumb stroking my cheekbone, "and we'll drop you off at Charlie's."

That woke me back up. Despite spending many hours together this week, Thom and I hadn't really gotten much time to talk. We'd been furry for most of it. And, when we weren't furry, he was managing the Full Moon Saloon.

"I'm not staying at Charlie's," I admitted. "Dixie Lee lent me her guest room."

Thom's eyebrows rose as his hand fell away. "Dixie Lee? Helps me run the bar? Has a kid? *That* Dixie Lee?"

"Do you know another one?"

Amusement curled around me like the questing pack bond had earlier. Thom's lips twitched. "No. I just wouldn't have thought...." Rather than finishing his sentence, he shrugged. "Alright, we'll drop you off at Dixie Lee's."

So I donned fur and rode in Thom's lap back to Gate City. His fingers curled behind my ears, soothing me as I drifted into the half-awake state of bodily healing.

The wound had really only been a scratch, though. Not like last time. Not enough to knock me flat on my back. So after a shower, I headed to the bar. The pack would be celebrating tonight and I wanted to celebrate with them.

"They're in the Moon Room," Dixie Lee observed when I strode into the dim, throbbing interior. It was Friday night and the place was packed. No wonder she thrust a tray overloaded with drinks into my hands. "Take this in and save me a minute."

Through the next door, I found a situation like yet unlike that within the bar proper. Most of the shifters who called Gate City home seemed to be present, but the lack of authority figures—Thom, Bertrand, Hank—gave the room an air of wildness. Still, Dixie Lee must have thought things were under control because Ava was parked in one corner. Her library book was open, but the girl's eyes sparkled as she watched the celebrating werewolves over the top of an ice-cream float.

I offered the girl a smile then scanned for danger as the timbre of chatter shifted like a moody wind. The only change I could see was Hank's kid brother ambling in from the parking-lot entrance, his litheness making him appear positively skinny beside all of the burly werewolves. The youngster had to be barely old enough to shift if you measured age by his complete lack of facial hair. But the adult werewolves included him...in a manner of speaking.

"Kid!" The shifter who'd snuck in the back of a human's house earlier in the week greeted the boy with a hearty back thump. The youngster stumbled and would have fallen if the backslapper hadn't grabbed his collar to keep him upright. Then, taking one exaggerated sniff, the older man bellowed: "Kid! You stink!"

Alcohol colored the crowd's responses. "Kid needs a shower!" someone else suggested. Three other shifters roared approval.

From the other side of the room and with the crowd closing ranks, I couldn't see who was involved now. Could only hear the youngster's fear when he squeaked: "No, that won't be necessary."

Unfortunately, his words were lost in the cascade of drunken shouting. "Shower, shower, shower!"

Shifters twice his size were dragging the kid toward the Moon Room's bathroom and he was trying so hard to wriggle free that I heard the distinct sound of a collar rip. "Please, stop!" The boy's shriek gritted against my teeth.

Okay, this had passed straight out of friendly ribbing and into uncool hazing. I eyed the tray of drinks Dixie Lee had given me, decided it was more of an impediment than an asset, and dropped it on the closest flat surface before spinning...right into a werewolf's unyielding chest.

"Not your problem." Tall, bald, and one of the shifters who'd muttered loudest about how crazy it was to let a kitsune stay in Gate City. This was the worst person I could have run into right at the present moment.

Still, I was faster than any over-muscled werewolf. Or I should have been.

I tried to dart around the wall of werewolf, but the energy I'd used up healing the wound on my cheek into a thread-thin scar caught up with me. The werewolf's hand latched onto my shoulder even as the door to the bathroom slammed into the Moon Room wall.

Chapter 24

The gush of running water and the hoots of werewolves swirled around me as I considered a knife at the neck or a knee to the groin. Both were beyond the pale in a non-lethal fight against a semi-friendly pack mate.

But the scent of the kid's fear was so strong it scratched against the inside of my nostrils. And, after all, I wasn't really pack....

To everyone's surprise, Ava was the one who put a halt to the hazing. Her laughter started quietly then trilled higher and louder. The shower didn't stop, but the hooting did.

"What's the joke?" someone called. From the way his voice was no longer muffled by intervening walls, it was clear he—and maybe others—had reemerged from the bathroom.

"You are." Ava's voice was choked with barely repressed laughter. "*You*, who I saw rolling in rabbit poop last week, are making fun of someone else's body odor?"

"Well...."

Rather than letting him make the point that wolves roll in shit for several very functional reasons, Ava moved on. "And *you*." I presumed she was pointing at another werewolf, not that I could see around baldie, who'd swiveled to watch but hadn't let go of me in the process. "You ate opossum guts last fall. In *public*. That's pretty disgusting if you ask me."

Sheepish scents proved Ava was onto something. If she really was able to shame this pack into letting Hank's kid brother go, I'd beg Mai to dig deeper into kitsune history to figure out if there was any chance of the offspring of a human shifting

Never mind that Dixie Lee wanted nothing more than for her daughter to grow up with her shifter blood tamped down out of sight.

The overall mood of the crowd, though, was undecided. Ava was, after all, just a thirteen-year-old who might smell slightly of fox on occasion. And these were not only werewolves but the rough-and-tumble sort who'd lived outside packs for months or years before washing up on Thom's doorstep.

Ava clearly needed backup. So, as soon as the bald shifter's hold on my shoulder loosened, I wrenched myself free and headed in the kid's direction. Not that I needed to. It turned out Thom had gotten there first.

He must have felt something going on through the pack bond. That's the only explanation I could give for him showing up in the nick of time. Whatever the reason, his presence now resolved the room's mishmash of conflicting odors into instant attention.

"*Let the kid go,*" he commanded, pressing alpha bite into the few short syllables. "And head home. We've all been invited to a wake tomorrow. I expect you to show up in suits and on your best behavior." Then, turning to the kid, he offered one final order: "You will come smelling of soap."

The reason Ito had invited us to his brother's memorial service became clear the following morning when I pulled into the driveway of the burnt-out house. Most obviously, the ashy ruins were within Thom's territory and no one even shifter-adjacent would be wise to enter without his permission. Add to that the fact that the funeral party—minus shanghaied werewolves—was tiny. Just Ito and Jessie, as far as I could tell.

Which meant the lack of social graces of our contingent turned the entire event awkward. Ties and collars were loosened...then retightened as Thom glared at the offending parties. Half-assed condolences were offered by shifters who had very clearly never met the deceased. And one socially inept werewolf mistook the shrine topped with Kaito's favorite foods for a tableful of hors d'oeuvres.

Ito's beeline was so rapid he almost moved like a shifter. "Please don't eat that." Despite his mild tone, his eyes flashed.

And rather than apologizing, the werewolf in question spit out the entire mouthful he'd already started chewing. His face wrinkled up in disgust as he clapped Ito on the shoulder. "Thanks for the warning, man. That stuff tastes like dirty feet."

"As opposed to clean ones. Since you've tasted both and have such a discerning palate." Thom's tone was wry as he smoothed over that faux pas. Which left me free to address a different potential powder keg.

Because Charlie had joined us, but she wasn't alone. Instead, another woman gracefully emerged from the passenger side of the vehicle, her skin darker than mine and her hair shaved on the sides.

I was instantly intrigued but also wished Charlie hadn't chosen this moment for introductions. Because Thom was a gentleman, but some of these werewolves? Well, I could see feet yearning to become acquainted with mouths.

I'd rather be by Charlie's side if anything untoward happened. But muddy lawn squelched beneath the dress shoes I'd donned out of respect, a recipe for moving just a little too slowly....

Sure enough, the girlfriend was already deep in conversation by the time I was close enough to hear what was happening. She appeared to be making small talk about plant-based diets with someone who ripped the throats out of deer on a regular occasion.

"Protein levels are essential," she concluded.

Rick—not one of the sharpest werewolves in the pack—frowned once, then offered what he seemed to consider a suitable rejoinder. "So you're, like, one of those Mexicans?"

"I think the word you're looking for is *Latina*. Are you aware of how many countries there are south of the U.S. border?"

Rick wasn't. I could tell by the way his face screwed up in deep thought.

But the girlfriend had already turned away with a murmured "Excuse me" while Charlie whispered in her ear. I waved as my friend's head rose. Our eyes met...and Charlie shook her head once, fast and clear.

No, she wasn't going to introduce me to the new significant other. Instead, she guided her guest in the opposite direction. Toward Jessie, whose scent was so pained I could smell it out in the open where odors usually dispersed quickly.

Which made sense. Twins before...well, anything. And, at first, it appeared that Jessie felt the same way.

"I'm so glad you're here, Charlie," she murmured, tears welling up but not quite falling. "I'm so grateful...."

Unlike her honest-smelling words, Jessie's actions were calculated. She pushed between the two women, hugging her sister while presenting her back to the girlfriend.

I winced and lingered, ready to ride to the rescue if Charlie wanted me to. But the truth was that my presence would likely make matters worse.

So, after a few moments, I drifted in a different direction. Toward Ava, who looked just as pained in her prim, flounced dress as the werewolves did in their ties and dress shirts.

"Not your idea of fun?" I asked.

Among so many people, Ava had turned silent. She shook her head, library book hugged tighter than I'd seen her hug it for quite a while.

So I took pity on her. "I don't think your mom would mind if you read in the car for a while."

The relief on the girl's face was enough to fuel the next hour of wishing I was also young enough to hide behind a library book. But awkwardness was manageable. Gently suggesting that it wasn't a good idea for high-energy werewolves to turn the charred timbers of the house into a jungle gym was manageable.

What wasn't manageable was the way my eye caught on the waning moon, hanging half full in the sky, and my stomach dropped into my too-tight shoes.

Suddenly, I didn't care about werewolves unable to embrace the solemnity of the occasion. I didn't care about new girlfriends who weren't finding this gathering as welcoming as they'd anticipated. I didn't care about the way Ito had taken one look at me as I advanced to present my condolences and suddenly found the remembrances of a shifter who'd once driven by the nursing home where Kaito had been maintained during his coma deeply riveting.

Instead, all I cared about was finding Thom. Ripping his clothes off. Consummating the attraction that had been coursing between us for three long months now without a shred of resolution.

Skin on skin. Mouth on mouth. I wasn't waiting any longer.

I was taking what I wanted, what I needed. *Now.*

Chapter 25

"**H**ey!" The shifter I'd elbowed out of my path shouted further complaints after me, but I didn't answer. Just barreled forward, peering left and right as I searched for Thom.

"I'd thought Ava's father might be here." That was Dixie Lee, who I strode past without acknowledging. Beside her, Ito's scent was redolent with resigned pain I couldn't care less about.

"He returned to Japan years ago." Ito's words trailed after me, meaningless. Well, almost meaningless. Some tiny fragment of self latched onto them, filing the information away for later as he continued. "The kitsunes there are always glad to expand their honor guards. Being with a mistress is...addictive."

"I know." Dixie Lee's voiced faded behind me. "I'd just hoped he could resist."

The fragment of self wondered if perhaps this was why Ito had kept me at swords' length back in Charlie's backyard. If that might be why he'd been so opposed to my presence in the Raven twins' lives back in college and was resolutely avoiding me now.

But the moon was tugging me harder than ever. I found myself panting, my mouth hanging open as I heaved in great gulps of air, tasting, testing. Suddenly, even that fragment of self was submerged by the hunt for...*wolf, wolf, wolf, but where was the alpha?*

There. He was talking to three other werewolves, not that they mattered. All that mattered was Thom's proximity. The electricity that sparked up my spine the moment he glanced in my direction. The alpha was here and he was mine.

"Kira." Thom greeted me with the warm smile that always turned my stomach a little gooey. This time, though, I gasped, the indulgence of a single word sealing my tongue against the roof of my mouth.

I couldn't speak. Couldn't demand what I wanted.

Well, not with words. I was close enough to touch him though. To climb his delicious body like a tree until I was high enough to clench my legs around his hips, to rub my center against a ridge that hardened the instant I touched it. With one hand, I clung to his shoulder. With the other, I fumbled at his belt.

The intricacies of the buckle evaded me. I growled, nipping at the flesh just beneath his chin. *Now, now, now, open!*

Rather than helping, a hard hand clenched around my right wrist. "Kira. Stop this."

I whimpered out pain, anger, denial. Thom must have only heard the pain because he swore and released me.

Then air was brushing past my skin. Powerful hips jolted as he carried me away from the crowd.

Not that the where mattered. What mattered was the way Thom's movement rubbed me just the right way.

This time the sound I made was pure pleasure. I grabbed onto the tie that might as well have been invented to assist in kissing. Pulled until Thom's head lowered toward mine.

He smelled like wood ash and alpha. No, the ash wasn't coming from Thom, but from all around us.

That would be sensually intriguing. Slick ashes against naked bodies. The sun above, the earth below, we'd merge and....

I growled. Thom's head hadn't lowered after that first inch. His belt was still buckled.

And now something invisible yet fully tangible looped around my upper arms. First loose then tighter and tighter....

I was immobile before I knew what was happening. Was being lowered to the ground just slowly enough for me to get my feet under me.

I strained forward but found myself unable to advance toward my target. I was bound by the unaccepted pack bond.

"The moon isn't even full."

Thom's words made no sense as I battled against the inflexible bindings. Battled then ceased as a method of escape grew clear.

"Are you feeling better?" Thom's piercing blue eyes met mine, his head cocked just a little.

Better? I had no idea what he was talking about. But I nodded, and that appeared to be the correct answer.

Because the invisible tether loosened just the tiniest fraction. And I leaned into that weakness, shifting to fox form as I wriggled free of both bonds and clothing, regaining my humanity as soon as I was free.

Bare feet sank into ash that was just as soft as I'd imagined. Yes, this would form a delightful cushion for both of us.

I tackled Thom and he grunted as I struck him. But he didn't topple over. Too strong, too stable.

Too *alpha*. I purred. I'd lost that move, but I'd also won.

My hands splayed across his chest. Slid into the gap between buttons. Thom muttered another curse, followed by: "I should have sent you home when I had the chance."

The word *home* was an icicle slicing through my passion. I hesitated, almost understanding. Shaking my head hard, I managed a single word: "No."

Then Thom was walking again, and this time he was holding me in his arms rather than letting me slide up and down against his arousal. I wriggled around, trying to regain the craved connection. I was naked. This should be easy.

When Thom dropped me, I wasn't ready. Couldn't twist and get my feet under me. Instead, I landed butt first in ice-cold water. Spluttered out shock and anger as he dunked me once, twice, three times in a flowing stream that stank of muck.

Muck and oil. Some sort of dark substance washed off my skin, sluicing away atop the stream. As it did so, frigid reason reasserted itself.

"Okay." My teeth chattered. I was freezing...and mortified. "It's gone. You can stop."

Thom did. Drew me out of the water, tugged off his suit jacket, and wrapped me up in it. Pulling me close, his body heat stilled my shivers. Chin resting atop my head, he murmured, "We have to find a way to prevent this from happening."

"Or," I countered, "we could just let it happen." Because, despite the dunking, despite having chosen the absolute worst moment to try to tear Thom's clothes off...I didn't want to let him go now.

Not when his warmth was so seductive. His strength so tantalizing. Even without the moon's influence, I craved this connection to Thom.

And, yes, there was the issue of consent. But if we both agreed beforehand....

"No." Thom's muscles tensed, and at first I thought he was going to push me away again. Argue the point I'd raised the same way we'd argued it before.

Only, he addressed someone else over my head instead of me. "Dixie Lee, I'm afraid this is a bad time."

"I can see that." Her voice was just as curt as ever, her scent containing a seesaw of fury and terror. No amusement, though. No smugness at catching me naked at a formal event.

I was the one who pushed myself away from Thom, ignoring my lack of clothing. "What is it?" I demanded, shivers starting back up again. I was only half dry and the air bit like wolf teeth.

Plus, something about the wildness of Dixie Lee's eyes suggested our world wasn't going to get better in the near future. Instead, the icy slither of cold air down my back warned it was about to get much, much worse.

Sure enough, Dixie Lee swallowed hard before finding words. Then she told us, "I can't find Ava. I've looked everywhere, but she's gone."

Chapter 26

For an instant, I relaxed. "I sent your kid back to read in the car. She was miserable."

"So you're responsible. I should have figured as much." Dixie Lee spun away from me, facing Thom only as she explained. "No one has seen my daughter in over an hour. Her book is on the front seat, but she's not with it. There are fresh tire tracks in the mud...."

Dixie Lee's words choked off, her strength crumpling. I reached out to console her but she recoiled as she had every right to do. Okay, so I'd instead focus on getting Ava back.

The task should be far easier than tracking down Kaito's killer. Because it seemed that Thom's initial impulse—to doubt his own pack mates—had been wise.

After all, who had known about today's wake? Charlie, Jessie, Ito...and every werewolf who lived in Gate City. A glance across the crowd proved that my human friend and her family were still very much present.

The question became: which werewolf was not?

It was impossible to count heads in the crowd, but Thom could solve that problem easily. "The pack bond...." I murmured.

Three months ago, I would have needed to explain, to point out that an alpha's invisible connections to other Gate City werewolves would allow Thom to nail down everyone's current location. Now, three words and a nod were enough to let me know he was already on top of that trick.

He worked fast too. His right eye twitched and then he gritted out the name of someone I hadn't expected: "Hank."

Dixie Lee lifted her head out of her hands to demand, "He has Ava?"

"Don't know. But Hank's not here and his little brother has severed the bond between us."

Why hadn't Hank also severed his bond? The why didn't matter so much as the result however.

"Can you tell where he is?" I asked.

"Better." Thom's teeth sharpened as he smiled. "I can pull him back here. Perhaps you wouldn't mind evicting Charlie's family?"

Then his fist clenched down around something invisible. Muscles rippled as he yanked the tether toward him. Reeling in Hank. Drawing—we hoped—Ava back toward us as well.

I glanced once at Dixie Lee. Her bottom lip trembled, but she'd regained enough of her composure to glare at me. "Go," she demanded.

I couldn't do anything here to help matters, so I went.

"You have no pants," Charlie's girlfriend informed me as I joined their little huddle.

"Fell into a creek," I lied. Well, I guess it wasn't a lie, just a mere fraction of the truth.

Charlie shook her head, used to shifter shenanigans. Then she provided the introduction I'd craved an hour ago: "Nora, meet Kira. Kira, Nora."

Unfortunately, I couldn't afford to waste time getting to know this very interesting human Charlie had found worth revealing her sexuality for. "Great, good," I said quickly. "Look, I need you guys to go."

Rather than obeying, Nora tapped one finger against her lips. "Hot chocolate."

"Excuse me?"

Ignoring my question, Nora rooted around in a purse that didn't look nearly large enough to disgorge the shiny silver thermos that came out of it. She unscrewed the cap and poured out a steaming portion of what did, indeed, appear to be hot chocolate.

"You're suffering from hypothermia," she informed me. "I'm an EMT, so you can trust me on this one. Drink this then we can see about finding you a blanket. Or pants. Charlotte, do you have anything in your trunk?"

"Charlotte?" I couldn't help myself. My eyebrows shot up as I considered the friend I'd only ever heard referred to as Charlie.

"It's her name and it suits her." Nora thrust the metal cup into my hand, forcing my fingers around it. "Drink."

I drank. What else could I do? Gulped down the whole thing—it was delicious—then returned the cup to Nora while addressing Charlie.

"Can you and Nora take Jessie and Ito out to lunch?"

"Now? What's going on?"

I didn't want to draw these two into our mess. I had a feeling neither would leave as easily once they knew what was happening.

But the mood of the gathering had already shifted. Werewolves were assembling rather than pretending to mingle. A sharp exclamation drew my gaze to Thom as he stumbled backwards, barely catching himself before he ended up in the same creek I'd been dunked in.

If I didn't miss my guess, Hank's pack bond had become so strained it had broken. Which meant we'd need to hunt for the culprit and the missing girl the hard way.

Which, in turn, meant it was even more essential for those who didn't know about the existence of werewolves and magic to leave.

Unfortunately, my friend's feet were planted. She wasn't going anywhere without an explanation. So I admitted the truth, or the part of it that was suitable for public consumption. "Dixie Lee's daughter is missing."

Nora's phone was in her hand and she'd dialed two digits—9-1—before I barked out a sharp, "No!"

"Calm down." Nora's tone was firm as she stared me down, but she didn't hit the last number either. "If a child is missing—I assume this daughter is under-age?—we should contact the authorities. They can put out an amber alert."

I glanced at Charlie, who shrugged. In the human world, yes, that made perfect sense. But—the lie bubbled up before I thought it through—"Immigration issues. They'd deport Ava and her mother as soon as they found her."

Nora considered Dixie Lee, whose tear-streaked face made her the obvious bereaved parent and whose blond curls and sweet southern accent made her the most unlikely immigrant present. "You don't say."

"I do say." When deeply committed to a paper-thin lie, the only solution I'd ever found was to turn the paper sideways until it cut. "I'm surprised that you, of all people, would judge someone's ethnicity by their appearance."

"So you're, like, one of those Mexicans?" The tone-deaf jibe from earlier hovered in the air between us.

A werewolf would have snarled at me. Nora just went still.

Then she turned to face Charlie. "I do believe I'm done here. I'll wait for you in the car."

"I thought you were the one person I could count on to make Nora feel welcome," Charlie said as we both watched the girlfriend I hadn't wanted anyone to hurt walk away, injured by my own sharpness.

"I should have been," I started. But Charlie was already following Nora. Was gathering up Ito and Jessie, clearing the area of non-pack humans by the time werewolves began slamming into vehicles.

Ignoring the ice block in my belly, I slipped into the passenger side of Thom's pickup. I'd collect my own car later...along, I hoped, with the shreds of my friendship.

"Where are we going?" I asked.

"Reed boundary." Thom's voice was grim. "Well, almost."

He told me the rest in bits and spurts as we sped down the road, heading east then north. Hank had been near the far corner of Gate City territory when Thom latched onto his pack bond.

"With Ava?"

Thom shook his head, not slowing the tiniest bit as he took a curve wide then veered away from half of the pack. "I don't know. But he won't be going anywhere anytime soon. Not in his car at any rate."

Because it turned out Thom had done more with the pack bond than I'd thought was possible. First he'd dragged Hank toward him for a good long while. Then, when Hank started fighting back, Thom had let up for a moment before latching onto Hank's fine motor controls. With a quick twist, he'd piloted Hank's vehicle straight into a tree.

I almost laughed but didn't, imagining Ava's screams as the car collided. I hoped the girl had buckled her seat belt. Hoped she'd been able to hold tight to her wish to be a hero rather than collapsing in terror like an ordinary thirteen-year-old.

Hoped she'd been in that car with Hank. Because the location he'd been found in was deeply suspicious.

For a split second, I remembered that bottle of blood the Reed alpha had taken from me. Remembered Ava's kitsune heritage and the fact that, to me, she smelled like fox.

Well, if Chief Reed was involved, we'd cross that bridge when we came to it. Which would be soon at the rate Thom was driving.

In fact, his enjoyment of the thrill ride I'd engaged in on the way to that West Virginia post office suddenly made more sense as he continued to take curves so fast the car's inside tires lost contact with the pavement. Three more turns and the rest of the pack was no longer eating our dust.

"They're splitting up," Thom answered without me needing to ask. "Blocking potential avenues of escape."

He wasn't even breathing heavily. I was. In fact, I was ashamed to see that I'd grabbed onto the oh-shit handle...and I couldn't quite seem to let go.

Then we saw it. A crashed car—Hank's car—crumpled against a tree trunk so solid it barely looked scratched by the impact. Thom slammed on the brakes and we both sprinted forward.

The frame was crumpled. The door I yanked refused to open.

But a window was rolled down, the driver's side window. I leaned in with my entire upper body only to discover that the vehicle was empty.

If Ava had ever been present, she wasn't any longer. And Hank? He'd cut his losses and fled.

Chapter 27

There was blood on the steering wheel, its metallic scent overwhelmed by the reek of spilled oil and gasoline. Thom and I shifted in tandem, sniffing the ground as we hunted for a trail....

There it was. Well, Hank's trail at least.

I continued circling, hoping to find Ava's scent veering off in a different direction. For a moment, I thought I caught a whiff of female, so faint the girl's identity was indeterminate. But it was gone as quickly as it had wafted up my nostrils. Tracing the aroma back to its source, I found only the barest hint of someone who wasn't male lingering in the car's back seat.

Ava—if that had been Ava—hadn't gotten out after the accident. There was no scent other than Hank's and ours on the scene no matter how many times I circled around the vehicle. Sniffing hard at the trunk turned up no odor other than mold and exhaust.

So Ava must have been stashed somewhere before Thom grabbed onto Hank's pack bond. We could go off half-cocked, invading the territory of an alpha who'd made it clear how he treated invaders. Or we could force Hank to give us more information first.

The path forward was clear even though the inevitable delay clawed at my gut. Thom must have come to the same conclusion because he yipped once from the spot where Hank had dripped blood onto the leaf litter. The sooner we found the kidnapper, the sooner we found one scared child.

Without further discussion, Thom's nose and mine drifted down to the scent trail. Together, we ran.

Well, not together for long. Thom's legs outpaced mine within fifty yards and soon I was alone in the winter woods, following a path that was as clear as it was erratic.

Hank, I guessed, had been dazed by impact. He was fleeing, but in an ungainly almost drunken fashion. Thom should catch up to him easily.

Sure enough, a howl drew me forward, a howl that was more than mere sound. The pack bond curled around me, turning my feet in a subtly different direction. Toward Thom. Toward Hank.

Toward, I learned as I crested the final rise and peered down upon a scene of werewolf wildness, the entire pack.

They formed a roiling mass of fur, ruffs raised, teeth bared. In the midst of the melee, dead center, two wolves fought.

Thom and Hank. Blurs of gray moving so quickly I couldn't see who was winning. I caught my breath and found myself human, sword grasped in one tense hand.

The watching wolves didn't move out of my way when I approached but they didn't purposefully trip me up either. Instead, their shoulders bumped against my hip, their warmth pressing against my nakedness. Each wolf was jostling for space, content to watch rather than join the single combat.

As best I could see between the muddled mass of bystanders, both fighters were brindled gray. Both were large and powerful. Both moved so quickly I only caught the blue of Thom's eyes once, his alpha scent arriving in erratic bursts.

Then I lost track of identities altogether. It was hard to keep the fight in view, even though I was taller than the rest of the watchers. Uninvolved wolves kept waving their tails across my sight line, accidentally or on purpose. I pressed in closer as one of the fighters latched onto the other's jugular. The loser was slammed to the ground, panting and trembling as he whined on his back.

Was that...? Yes, Thom had won.

I released my pent-up breath...what appeared to be a moment too soon. Because Thom didn't release Hank's throat despite the obvious signs of submission.

Instead, he clenched down harder, growling. When the wolf in front of me tilted out of my way, I caught a glimpse of Thom's eyes.

His irises had transitioned from pure blue to dark lupine rage. Had filled with the willingness to rend and tear and end the life of someone he'd treated like a friend only yesterday.

I was furious too, but we couldn't afford to kill Hank. Not when he was the only one who knew where Ava was located.

Plus, Thom had been raised human. He wasn't ready to face the aftermath of murder in the skin of his wolf.

I pushed harder against the wolves between me and our alpha. This final ring, however, didn't want to give up their prime viewing stations.

Meanwhile, on the other side of the wolves, Thom growled, teeth biting down deeper. As if catching the mood of his alpha, the beast in front of me turned to snap at the air an inch from my knee.

Among shifters, aggression was as contagious as the measles. All it would take was one wrong move and this entire pack could turn on each other like so many lone wolves. They were, after all, only partially pack mates. I didn't possess even that dubious distinction.

Luckily, I was a fox, not a wolf. Impervious to lupine rage and barely earthbound, even in human form.

So I stopped fighting my way forward. Pushed off instead and leapt over the snappy wolf, landing beside Thom and Hank.

My sword slid across the submitting wolf's throat just above where Thom's teeth disappeared into fur. "I've got this," I told Thom. Then, to Hank: "Shift. But I recommend you do so without moving. No one here seems to like you very much."

I hadn't been sure either would listen, but both blinked acknowledgment. Thom growled then eased his teeth out of his enemy's fur. And Hank's fur receded, arms and legs straightening as his torso lengthened to human size.

Then there were two naked men beside me. Hank, still flat on his back with my sword at his throat. Thom crouched beside us, his blue eyes clearing but not clear yet.

"You talk," he managed.

I could do that. I turned all of my attention on Hank, noting without pity that he'd begun to shiver. "Where is she?"

"I don't know who you're talking about."

And I didn't know why Hank bothered lying when the scent of mistruth was so foul it made the closest wolf sneeze. Instead of replying verbally, I dug my star-ball sword in deeper, sawing little by little until blood welled up.

Forcing a pack mate to obey me by drinking their blood was a last resort, but Ava's face hovered in my memory. Her animated smile as we hunted stink bugs together. Her shut-down body posture when she hunched behind her library book.

Wherever she'd been caged, the child didn't even have a fictional world to lose herself in at the moment. She'd trusted Hank as a member of her pack and he'd betrayed her.

So I reached out with my free left hand and scooped up a fingertipful of blood.

Out of the corner of my eye, I noted Thom's body posture tensing and I hesitated. He was the alpha and, more than that, I trusted his judgment. If he didn't want me to take this step....

"Drink it." Thom's rumble was low, but every wolf heard. Ears pinned against skulls, but no one made a move to stop me as I sucked the liquid into my mouth.

Hank's blood wasn't as foul as I would have expected. Didn't taste like the blood of a murderer, so maybe the suspicion hovering in the back of my mind that whoever took Ava had also killed Kaito was wrong.

I could only hope that meant the fox-scented child would turn up safe and sound and only mildly traumatized. The sooner the better.

To that end, I asked the same question a second time. "Where is she?"

Hank fought against replying. His face twisted, his body jerking convulsively against the ground.

I'd never seen someone resist so hard. But I was a kitsune and I'd stolen blood. Hank couldn't deny me.

In the end, he only managed vagueness. "We went into Reed territory."

Vagueness, then unconsciousness. Hank passed out before I could wrest further information from his lips.

Chapter 28

I t was enough. Enough to prompt us into leaving the bare minimum number of shifters handling Hank while the rest of us raced back to vehicles.

After all, the road Hank had been traveling led directly from Thom's territory to Chief Reed's.

"We can't go in as a pack," I argued as Thom once again drove faster than seemed safe down windy country thoroughfares. Already, two other vehicles had sped in off side roads to join us. Soon, the whole pack would be at our heels and we'd be passing from Thom's territory to the land ruled by another.

By an alpha who'd scarred my cheek in exchange for our last incursion. This invasion—in human form, no playfulness involved—would spur harsher repercussions.

Still, Thom didn't reply to my argument. I listened to gravel spinning out from under the pickup's tires for a moment, then I elaborated.

"Gate City is a tiny territory. Your pack is incohesive and young. If Chief Reed considers this an invasion, he'll wipe us off the face of the earth."

The scent of alpha aggression that had filled the cab ever since we got back into the vehicle softened. When I raised an eyebrow, Thom shrugged. "I like to hear you say *us*," he murmured. Then he added, "And I appreciate the warning. We won't enter as a pack. I'll go in alone."

"That will still be considered an invasion, but a stupid invasion." I didn't have the energy to mind my tongue. "You wouldn't make it out alive."

Thom's fingers drummed against the steering wheel. "Recommendation?"

"Send in an envoy. Someone unassuming enough not to be considered a threat while they request an alpha-to-alpha meeting. I'm willing to be that person."

"I'm not willing to let you."

Our conversation slammed to a halt as we rounded a curve and found a truck parked crosswise on the road. This was the border and apparently Chief Reed expected exactly what Thom had intended.

Expected it and was shutting down any invasion before it could begin.

Only...Thom hadn't slowed. Did he really intend to ram the other vehicle, shoving it out of our path through the sheer force of his impatience?

No. At the last possible second, Thom hit the brakes. One arm straightened to protect me even though my seatbelt was doing the same job quite admirably.

Nothing stopped me, however, when the truck screeched to a halt and I hopped out.

There were other vehicles behind the roadblock. I understood that when multiple doors slammed and at least a dozen shifters strode around both sides of the crosswise truck to greet us.

"Chief Reed is expecting you." The speaker was about Thom's age, nearly as well built, but much more submissive. His gaze remained averted as he spoke, gesturing to the narrow pathway between his pack mates leading back the way he'd come.

"He is?" Thom's tone was flat. "Then perhaps he should have come to meet me."

"Not you, Chief Faris." The submissive wolf raised his eyes off the gravel for one split second before dropping them again. "Kira Fairwood has been granted an invitation to visit our alpha's villa. We will leave a pack mate with you in exchange."

Someone was pushed forward out of their line. A teenager, not much older than Ava. She was pale-cheeked and terrified, but she obeyed the hissed command from behind her. Walked past her pack mates and toward ours with wobbly knees.

Thom growled, not at her but because of the situation. I knew that. She didn't. The girl flinched, froze, then swallowed hard and started forward once again.

"This is Chief Reed's grandniece," the same submissive wolf explained. "She is his blood."

His blood...or his sacrifice. Still, this was what I'd wanted. I stepped forward. ..or started to. Thom's hand clenched down around my wrist.

"Kira...."

Wolf ears strained both before and behind us. A pack bond, now, would have been a great asset.

We didn't have one, so I fudged it for the sake of our audience. "Yes, alpha. Of course I will be careful."

His nostrils flared, gaze meeting mine. We couldn't speak silently, but maybe we could communicate after all. Because I knew what he was thinking.

Thom's eyes told me walking alone into enemy territory was unbearably dangerous. My eyes replied that Ava was less able to defend herself than I was.

For another second, Thom's grip warmed my skin. His fingers were ever so slightly rough against the soft underside of my wrist, his thumb stroking my pulse point.

Then he released me, nodded. "See that you are."

Chief Reed's underlings patted me down as soon as we were hidden from view by the roadblock. They took my cell phone, which I'd reclaimed along with my clothes before we started chasing Hank. They also took my ace in the hole—the vial of alpha blood I'd harvested last autumn from three alphas including Chief Reed.

I'd hoped not to need the blood, but losing it made me feel naked. Not defenseless, though. I still had my star ball, which could turn into a sword or dagger.

"No weapons," the woman who'd searched me reported.

"No obvious weapons," the submissive wolf countered. Now that we were separated from Thom by a good distance, he seemed to be regrowing his backbone. His shoulders widened. The pinch to his face opened to reveal a mouth wider than average and teeth ever so slightly pointed.

When his attention turned to me, his scent turned anticipatory. "Your star ball goes in here," he told me, pulling a metallic reddish object out of his pocket.

I considered the two hollowed-out half-spheres, joined by a hinge then strung onto a chain. The item was small, clearly intended to hang around someone's neck after being closed. Could I stuff my star-ball magic into that tiny space? Probably. Did I intend to? If that's what Chief Reed required to discuss Ava, I didn't see that I had much choice.

"I'll pass out if I'm separated from my star ball for long," I admitted at last. "That would appear to defeat the purpose of being brought to your alpha."

"You won't be separated." The shifter's words said one thing, but his scent said another. He was a hunter who had dangerous prey in his grip and who knew just where to bite to turn the tables.

Nonetheless, he was true to his word. He jerked his chin and the woman lifted my hair so she could clasp the chain around my neck. Unlike Thom's touch, hers was cold, impersonal.

Just like the male shifter's tone as he continued. "You will remain in contact with your star ball at all times. You will simply be unable to access the magic."

Those extra-wide lips quivered as they tried but didn't quite manage to hide a smirk. He thought he was pulling the wool over my eyes. He wasn't. But what choice did I have?

For a second, I considered forcing only part of my magic into the necklace. But if this pack possessed an item able to contain my star ball, they clearly knew more about my kitsune heritage than I did. Chances were they'd test for residual magic and be sorely displeased if I tried to trick them with half measures.

Sorely displeased enough to injure Ava? I couldn't risk it.

So I drew my entire star ball to my fingertips, condensing the blazing light smaller and smaller until it flared so bright I couldn't look at it directly. The walnut-sized nugget fit into the orb, just barely.

The male shifter unbridled his smirk as he reached out and snapped the cage shut.

Chapter 29

I wasn't at all surprised when my minder's behavior took an abrupt left turn once I was no longer armed and dangerous. "In the car," he demanded. When I didn't move fast enough, he shoved me in the direction of an idling vehicle, pressing in after me and slamming the door so fast it nearly clipped his own heels.

The backseat should have been plenty large enough for both of us, but somehow he managed to impinge on my personal space while the driver steered us up a narrow mountain road entirely lacking in guard rails. Looking out the window was making me queasy and it felt childish to tell Chief Reed's spokesman to get back on his side of the line. So, instead, I focused on Ava. "The girl who was brought here. Is she safe?"

I wasn't particularly surprised that he shrugged in answer, so I tried a different tack. Lifting the necklace that caged my star ball, I considered at the peculiarity of a wolf pack having such an item on hand. "What is this? Does your alpha have a history with kitsunes?"

"Be silent," my minder growled, "or be silenced."

Instinctively, my fists clenched, but magic didn't fill them. Instead, the orb was the only thing inside my fingers, the tiniest trickle of star-ball energy oozing back and forth through pore-sized holes in the metal. Enough to keep me upright and active. Not enough to materialize a sword or even a knife.

And a weapon wouldn't help Ava. I was here to negotiate, not to fight.

So I was silent. I didn't protest when Chief Reed's spokesman manhandled me out of the vehicle at the top of the mountain. Didn't argue when he twisted one arm behind my back in a way that was entirely unnecessary and marched me up what felt like a thousand steps to the column-flanked front door of a villa that looked like it should have been planted on a Greek mountainside.

I wasn't invited in. Instead, my handler led me around the side to a patio with a view so breathtaking I forgot for a moment what I was doing there. The exposed space should have been frigid, but a fire had been lit in a tall, skinny heater while the sun pounded down, warming the stones. The result was surprisingly comfortable for a mountaintop in January. I could imagine Chief Reed basking here as wolf or man.

Then I didn't have to imagine him. I turned to find the nameless shifter gone, Chief Reed in his place. "Sit," he commanded, "and we will discuss what you have that I want."

Despite his opening, Chief Reed beat around the bush for a good long while, teasing me with tidbits about Ava. "Yes, Faris's wolf brought a young woman across the line into my territory this morning. Yes, he left without her. Yes, I know where she is."

Yes, I did notice that Chief Reed hadn't actually told me he had control over Dixie Lee's daughter. But I couldn't very well sneak away and find Ava for myself, so I smiled and nodded and let the alpha indulge in the upper hand.

My patience faded, however, when a woman drifted out of the manor to offer us refreshments. A woman whose fingers trembled as she poured a drink I wasn't interested in.

This was Chief Reed's pack mate, terrified to spend time in his presence. What was Ava feeling, surrounded by similar werewolves? The girl was young, small, and entirely lacking in power. She'd be ten times as scared as this grown woman who kept her gaze resolutely focused on the ground.

As if in response to my mood, the sun moved behind a cloud and a chill fell over the patio. We could dance around the topic forever, or I could broach it. "Why am I here?" I demanded.

Rather than answering immediately, Chief Reed laughed. His throaty guffaws were magnified by the stone of the patio and the towering edifice behind us. He laughed until my silence grew awkward, but I let that awkwardness linger in the rapidly cooling air.

And, finally, Chief Reed told me. "You, little fox, are here to become my heir."

So he wanted to bandy words? I could bandy. "Your heir? I find it hard to believe you don't have one already."

"I've had several." He sipped at his drink, set it down and continued. "My current heir brought you here today. He's not worth much."

"And you think I'll be worth more?"

Rather than answering, Chief Reed hunched in on himself for one split second before smoothing the pain out of his features. This alpha, I suspected, was clinging to power through the force of personality and theater.

Sure enough, his words—hoarse at first then stronger—suggested as much. "I think you'll confuse my enemies. You're small and scrappy, powerful and powerless. Plus, you don't want my job."

That last part was true. As beautiful as the view was down into a seemingly endless valley, I would have given anything to find myself back within the close confines of the Full Moon Saloon instead. Thom would be half-visible as he served drinks in the dim warmth while Ava would read by lamplight in one corner. Lone wolves who were slowly being molded into pack mates would fill the Moon Room with only slightly dangerous antics. And humans like Charlie could come and go without worrying the supernatural would snap them up.

Not so here. I considered Chief Reed over the top of the glass I hadn't bothered drinking from. "You'll give Thom the girl Hank brought in exchange for me being your heir."

"You're more clever than you look."

His backhanded compliment wasn't what made me flinch. It was the commitment he was demanding from me, the exact type of commitment I'd been running from for months.

Because you don't become heir to an alpha without building pack bonds. Pack bonds that would wipe away my ability to reconnect with my sister, niece, and nephew. Bonds that would block the inklings I was beginning to harbor of connecting instead with Thom and his clan.

If I chose a new place to belong, I didn't want that place to be Reed territory. There had to be another way to help Ava escape.

I was shaking my head when Chief Reed drew a familiar glass bottle out of his jacket pocket, one I'd last seen when the scar on my cheek was a fresh cut. He unscrewed the miniature lid, raised an eyebrow, then shook his head at the blank expression on my face.

"You don't know much about being a kitsune, do you?"

"Perhaps you could educate me." My voice wasn't as steady as I wanted it to be. The chill wasn't just from the cloud shadows now; cold started inside me and radiated outward. I didn't know what that bottle of blood meant, but I was starting to guess.

"Of course." Chief Reed tapped the bottle on the cast-iron arm of his chair, considering the contents for much longer than he really needed to. When he finally met my gaze, the faintest of smiles curled his lips. "It is my role to educate an heir after all. My role and my pleasure. So I'll tell you what you already know first. Werewolf blood on a kitsune's tongue gives her power over the wolf, as you're well aware."

I nodded, the cold within me turning to ice. I was starting to remember just a little about one of Mai's adventures when I was a cossetted child who didn't have to pay attention to unfolding disasters. There'd been something about kitsune power working in the opposite direction under very specific circumstances....

"Did you know," Chief Reed continued, "that freely given kitsune blood allows a werewolf to command a fox?"

Ah, yes. That was the specific set of circumstances. Still.... "You stole that blood."

"Did I?" Chief Reed's smile widened. "As I recall, you pretended to stumble in order to get close to me. You could have fought back before I sliced your cheek, but you chose not to. I consider this blood to be given, not taken."

The ice in my gut expanded, sending tendrils into my toes and fingers. If I had to flee now, I'd be slow as well as weaponless. I wiggled my extremities surreptitiously while I gave Chief Reed the question he likely expected.

"And you intend to use the blood to force me to, what, stand up in front of your pack and promise to be your heir?"

"That's the tricky part, isn't it?" Tap, tap, tap went the bottle against the cast iron. Wiggle, wiggle, wiggle went my toes under the table. They were still blocks of ice.

Chief Reed smiled as if he could see the chill dragging down my body, the way my brain was racing without finding any path out of his trap. "It would be easier all around if you gave me what I want willingly," he murmured. "Then I'd have an incentive to release the young woman, wouldn't I?"

A frigid wind cut through the heat roiling off the propane fire and Chief Reed closed his eyes for one split second. When he reopened them, the scent of nearing wolves was carried on that wind.

His pack was approaching, ready to hear our announcement.

"We can do this the easy way," Chief Reed said, "or the hard way. Your choice."

Chapter 30

Without waiting to see if I'd follow, Chief Reed led me back the way I'd entered, around the corner of his villa and into view of those endless steps.

Endless steps that were now covered by a sea of shifters. They stood in silent stillness, no feet shuffling, no curious whispers. A snap of Chief Reed's fingers and the underling who'd caged my star ball stepped out of the crowd and onto the flat expanse where his alpha now stood.

"Uncle." The younger man's head bowed the same way it had when he'd faced Thom. His scent was obsequious, his tendency toward bullying hidden beneath submissive body language. That too-wide smirk was clenched down once again into a firm line.

Chief Reed ignored him, motioning me forward instead as he addressed the crowd at large. "You have gathered here today to meet my heir."

At this, the younger man's head snapped up, the scent of fur roiling off him. "You're not thinking clearly, Uncle. Perhaps you should sit down...."

The pack appeared to hold their breath at this insolence. But Chief Reed merely smiled. "So you're afraid to fight for your role?"

"I'm not." The current heir's mouth turned down in a long slash of anger, his sword rasping as it exited its sheathe.

He advanced toward me on feet lighter than his bulk would have suggested. In contrast, I was defenseless. One hand rose to finger the necklace that caged my star ball. The orb remained impenetrable and cold.

Meanwhile, the crowd's scent turned hungry. They were amused by this spectacle even if obedience to their alpha kept them silent. Whatever they thought of Big Mouth, they certainly weren't going to help me out.

Good thing I was adept at attacking with words.

"I can understand striking down an unarmed woman," I mused. "But don't you think it's rude to fight without being properly introduced first?"

Chief Reed laughed, another extended bellow that seemed to give the crowd leave to titter alongside him. Unfortunately, my verbal blow slid off my enemy. Rather than answering, Big Mouth doled out his first attack.

I had no weapon, which meant I couldn't block a blow. So I shouldn't have been surprised that my enemy went straight for the obvious. His sword jabbed toward my unprotected chest.

I let him come. Stared down the blade until it was too late for him to change trajectory. Only then did I leap out of the way.

As I'd known it would, his sword clanged against one of the marble pillars, providing an opportunity for me to try to wrest it out of his fingers. I didn't take that opportunity however. I'd learned long ago that, in hand-to-hand combat against a stronger opponent, I had no chance of success.

Instead, I danced away, toward the watchers, many of whom had swords belted at their hips. The question was, how to gain possession of one of those weapons? The complete lack of sympathy in their expressions suggested words weren't going to work any better here than they had against my primary opponent.

Instead, I brushed up against the closest armed shifter, letting my breasts rub against his shirt front while my hands fumbled lower. His eyes widened and Chief Reed bellowed out a laugh that almost, but not quite, covered up the din as the entire sword belt clattered to the ground.

"Thanks bunches." I swooped up the sword, testing its weight with a few quick swipes in the air. The weapon was longer than I preferred, unbalanced in my grip.

Definitely much better than no weapon at all however. And just in time.

Because Chief Reed's former heir was upon me. He fought like he bullied—barreling his way into my personal space, doing his best to slam through my guard via brute force alone.

I couldn't out-brute him, so I stuck to my strong suit—finesse. Each time my opponent attacked, I evaded. Only when he started breathing heavily did I strike.

Not at him. At his weapon. He'd reached a little further each time I retreated. Had stopped worrying about guarding his own weaknesses until....

Ah, there. He'd overextended just far enough.

All in one quick move, I locked our hilts. Flicked my opponent's sword away with a twist of mine.

The blade flew out of his hand, over a crowd who ducked to avoid its sharp, spinning surface. Out of the corner of one eye, I saw a particularly coordinated shifter reach up to catch the discarded weapon without cutting himself. *Impressive.*

But monitoring the sword's path only required a small portion of my attention. The rest was focused on beating back my opponent, step by step, until he ran into a column and could retreat no further. My sword settled into the hollow at the base of his throat. Pressed just the tiniest bit, not even breaking the skin.

I expected to need to prove my point, but it wasn't necessary. "I surrender," Big Mouth gasped.

"Do you?" I cocked my head, considering submissive body language that I knew my opponent could turn on and off at will.

"I do." His face twisted as if in pain, even though I knew I wasn't causing him more than minor discomfort.

And I understood why when Chief Reed's command rolled over us. *"Kill him."*

I was a kitsune, so I didn't have to obey alpha orders. But if I wanted to find Ava, I had to act as Chief Reed's heir, which put me in a pretty pickle now.

Keeping my sword arm straight, I turned my head until I could meet the older man's gaze. "Alpha. I..."

Words cut off as my opponent—my *surrendered* opponent—moved faster than I'd thought he was capable of. Something flashed. A dagger he'd hidden about his person?

I'd let him within arm's reach in order to subdue him, which meant the blade aimed at my gut wouldn't even need to be thrown in order to strike its target. He could punch it in deep with the full force of his longer arms and I'd be unable to defend myself. I'd die slowly and painfully.

All of this spun through my mind in a millisecond. The same millisecond in which Chief Reed repeated: *"Kill him."*

I struck without premeditation. My sword pierced the soft skin of my opponent's throat as if his flesh was butter. Sharp steel caught on the hard jut of his spine, but I put my entire body weight behind the move as I hacked at the obstruction.

My would-be-killer's mouth gaped wider than I'd ever seen it. His eyes bugged out in surprise. Blood spurted across both of us, across the white marble, droplets splattering the closest onlookers.

Above it all, Chief Reed's laugh rolled long and merry. As his chuckles faded, he announced me with an expansive arm gesture. "Meet Kira Fairwood. My heir."

Chapter 31

"I killed him." The words gushed out like blood from a shifter whose name I'd never learned. A shifter who, yes, was a bit of a bully. But he hadn't deserved to be put to death.

Still, Big Mouth was very much dead. And I was very much the murderer.

The contents of my stomach spewed across the marble, mixing with blood and splattering the shoes of the woman rushing out the front door and falling to cradle the man at my feet.

"Quentin!"

So I guessed I knew his name now. Knew his name and knew that the woman who'd served us on the patio was what, his mate?

No, his widow.

For a long moment she clutched at the dead man, trying to force the wound in his neck back together. The effort was grisly and awful, blood coating her fingers, tears streaming from her eyes.

Then she glared up at me. "You...." she started.

"Now, now." Chief Reed stepped between us. His hand dropped onto the woman's shoulder and she flinched beneath his touch, seeming to shrink further as he continued speaking. "Don't say something you'll regret later. And clean up this mess before we return."

Then he turned to face me. "As for you, I'd expected a stronger stomach. We'll work on that."

His words unfroze me sufficiently to remember that we had an audience. That I'd chosen to be a cold-blooded bastard's heir to save Ava from being turned into a quivering heap like the woman who was already beginning to scrape her mate's blood off the marble.

It didn't matter that I'd never before taken a life. That I'd thought murder was a hard line I wouldn't cross, one I could always manage to avoid through words and humor.

I hadn't avoided. Hadn't even tried to. The man splayed across the ground at my feet was proof of that.

The emotional aftermath racked my body. But I couldn't afford to look weak now. Not if I didn't want to be forced to repeat this proof of my bloodthirstiness over and over again.

So I turned to face the crowd...only to find the stairs empty. "I sent them away," Chief Reed told me. "Before you ruined all of my hard work."

His hard work setting up a memorable transfer of power. His hard work removing a no longer effective heir.

The alpha's eyebrows rose at my silence, then he crooked his elbow as if he was a gentleman leading me to a ball. "Shall we find your young woman?"

I didn't want to go anywhere with this alpha. I certainly didn't want to touch him.

But Ava needed me. I settled my fingertips onto Chief Reed's arm and walked beside him down the steps.

The ride away from Chief Reed's villa was nothing like the ride toward it. For one thing, the man I'd sat beside on the way up the mountain was dead. For another, Chief Reed dismissed his driver and took the wheel in his own two hands.

"You will call me Uncle," he ordered as we wound down a different steep hillside. We weren't traveling back in the direction from which I'd come, giving me hope that we really were heading toward wherever Ava had been stashed.

Which meant I needed a solid promise from the man beside me. After seeing how easily he'd turned on Quentin, I wasn't willing to leave anything to chance.

So I swallowed down residual bile and clarified the deal we'd struck. "You said that if I became your heir, you'd allow Ava to return to Gate City. I want her released into Thom's hands today with no strings attached."

"You're referring to the young woman your stray delivered?" Chief Reed's eyes left the road, never mind the drop-off that, from my point of view, appeared to be inches from his wheels.

Ignoring the potential for imminent death, I spoke between gritted teeth. "Yes." When Chief Reed merely waited, I added a word that tasted like shit on my tongue: "Uncle."

The sweet scent of approval suffused the air between us. "Very good. And, of course, if the young woman wants to go, I will deliver her to Faris personally. Today." This time, his pause smelled like a hardening. And, sure enough, when Chief Reed continued, his words bit deep. "In return, little fox, you will swear a binding oath to obey me as heir."

Obedience wasn't my strong suit, especially not when I suspected all of Chief Reed's commands would be as distasteful as his first one. Plus, as a kitsune, if I swore an oath, I'd be forced to abide by it.

So I didn't agree, not immediately. "You expect me to do whatever you say without argument."

Chief Reed's booming laughter filled the car and he took both hands off the wheel to wipe tears of mirth out of his eyes. "I expect no such thing," he admitted as the car veered toward the drop-off. Only at the last moment did he steady our trajectory and keep us on the road. "I expect you'll argue with me in private until my ears bleed. But, in public, you will obey my commands."

It was better than I'd expected and, also, clearly the best I was going to get out of him. Ava's thin shoulders filled my mind's eye and I accepted the inevitable.

"I swear," I told him, feeling the tug of an oath kindling inside me. "If you uphold your end of the bargain, I will obey you as heir."

After that, we rode in silence. Down into a valley that looked vaguely familiar, especially when we turned onto a road I'd traveled not much more than a week before.

"She's *here*?" I demanded when the car rolled to a halt just at the edge of Reed territory. The gravel in front of us continued for another tenth of a mile, but I could see what sat at the end of the line.

A three-story farmhouse turned woman's shelter. One located on Gate City land.

"I never said she was in my territory." Chief Reed's smugness filled the air between us. "Or that I had her under lock and key. I'm afraid you'll have to cross alone, however. I respect boundaries."

Unlike some people. His unspoken words hurried me forward. I'd been tricked into an oath, I now realized, that bound me even though it would have been possible to save Ava without it.

In fact, the girl should have been able to figure out her own way home. That puzzle tugged at me as I tapped on the farmhouse door. As the door was opened by the same old woman who'd greeted me a week ago.

"Oh dear. Back again?" The few short words somehow managed to convey both her sympathy and her kindness. She couldn't be complicit in a kidnapping attempt. Could she?

"Not for myself," I told her. "I'm here to pick up Ava."

"Ava?"

The old woman looked befuddled, so I clarified. "The girl who arrived this morning." I was already toeing off my shoes, pulling out my pockets to show they were empty. "Can I see her?" I continued.

"She's in your old room. Go on up if you wish."

I wished. I wished my way up the stairs so quickly I almost knocked over a priceless antique. Catching it just in time, I propped the ceramic pig back on its shelf and tapped on yet another closed door.

Whatever was going on, Ava would be scared and upset. I was ready to console her. To promise library books by the dozen. Her mother's sheltering arms in short order and mine until we reached safety.

But the door didn't open to reveal Ava. Instead, I blinked for one long moment at someone who both was and wasn't familiar. Then I spoke the only name I had for her.

"Kid?"

Chapter 32

"I t's Lily," the young woman admitted after a long pause. The bangs of her silky blond hair tipped forward to cover eyes that, I now noticed, were rather well lashed for a boy. "Lily Randolph."

"The missing pack princess." The one Mai's neighbor wanted to search for within Fairwood territory. From what I knew of Lily's situation, she would definitely be desperate enough to kidnap Ava. But—"Why didn't you just slip across the closest border and ask my sister for help?"

"As if that would have been so easy." Lily's slender hands landed on slim but rounded hips, making me wonder how I'd ever mistaken her for a boy. Perhaps because I'd only run into her when she wore baggy clothes that clearly belonged to someone else? Or because I'd seen what I expected to see.

Now, though, Lily was all young woman…just as Chief Faris had said, the wily old dog.

"Your pack has one goal," she continued, "protecting kitsunes. If Hank and I had asked for help, your alpha would have tossed us back."

"They're not my pack and Gunner's not my alpha." The words slipped out before I could stop them, leaving a foul taste behind. A taste that wasn't relevant at the present moment. "What about Thom?" I continued. "He would have taken in a mated pair even if they were running from another pack leader."

Because Hank wasn't this woman's brother. He'd fought against my compulsion with all the desperation of a devoted lover.

Plus, the Randolph heir wasn't named Hank and he wouldn't have helped his sister wiggle out from under their father's thumb. More like offered to help, tripped Lily up, then laughed about it. The one time I'd met Randolph Junior, it'd been clear he was a dick.

For the first time, Lily's eyes evaded mine. "Hank's not my mate," she mumbled. "He said it wouldn't be fair to pin me down when I'm young and desperate."

That did change things. An unmated pack princess was seldom allowed outside her guarded compound for very good reason. Her scent alone turned some males so crazy they tended to take whatever they wanted by force. Among lone wolves like those in Gate City—yes, I could imagine Lily had felt it necessary to hide her sex.

How she'd done that around wolf noses, though, was another matter. "The stinky clothes you wore to cover up your scent were Hank's?"

Lily's fire returned with a vengeance. "Of course they were his. That's why we had to go. Because Chief Faris ordered me to show up this morning smelling like soap. I couldn't do that."

She started pacing, toward the old metal radiator then away again. How this led back to Ava I wasn't sure, so I let silence draw more information out of the young woman in front of me.

"I told Hank it wouldn't work," Lily spat out. "He intended to find a place for us then send for me. But this house is too close to Gate City, never mind the Reeds."

I wanted to sympathize, but you don't kidnap a child to save your own skin. That turned you from victim into villain. "And Ava?" I demanded when the confessions didn't seem to be veering in the proper direction.

"Ava?" Lily turned back toward me, face as confused as mine had been when she opened the door and revealed herself to be female. "I didn't tell her about any of this. She's just a kid."

A kid who wasn't here. Who had never been part of Hank's plan. Lily let me drink her blood to confirm that fact, which made me like the young woman a little better. After all, self interest should fade when one learns a child has been snatched.

Lily only balked when I offered her a ride back to the border. "Thanks but no thanks. I'll catch up with Hank and...."

"The only place you'll catch up with Hank is at the border. How do you think we tracked you down?"

I was tempted to leave her there. Let Lily sleep in the bed she'd made for herself. After all, Ava's absence gnawed at my gut while my oath to Chief Reed tugged me in the diametrically opposite direction. I had enough problems without adding this potentially problematic pack princess to the mix.

But, despite everything, Lily was young. Likely not much more than eighteen and a very sheltered eighteen at that. She'd done the best she could in a desperate situation. In her shoes, could I be sure I wouldn't do the same?

So I ignored the contradictory yearnings and sat Lily down on the bed for a few torturous minutes. Held her hand and promised that Thom would make a safe place for her and Hank in Gate City. All she had to do was ask.

"But you're not even willing to commit to him," Lily countered. "Why should I do what you won't?"

Was that how the pack saw things? "It's not Thom I won't commit to. He wants me to bond with a bunch of lone wolves instead of my family."

"Oh yeah?" Lily snorted. "You think that's really the bond he wants?"

Despite her snark, in the end she willingly walked with me out of the farmhouse. Rode in the back seat of Chief Reed's car while I did my best not to pummel our driver with anything other than words.

Because Chief Reed had greeted me with an ultimatum. "You will remain in my territory." The command bound me both physically and ethically, leaving me no way to fight back other than venting my outrage.

"You knew Lily wasn't the girl I was looking for," I gritted out as we sped toward an alpha I now could do no more than say farewell to. "That's why you kept calling her a young woman."

"Is it my problem Faris sheds females like couch-swallowed pocket change?"

Chief Reed braked as we approached the back side of the same roadblock Thom had nearly run into from the other direction. Half the Reed vehicles were still there, holding the boundary against a potential invasion. Waiting for Thom to make one wrong move so they could attack.

"I need to speak with him." My hand was on the door handle, but I didn't push it open. Couldn't, actually. My oath required me to obey Chief Reed's demands.

As such, he could have refused this request and I'd have had no choice but to ride back up to his mountaintop manor without fulfilling my promise to Lily. Instead, Chief Reed shrugged. "Five minutes."

It would have to be enough.

Chapter 33

"That's not Ava." Someone stated the obvious as Lily and I stepped over the invisible line that separated Thom's and Chief Reed's territories. My oath tugged at my shirtsleeves, trying to pull me back toward the idling vehicle in which my new pack leader waited. I quelled the urge but still felt seconds starting to count down in my gut.

"It's not," I said, my gaze meeting Thom's clear blue eyes. There wasn't time to explain Lily's story detail by detail. Nor was there time to manage my words so they didn't tilt a ragged pack off kilter. I hesitated, unsure what, exactly, I hoped to get out of five minutes on the Gate City side of the line.

Or, rather, four minutes and thirty-three seconds. *Thirty-two. Thirty-one....*

Then Thom was beside me, his long strides eliminating the distance between us. "Walk with me."

Another thirteen second passed in silence as we separated ourselves from listening werewolves. Thom's proximity buoyed me up in ways I couldn't quite put my finger on, ways that pointed to a gaping loneliness ahead.

The remaining four minutes weren't about me, however. Couldn't be about me. Instead, I told Thom as quickly as possible how I'd promised Lily that he would offer her a place in Gate City. I acknowledged the drama bound to ensue among his lone wolves, plus—if the secret got out—the danger that would come his way from the Randolph pack.

"Of course." Thom turned to face me in the middle of the gravel road, his body language intent, focused. Unlike Chief Reed's mountaintop, this whole valley was already drenched in winter shadow. But Thom's presence warmed me. His broad shoulders seemed to shield me from the darkness. "Now will you tell me what's wrong?"

"Besides the fact we don't know where Ava is? That I wasted enough time so her kidnapper could be anywhere at this point?"

"We'll find Ava," Thom promised, his words bringing feeling back into digits that had been frozen seemingly forever. "And that's not what's bothering you right now."

Thom wanted to know and I wanted to tell him. But I couldn't. Not while looking at his face.

Instead, I closed my eyes and spoke into the darkness. "I've been an idiot, Thom. Every time you offered me a pack bond I refused it because I was afraid of losing a connection that I'd already lost. And so"—I took a deep breath, this last part almost too painful to speak out loud—"when Chief Reed demanded I stay in his territory and become his heir if I wanted to free Ava—well, Lily, but I thought it was Ava—I said yes."

I wasn't sure my explanation made sense. All that made sense was the emptiness in my gut that promised I'd thrown away my one chance for true happiness. That I hadn't valued the treasure I possessed until I lost it. Salt prickled the undersides of my eyelids.

Then a finger of warmth slid across my cheekbone. "I've been an idiot too." Thom's rumble vibrated through our tiny point of connection, warming me even though the countdown was approaching zero. *One minute and twenty-seven seconds. Twenty-six. Twenty-five. Twenty-four....*

Blinking my eyes open, I soaked up Thom's presence. Shadows had turned his face even more beautiful, emphasizing the strength of his bone structure. "An idiot?" I parroted back at him.

"An idiot," he confirmed. "I've been pretending not to notice that my life expands every day you're part of it. I've been pretending not to notice that you're different from anyone else I've ever met."

I couldn't help it. I barked out a laugh. "Different, yes. I've heard that before."

Thom frowned and I should have flinched. Instead, I grinned and waved him silent before he could reframe his words. "Never mind. I get what you're saying."

"Do you?" That heat-giving finger slid down my cheek. At the corner of my mouth, it lingered for one split second before leaving my skin behind. "You've been shielding your heart these last three months and I've been shielding my heart for two decades. But who's to say that if you did what I asked and committed to our pack, you wouldn't be hit by a bus tomorrow?"

Despite the seconds fading faster than daylight, I couldn't help chuckling. "I hope my reflexes are better than that."

"I hope so too. But that's not the point." Thom reached up now to cup my face in both of his hands. His blue eyes blazed out of the darkness and I'd never felt closer to anyone than I did to Thom in that moment.

"The future is unknowable," he murmured, words like nets drawing us together. "The past is unchangeable. All we can count on is this present moment. And in this present moment, I want you."

I itched to take what he was offering, to seize it and clutch it close to my heart. But, in all fairness, I had to point out the obvious. "I can't bind to your pack," I admitted, the words like a rusty lock being forced shut around me. "Not while I'm heir to a different pack."

Thom's answer came fast. "Doesn't matter. I'm not asking for anything from you, Kira. Instead, I'm giving what I've wanted to give from the first moment I met you."

What he was giving me—his heart, his commitment—I felt sizzling in the air between us. Words were unnecessary. Bonds were irrelevant.

Then he was kissing me and I was kissing him and the darkness of night might as well have been fireworks. The pack, too far away to hear our words but close enough to see two silhouettes merge into one being, whistled and catcalled. In my gut, my brief allotment of time outside Reed territory slithered away to zero.

And it didn't matter. Nothing mattered other than Thom.

Thom walked me back to the boundary, a location he seemed to feel as easily as I did. Because he stopped just as his toes touched the invisible barrier. Stopped there and called past the border guards. "Reed! Get your ass over here."

I couldn't see Chief Reed's face in the darkness of his vehicle. Didn't expect him to respond well to Thom's order. But, after the tiniest pause, he laughed and emerged. Strode forward until he was closer to me than I was to Thom.

After all, my oath had pulled me away from the man I wanted to cling to, dragging me unwillingly back into Reed territory. My oath didn't let me sidle away either when Chief Reed draped a possessive arm across my back. Instead, I braced myself beneath the weight of my freely given word.

"Yes?" This time when a man's deep voice vibrated through me, it knocked my organs out of alignment. Tried to wobble my knees until I had to lock them to stay upright.

Thom noticed all of this and I expected him to argue for my release, something that I knew wouldn't work but could have used hearing. Instead, he demanded something different. "Kira needs her things. I'll bring them by tonight."

"She needs nothing." Chief Reed's arm on my back grew heavier with the weight of not just my oath but his intentions also. One murder down, how many to go? "Do you really think," he continued, "that I'm unable to supply clothes and toiletries for my heir?"

The point was unarguable, so Thom didn't argue it. Instead, he pointed toward the Gate City side of the roadblock and tossed out his ace in the hole. "Your grandniece is still over there."

"Keep her. She's not worth much."

Thom's nostrils flared, but he didn't address Chief Reed's lack of family values. Instead, he refocused his demands on me. "Kira is under my protection. I won't send her away empty-handed."

The words Thom uttered were heavier than Chief Reed's arm, so why did they make me feel so much lighter? Unfortunately, the effect lasted mere seconds. Then Chief Reed shrugged, the gesture counteracting the headiness of Thom's growl. "If you wish, drop her possessions off here. I'll leave someone to wait for them."

After that, he steered me back toward his vehicle. Away from Thom, away from the pack who, I could hope, would find Ava while I was serving out an oath I'd sworn without thinking through the consequences.

As we got into a car that reeked of alpha musk and trickery, I could see Thom standing unmoving as the mountain that cast us all into shadow. When Chief Reed turned the car to head back up to his villa, I swiveled to crane my neck back toward the man who hadn't moved a muscle since I left him.

Thom was still standing, still watching, when the road curved north to block him from sight.

Chapter 34

I woke in a strange room to the certainty that someone had invaded my personal space. Heavy curtains blocked all light, leaving nothing but air whispers to hint at danger. They danced in eddies, refusing to pinpoint the invader's location. I flared my nostrils but caught no distinguishing scent.

The room was huge, more of an open-plan suite than a bedroom if my exhausted memory could be trusted. Whoever had crept in could be anywhere. Given yesterday, they could be anyone wanting to take out a kitsune turned alpha's heir.

The tiniest snick of something hard tapping against wood focused my attention. My hand clenched around the knife I'd swiped off last night's dinner table in plain view of Chief Reed. He'd laughed at my need to arm myself, hadn't responded when I tried to bait him into offering blades meant to be used for stabbing rather than sawing through bloody steaks. Had laughed harder when I suggested he open the necklace caging my star ball so I could create my customary sword.

Now I intended to be more secretive and also more aggressive. It was better to attack than wait and defend myself. No matter what, the covers—warm and comforting yet sure to slow my response time—had to go.

They were soft enough not to rustle. Soft enough to fold back as I let my bare feet chill silently against the wooden floorboards.

I was entirely naked because my possessions hadn't arrived before dinner ended and I hadn't been willing to accept the nightgown Quentin's widow had been forced to offer me. The well-washed seams had smelled like her, the faintest scent of spring sunshine out of place in January. Before today, I guessed, this woman had offered a kind word and smile to everyone. She didn't smile, though, when she pushed a gown she must have worn during nights spent beside her now-dead mate into my arms.

"I can't take this," I'd told her.

"Take it or sleep naked," Chief Reed had countered.

So I'd slept naked. And now, naked except for a steak knife, I padded across the room.

Luckily, I possessed the stealth of a kitsune even two-legged, so there was no problem remaining silent. But the blankets had a mind of their own. Despite the fact I'd stacked them carefully at the end of the bed, they slumped onto the floor as I left them. Air whooshed past my bare calves as the blankets landed with a very audible thud.

Whoever had entered my room paused. Paused then...meowed?

"Pumpkin?" I knew that throaty chirrup. Knew, now that he was closer, the fishy scent of his breath.

I dropped the knife and flung myself toward the place where I'd last heard a claw click against floorboards. Warm fur indented beneath my fingers. Pumpkin's purr thrummed pleasure through us both.

No wonder Thom had demanded I be allowed my possessions. Pumpkin wasn't a possession, but he was deeply necessary for a woman in exile. The cat settled onto my lap, digging claws into my bare knee deep enough to leave scratches. And, for one endless moment, I felt entirely at home.

Then a chuckle erupted from the direction of the door. Not Chief Reed's deep belly laugh. No, this humor was feminine and carried with it the faintest scent of sunshine.

Sunshine and smugness that lingered even after the door opened and closed behind her. Quentin's widow had seen my weakness. Had seen and taken the information with her back into the night.

Willow—whose name I learned at breakfast—didn't act on her knowledge right away. Instead, she faded into the woodwork, her posture in my presence staying just as submissive as it was around her alpha. But the glint in her gaze when she thought no one was looking made me imagine her poking pins into a kitsune-shaped voodoo doll as soon as I turned my back.

I also imagined her skinning Pumpkin and leaving his bloody body on my pillow. Luckily, the old tomcat was used to fending for himself. I pushed him out the window that first morning and he left the way he always used to when I was rooming with Dixie Lee or Charlie. Disappeared and didn't return until I was ready to go to sleep.

So I didn't worry about him. Instead, I worried about Ava, about how long Dixie Lee's child had been missing. About how every passing hour made it more likely she would turn up dead.

Not that I could do anything about it. I wasn't granted access to my phone or to the outside world in any other way either. Hard as I tried, my oath didn't allow me to try to escape.

Instead, I found myself drawn toward obeying even Chief Reed's unstated wishes. He wanted me to bind with his pack. Wanted me to become one of them.

He never said so out loud, though, so I was able to fend off the questing pack tendrils while dragging myself through the busy schedule Chief Reed set for me. And time slipped away, first an hour, then a day, then a week.

I toured a school where children lived separately from their parents, affection forbidden. I visited a sword-training facility where matches ended with a gush of blood.

When given a spare moment, I asked anyone willing to speak with me about kitsunes, about the orb that caged my star ball, about fox magic. Even those who'd been welcoming a moment earlier avoided those questions, which told me more than they suspected. There was something to learn here, something about my heritage embedded in the history of the Reed pack.

But I didn't learn the connection. Instead, every night I ran two-legged behind vicious werewolves. We hunted, not the mice and rabbits I was used to catching with fox teeth, but bigger prey wolves could flush out of the mostly wild mountainside. Usually, our chases were painless for everyone except the unlucky source of dinner. But as the moon grew larger, one wolf was speared by the antlers of a bull elk defending his life by taking another. Breathless, I caught up just in time to see the squiggle of intestines trailing across bloody leaves, the clouded eyes of someone who'd been in his prime moments before.

Chief Reed changed back to human form so he could laugh and laugh and laugh.

That night, I dreamed of Quentin. Of my own hands-on awfulness, worse than Chief Reed's humor. Scarlet slipped into the stream of images as well, her pain beneath the Executioner's knife, the fact I'd never checked afterwards to see whether she was alive or dead.

Come morning, I was sick from lack of sleep and self-loathing, but Chief Reed set me the same sort of timeline as ever. I toured workshops and gardens and tried out each task underlings were assigned to. I learned how Chief Reed built a machine out of living beings, each shifter fitting together like gears so their alpha could sit in his manor at the top of the mountain and gloat.

I was another cog in that wheel, a cog that Chief Reed intended to keep pushing into place until I stuck there. He pushed and I resisted. Shoved harder and I dug my heels in deeper.

Our impasse might have gone on forever if the moon craze hadn't struck.

Chapter 35

We'd been hunting every night that week, so I really should have known the full moon was nearing. But, days ago, heavy clouds had settled like a wool hat atop the mountain, blocking all view of celestial bodies. Plus, sprinting after werewolves in human form kept my attention riveted on my feet.

Until, that is, a break in the clouds revealed a perfect orb of reflected sunlight. The moon smiled down at me and yearning erupted deep in my gut.

I wanted. I needed. I craved Thom *now.*

Pivoting, I sprinted away from the pack, toward the only thing that would ease the yearning. My stomach knew where Thom was located. My fingers, trailing across a beech trunk as I rushed past it, remembered the minor roughness of Thom's thumb against my cheekbone. I panted, not from need of oxygen but from need of touch.

Then something slammed into my back. Something huge and hot and heavy.

The weight atop me was furry...then not furry. Hands spun me around, an alpha's irate face settling inches from mine. "What the hell do you think you're doing?"

I bucked rather than answer. This wasn't getting me closer to Thom.

Unfortunately, the alpha's weight was immovable, by me at least. But he'd move himself if I provided enough incentive.

My teeth refused to sharpen. Shrugging, I decided blunt human dentition would have to suffice.

Wrenching my neck around until I could reach the closest exposed flesh, I bit down hard....

I was free. Then I wasn't. A forearm on my throat slammed me back to the ground, knocking away my breath for one split second. Another hand fumbled at my cleavage.

No, not at my cleavage. At the red metal orb on a chain around my neck. He thumbed it open as easily as if I hadn't gnawed at the metal for hours without making headway. My star ball erupted, a globe of light more brilliant than the moon.

"Shift, damn you," the alpha above me growled. "That'll clear the crazy."

Shifting was a good idea. Shifting would make it easier to wriggle free and find the man I needed.

Star-ball light suffused me, then I was vulpine. And Chief Reed was right. For one split second, the relief of shifting for the first time in weeks cleared my head.

We were far from the rest of the pack, I noted, just me and Chief Reed halfway to the Gate City border. How had I overcome my oath long enough to make a run for it?

The moon craze. Its strength must have shunted aside magically-induced obedience.

And if I gave in to that craze now, could I evade the oath entirely?

This time, when the yearning struck my belly, I embraced it. I filled my head with *Thom, Thom, Thom,* wriggled free, and ran.

Wind whipped past my questing nose. My feet were light as feathers. I'd find Thom and we'd....

Wolf teeth clamped down on my ruff. My body shook like a rabbit in the teeth of a predator, but the motion wasn't enough to block out the need strumming through my body.

His hands, his lips, his hot breath....

The wrong hot breath seeped into my nape as wolf teeth carried me through the darkness, away from my destination. Into a cold marble edifice. Into a room with no windows and one closed door.

"Now shift back and put the star ball away."

The alpha's demands were irrelevant as I leapt from bookcase to floor lamp. There had to be a way out. A way to leave this cell and find the man I needed.

Thom, Thom, Thom....

"I'm warning you." The alpha's growl barely impinged upon my moon craze. But when he grabbed me in hands that were gloved against teeth and claws, I was forced to pay attention.

"The. Star. Ball. In here. Now."

He held that red metal orb so close to my nose I couldn't focus. Shook it menacingly.

Star-ball magic wasn't necessary for my goal tonight. To shut the alpha up, I slid back to humanity, oozed light into the necklace.

Then I was alone in the room whose door knob refused to turn no matter how many times I yanked it. I kicked the door, the wall, only managing to injure my toes.

Thom, Thom, Thom. I wanted. I needed.

Unable to reach the man I craved, unable to leave the room I'd been caged in, I subsided, gasping. Reached down to find pleasure in the wet spot between my own legs.

"You have a visitor."

Willow loomed, her words knocking me out of the restless sleep that had eventually consumed me. She nudged my bare hip with a shod toe, then dropped clothes onto my naked body. "Get dressed and join them in the blue sitting room."

A visitor. The word cut through my aching head. Through the memories of last night—had Chief Reed left the room before I started masturbating? I thought so. I hoped so.

Then the possibilities presented by Willow's bombshell struck. If I had a visitor, it had to be Thom....

I dressed faster than I'd ever thrown on clothing. Sprinted through the echoing mausoleum of a house to the blue sitting room where my host and I had wasted hours reading in silence. Willow kept the space spic and span, but to me it reeked of heel-cooling frustration.

Even more so when I peered through the open doorway and found Chief Reed relaxing in his customary armchair. That wasn't right. Surely his limbs wouldn't be so languid in proximity to another alpha. Surely his face wouldn't be so smug.

Still, I stepped inside. Turned to face the part of the room that had been invisible from the doorway.

My visitor perched on the arm of a sofa in a way that could be construed as sitting while giving her instant access to her half-sheathed sword. Not Thom, but....

"Charlie, what are you doing here?"

My entirely human friend pointed a thumb at Chief Reed. "I'm the only one hot stuff over there would let into his territory."

Because he could snap her spine in seconds, sword not withstanding. Chief Reed's toothy smile proved he understood what I was thinking. His words said the opposite.

"Sit. You have a guest. After last night, I have my doubts, but surely you know how to act in a civilized manner."

"Last night?" Charlie's eyebrows rose, but I ignored her question.

After all, if the pack had news important enough to risk Charlie's skin to tell me, it could only be about one person.

"Ava?" My hand grabbed onto the door for support. "You found her?"

Alive? I didn't say the word. I couldn't.

Charlie shook her head, answering the question I'd asked, not the other. "No. We've all hunted every day, but there's no sign of her."

The silence after my friend's admission filled the room like fog. Fog that reminded me how dangerous it was for a human to linger in this den of werewolves.

I needed to get Charlie out of here before Chief Reed thought of a way to twist her presence around to his benefit. So I cleared my throat. Forced out words. "Then why did you come?"

"Because something emerged last night in the Moon Room. Glowing. Bouncy. Here."

My friend tossed her cell phone toward me, a photo pulled up on the screen. I glanced at it, but I didn't need to.

As impossible as it sounded, I knew already what I'd see there. Despite the fact Mai and I were the only active kitsunes in North America, despite the fact our magic was so rare we didn't even understand all of its abilities, the image was exactly what I'd thought it would be.

A luminous, impossible star ball.

Chapter 36

"Ava's alive." The relief in my voice matched the bounce in my step as I headed for the door.

"Really?" Charlie met me halfway, her grin so wide it seemed to split her face in two. "You're sure?"

"Pretty sure. New star balls don't emerge out of thin air. They're attached to kitsunes—generally teenagers just old enough to come into their magic for the first time."

"So Ava is at the bar?"

I shook my head, thinking through the possibilities aloud. "Usually, that's what it would mean. But Ava's mother isn't a kitsune, so the star ball had to come from some source other than Ava herself. It's still linked to a kitsune though. Which doesn't 100% mean Ava. It wouldn't hurt to get Ito and his kids over to Gate City just in case one of them is foxy."

Charlie was already tapping away at her cell phone while I considered my newborn niece, also a kitsune and possible link to this rogue star ball. I'd call Mai, but the age at which kitsunes traditionally materialized their magic said Ava rather than Chipmunk was the partner of the Moon Room's glowing ball of light.

And if Ava was its focus, I could use the star ball to find her. I'd....

My right foot rose but didn't fall again. It felt like I'd run into a very invisible yet very tangible wall.

A deep growl. "Aren't you forgetting something?"

My oath. I winced, turning to face the alpha who had me bound to his presence as thoroughly as if he'd locked me in the basement. And I forced myself to use the honorific that carried with it memories of blood. "I have to do this, Uncle. It won't take long."

I hadn't expected my argument to make headway, honorific or no honorific. After all, I'd tried browbeating, trickery, and sullenness over the course of the many days we'd spent together. No attitude of mine had changed Chief Reed's tune one bit.

So my spine chilled when he smiled and agreed. "Of course."

"You're letting me go?"

Because he wasn't. In fact, whatever Chief Reed had been doing to my oath to manipulate me accelerated rather than slowing. I found myself being dragged closer to where the alpha lounged, further from the door and Charlie.

Chief Reed's grin grew. "I can see how important this is to you. All I ask in return is two small favors."

And there it was. The reason he'd been so smug from the moment I entered this room. "What favors exactly?"

Rather than answering, Chief Reed dug into his jacket pocket, drawing out a small glass bottle just like the one he'd used to harvest my blood weeks ago. "First, you'll fill this back up."

Back up? I blinked, the past rewriting itself. Quentin's head being cut nearly free of his body—I'd thought that action was entirely my own fault, proof that I could be as monstrous as my jailer given the proper set of circumstances.

But if this bottle didn't just resemble the bottle Chief Reed had stored my blood in.... If it was instead the exact same bottle....

Anger warred with relief, my stomach trying to leap with joy and drop at the exact same moment. "You forced me to kill your nephew."

"Oh, did you not realize?" Chief Reed smiled nearly as wide as Charlie had when I swore Ava was living. "I do hope you haven't lost any sleep over that." The master manipulator's voice hardened. "Now, give me what I want."

The empty bottle spiraled through the air toward me. I caught it one-handed, my fingers clenching tight. I wanted to fling this seemingly innocuous vessel at my so-called uncle's head, to shatter it beneath my feet and dance on the shards. Not fill it knowing I'd someday be forced to repeat past horrors.

But if I didn't fill the bottle? Then I'd never find Ava. *We'd* never find Ava.

After all, only a kitsune could handle a star ball. Mai might be able to do the job, but I wasn't about to ask my sister to leave the safety of her pack, not when my niece was nursing. Not when this was my problem to fix, not hers.

So I swallowed down bile and memories, tabling relief and anger to be digested at a more conducive moment. Nicking my thumb on the jewel-handled letter opener Chief Reed kept on the reading stand beside his chair, I squeezed out fat drops that slithered down the wall of the bottle like so many slugs.

"Is that sufficient?" I demanded once the bottom was covered.

"Certainly." Chief Reed snatched the returning bottle out of the air as easily as I had. "And the second favor is equally simple. I'll let you hunt the missing child as soon as you bond to a member of this clan."

Chief Reed, of course, was the only member of his clan present. He sat there smug in his armchair, waiting for me to accept this second inevitability.

The inevitability I'd been fighting against for weeks now. Because that was what Chief Reed had been angling for with his hunts and his training. Tie myself to even a single member of the Reed pack and I'd find it difficult to return to Gate City. Tie myself to the Reed alpha and I'd be instantly connected to every one of his pack mates. My chances of leaving this territory permanently would become nil.

Unlike with his demand of blood, however, Chief Reed hadn't driven me all the way into a corner this time. Because he wasn't the only member of his clan in this house, no matter what he thought. Willow would be hovering somewhere nearby, ready to jump at any hint of a wish from her alpha. Willow, who detested me for a very good reason but who I'd found to be kind when the memory of murder wasn't directly in her face.

Because she'd never harmed Pumpkin, even though she knew doing so would shatter something inside me. Instead, I'd walked in on the widow yesterday as she tempted the orange tomcat into the kitchen to offer him a bowlful of meat scraps. She hadn't seen me when she lifted a tentative hand to stroke Pumpkin's neck. Hadn't seen me when she gasped in pleasure at the way he arched into her touch.

Anyone who was kind to an enemy's cat, I was willing to bind to. So I took yet another step closer to Chief Reed, this time of my own volition. And I felt blindly for the pack bonds I knew radiated out from the alpha like rays of the sun.

Most slid through my fingers. Distant shifters were barely connected to their leader, and Chief Reed wasn't the type to nurture personal connections that would strengthen pack tethers.

But if Willow was physically close enough….

She was. I tasted sunshine in the back of my throat as my palm caressed a pack bond thicker than the others. Picking it apart with my thumbnail, I frayed the tendril just a hair.

Enough for me to pinch a thread and wrap it around my hand. Enough for me to….

Well, to *try* to form a connection. Willow fought the attempt the instant she realized who was messing with her tether. The thread whipped itself against my fingers, struggling to rejoin the thick bond leading to her alpha.

But I didn't let go. *I promise to make Quentin's death up to you,* I thought, forcing the words toward her down the pack bond. *I deeply regret that action. I will find a way to make your life better in the future than it's been in the past.*

I doubted Willow could hear my thoughts, but maybe she felt them. Because the thread calmed. When I wrapped it around my wrist, it didn't fight against me. Instead, it lay quiet as a sleeping cat while I tightened the knot with my teeth.

Only then did I turn to face Chief Reed. He hadn't gotten what he wanted, but I'd obeyed the letter of his command.

And…maybe he'd gotten what he wanted after all. Because this connection to Willow filled me with her needs, her wishes. She itched to have a cottage of her own where she could grieve in solitude. Even if I hadn't just promised to make her life better, I wanted to make that happen for her.

I wanted that even though getting involved would require me to return and deal with what I now left behind. I wanted that even though it meant not wriggling away from my oath to Chief Reed if the opportunity presented itself.

No wonder the alpha in question smiled his sly, cunning smile. No wonder his belly laugh slapped my face like an ocean wave I hadn't seen coming.

"Twenty-four hours," he warned. Then he turned his attention back to his book.

Chapter 37

The moment we left Chief Reed's presence, Charlie handed over her phone again and strongly suggested that I call my sister. It seemed Mai had been hounding her like crazy while I was incommunicado, accepting the story that my phone had broken but demanding I make contact sooner rather than later.

I itched to make that call…but I itched even more to mend the fence right in front of me.

Because Charlie hadn't asked me how I was doing. Had deflected my questions about herself. The silent treatment settled between us, making her car feel much smaller than it was in reality.

So I didn't call Mai. Instead, I told Charlie the unvarnished truth. "Look, I'm so sorry. You have every right to be furious. I was a bitch to your girlfriend."

For a moment, the silent treatment continued to press down on my eyebrows. Then, just like when we were kids, my friend softened. "I get it. I got it the instant I learned what was up with Ava." Charlie glanced up from the road for a moment, lips quirking, before refocusing on the winding route down the side of the mountain. "Nora isn't your biggest fan," she admitted, "but we'll work on that."

"You haven't told her about what's really going on in Gate City?" My question was pretty irrelevant given current circumstances…but I couldn't help asking given the circles Charlie moved in.

"About werewolves and fox shifters and strange magic imbuing the neighborhood? Nope." My friend popped her P then reached across the console to tap the cell phone. "Please call your sister before she rings to tell me how *disappointed* she is again."

This time, Charlie's words were just as pointed as they'd been earlier, but the sweet scent of forgiveness filled the vehicle. So I took my friend's acceptance of my apology at face value and I contacted one of the people I'd missed the most while stuck on Reed land.

"Charlie?" Mai's voice was clipped in what I called Scary Sister mode. She'd used that tone on me when I climbed trees in fox form and refused to come down for dinner, when I impersonated her to call us both in sick at school so she'd take me to the circus, when I let her talk for long periods then interrupted her with *"Huh? What was that? I had my ears turned off."*

No wonder Charlie had begged me to pick up the phone.

"It's me," I corrected. "Kira."

"Kira!" Scary Sister fled, replaced just as quickly by Worried Sister. "Breaking a phone is no excuse for not calling for *weeks*, young lady. Why didn't you use the new phone Gunner express mailed?"

"It must have got lost in transit." I cradled Charlie's cell a little closer to my head, wishing I could breathe in Mai's scent or at least see her face. Because Scary Sister or Worried Sister, the important part was *sister*.

Okay, and, yes, *sister* wasn't the only family member I'd missed. "Hey, could I talk to Grub?"

My favorite nephew must have been listening in the background because he caroled: "I'm here, I'm here, I'm here, Keeeeera!" so loud even Charlie chuckled.

"You sure are," I answered. "Are you being nice to Chipmunk?"

Silence. I tried again. "Chippy? Your sister?"

"Oh! Rorora." Grub mangled my niece Aurora's given name adorably, but a pang shot through me anyway. I'd thought for sure Grub would help cement the infant's nickname, but it appeared he hadn't. "I'm nice to her *always*," he rambled, "even though all she does is eat and poop. I'd rather play with you, Auntie Kira. When are you coming home?"

A rustle as the phone exchanged hands. A muffled *"Go ask your father for a cookie."* Then it was Noticing Sister who murmured in my ear. "Nicknames don't always stick, Kira. Remember how many you went through before settling on Grub?"

"Yeah, of course." I'd tried out all kinds of silly monikers before glomming onto the current one for my nephew. But I'd also been there to see Grub grow out of one baby stage and into another. Not so with my niece.

"Aurora's just like you," Mai continued. "Always doing crazy things that make no sense but that turn out to have their own sort of internal logic. She's going to be a handful when she's older. I can tell."

And, just like that, something clicked into place in my memory of Ava. Something that suggested where she might be and what might be going on.

But Charlie's car was crossing over the border into Gate City territory and a very familiar pickup was waiting on the other side. "Gotta go," I told my sister. Then I jumped out of the car and into Thom's arms.

"You look like you haven't slept for a week," I said an hour later as we neared Gate City. I was once again riding shotgun, this time in Thom's vehicle instead of Charlie's. In the interim, I'd debriefed him about the past few weeks and he'd caught me up on Gate City goings-on.

What we hadn't done was touch beyond that initial bear hug and, now, intertwining our fingers atop the gear shift. My twenty-four hour deadline mandated that I stick to business until we found Ava. And Thom, I got the distinct impression, was ashamed not to have fulfilled his own promise to find the missing child before this.

Sure enough, his scent was ragged as he answered. "I'll sleep when Ava's home."

Then we were pulling up in front of the Full Moon Saloon, Thom's designated spot empty even though the rest of the street was packed. It was Saturday, I realized, days of the week having run together while I was cooling my heels in the blue sitting room. Despite being barely lunchtime, the bar thrummed with life.

Thom opened the front door before I could reach it. "After you." Inside, dozens of heads turned to consider us. The space smelled furrier than usual, as if every werewolf had chosen to sit out here rather than in their customary seclusion within the Moon Room.

Which made perfect sense if a star ball was bouncing around in there. A star ball that wouldn't be a fan of werewolves.

I smiled back at the few who greeted me but I didn't stop to chat. Instead, I pushed through the moon-marked door into the shifter-only section, hoping Ava's magic would take to me better than to a member of Thom's pack.

I saw it the moment I entered. An untethered star ball floating midway between floor and ceiling. The key, I hoped, to bringing Ava home.

As if it felt the intensity of my interest, the glowing ball skittered away from me. Nearly skittered through the door into the main part of the bar before Thom's quick reflexes blocked that avenue of escape.

"It does this with everybody," he rumbled, closing the door firmly behind him. His tone likened the star ball to a feral cat scared of human companionship.

Which perhaps wasn't a bad analogy. I held out an empty hand...which spurred the magical sphere to zip away and hover in the corner where walls met ceiling. Out of anyone's reach. That wasn't going to work.

On a whim, I tugged my own caged star ball out from beneath my shirt and held it out at arm's length. "I'm like you," I promised. "Look."

For a moment nothing happened. Then the rogue light pulsed brighter. The star ball drifted downward. Air kissed my palm as magic landed as gently as a butterfly coming to rest.

I didn't grab it. Instead, I spoke through the strange sensation of someone else's star ball engulfing my fingers. "Ava is my friend," I murmured. "She needs you so she can escape a bad situation. So she can be a hero."

I doubted the star ball understood my words, so I filled my mind with images. Ava decked out in a cape and spandex, a big S emblazoned on her chest. If what I thought was true, she needed to believe in her own abilities while she waited for us to come rescue her.

She also needed to understand that what she was doing was the wrong path forward. Otherwise, chances were we'd find her and she'd send us packing. So I envisioned Dixie Lee sobbing. Imagined the adult human alone and sad, yearning for her daughter. Imagined....

Ava's star ball flared, scalding my fingers for one split second. Then the red orb caging my own magic popped open, releasing the other half of myself.

I laughed, delighted. I was a kitsune again. Could be a fox if I wanted, could bear a sword as easily as snapping my fingers. Even after returning to Reed territory, I'd no longer be completely under the alpha's thumb.

Now, though, I had to focus. So I tamped down bubbles of joy and considered the way my star ball and Ava's star ball twisted around each other to form one glow instead of two.

They seemed to be communicating. Never mind that I'd always thought of my star ball as merely a facet of myself rather than a being with its own personality and volition. Now, as two orbs of magic twirled around each other then separated again, they seemed to have minds of their own.

Together, they sipped at my fingertips and pulled me toward the back door the way Grub might tug me toward the ice-cream freezer in a gas station. Which was all good and well, but the worst that had happened when I indulged my nephew was a bellyache. If I opened this door, Ava's star ball might disappear for good.

Or it might carry my message to the child. Might travel slowly and let me and Thom follow. Might be the key I'd hoped for to unlock her cage.

"Be ready to run." I didn't dare glance back over my shoulder but I smelled the moment Thom twisted into fur form. That was clever. A wolf on the streets of Gate City might turn heads, but he'd sprint faster lupine than either of us could two-legged.

I turned the knob and opened the door, revealing blue sky and a sun so brilliant it hinted at springtime. For one split second, Ava's star ball hovered there, uncertain.

"Go to her," I nudged. "She needs you. But...slowly please."

Ava's star ball shot away so fast neither Thom nor I could tell where it had gone.

Chapter 38

"We still have the backup plan," Thom reminded me as he drew his clothes back on just out of sight before joining me in the open doorway.

"You're right." And when I'd imbued Ava's star ball with the image of her as a superhero, I'd really thought the backup plan had a good chance of working. After all, what I'd realized when talking to Mai was that Ava reminded me of myself at that age. Impulsive with her own sort of internal logic that got her both into and out of trouble. Once able to shift, surely she'd be able to wriggle out of captivity and make her way to a place visible enough for the pack to find her....

But the cold air reminded me that Ava hadn't spent her entire childhood learning how to manage her star ball. She hadn't been nurtured by an older sister who treated her abilities as assets. Instead, she'd been raised by Dixie Lee, who adored her daughter but considered kitsune heritage an ignorable curse.

Still, our backup plan was the only thing going at the present moment. So I wasn't surprised when the hum of conversation picked up on the bar side of the wall. When Thom turned to me with eyebrows raised in question.

"Go," I answered. I began closing the door as he left my side, intending to shift and join the hunt. But a minivan was pulling into the parking lot. A minivan I'd last seen in front of Charlie's house, one that suggested my unvoiced suspicions were about to prove accurate.

Because I'd had a lot of time to think while cooling my heels in Reed territory. I'd had time to consider the seeming push and pull of Kaito's willingness to speak with me. The way he came toward my voice when hiding in the rock maze then fled when he realized Thom was present. The way he'd contacted me so quickly after I'd left that note in the West Virginia post office, quickly enough that he might have seen virtual sparks fly as Thom and I intertwined our fingers on the way to and from my car.

Ava's kidnapping hadn't clicked into place until I'd seen the star ball on Charlie's cell phone. Then, the memory of Ito's words had come rushing back:

"My brother seeks a mistress."

That had been Kaito's motivation all along, to become part of a kitsune's honor guard. I'd been the original focus of his attention, but he must have realized my affections were promised elsewhere.

So he'd pivoted to fixate on someone else instead. A child who could be easily manipulated. A child with fox blood if not a star ball...at the time.

Now, I waited until Ito was close enough to hear normal speech, then I tossed out the question I'd wanted to ask ever since crazy possibilities had started invading my dreams.

"How about it, Ito? Are you finally willing to admit that your brother isn't dead?"

Ito's stride hiccupped, his face paling. But he continued drawing closer and closer until our toes touched.

Even through two sets of shoes and socks, I could feel the contact. A shock spun through me, much like the shock when I'd first touched the Gate City artifact. Electric and painful and powerful all at once.

Ito must have felt it also because his body quaked as he admitted. "It's true. He's not."

"What happened?"

For a moment, Ito just looked at me. His body leaned in closer as if he craved physical contact, but I glared and he spoke instead.

"You have to understand, Kira-san, that Kaito is my brother. I keep his confidences."

"You do his dirty work for him, you mean."

"Yes, I gathered you together for the funeral," Ito admitted. "I knew Kaito needed a mistress and you'd already sworn to be kind."

I didn't need explanations. I needed information about Ava. "But Kaito didn't take me. He took a child. Where is she?"

Ito shook his head. "I don't know."

"Shit." I tried to wrench myself away, but our shoes seemed to be superglued together.

Meanwhile, Ito reached toward me in a gesture that aborted a hair's breadth from my shoulder. "I can explain," he murmured. "About how I knew Kaito was alive at least."

This wasn't what I wanted clarified, but I nodded anyway. My head was spinning, trying to figure out how to use Ito's bond to his brother to reclaim Ava. While I thought, the man in front of me spoke.

"When we were children, Kaito broke his leg and spent many hours in bed thinking," Ito started. "Afterwards, he would joke that the pin embedded in his flesh was his greatest asset. All he had to do was track down a similar pin, then he'd be able to get away with anything. Rob a bank then light a huge fire and toss the spare pin in it. Afterwards, everyone would assume he was dead."

"Rob a bank...or steal Ava." Okay, so keeping my voice nonconfrontational wasn't working. I wanted to punch Ito, but something told me that if we touched the gesture would feed him more than injure him. So I kept my hands to myself as I demanded, "How could you let him molest a child?"

"Molest?" For the first time, Ito appeared confused. Then realization dawned. "You think that Ava is feeling the same"—he cleared his throat—"sexual confusion you're suffering from?"

The low hum of another car engine approached, but I ignored it. If a Gate City werewolf was showing up late to the hunt, Thom could guide him into place via the pack bond. I had a more pressing issue to deal with right now.

Because it was possible Ito had a clue about Ava's location, perhaps one he wasn't even aware of harboring. Keeping him talking seemed like the wisest course of action. "What else am I supposed to think?" I asked.

Ito's fingers brushed the air inches from my cheek, as if he wanted to soothe me the same way I soothed Pumpkin. When I flinched backwards, he turned to words instead of touch.

"Kaito is using a simple spell meant to please a mistress," he offered. "It helps the focus of his attention unlock her deepest desire so he can give her what she wants. Entirely harmless. No long-term ill effects."

For the first time in weeks, the muscles in my neck relaxed a little. A child wouldn't crave sex the way I did every time Thom's scent wafted into my nostrils. A child would want something age-appropriate and entirely different.

Like a star ball so she could become a hero. A star ball that had materialized on the same night my most recent moon craze struck.

That should have been a heartening thought...only, Ito had found a way to wriggle in a little closer. His shoulders cupped as if he wanted to embrace me but was holding himself just shy of touching. Each of his exhales flared hot against my skin.

Is that how Kaito would react now that I'd sent Ava the star ball? I'd meant the child to use it to free herself, but the magic might instead turn Ava as irresistible to her jailer as I appeared to be to his brother.

"I think I just made a terrible mistake," I muttered as a car door slammed in the parking lot.

Then a hand ripped me away from Ito. A hand with short, slender fingers that matched up with a recognizable voice.

"You sure did," Jessie said.

Chapter 39

Charlie's sister turned her attention to Ito as quickly as fire had licked through the house Kaito used to stage his own death. "I can't believe you're cheating on me with *Kira*."

"I'm not cheating." Despite his words, Ito was already edging around his wife, trying to get back into my personal space. If this was how his brother felt, it was no wonder he'd snatched Ava. The girl's lack of a star ball might have protected her during the last few weeks, but now that she'd come into her full potential....

I spun away from the marital conflict erupting behind me, paying attention with only half an ear as Jessie lambasted Ito for sneaking off with the kids. Apparently, it was a bad idea to pretend you were going to the park when your wife knew you hated dirt....

The kids. That was why Ito was here after all. I'd asked Charlie to summon him so I could ensure his children weren't in any danger.

Despite the strumming urgency inside me, I made a quick stop at Ito's vehicle. Sniffing the heads of two sleeping children, I determined they didn't smell fox-like at all.

No, Ava was the one that untethered star ball would be arrowing toward. Ava was the kitsune who'd been primed by Kaito and ignited by me.

And I knew of only one source of magic stronger than both of us. Leaving Ito to fight his own battles, I strode back into the Moon Room. Shoving aside the wardrobe, I ripped up the trapdoor that hid the fox-skull artifact.

The artifact which I suspected had been instrumental in materializing Ava's star ball. Likely with a healthy nudge from Kaito's moon ritual and maybe even a little help from Ava herself.

After all, the girl had stumbled upon me visiting the skull. She'd felt its power. What teen itching for a path to heroism could resist sharing a secret with someone offering her exactly what she craved?

"You know something." The angry female voice this time around wasn't Jessie's. Instead, it appeared Dixie Lee had been clued in that the hunt for her daughter was once again underway. Or so I assumed when she stomped through the bar-side door with all the finesse of a charging mother bear. I half expected her to tackle me, but instead, she stopped by my side, peering down with me into the dark beneath the floor.

So much for secrecy. I pursed my lips and hopped into the pit rather than answering. Used my star ball—it felt unbelievably good to have magic once again at my fingertips—to illuminate the stone walls and locate the artifact.

"I'm guessing," I answered while running my hand over the ancient bone. "Guessing that the kitsunes my sister defanged twelve years ago have something to do with this. One of them was my grandmother, so she wouldn't have had a spare star ball inside her. But the other one never bore children. When she lost her magic, that unused star ball might have somehow ended up here."

"And in me also." To my surprise, a whump of air preceded Dixie Lee landing beside me. She might detest kitsunes, but she was apparently willing to do whatever it took to get her daughter back. "That's why you thought Ava smelled like fox."

I nodded. "It must have been a lucky break that someone with kitsune blood was young enough to capture that remnant magic."

"Not so lucky," Dixie Lee answered. She reached out as if to touch the skull, then drew her hand away without making contact. "Ava had a terrible fever when she was around a year old. The doctors couldn't diagnose or treat it. She almost died."

I winced. Yet another way kitsune magic had harmed Dixie Lee's daughter. The question was, could the same magic save Ava from Kaito now?

I considered the fox-skull artifact that had shocked me the first time I touched it months ago. After that, it had seemed quiescent. But as I stroked the smooth bone, I thought I felt a hum of pleasure at my touch.

Pleasure...and a burst of images. A fox leaping from an upper-story window onto a gutter. A fox scampering across a porch roof, easily bridging the gap between house and tree then tree and ground.

That wasn't just any fox either. The animal was slightly gawky with youth, moving unevenly as if paws were a new addition to her body.

"I think Ava just escaped."

I shouldn't have spoken. Because the artifact provided no further information. And the hope in Dixie Lee's eyes dimmed in slow, painful increments as we waited through the night for a child who didn't come.

My oath was beginning to remind me that this wasn't home, that I was due back in Reed territory not long after daybreak, when something scratched at the parking-lot-side door.

In the interim, wolves had come and gone, reporting in about sectors patrolled and the complete absence of Ava. Jessie and Ito had united long enough to decide they and their kids should spend the night at Charlie's house then had started bickering again before they'd even made it to their separate vehicles. And Dixie Lee had become so agitated that she'd stopped noticing the psychological tricks I'd unveiled to keep her from rushing out into the night to join the hunt for her daughter.

Through everything, I made frequent pit stops of the literal sort, but the fox-skull artifact provided no further information or assistance. After the seventh attempt, I started wondering whether Dixie Lee wasn't right. Perhaps we would be better served pounding pavement after all.

Then that scratch, the scratch of an animal claw. I flung open the door and peered out into the darkness.

Not pitch dark. There were enough nearby streetlights so I could make out who'd come calling. "Dixie Lee, you'll want to get over here," I said, unable to take my gaze off the kitsune who had indeed saved herself.

Ava's fox tail was darkened on the tip, as if she'd dragged it through something vile. And she winced with each step, suggesting she'd worn her pads raw running on cracked pavement.

But she was whole and healthy. And as her mother approached, Ava rapidly shifted to join us on two feet.

Rapidly, but not entirely efficiently. A paw turned into a hand then into a paw again. When Ava finally figured out full humanity, she slapped one arm across her buds of breasts and the other across her privates. First lesson I'd have to give her was how to turn her star ball into emergency clothing.

But that wasn't relevant now. Instead, I moved out of the way, waiting for Ava to run into Dixie Lee's arms. To crow about having escaped all on her lonesome.

Instead, Ava's weight shifted from foot to foot, her gaze staying on her bare feet. "I know you didn't want me to be a fox, Mom."

"Are you kidding?" Dixie Lee was the one who grabbed her daughter into a hug so tight I could hear the breath whooshing out of both of them. "I want you to be exactly what you are, Ava. I'm so grateful you're home. I'm so *proud* of you."

"But I was dumb," Ava said into her mother's shoulder. Dixie Lee hadn't let go of her and didn't appear likely to in the near future, so the girl's voice was muffled as she continued. "Kaito told me I could be special, so I left the funeral with him. It wasn't until my star ball showed up that I realized he didn't want me to be special for myself. He wanted me to be special for *him*."

"You were always special," Dixie Lee promised into her daughter's hair. "And you're even more special now."

"You mean it?" Ava drew back so she could see her mother's face.

"I mean it," Dixie Lee answered, every word encircled with the sweet scent of truth.

After that, Dixie Lee drew her daughter into the Moon Room, murmuring endearments while gathering spare clothes out of the rolling wardrobe. I wanted to follow, but something was pulling me in the opposite direction. Out the door, which I closed quietly behind me. Through the nearly dark parking lot and around the corner of the next building until I'd entered the alley proper.

Midweek, there would have been at least a few people around. But before dawn on a Sunday morning, I had the place all to myself.

To myself, except for the alpha who loped toward me two-legged but with all the grace of his wolf form. "Kira," Thom called, voice gritty with tiredness and something else I couldn't quite put my finger on. "We found Ava's trail then lost it. I called the bar in case she'd turned up there but no one answered."

"It's okay. She's here." My stomach fluttered, not quite in the way it usually did in Thom's presence. Instead, my veins felt fiery. My feet refused to stay put.

"She made it before he caught up then." The dull thud of Thom's steps on the pavement slowed. Relief was evident beneath the lack-of-sleep burr in his voice.

"He?"

Then, behind me, someone else spoke. Someone whose words turned flutter into shudder. "Mistress. Finally. Get rid of the wolf, then we'll talk."

Chapter 40

The voice tugged at my oath like the reins on a horse, momentarily quieting the countdown clock tugging me back toward Reed territory. Because this was Kaito and I'd sworn to make him happy. Expelling Thom would do just that.

No. I shook my head. Kaito's best interests were important, but I didn't have to slavishly obey him. Not when he'd imprisoned a child for weeks on end. Not when, I could tell, he was hoping to do the same with me now.

Instead, I surged star-ball magic into sword form and whirled, aiming for the dark alcove off the alley that the voice had emerged from. I didn't intend to injure Kaito. Just to threaten him until he surrendered. Until Thom could draw the rest of the pack here to deal with this man who'd run rings around all of us.

Only...none of that was in Kaito's best interests, was it? My oath fought the momentum of my own sword stroke, twisting my blade so it struck the pavement with a cascade of sparks. Inside the darkness only feet from me, the shape that had to be Kaito murmured, "The wolf. Send him away."

"She can't send me anywhere." Behind me, Thom's voice was rapidly approaching. "Not before the rest of the pack arrives. You might as well come out and face the music."

Ignoring Thom, Kaito spoke directly to me again. "Take his blood, mistress. Take his blood and use it to get rid of him and his pack."

I had absolutely no intention of stealing Thom's will from him via blood magic. And then...my intentions changed. The closest streetlights flickered, something I'd begun to associate with the fox skull in the Full Moon Saloon's crawl space. Then my sword arm was acting without my permission. Was rising with blade extended as my feet danced around in a circle. The tip would have sliced through Thom's bicep if he hadn't met my blow with his own sword.

The clang of metal on metal knocked a little sense into my brain. Into my brain, but not into my fingers. They kept straining to push my sword forward even though I had no chance of succeeding in a brute-force contest against Thom's greater strength.

"Yes, just like that," Kaito murmured. Out of the corner of my eye, I caught the flicker of candlelight where he was standing. Candlelight combined with an overwhelming wave of fox scent. Whatever magic the honor guard member had used in the Reed forest, he was spinning a similar web now.

A web that fogged my brain again until the only words I could think were: *Take Thom's blood.*

A hum of pleasure rose from beside me. Then: "A little faster, mistress. Faster and slyer. Remember, you're a fox."

My feet and arms remembered. And even though I'd never sparred with Thom, I knew him. Knew he wouldn't want to hurt me. Knew he'd expend only the barest modicum of energy defending himself while trying to draw me down the alley away from Kaito.

So I followed Thom's lead. Followed then used his own momentum to guide my blade toward his chest.

It was an idiot's move on my part. Such an overt attack turned me defenseless. Thom could have landed blows on three different parts of my body without breaking a sweat.

He didn't, though, just as I'd known he wouldn't. Instead, he tried to block my offensives, even though doing so meant bringing his sword so close to his face it nicked his own chin.

I laughed out of pure pleasure. Yes, this was what I'd wanted. The wound was the merest of scratches but sufficient for our purposes. Reaching out with the hand that didn't clasp my sword hilt, I knew Thom wouldn't bat away my finger. Knew he'd let me stroke his skin...and steal a single drop of precious blood.

I held my finger up to the closest streetlight to consider the ruby semicircle. I had to drink it. I knew that. Had to drink the blood and force Thom and his pack mates out of Kaito's proximity.

But whatever magic Kaito had conjured in his alcove, it had been cast in haste and didn't have the full force of the full moon behind it. So my thoughts, although muzzy, were increasingly my own.

I didn't want to send Thom away. Not now, not ever. He was the anchor who'd moored me during the past three months cast adrift from my family. He merged the best characteristics of an alpha werewolf with the chivalry of a southern gentleman. And when he'd finally dropped his guard and kissed me without reservation, we'd simply *fit*.

All of this ran through my mind even as my finger rose toward my lips. I might want Thom by my side, but I couldn't work against Kaito's wishes.

I could, however, twist as best I could beneath the web of his demands.

So I forced myself into mental blinders. Reminded myself that Ito was his brother's strongest ally. Sending for Ito now would only help the man I was oath-bound to. Would be in Kaito's best interests.

I held that thought close, forcing myself to forget the flip side of the coin. Forcing myself not to dwell on the fact that Ito, as the one who had pinned me down to putting Kaito's welfare above my own, could also release me from that oath.

Forgetting allowed me to whisper a request to Thom. "Send Ito here."

But I couldn't resist the urge to draw my bloody finger between my lips. Couldn't prevent myself from licking up salty fluid then demanding, "Go far away and take the entire pack."

"Well done, mistress." Kaito emerged from the alcove and together we watched Thom struggle against the marionette movement of his own limbs. The hole in my stomach deepened as Thom rounded the corner and disappeared from sight, but Kaito's voice just turned more seductive. "Now call for your apprentice."

"Apprentice?"

"Ava. I smelled your magic on her. She's yours and I'm yours and together we'll be an unbeatable force."

"No." Somehow, I found a way to raise my sword against Kaito a second time. Found a way to aim for his throat.

Because Thom and I were adults able to deal with the repercussions of this night. Ava was just a child who had gone through enough already. I couldn't draw her back into this madness. I *wouldn't*. I might not have made an overt promise to that effect to Dixie Lee, but I made that promise now inside my own head.

And it was enough. The countervailing oath allowed me to clench my lips shut then thrust cold steel into the space between me and Kaito.

Unfortunately, Kaito had been a member of a kitsune's honor guard just like his brother had. As such, his knowledge of swordcraft was so deeply ingrained I shouldn't have been surprised when a blade I hadn't noticed countered my blow so quickly I barely took in the flash of movement before metal connected.

It was impossible to ignore the electricity spinning down the crossed weapons from his fingers to my fingers. And in the other direction also, I suspected, when Kaito's scent became suffused with pleasure. "Yeeessss, mistress," he groaned, his words forcing heat into my body. "Fight me this way, not the other. Surely you want something more than a useless alpha. Forget him and focus. What is it you crave? What is it you truly want?"

As he spoke, Kaito's sword slid along the length of my sword like fingers caressing from hip to ankle. Withdrew and feinted while tempting me forward in a dance of bodies and blades.

"Ava mentioned your family," Kaito murmured as we pirouetted away from the alcove and into the daylight beginning to creep up the length of the alley. "Family is the heart of all of us. Tell me and I can help you achieve your wish."

As he spoke, for the first time in over a decade, I was able to see Kaito's face clearly. His dark eyes were squinched up with the same glee I'd seen in Grub when my nephew figured out how to stack a stool atop a counter to reach the cookies hidden nearly at ceiling level. Kaito's black hair gleamed beneath the closest streetlight like Mai's had after I brushed it with a hundred careful strokes.

Love suffused me. "Yes," I answered, dazed by the past layered atop the present. "I want my family. But I can't have them. They're not safe near me."

"But they could be." Kaito dropped beneath the swirl of my blade, ignoring the easy opening I'd accidentally left for him. He didn't want to end our match...and I found I didn't want to either. This connection between us was so heady it rivaled the moon craze. Headier yet was the picture painted by his subsequent words.

"Together, we're a force to be reckoned with. No more hiding, no more scraping by. We can live wherever you wish to live. With your sister. With my brother. We'll build an enclave safe from the world and there we will do as we wish."

An enclave where I could watch Aurora grow up the same way I'd watched her brother's early childhood. An enclave where I wouldn't have to worry about the overwhelming danger presented by angry werewolves if I dared to spend time with my sister.

Something inside me niggled warning. This wasn't right. I was forgetting a very important part of that rosy picture....

Then Kaito's sword guided mine into a spiraling display that left us both laughing from pleasure. What had I been thinking? Oh, yes. That Kaito was correct. That the solution wasn't to fly beneath the radar the way I'd always thought it was. The solution was to appear powerful rather than weak.

Our blades chimed together again and again. Then they met in an X and I found our faces sliding closer and closer through the gap above where the swords crossed.

Something wasn't adding up, but I didn't know what that could be. Only knew that Kaito's promise strummed through me like a plucked guitar string. Living with my sister without worrying about her safety was my top priority. I wanted what Kaito was offering.

"Make me yours, mistress," he murmured, twisting his chin upwards to bare his throat. He let my sword settle there, nestling against the soft skin that hid his jugular. Would taking Kaito's blood grant me everything I wished?

Chapter 41

"**B**rother."

Someone stood behind Kaito, blocking the glow of the rising sun. I cocked my head, trying to make out who it was. But Kaito murmured, "No, mistress," and I refocused on him instead.

"*Brother.*" The familiar voice grew louder, more adamant. Then rapid footsteps preceded the addition of a female voice.

"Is that Kaito? I thought he was dead."

"Not now, Jessie. Kaito needs a mistress badly. He's losing himself to the craving."

I felt like I should be doing something. Saying something. But the heady surge of whatever-it-was rushing down the blade turned me sluggish.

Instead, Kaito was the one who spoke for both of us. "I've found a mistress. I don't need your help."

"You've found a kitsune," Ito corrected. His voice was firmer than I'd ever heard it. Something about his words started clearing the fog in my head. "Two of them, actually. But neither wants an honor guard. You can force what you want in the moment, brother. But the connection won't stick."

"And you have a better solution? Bind yourself to a human who will never understand you?"

Jessie's voice intervened again. "Ito, what is he talking about? What do you mean by a mistress? Is Kaito cheating? How could he have a wife I'd never heard of after being in a coma for so long?"

A long-suffering sigh was followed by the repetition of a sentence I'd overheard half a dozen other times during the last twelve hours. "No one is cheating, Jessie."

Kaito's breath caressed my cheek as he laughed. "Mistress, perhaps you could demonstrate what we are for the human's sake."

Demonstrate? Sure, I could do that.

I hated to pull my sword away from Kaito's, so I merely withdrew a sliver out of the center. Turned the fraction of my star ball into a glow what coated my fingers and skittered up my shoulder to caress my own neck.

"What's that?" Jessie's voice grew fainter, as if she'd lost track of the vengeful wife persona that had sent her rushing after her husband. As if she'd sank down onto the curb when her legs grew weak.

"It's kitsune magic," Ito answered, his voice choked. "Stop it, Kaito. You know I can't resist this any more than you can."

Sure enough, his voice was a little closer than it had been a moment earlier. Inches from my nose, Kaito smiled. "Don't resist then, brother. Our mistress will be doubly powerful with both of us in her honor guard. Think how wonderful it will be to work together again."

I shook my head. Honor guard? Was that what I wanted? I didn't think so....

And it was almost as if my confusion had given Ito the strength to reject me. Because his voice was no closer when he refused his brother. "That's not what I want, Kaito. I've found a new life. I've come to peace with the yearning." His voice grew muffled then, as if he'd turned away from us and toward his wife. "I only hope Jessie can come to peace with it also. I know this is a lot to take in, Jessie, but the part that matters is simple. I love *you*. You and the kids."

A pause, and when Jessie spoke her voice trembled. "You could have told me."

"I should have told you. Can you forgive me?"

No words emerged in answer. Just the sweet scent of marital affection. Of unity and understanding. Of love that started with the physical then deepened into something much more.

And their reconciliation woke in me a memory of what I truly wanted. Yes, I yearned for the future Kaito had painted where my presence wouldn't be a danger to my sister. But, more, I yearned to ask Thom the question that had sat on the tip of my tongue since the moment I'd set eyes on him yesterday on the Reed border.

Thom, who had managed in three months to turn a hodgepodge of lone wolves into a pack without a single bloodletting. Thom, who knew me more deeply than anyone ever had before or might ever again.

Thom, whose piercing blue eyes and subtle smile brought everything back into focus. The reality was that Kaito had manipulated first Ava then me. He needed to be neutralized and, from the murmurs and lip smacks behind me, it appeared Ito wasn't going to be any help in the matter.

Which was fine, because my mind was clear now. And, with a clear mind, I understood that I could defuse the Kaito situation while also giving him what he truly craved.

A mistress. Not me, not Ava, but another kitsune who had willingly taken on an additional honor-guard member not so many years ago.

After all, back at the funeral, I'd overheard Dixie Lee learning how Ava's father had been unable to resist the draw of past behaviors. How he'd returned to a country where kitsunes were numerous and honor guards were customary.

Withdrawing my sword from Kaito's sword, breaking the connection that had fogged my brain and strengthened his magic, I observed, "I'm buying you a plane ticket to Japan."

Ito and Jessie promised to escort Kaito on his journey, an issue I couldn't take care of personally because my time in Gate City was waning. With every passing second, my oath to Chief Reed was doing its darnedest to draw me north and east.

I fought the pull long enough to break my blood command exiling Thom and his pack mates from their own territory. Then, while I waited for them to return to Gate City, I headed back into the Moon Room to speak to a chunk of bone.

Because the fox skull had fueled Kaito's spells. I knew that in my gut and knew, also, that the artifact could be manipulated toward even worse ends if I didn't do something to prevent that eventuality. A trap door apparently wasn't nearly enough.

So I spoke to the skull the same way I'd speak to a partner. Explained that it had been used to kidnap an unwilling kitsune. To force me to the brink of making a decision I'd always regret.

"I can't stay here," I told what I hoped wasn't just an inanimate remnant of a long-dead kitsune. I hoped I wasn't wasting my final moments in Gate City on a flight of fancy. "But I can protect you," I continued. "If you'll let me be your gatekeeper, I'll prevent others from taking advantage of the power you've stockpiled."

I drew the necklace that Chief Reed's dead heir had given me out from under my shirt. Tapped the open halves against the orbital ridge of the fox skull. Then I explained what I hoped to do. "This necklace binds kitsune magic," I told the artifact. "It can bind you if you let it. I'll ensure you're not manipulated another time to harm a child."

I waited. Nothing happened. Well, nothing other than the door to the outside blowing open. The scent of alpha wafting in.

I itched to jump out of the pit and spend my last few minutes with Thom. But I didn't. Not yet. Instead, I waited...

...And the tiniest chip of bone fell away from the artifact. Fell straight into the open orb of my necklace. I snapped the two halves shut, not expecting much. After all, I'd tried to pry the necklace open for days, had no clue how Chief Reed had locked it closed or what Ava's star ball had done to release my magic.

But just completing the circle worked. Something shot through me, a shock ten times stronger than the one that had greeted me the first time I touched the artifact. A shock that almost felt like a female voice.

"Welcome, Keeper of the Gate."

I'd have to discover the meaning of those words later. Because my time had nearly run out.

I didn't have the hours I wanted to make my proposal to Thom special. All I could do was whisper a question in his ear then grin as he whirled me around and around and around.

"Of course I want that," Thom told me when he finally let my feet settle back onto the floorboards. "I want that more than anything."

"I have to leave again," I reminded him. "Pretty much immediately afterwards. I can't bond with your pack while I'm on Chief Reed's hook."

The ecstatic sweetness surrounding both of us dampened just a little, but Thom nodded. "I know that. And I still want this. If you're part of the deal, I'll take whatever I can get."

So I woke up Mai with a sunrise phone call. Gathered the people I cared most about together even if some only tuned in virtually. And with Mai's kids and mate, Charlie and Dixie Lee and Ava, Thom's entire pack, and even Chief Reed's grandniece watching, I poured everything I felt for Thom into my right hand while he poured everything he felt for me into his left hand. Our palms clasped together and a mate bond ignited, its brilliance eclipsing the rising sun.

The new bond joined tethers I'd accepted willingly. The pack bond to Willow that niggled at the skin of my wrist, requiring attention. The whatever-it-was between me and the artifact that twitched every time I thought about leaving Gate City. The oath I'd sworn to Chief Reed that meant I couldn't stay here more than another twenty minutes.

My mate bond to Thom layered on top of and around all of them. It warmed me even before he—my *mate*—slipped his mother's medallion over my head then kissed me soundly. Even before our audience started laughing and Grub shouted, "Gross!"

Then I left them, all the people I loved plus the alpha werewolf who was the other half of my soul now. I got into my car and drove myself across the border between Gate City and Reed territory, back to a pack leader who was thoroughly distasteful but who might one day tell me more about who I was and how my magic worked.

More important, though, was the bond that stretched tight between me and Thom. The bond that strained but didn't break as distance yawned between us.

This time, even leaving my heart behind, I no longer traveled alone.

Rock Mazes

Yet another note from the author...

The rock maze in *Rogue Moon* is a real natural feature that can be found in several locations in the Appalachian Mountains. The next two pages contain photos of a couple of the rock mazes I merged together to create the one Kira faced. First, The Ledges inside Cuyahoga National Park in Ohio. And on the facing page is a photo of me taken by Jennifer Rusche along the Rock Maze Trail in Garrett County, Maryland.

MOON DUEL
KIRA FAIRWOOD: BOOK 3
USA TODAY BESTSELLING AUTHOR
AIMEE EASTERLING

Moon Duel

Chapter 1

I t all started with fox pee in Italian leather shoes. Fox pee and a very pleasant kiss...

Thom's broad hand cupped my cheek, fingertips stroking circles of pleasure beneath my hairline. I was half turned away because *noses.* Every bodily protrusion risked crossing the boundary between Gate City territory and the land belonging to the endlessly unpleasant Chief Reed, the land Thom couldn't enter but that I had to stay on as Reed heir.

"Neck," Thom growled and I arched the requested body part out to meet him. Heat, lips, the scrape of teeth against sensitive skin. I hummed my pleasure, reciprocating with fingers sliding down the hard line of side toward his hip...

And my cell phone erupted into jangly music.

Reluctantly, I pried my eyes open, blinking against the brightness of late April sun filtering through tiny, unfolding leaves in the canopy above us. My phone lay at my feet because Thom and I had both run here in fur form, which meant no pockets.

It also meant nothing to cover the magnificence of Thom's lean, muscular body. Lifting one foot, I daintily tapped the end-call button with my big toe. Then I smiled at my mate. "Face me," I demanded.

We both knew this stance had major technical difficulties. Still, wordlessly, he obeyed.

Full frontal, one part of Thom jutted out further than all others. Which meant I couldn't touch skin without crossing that dratted dividing line between two pack territories. Well, I couldn't touch skin save one square inch of rounded, luscious tip.

I touched. And the phone blared a second time. "Answer it," Thom suggested, his voice slightly choked, "or he'll dream up another sadistic punishment."

"I don't care."

"Well, I do."

So I accepted the call with the same toe I'd used previously. Headed off Chief Reed's complaint with the honest truth. "We did not cross the line."

I knew this because I'd learned the hard way over the last few months that putting so much as a fraction of a toenail over the boundary line caused a jolting shock to my system. Thom wasn't oath-bound the way I was, so he *could* cross without physical pain. But Chief Reed was glad to use any intrusion as an excuse for inter-pack aggressions. It was a good thing my mate had an instinct for the boundary coordinates the same way he did for the locations of members of his pack.

Unfortunately, the other pack leader in my life, the one who I was oath-bound to obey but whose rules I wiggled out from under on a regular basis, didn't bother responding to my parry. Instead, his voice went just as deep and growly as Thom's had been but for a very different reason. "You peed in my Ermenegildo Zegna last night."

"Your ermine zelda?" I twirled my spare hand around in a demanding circle, halting Thom once I'd gained a few more inches of skin to play with. And while my honorary uncle griped, I played.

"Don't pretend not to know what I'm talking about," Chief Reed ended. "The scent is vile."

"Doesn't wash out either," I commiserated. "Such a shame. But that's what happens when you coop up a fox."

Rather than arguing the point, Chief Reed's voice turned darker. "A pack hunt is beginning as we speak."

"That's nice."

"I expect you to join us." This wasn't a request. It was a demand from my alpha. Since I wasn't a werewolf, though, the words didn't wrap around my gut and yank me into line.

"You know what they say," I answered, allowing the pleasure I felt at being here with Thom to warm cold words. "Expectations are premeditated resentments."

Thom swayed slightly, and I don't think it was because of my verbal cleverness. One of his hands reached out in my direction, stuttering to a halt at the boundary line we couldn't cross without risking repercussions from my pack leader. The other hand clenched itself into a fist.

Over the months, Thom and I had found ways of sating our frustrations. We could separate, lie on either side of the line and watch the other bring him or herself to completion. Gaze never wavering, it was possible for me to imagine the hands roving across my body were my mate's.

But today we didn't go there. Because the faintest slurp emerged from the cell-phone speaker. And this time when Chief Reed spoke, his words compelled me as easily as if I was a puppet. "Join the pack hunt. *Now.*"

I was barely able to delay long enough to strap the cell phone to my suddenly furry back with a tendril of star-ball magic. Then I was four-legged and sprinting toward werewolves I neither liked nor trusted as they hunted prey for status rather than food.

Chief Reed had compelled me to join the hunt, but by the time I made it back to the villa I'd lived in for the last four months, the premises were vacant. Lungs billowing and pads throbbing, my body didn't let me pause long enough to catch my breath or soothe my throat with a sip of water. Instead, I set my nose to the ground and followed the trail of wolf back down a different side of the same mountain I'd just run up.

Only, the pack had doubled back over and over, crossing their own footsteps and setting me a chase as if they were the prey and I was the hunter. At this rate, I'd be trailing behind snickering werewolves all afternoon. But there was no alternative. Not when Chief Reed had frittered away a sip of my freely given blood to force me into an endless hunt.

Frittering was good though. Frittering meant sore paws and a parched throat instead of...

Blood on marble. Pain in my fingers a tactile reminder that I'd recently hacked through the neck of a living being. Vomit lingered on my lips from where I'd tried and failed to repeal the past...

I squeezed shut the faucet gush of memory, my breath now wheezing in and out for a reason other than exertion. Yes, it was a good thing that Chief Reed was using up my blood one sip at a time. Maybe soon he wouldn't have enough left to make me do something I'd regret for the rest of my life.

Something *else* I'd regret for the rest of my life.

The sip this time must have been infinitesimal, however. Because, soon thereafter, the blood compulsion lifted sufficiently to let my brain work the problem rather than my feet merely stumbling mindlessly forward. I still had to find the pack, but I didn't have to follow Chief Reed's tortuous route back and forth through the same patch of forest to get there. Instead, I tapped into my sole pack bond, the one I'd built between myself and Willow, the mate of the man I'd killed.

Killed without remorse or warning. Killed because he stood in my way, not because he was about to harm another...

I choked down the past, focusing on cutting across country the short way. The sooner I got this over with, the sooner I could return to Thom, who was likely waiting impatiently in the same sunlit patch of forest where we always met.

That was a much more palatable image to focus on. My naked mate, his blue eyes lighting up when he saw me running toward him between broad-trunked tulip-trees. He always hummed when I shifted upward into humanity. Even the memory of his rumbling "Hello" warmed my bones.

I was so intent upon replacing bad memories with good ones that I wasn't paying attention when I stumbled into real, present-day carnage. *Blood, blood, blood...* I teetered on the brink of awfulness, about to fall fully into the pit of the past.

Then I swallowed hard and forced myself to see what was actually there rather than what my horrified brain was trying to turn this into. Yes, something had been slaughtered in this wooded hollow, but the deceased hadn't been human. Instead, deer parts were strewn across the ground, red streaks painting tree trunks with lewd words and imagery. The typical end of a Reed hunt, where the pack played out the sadism inside their alpha's head.

The culprits were largely absent, however. Only one underling—Willow—lay in wolf form at her fully clothed alpha's feet.

Like the tree trunks, Chief Reed was painted red from his fingers to his three-piece suit and watch fob. But he must have licked his teeth bare because they glinted white when he greeted me. "You were slow."

I shifted upward and waited to speak until I was sure my voice wouldn't quaver. "You don't appear to have been bored."

"Never." My nemesis stalked toward me, Willow trailing behind like a well-trained lap dog. "I called you here to discuss the Moon Trials."

Not fancy Italian shoes? I cocked my head, unsure what he was referring to.

When I failed to answer, Chief Reed sighed. "You really know very little about our world. Good thing you have me to educate you. The Moon Trials are a long-lived tradition. Once a decade, pack heirs from across the United States converge to fight for status. Admission to the Trials is an honor I have worked hard to achieve for you."

"Not interested."

"No?" He lashed out with one bare foot and struck Willow hard in the softness of her belly. Pain ricocheted down our pack bond, but she didn't cringe away or yelp. Chief Reed, who would have felt the same thing through the bond he also shared with her, smiled then continued. "Maybe if you're lucky, your Thom will meet you there. Wouldn't that be nice—a honeymoon bathed in blood?"

The verbal imagery forced me to rise to bait I knew I shouldn't have. "I doubt our host will allow another pack leader to enter his territory uninvited."

"It's true that each heir is allowed only a single plus-one. Willow will be yours. But I hear Thom is quite resourceful."

Chief Reed waggled his eyebrows but I ignored the subtext this time. Kept my words simple. "Same answer. Should I spell it out for you? N. O."

Willow and I both tensed, waiting for another physical outpouring of displeasure. Instead, Chief Reed lowered his voice. "I will reward you for your wholehearted participation."

I wasn't so sure I wanted any reward Chief Reed was offering, but I didn't want him to kick Willow again either. So—"I'm listening," I said.

His scent sweetened. He thought he had me with whatever he was about to offer. And he was almost right.

"Win three battles at the Moon Trials," Chief Reed murmured, "and you will be granted one day per week to spend with your mate."

"In Gate City?"

"Wherever you choose."

I wanted that. I wanted it so badly. Not just to see all of Thom rather than the inches that brushed up against the boundary, but to hang out with friends new and old at the bar my mate managed. The warmth, the life, the camaraderie... Gate City was nothing like the cold, hard marble within which I now lived.

But I could read between the lines. The Moon Trials wouldn't consist of gentlemanly fencing matches. Heirs would fight tooth and claw, lacking face guards and armor. There would be pain and blood and possibly even death.

It wasn't my own death I was afraid of. I swallowed down memories before they could latch on with pointy teeth, fighting back the haze of red that threatened to cloud my vision. "Not interested," I repeated, mentally apologizing to Willow.

But Chief Reed didn't attack physically this time either. Instead, he offered the stick to go with the carrot. "No? Then you won't mind slaying this useless wolf at my feet."

He reached into his vest pocket and removed that awful little bottle, still half full of my freely given blood preserved in alcohol. If he downed the whole thing, he could force me to do anything.

I closed my eyes, opened them again. "I'll go," I promised.

Chief Reed smiled so wide I could see blood resting on his tongue. "Of course you will."

Chapter 2

One week later, the descending airplane left my stomach behind as it carried me toward violence, mayhem, and hopefully some long-delayed hanky-panky with my mate. Because Thom had promised to be here waiting for me, and I'd chosen to ignore everything else that might possibly go wrong.

Now, I unsnapped my seat belt and surged up onto my knees, craning around the man on my left for a view of our destination. Beneath us, water butted up against city, the crazy-quilt pattern of reds and oranges in the San Francisco Bay salt ponds sunlit except for one tiny shadow that matched the shape of our plane.

That was what I'd be soon—a speck in an overcrowded field. A single not-so-interested Moon Trials participant facing down dozens of cutthroat fighters willing to battle to the death for a decade of bragging rights. Unlike them, I intended to use every asset at my disposal to fly under the radar, win Chief Reed's mandated three contests, then return to Virginia a much happier fox.

"Looking forward to a second murder?" Willow didn't even glance up from her in-flight magazine while raising memories like ghosts in a graveyard. *Spilled blood, unseeing eyes, a too-wide mouth frozen in a leer of endless surprise...*

I shook my head to cast off mental images while Willow flipped to another page and continued taking me to task. "The flight attendant will be here momentarily to remind you, *again,* to fasten your seatbelt."

"You don't sound happy to be along for the ride," I countered, obediently sinking back down and clipping the restraint around my middle. "I thought you were itching to get out from under Chief Reed's thumb."

And, sure, as best I could tell, Willow's purpose as plus-one was mere window dressing. An alpha is nothing without a pack, so an heir must travel with some sort of entourage. I supposed that was why her lips pursed up even tighter as she offered five clipped words by way of reply.

"I'm not. And I was."

That was all Willow gave me while our plane dipped lower, the view suggesting we were about to crash into water until the instant our wheels touched down on tarmac. In silence, Willow and I cooled our heels through several interminable deplaning minutes. In silence, we stepped out into an airport that stank of barely repressed fur and claws, catching fleeting glimpses of other Moon Trials contestants as they stalked through crowds of innocent humans while considering each other with murder in their eyes.

And when Willow finally broke the silence, she didn't acknowledge the fact that this was a dangerous place for a kitsune and a pack princess to linger. Instead, she addressed the elephant in the room...or, rather, stabbed that elephant with a cattle prod. "Today would have been my mate's birthday, you know."

"I didn't know." All I knew was the way my stolen sword had sliced through Quentin's neck four months earlier. The blade hadn't bit in easily the way swords do in movies. Instead, I'd had to brute force my way through flesh and bone.

But cinematic blood had indeed spurted through the air as the previous Reed heir fell, dead on contact. It didn't matter to either me or Willow that Chief Reed had forced my hand, drinking blood to make that death happen. I'd become a murderer last winter and now I was protecting my victim's mate by willingly walking into a situation that might force me to repeat that awfulness. Did that make me a better person than I'd been four months ago or worse?

A sharp pain in my side brought me back to the clatter of the airport. Willow's hand retreated, the indentations of her fingernails in my skin the only proof that she'd dealt a particularly vicious pinch.

Right. This wasn't the time to lose myself in memory. The scent of aggressive wolves was stronger here in the baggage claim, as if we'd caught up with more heirs in the moments I'd lost to nightmare. Willow and I needed to collect our luggage, find Thom, and get the heck out of Dodge.

Only, the aggressive alpha scent stuffing up my nostrils didn't emerge from distant shifters this time. Instead, my path was blocked by a man who I'd hoped never to see again. A man whose name I didn't even know.

"Executioner," I greeted him. He seemed to be playing up his title today, dressed in a stark black suit that blended with the ebony of his close-cropped hair and the charcoal of his eyes. The only color on his person was a bright red pocket square. The shade of a freshly picked rose, or of newly spilled blood.

Because, like me, this man was a murderer. In fact, he killed for a living. He wasn't, as far as I knew, heir to any pack however. What he was doing in San Francisco was beyond me.

As such, the Executioner was irrelevant to this week's drama. I pushed Willow into the shelter of my body as I started to step around him. "Excuse us," I murmured.

The low-key evasion didn't work. The Executioner's arm flashed out faster than it really should have among people who weren't privy to the paranormal. Hard fingers closed around my sleeve-covered upper arm.

And while I could have magicked up a sword and fought back, this was neither the time nor the place. So, instead, I summoned up my most contagious smile. "Are you here to kill me or protect me?" I asked, ignoring Willow's gasp as she tried even harder to sink into the floor.

To both of our surprise, my boldness worked. The Executioner's eyes twinkled just the tiniest bit as he relinquished his hold on me.

Or maybe I'd only imagined that flash of humor. Maybe the scent of Thom finally wafting toward me out of the crowd just made me see dewdrops and flowers in an arid desert.

Because the Executioner's answer wasn't heartening. Or explanatory. In fact, he offered me one word only: "Yes."

"Okay. Whatever." I turned my back on the hulking shadow of danger. Willow and I couldn't bull our way past the scary shifter but we could retreat into the crowd of humans, give the Executioner a wide berth, then get back on track on the other side.

Could and planned to, because my mate bond tightened and sang like a plucked guitar string. I knew even before picking Thom out of the crowd that the man I'd been yearning for had finished tugging our luggage off the carousel. His blue eyes were even now lifting to find mine, sending a wave of pure heat through my body. And while other alphas were busy jostling for position, space opened in front of Thom the instant he took a step forward. I aimed for an intersecting trajectory and...

The shriek of a sub-audible dog whistle pierced the room. Humans failed to notice, but every shifter winced, most dropping whatever they were holding so they could press their palms over their ears.

Willow's lips formed words I'd never imagined she knew the meaning of. Thom's cheek twitched as he barely managed to cling to our luggage. Meanwhile Rupert—my former co-worker and Thom's current pack mate, best known for his unerringly grumpy life outlook and surprisingly accurate moral compass—stepped out from behind my mate and proved himself to be the only shifter properly prepared.

"Noise-canceling headphones," Rupert mouthed smugly while tapping what appeared to be black earmuffs cupping his angular head. "Never leave home without them."

As if on cue, the whistling ceased. From behind my back, the Executioner's words descended like an icy chill over every shifter in the crowded baggage area. "You are here on a very limited invitation from the San Francisco alpha," he began, speaking at a normal volume despite the distance yawning between himself and the furthest werewolf. The humans around us hadn't stopped talking, but we all caught the gist well enough.

"Fail a fight and your invitation is rescinded, effective immediately," the Executioner's saw-rasp voice continued. "Losers and their plus-ones will be ferried back to the airport, at which point their immunity from trespassing becomes null and void."

I winced, relinquishing any hope that Thom and I would get to spend at least a little time together. I'd have to focus on the bigger picture instead. On Chief Reed's promise that if I won three matches I could enjoy one day a week in Gate City.

That plus the real reason I was here—the promise that Willow's death sentence would be lifted upon my third triumph.

Meanwhile, the Executioner was cracking his metaphorical whip. "Moon Trial participants will be on the vans out front in three minutes," he concluded. "Too slow and you will forfeit your spot."

Chapter 3

A stampede of werewolves erupted in the indicated direction even as I tried to turn backwards against the tide. Willow's fingers on my sleeve halted my backward momentum this time. "Your mate can afford to dally," she groused, tugging me toward the exit along with everyone else. "We can't."

Then we were outside the airport, in a busy loading zone. There, a clipboard-bearing woman considered the two of us for a moment before opting to ignore Willow while demanding of me: "Name?"

"Kira Fairwood."

"Fairwood?" The other woman's brows drew together. "I don't see you here."

From behind me, the ice of a predator's presence prickled hairs on the back of my neck. Before I could decide whether it was better to turn and face the danger or maintain the illusion of toughness, the Executioner's rough voice cut through Clipboard Lady's confusion. "Reed heir. She's been vetted."

"Reed heir," the woman agreed, checking the surname I hated off her list. "Van four."

"We'll be on van four also." Somehow, Thom had caught up to us, despite pulling far too many suitcases behind him. Somehow, his deep rumble melted away the ice shards that the Executioner's predatory intensity had sent shivering down my spine.

Some of that heat must have warmed Clipboard Lady also because she dimpled. "Yes, of course. And you are?"

"Thom Faris."

The woman flipped the page over, frowning. "Are you sure?"

My mate's cheeks crinkled into a half-smile that drew the woman's upper body subtly toward him. "Of my name?" he rumbled. "Positive."

"Ahem." I'd failed to notice Rupert's reappearance until his theatrical throat-clearing, but none of us could miss the way he drew himself up to his full height of approximately five feet zero inches while intoning: "*I* am the participant. Rupert Rumfelt."

Clipboard Woman appeared even more dubious about Rupert than she'd been about me. "Which pack?"

"Rumfelt, of course." Before the woman could ask for additional information, Rupert popped open his briefcase—the only item he carried—and drew out what appeared to be a certified deed. "I recently purchased an island."

"Oh, well, that's not exactly..."

"Eh, eh, eh." He held up a finger in the universal demand to wait while flipping through further paperwork. "According to the Treaty of 1914, alphas are considered heirs during the period between claiming their property and the moment they physically set foot on said property."

"Sir, I'm afraid the Moon Trials are for..."

Unlike Rupert, the Executioner didn't have to clear his throat to gain everyone's attention. "Write him in."

Clipboard Lady's polite refusal stuttered into silence. She averted her eyes from the Executioner while scribbling something on her paper and grimacing what was likely intended to be a smile in Rupert's general direction. "My apologies. Van three."

Thom and I rode in separate vehicles to a gymnasium that was nothing special. Just a big echoing arena with paired names sharpied onto posters spaced evenly along its length. The fighters had been set up in alphabetical order, so I zeroed in on the Fs, hunting first Fairwood then Faris before realizing I should have been looking for Reed.

Reed...one down from Rumfelt. Just outside the taped square where he'd be fighting, Rupert dribbled a big red ball that created painful non-harmonics no human would be able to hear. His headphones meant he either didn't know or didn't care that everyone around him was wincing and growling each time the ball and floor made contact. Willow muttered a complaint, but all I cared about was Thom.

Because my mate was waiting for me beside Rupert, no boundary separating us. We did have an audience, but I didn't particularly care about that. I strode forward...

Then—"Rules." The Executioner's voice cut across the room, stilling chatter and leaving nothing but the sound of Rupert's reverberating ball to fill the silence. A single dark eyebrow rose and four shifters dove forward to snatch the offending object before Rupert could slap his hand down yet again.

"You could have *said* something," Rupert complained, slipping his headphones down to hang around his neck. "No need to get physical."

As if the Moon Trials weren't going to become far more physical than that.

Physical in more ways than one. I'd finally reached Thom's side and his right arm rose to enfold me. The side-hug was simple, but it was more than we'd been able to do for months now. I half-listened as the Executioner continued speaking but mostly just reveled in contact with my mate.

"Thirty-two contestants," the Executioner rasped. "Elimination contests."

Beside us, Rupert pulled a calculator out of baggy cargo-pants pockets, typed in a few digits, then reported: "That would be five matches, assuming each involves exactly two parties. Alternatively, we could make this more efficient by..."

"Winner of the final duel," the Executioner said, speaking over Rupert, "organizes the next Moon Trials. Loser dies."

And Rupert's chatter faded to silence. Thom's body tensed against mine as he growled, "You didn't mention a fight to the death when explaining the setup."

"I didn't mention it because it's irrelevant," I countered, keeping my voice low. Public displays of affection were one thing, public displays of discontent another thing entirely.

Sure enough, scents of interest sparked to life around us. I could feel hungry eyes on the back of my neck as I murmured further explanation into my mate's ear. "Chief Reed only requires me to win three battles," I told him. "If necessary, I'll purposefully toss the fourth."

My mate didn't quite relax in the face of my promise, but his voice did turn less gritty. "I'll watch your back through four battles then."

"And Willow's back. And Rupert's." We weren't just side-hugging any longer. Thom had enfolded me in a full-body embrace that felt like nothing so much as coming home.

"Of course," he agreed with both words and body.

"Rules for today," the Executioner continued, his saw-toothed rasp no longer causing goose bumps now that Thom's arms encircled me. I nestled deeper as the Executioner laid down the law. "To win, you will cause the other party to surrender or to step outside the taped area. At that point, victors and their plus-ones will be transferred to a hotel to prepare for tonight's entertainment."

I should have been assessing the competition, plotting out strategy. But all that mattered was Thom's hot breath on my forehead. All that mattered was...

The absurd shortness of the Executioner's speech. He ended with a single word.

"Start."

Chapter 4

My muscles twitched with the double-edged blade of anticipation. Because this was a shifter competition where the scariest predator won, blood was expected to spill, and I hadn't even taken the time to unearth a weapon from my checked luggage.

Good thing I possessed something no werewolf had access to—a star ball that not only helped me shift into vulpine form but could also be molded into any shape I pleased. A flash of light and I was holding a sword no less sharp because it was magical. Then, meeting Willow's eyes and silently promising to cling to my humanity no matter the consequences, I took a deep breath and recentered on the upcoming fight.

I expected to face a stranger as I hopped into the taped-off square to face my opponent. But the werewolf in front of me was actually familiar. Liam Randolph, heir to the pack next door to my childhood home. The last time we'd met, Liam had been a gangly teenager. Since then, he'd filled out into a bear of a man.

He was also barreling toward me with all the finesse of a Viking berserker. Both hands gripped a broadsword, the weapon looming above his head while he greeted me with a wordless bellow.

And I grinned. I couldn't help it. I'd been worried about having to unleash my inner murderer to hold my own at the Moon Trials. But I could have won this contest bloodlessly while armed with nothing more than juggling scarves.

And words. Words were my greatest asset.

"You know," I observed, dancing out of the way of an attack that might have taken down a tree trunk but had little chance against more animate objects, "it's not as if we *stole* your sister. Lily fled from your pack. She asked us for help. You really should be thanking me."

No gratitude was forthcoming, which wasn't entirely surprising since I'd followed up my words with a couple of quick jabs of my star-ball weapon. Just a prick to his ribs. A scratch on his arm. Still, it was enough to set Liam growling and charging a second time. He slammed his sword into the spot where I stood...

I wasn't there waiting to be struck. I'd already vacated the premises as best I could in a square no more than ten feet on a side. Now, to keep my opponent blinded by rage...

"You're going to have to do better than that, *Shrimpy,*" I chided, trotting out the childhood nickname that had always tweaked his tail in the past.

Sure enough, Liam raised his hulking sword a third time, opening his entire body up for attack. Rather than diving in and fighting back, however, I peeked over my shoulder to consider what was going on next door.

Because if my own Trial was going to be this easy, I might as well see what I could do about keeping Rupert—and, by extension, Thom—in San Francisco for one night longer. Sure enough, Rupert's opponent was being cleverer than Liam, playing on his obviously superior dominance. *"Surrender,"* the tall redhead demanded with alpha bite in his voice...which totally should have done the trick.

But Rupert tapped his noise-canceling headphones with a smug smirk. "Eh, eh, eh. If you want to win, you'll have to fight."

So we fought, me against Liam and Rupert against an alpha whose name I hadn't bothered learning. I dodged with ease, letting Liam wear himself out while sparing plenty of attention for commenting on the contest on the other side of the taped line.

"Ooh, that looks like it hurt," I called as Rupert landed a surprise cut to the redhead's calf. My goal was simple—push the other alpha off the deep end Liam had already tripped over and into a pit of testosterone-laden brain fog.

Unfortunately, my nudge had the opposite effect from the one I'd anticipated. The redheaded alpha feinted then lunged forward, leading with his weaponless left hand. "What are you doing?" Rupert shrieked as his protective headphones were forcibly ejected from his scalp along with a sizable handful of hair.

At which point the redhead spat out yet another alpha order. *"Surrender,"* he told Rupert. *"Now."*

Among werewolves, alpha commands are a quick and easy way to determine pecking order. If you're dominant, you can force those with less oomph to do pretty much anything you please. As a kitsune, I was immune, but until last fall I'd thought werewolves were bound by alpha commands as a fact of life.

Rupert was the one who'd shown me that wasn't true. If a weaker wolf distracted himself sufficiently, he could wiggle out from under even the most powerful order. In Rupert's case, his preferred distraction was nursery rhymes.

Sure enough—"Jack Sprat could eat no fat," Rupert shouted at the top of his lungs. His eyes were closed and his fingers drummed against the sides of his thighs to double the distraction.

So, yeah, Rupert wasn't surrendering. But he'd also turned himself into a sitting duck. Redhead cocked his head in disbelief for one long moment, then he shrugged and stalked around his opponent. The stronger alpha still had a sword and a near 100% chance of winning the Trial the physical way.

Uh uh. Not happening. I continued dancing out of Liam's path, noting that my opponent's grunts and roars were starting to turn hoarse. The floor within our taped square was now marred by sword strikes in several locations and his blade had developed obvious dings and dents.

Looked like my opponent was ready to be used as a bowling ball.

"Hey, Shrimpy." I edged myself around to line Liam up while pulling my star-ball magic back inside myself. "Remember those slugs in the salad eight years ago? I put them there."

The reminder from our shared childhood was a lie and Liam should have been able to smell as much. But he was far past paying attention to subtle cues.

All he noticed was my hands, spread out to my sides and entirely empty. I shimmied around one more time then planted my feet into sudden stillness, hoping that would turn me irresistible to my brain-fogged opponent.

I hoped right. Liam charged; I sidestepped; he crossed the line—granting me an immediate victory in Moon Trial Number One.

Meanwhile, a roar from behind me suggested the rest of my plan had come to fruition as well. Spinning to take in the view, I laughed out loud. I couldn't help it. Because Liam had knocked Redhead all the way into the next square, disqualifying Rupert's opponent also. In fact, the losers were now in the center of a four-heir pileup, teeth turning lupine and hands squeezing throats.

"Crude yet effective," Rupert observed, which was high praise coming from Mr. Discongeniality.

"You're welcome," I started, only to snap my mouth shut as the red-gold necklace bearing a fragment of Gate City's magic turned icy against my collarbone. Above us, the lights flared blindingly bright for one split second then quenched to plunge the gymnasium into the approximate light level of a supermassive black hole.

Chapter 5

E ven shifters can't see in total blackout conditions. But we have other senses and other ways of communicating with our mates.

The bond between me and Thom formed an invisible yet very tangible rope connecting the two of us. Using it, I could gauge my mate's proximity—roughly twenty feet to my right and behind my back—while also sending silent words in his direction. *"Do you know where Willow and Rupert are located?"*

His answer came quickly, in his usual warm—if silent due to our use of the mate bond—rumble. *"I have Willow..."*

A squeak that wasn't Thom's emerged from his general direction. A quiet, "Hush." Then Thom continued our one-on-one conversation.

"Rupert also. Shall I draw you in?"

"No." Because if Willow and Rupert were under Thom's protection, then I had other priorities. Priorities like figuring out why my necklace had warned me one millisecond before the lights winked out. Priorities like discovering the source of the overwhelming scent of blood hanging heavy in the air.

I must have transmitted more of my thought processes than I meant to, because my mate's words in my head turned sandpapery. *"I would prefer that you didn't walk blind and alone toward danger."*

"Thom. You knew what you were getting when you accepted my mate bond."

"Kira. I could say the exact same thing."

As we spoke, I was shedding clothes and shifting down into fur form. Air currents on fox whiskers made it easy to dodge bumbling werewolves. Thom and his contingent didn't have nearly as much luck.

Or so I guessed when a stranger's growl emerged like fingernails on a chalkboard behind me. "Watch where you're going." Whoever this was, he was itching for a fight and I had a bad feeling about the identity of the person on the other end.

Yep—"*You're* the one who ran into *me*," Rupert replied. As if it was a good idea to antagonize someone I suspected was three times his size.

I closed my eyes in frustration then reopened them to the same darkness. Thom would need my help to keep Willow safe while defusing Rupert's bombshell.

I'd already spun to retrace my footsteps when my mate proved me wrong. "Make way for my alpha," he growled, imbuing his words with even more dominance than Rupert's foe had mustered before adding the clincher: "Please."

"For your *alpha*?" The stranger's tone turned considerably meeker. I could just see him imagining the werewolf who'd be mighty enough to lord over a dominant of Thom's caliber.

Grinning, I left my mate to his own devices. I shouldn't have doubted his ability to hold his own.

Since my voice was unlikely to scare off enemy combatants, I was even more careful to dodge werewolves as I sped across the gymnasium. Still, I was faster than Thom's contingent and it was no surprise that Rupert's complaints became indistinguishable from the general hubbub by the time the metallic reek of copper turned into wetness against my paw pads.

I'd stepped into the source of the smell and it wasn't just a sprinkle either. This was as much blood as had gushed out of Willow's mate four months earlier.

The question was, could I save whoever had been cut down today?

"No, the question is, who cut him down and is the killer still there beside you?" Thom growled. *"I would prefer it if you'd wait for me to catch up."*

I didn't wait. Instead, I inched forward until my nose struck an obstruction. Not solid but yielding. A clothed body, laid out flat against the cool gym floor if my whiskers were to be believed, which they generally were.

Tracing the outline of shoulders in total darkness, I found an ear. So the victim's mouth should be right about there...

Soft lips indented beneath my questing nose but no breath emerged from between them. I was too late to save whoever this was.

Blood on my face, on my hands, on my sword. I'd killed *him. I...*

Thom's voice broke into the panic-inducing memory as if he knew the dark path I was being drawn down. *"Dead?"* he asked simply.

The past popped in a soap bubble of relief that made my silent response run longer than it really should have. *"I suppose it wasn't entirely fair to dump protective duties on you while keeping all the fun for myself."*

"Stolen fun isn't the source of my complaint."

"No? I can't think why not."

Our banter was interrupted by rekindling lights flaring at blinding levels. I blinked furiously, catching streaks of red that slowly materialized into stomach-twisting butchery. This hadn't merely been a kill but an annihilation. Blood covered every available inch of the victim's skin and one arm had been totally ripped away from his body.

I'd been avoiding the face, avoiding finding out whether I knew this victim. But I finally forced myself to set my sights higher, sighing out a gust of relief as it became clear this was a stranger to me.

No, I didn't recognize the victim, but I did recognize the man crouched on the opposite side of the body. The man whose profession involved killing those who broke the rules, usually in bloody and awful ways.

The Executioner considered me across the dead man's body. "What a coincidence," he said, voice flat as his facial expression, "to find you here."

After that ominous start, the Executioner didn't grace me with any further words of warning or explanation. Instead, I was herded along with every other woman toward a hallway leading to the restrooms while Thom reported men were either being shuttled to the airport or to a hotel depending on whether they'd lost or won the recent battle. *"Rupert and I will wait for you here,"* he observed.

"They'll let you?" Because the musclebound guys keeping our line in order didn't seem particularly malleable.

"They're pushy but manageable."

I wanted to laugh but I didn't. After all, while I'd hastily pulled on clothes in my spot in line, other women had been ushered into the bathroom one after another. Each had emerged trembling, face pale and breathing rapid. They'd all been allowed to leave afterwards, but most had seemed likely to need smelling salts and a good lie-down to recover.

Willow was braving the bathroom now, having glared me down when I offered to join her. Or...no. She was coming back out into the hallway, shoulders hunched and hands clenched into fists so tight her knuckles were decidedly white.

Eyes on the floor, she started to pass me without acknowledgment but I didn't get the impression she was giving me the cold shoulder. Instead, she seemed to be struggling just to stay erect.

"Hey, are you okay?" I murmured, reaching out to touch her arm.

I'd kept my voice soft and my fingers gentle, but Willow gasped and jerked away. Only when her gaze met mine did the fear in the air lessen a trifle. Slumping against the wall, her words came in hiccups. "I...I...feel dizzy."

"We'll get you out of here." Despite our painful past, it felt entirely natural to slide my arm through Willow's and guide her toward the exit. We weren't friends, but we were pack mates. I wasn't about to stand by and watch her collapse.

Unfortunately, two burly security guards stepped away from their stations where the hallway bent to reenter the stadium. Between them, they blocked our path via body mass alone.

Or, no, they blocked *my* path. Likely because I hadn't yet taken my turn inside the horror chamber of the bathroom.

"Go," I told Willow, patting her on the back and retreating, hoping the security guards would let her pass unhindered as long as I wasn't beside her. They did. But once Willow rounded the bend, she'd be adrift in a sea of heirs amped up from their recent battles. She wouldn't last long on her own.

"Willow's coming out," I warned Thom. *"She needs to rest somewhere quiet. Food wouldn't hurt either. Can you take her back to the hotel?"*

"And leave you there with no backup?"

"We've discussed this, Thom. Once Rupert loses, I'll be alone until the end of the Trials. I can handle myself."

Thom's reluctance to accept the inevitable turned our mate bond slippery. But then he must have set eyes on Willow because I got the distinct impression of a sigh as he relented. *"Alright. But be smart about it. Look out for yourself and don't get involved in anyone else's business."*

"Who me? I'm the epitome of self-centeredness."

Thom's chuckle faded as he gathered up Willow and herded her away from the bathroom hallway. Meanwhile, my phone buzzed with a message from a far less enticing pack leader.

"I expected a full report as soon as the Trial ended. Status?"

With Chief Reed, the trick was to hop, but not too fast. It was a balancing act, neither pushing him into true awfulness nor acting like a pushover who could be manipulated at will. Tonight I estimated forty minutes would be just the right delay. To that end, I turned off my phone screen and surveyed the women in front of me, each of whom appeared to be moving one space forward to make up the gap left by whoever had just entered the bathrooms.

At the head of the line, a teenager bit her fist, eyes wild. I'd noticed her at the airport, one of only two other women who kept their chins up and their eyes steely. An heir, I presumed, not a plus-one like Willow.

Which was why her sudden posture shift tweaked my protective instincts. *"Thom?"*

"Yes?" My mate's voice was distant now, which was just as well. Our spotty connection hopefully meant he wouldn't pick up on my thought processes this time around.

Still, he was bound to guess what was going on once I spat out my final question. Shrugging, I pushed my request down the mate bond anyway. *"Will you ask Rupert what the rules say about interrogating minors?"*

A pause, then: *"Sounds like children have no special protection among werewolves. But you're not responsible for anyone there other than yourself. Do you hear me, Kira?"*

I heard him, but he was far enough away so I could pretend I didn't. Because young werewolves might have no special protection, but that wasn't the case if someone older looked out for them voluntarily.

The door to the bathroom opened, disgorging yet another traumatized plus-one. It was time for the teenager to enter that horror chamber.

"Wait!" I raised my voice even as I strode toward the source of unknown trauma. "She's not going in there alone."

Chapter 6

I wasn't the only one who'd had the idea of protecting the young, apparently. Because the other female heir—roughly a decade my elder and bearing a tray of cupcakes instead of a weapon—ended up shoulder-to-shoulder beside me as we attempted to push our way through the door.

"I know I'm irresistible," observed the hefty security guard blocking our path, "but I can only handle one girl at a time."

"Don't sell yourself short," I bantered back. But the door had already closed in my face.

Cupcake Woman and I weren't left fuming for long however. Because a raspy voice barked an order, the door was flung back open, and the same guard shrugged as he ushered us inside.

I scanned the space, seeking signs of whatever had terrified Willow and the other plus-ones. The L-shaped bathroom boasted stalls and sinks on the long leg plus a shorter, dimmer arm with no apparent purpose other than intimidating the young. There, the teenager had moved on from biting her fist to gnawing a thumbnail as she eyed the source of her discomfort—the Executioner himself.

For a moment, the reek of floor cleanser pressed so hard against the insides of my nostrils that I couldn't breathe. Then I lost track of aggressive cleaning products as the Executioner's gaze settled like a sodden wool blanket over my head.

Now it wasn't just my lungs that were frozen. My muscles refused to obey my urge to run, fast, in any direction except toward the scary shifter in front of me.

Relief came from an unexpected direction. A click of plastic as the woman beside me popped the top off her tray of desserts then a menu litany. "I've got strawberry, lemon, vanilla, red velvet, and chocolate either spicy or non-spicy. Pick your poison.”

To my shock—and the relief of my lungs, the Executioner’s attention moved away from me. “Poison?” he rasped. His single word crawled down the back of my shirt like a well-greased worm, but at least I now had the bodily autonomy to shiver.

“Metaphorical expression only,” the cupcake bearer answered. She tapped one finger against her chin as she reconsidered. “Although poison *is* traditionally a woman’s weapon. Perhaps you shouldn’t risk it if you’re worried about your health.”

A moment of silence, then that raspy voice filled with incredulity. “You’re daring me?”

“If it quacks like a duck…”

The Executioner was the last person I would have expected to fall for a childish goad. But he took one step away from the teenager and toward the cupcakes. Another. And another.

Well, if Cupcake Woman was able to distract the big, bad wolf, that left me with the much more palatable job of soothing the young. Sidling toward the teenager while staying as far away from the Executioner as possible, I finally got a chance to take a closer look at the girl we’d teamed up to save.

She looked to be about fifteen but a very tall fifteen. Her hair was a crazy mass of curls manageable only because it was shorn close to her head. The pimples I’d noticed earlier were red as if she picked at them often, but what she worried now wasn’t her face.

Instead, the hand that had been in her mouth stretched the neck of her t-shirt away from her throat. A tag popped up where it shouldn’t have been and she grimaced.

“Dressed too fast?” I asked, hoping to set her at ease. “Join the club.”

Then Cupcake Woman was padding toward us, one compartment in her tray empty and her steps slower and calmer than mine would have been if my back was to the Executioner. Only, the snacks seemed to have sweetened his disposition.

Ignoring all of us, the scariest werewolf I'd ever met stuffed half the pastry into his mouth like a greedy little boy at a birthday party.

Or, well, the dessert offensive had worked to give the teenager a short reprieve at least. Because the Executioner's cold gaze met mine shortly thereafter. His throat bulged as he swallowed. Then he ordered, "*Stay put.*"

At first, we three heel-coolers paid close attention as the guard interviewed woman after woman in front of a largely silent Executioner. We learned that this bathroom was home to a fuse box, one that had been doctored to produce a power surge mid-contest. The guard currently doing the questioning had stood outside in the hallway the entire time. He hadn't paid attention to specific faces, but he was confident no men had gone in or out.

Which meant any female was a suspect. Reliably, when presented with this fact, every plus-one broke down into agitated crying. It appeared they'd all needed to visit the restroom to refresh makeup or dab water on their hands. None was so crass as to suggest she'd peed, but eventually the Executioner's glare had gotten even that damning evidence out from between each pair of dainty lips.

As the questions became repetitive, I turned to the girl whose fingernails had once again found their way into her mouth. "I came in to use the bathroom before the fight," she whispered when our eyes met. "The circuit box was open. I...I closed it."

No surprise there. In the minutes since being released from the Executioner's clutches, the girl had turned her shirt around so it was no longer back-to-front then had undone one of her sneakers and realigned the lace ends so they matched up perfectly. It took a crazy amount of control for a teenage girl to hold her own at the Moon Trials. Having some of that control spill out into tidying up the bathroom seemed entirely within character.

"We won't let him bully you," I promised. Then, figuring introductions were in order, I added, "I'm Kira."

The girl scrunched up her face, muttered something I couldn't hear even with shifter ears. At my raised eyebrows she repeated it. "Pet. Short for Petunia. No, I don't like either option but Pet is better. Moving on."

She stuck her gnawed-upon hand out in front of her and I shook it. The girl had a firm grip, bordering on aggressive. Her fingers were only slightly damp.

She also, I suspected, needed to no longer be the center of attention. So I turned to the cupcake bearer for my second handshake.

Rather than meeting my hand with her own, though, the thirty-something stuck the tray of pastries between us. "I'm Ember. Choose and I'll tell you about my relationship to your mate."

Pet bit back a bark of laughter. This was definitely the distraction the kid needed.

And, okay, so I was interested also. As far as I knew, Thom's human father was his sole living relative.

No, that wasn't quite true. Thom also had a werewolf mother who'd abandoned him the day he was born. A mother who'd been afraid to tell her mate about past infidelity and had instead sent her sister to deliver the infant to his dad.

Was it possible Ember was that aunt? No, far too young. Still—"You're Thom's cousin?" I guessed. "Sister?"

Ember wiggled the tray meaningfully rather than answering. And I grabbed the most interesting cupcake, a dark chocolate confection with a dried chili pepper on top.

"My father sold your mate his territory," Ember observed as I picked off the decorative pepper and took a bite of cupcake that was surprisingly delicious. The kick at the end perked me up, rekindling energy I'd lost shifting back and forth from the form of my fox.

The flavor explosion wasn't quite enough to dislodge my attention from Ember's fascinating factoid, however. I'd wondered about the werewolf history of Gate City for quite a while. Because alphas don't sell off corners of their territory without ulterior motives. For months, I'd expected someone to show up with demands for Thom but no one ever had.

Now, I raised my eyebrows. "Why?"

"Dad liked Thom when he met him. Thought he might be a good mate for me, despite the age difference." Ember's eyes twinkled as she confided, "I had other plans."

Then she turned the tray toward the teenager, apparently done with our conversation. "None for me," Pet answered, pointing at her pimples. "Makes these worse."

"You should eat something though." Ember opened up a massive purse that appeared to be full of snacks of every type imaginable. Nuts. Jerky. Fresh produce of various persuasions. Pet hesitated then withdrew a grapefruit.

"Interesting." Ember smiled, revealing dimples that made her look just as soft as the dessert-bearing persona indicated. And yet...I didn't believe she was soft at all. Instead, I got the distinct impression she'd just drawn more information out of me and Pet than she'd given about herself.

As if to prove me correct, the cupcake pusher observed, "Sweet and spicy. Sweet and sour. I like women with hidden depths."

Before I could decide how to respond to such a succinct sum-up of my personality, a shiver-inducing voice intruded. "I don't."

We jumped. Well, Pet and I jumped while Ember snapped the lid back over her cupcakes and latched her purse. She seemed unconcerned by the fact the Executioner had crept up on us, something that should have been impossible while crossing loud tile and approaching three women who boasted shifter senses.

Impossible, yet he'd managed it. And now he exuded so much danger that I couldn't bear to look at him straight on, the dark cloud of a man raising hairs on the back of my neck with his proximity alone. I felt more than saw as he considered me, Ember, and Pet in quick succession before gesturing with his chin toward the exit.

That was it? We were dismissed? After a quick glance at each other, we started filing out, giving the Executioner as wide a berth as possible in the narrow space.

My head was averted, so I only saw a flash of movement out of the corner of one eye as a cold hand came down on my arm. The Executioner's fingers clenched shut like iron pincers.

His words were even harsher. "Not you, fox."

"**I**f she stays," Ember said, planting her feet decisively, "I stay." Even her cupcake tray jutted aggressively in the Executioner's direction, which was far more support than I'd expected from a werewolf who was a stranger to me.

Still, I shook my head. "I'll be fine. Make sure Pet makes it back to her hotel room safely."

Because the kid was fading. If her *Live free or die* t-shirt plus subtle dropping of Rs at the end of words were any indication, Pet hailed from New England. The other side of the continent, where it was three hours later than the clock on the wall currently posited. Since Pet seemed to have come here on her own without a support network, she'd likely had to stay alert for the past many hours. She was overdue for a break.

Ember considered us both then pulled out her phone. "Okay, but let's start a group text. Numbers?"

Pet rattled off hers and I countered with mine, noticing as I input digits that Chief Reed was getting antsy. My forty minutes had ballooned out of proportion and his texts had definitely escalated. I waved farewell to Pet and Ember then prepared to calm my pack leader.

Unfortunately, before I could type in more than a single word by way of reply, that iron hand had lashed out and snagged my cell phone. "Hey!"

The Executioner didn't bother answering, just pointed toward the row of stalls. With no cupcakes available as mood softener, I instead tried humor.

"You need to use the bathroom?" I misguessed. "Little boys' room is on the other side of the hall."

One blink. The finger never wavered.

"Oookay. How about this? Give me back my phone and I'll go willingly."

The Executioner didn't do anything, but the air between us turned so cold it choked me. I could have sworn ice crystals were forming inside my nose.

And while I could have tried something rash, this man was apparently in charge of crowd control here at the Moon Trials. I needed to stick it out for three more contests before I could shoot him the middle finger with impunity.

So I went. Tried not to wince as my phone clinked onto the counter. Resisted looking back as a jangly ringtone suggested Chief Reed had run out of patience with texting and resorted to a call.

Would he find a way to harm Willow when I didn't answer? I would have liked to say that was impossible since she and I were the only members of the Reed pack currently located in San Francisco and we weren't even in proximity to one another. But I wouldn't put it past the ornery old cuss to use up a favor and have Willow killed just to prove a point.

I turned back to face the Executioner, or tried to. But the floor tiles had gone slick beneath my feet. This wasn't kitsune magic, merely alpha dominance so great it sucked heat out of the air and iced over all damp surfaces.

The gesture could have been unconscious, but in this case I got the distinct impression it was purposeful. Because the icy ground used my momentum against me. I slid into the last stall on the end without meaning to. Slid there and almost hopped right back out.

Reason reasserted itself first. Chief Reed wouldn't kill Willow because then I'd have no reason to play his games at the Moon Trials. And while there was a lot of leeway between dead and safe, the smarter route at the moment involved biding my time.

So I sat in a grubby little stall where at least the floor-cleanser scent had faded enough to keep my nostrils from imploding. There, I twiddled my thumbs as every other woman in that long line was debriefed. There, I imagined Chief Reed's reaction to my extended silence while hard-won seconds I'd intended to spend with my mate slipped through my fingers to splat unused onto the dirty bathroom floor.

Only when worry and frustration were about to make me do something unwise did the door to my stall slam open. The Executioner and the guard crowded in, their bulk intimidating me into pulling my legs up onto the toilet seat. One chin jerk apparently meant something to the guard because he invaded my personal space until his meaty nose poked my collarbone. He inhaled hard then nodded.

"Yep, she smells like the breaker box."

I tensed, drawing magic out of my star ball to turn into a sword. This was it, the moment I'd have to fight my way free of two overbearing werewolves while enclosed in far too close quarters. My strengths relied on speed and space, so the task wouldn't be easy. But I'd manage. I'd...

...wait it out while the Executioner considered me with those flat charcoal eyes. "Go," he said at last, stepping aside to allow me space to exit.

I'm not ashamed to admit I scurried toward the hallway faster than a terrified jackrabbit flees a hawk's talons. Snatching up my phone, I waited to glance back over my shoulder until my other hand came down on the door handle.

Behind me, the guard had turned aside, yawning. But the Executioner hadn't moved a muscle. He stood watching my retreat, ice in his gaze and that scent of floor cleanser so strong it choked me. I didn't need a verbal warning to know I was on his shit list.

Still, the Executioner let me go. And a chatty driver waited outside, ushering me into the back seat of a car slated to take me wherever the other heirs had already been ferried. I greeted him briefly then typed up a report I hoped would keep Chief Reed from dreaming up punishments. Finally, meeting the driver's gaze in the rear-view mirror, I offered a flirty: "So, about my keycard..."

"Don't you worry your pretty little head about logistics," the driver answered. "I'll get you where you need to go."

Okay, so maybe flirty hadn't been the right approach to achieve what Thom had reported every other heir was offered the moment they left the gymnasium.

Still, I dropped the issue because I didn't really need my keycard, not yet anyway. I had no intention of holing up in my room tonight, not when the hours Thom and I had carved out to spend together were already almost half gone.

Because Rupert was bound to lose tomorrow, at which point Thom would be sent home from the Moon Trials. And if I didn't manage to ace my own mandated three matches, there would be no consolation prize. It would be back to meeting my mate at the border with the invisible yet entirely tangible territorial wall between us. Tonight might be our one chance to steal more than a peck on the cheek for a very long time.

So I hit up my phone again, ignoring a long thread of back-and-forth between Ember and Pet and scrolling past Chief Reed's terse reminder of the house cat he held hostage for my good behavior. As threats went, it was a mild one. Not that I didn't cherish Pumpkin, but that old tomcat was quite capable of holding his own in contests against alpha werewolves.

The strange absence of messages from Thom, though, cut through my smugness. Well, if my mate hadn't reached out, then I would. *"Sprung at last,"* I thumb-typed. *"Where should we meet?"*

No answer, which I supposed wasn't entirely surprising. Thom had a lot on his hands between propping up Willow and getting Rupert situated. No matter what hotel the organizers had booked us into, sheets wouldn't be high enough thread count and the room-service menu was almost certainly too low-brow for Rupert. The entitled werewolf would have pitched a fit and I could see him taking full advantage of having a plus-one alpha along in order to win special treatment.

Still, Thom had flown across the country to spend this night with me. Surely he'd keep his phone at his fingertips?

When my mate still hadn't responded ten minutes later, a dark thread of worry prompted me to open the locator app we'd both installed and linked together months ago. When we were first separated by my oath to Chief Reed, I'd spent hours staring at the screen. Later, I'd decided watching Thom's movements from afar was worse than no contact.

Now, though, the app came in handy. Because the red dot representing my mate wasn't in our current neighborhood. He appeared to be halfway across the city instead.

"Change of plans," I told the driver who, like all the other Moon Trials guards, smelled of San Francisco fog and was twice as wide as me across the shoulders. "Can you head here?"

We'd paused at a stop sign, but the driver didn't even glance over at the phone screen I'd angled up toward him through the window between front and back seats. Instead, he shook his head. "No can do. Tardy plus-ones go directly to the mixer. Gotta look pretty in front of those heirs."

"But I'm not a plus-one."

He didn't bother answering. Just depressed the gas pedal and continued carrying us away from my mate.

Away from my mate...who had finally answered my text. Only Thom's reply was oddly out of character. *"MISS U,"* he'd sent, all caps and with the single-letter abbreviation we both found abhorrent.

Well, that clinched it. I grabbed the door handle, intending to jump out and find my own way to Thom.

I hadn't counted on a child lock. A child lock plus the transparent barrier my driver slammed shut between us. Neither door nor divider gave way beneath my questing fingers and my demands had no effect either.

I'd come to San Francisco to participate in the Moon Trials. But it appeared that in the eyes of the support staff, I was a recalcitrant woman to be delivered to the hotel whether I liked it or not.

Chapter 8

Well, the driver might think I was an easily managed woman, but I only identified with the noun not the modifier. A childhood obsessed with magic tricks meant I'd come up with all sorts of fun ways to put my star ball to use.

Now, I pounded on the barrier between me and the driver to sidetrack him from the glimmer of light sliding into the crack between door and window. A twist of my fingers and the lock disengaged. Another twist and I didn't even have to yank on the handle.

I was already ducking and rolling when the door flew open. Pavement ripped through the knees of my jeans, but pain—if there was pain—didn't have a chance against the adrenaline coursing through my bloodstream.

"Hey! Wait!" the driver yelled. Horns honked, suggesting he'd stopped dead in the road, obstructing traffic. Someone shouted complaint as a door banged shut, then the driver's heavy footsteps pounded down the sidewalk toward me.

I didn't look back. Just sprinted for the subway sign I'd noticed one block before managing to open the car's door.

Because foot traffic here was too sparse to lose myself in. And if I shifted out in the open...well, the Executioner would be thrilled at the excuse to put me out of my misery. He might even crack a smile.

Only, it turned out I didn't have to broach the gray area of going fox far too close to non-shifters in order to get rid of the scent of fur gaining on me by the second. Instead, the necklace containing a shard of Gate City magic shocked me just before a sea of people rushed out of the station's entrance. I barely made it to the down escalator before the sidewalk was engulfed by fast-moving masses of people on foot.

I'd entered the station before the surge but the driver hadn't. His salty-fog presence in my nostrils dulled as the exiting humans cut him off from following me in. And luck was with me for more reason than that. At the bottom of the escalator, an open train door yawned. I hopped on without looking to see where it was headed.

Hopped on and peered behind me to see my werewolf driver jogging down moving steps even faster than I had. The sea of people must have let him pass, which meant he'd catch up to me in seconds. He'd corner me in this train car containing people who couldn't be allowed to observe shifter fur or kitsune magic...

I tensed, reconsidering my options. Was there time to dart back out the door and make it across the platform into the darkness on the opposite side before the driver collared me? Could I...?

One more time, my necklace tingled with electricity. Then the door slammed shut one instant before my driver would have stuck his foot into the gap.

I had to change trains to reach the spot where my app promised Thom was located, and he'd moved a few blocks over in the interim. Sitting in the second train car, I texted my mate multiple times. But there was no reply.

No, that wasn't quite true. Thom responded once—a random string of letters and numbers that looked like he'd swiped a finger across the screen in the texting version of a butt dial.

That wasn't like Thom, who was intentional about everything. Something was very wrong. He needed me by his side.

But first I had to brave the world outside the subway station, a world that had turned pea-soup foggy while I was in transit. The clinging damp accentuated scents while making their sources uncertain. There were werewolves here, but I couldn't pinpoint their locations well enough to dodge them or ascertain their identities. I could only assume the driver had sent backup to catch me. That he'd looked at my phone screen when I tilted it in his direction after all.

Luckily, I'd prepared for the worst before exiting the subway. My star ball had become not only a sword but also a sheathe at my back now. The hilt of the former was hidden in my hair, reminding me of its presence each time I turned my head to check the source of fleeting movements. Meanwhile, I'd memorized the turns I'd need to take in order to reach Thom, not wanting to stick my face in my phone while walking past a not-so-welcoming committee.

Strangely, though, there was no line of werewolves waiting to apprehend me. Just fleeting whiffs of fur and fangs that failed to materialize into tangible danger.

Until, that is, music drew my attention to a hopping nightclub, its door closing as three shifters strode out in a jostling group of testosterone. For one split second, I thought I saw Thom among them. Their bodies were backlit, details blurred by fog and distance. But the man on the left moved just like Thom did. Graceful, predatory, and uniquely my mate.

Or not. Because the man I'd focused on laughed, an edged chuckle filled with razor blades. That wasn't Thom. Wasn't anyone I wanted to meet alone on a dark night like this one.

So I took a right I hadn't planned to, away from men whose fur scent chased me for three turns before receding. Glass crunched beneath my boots as I tried to get a feel for Thom's location along our mate bond. I'd lost the thread of where he was in relation to the hastily added dogleg and I still didn't trust my surroundings enough to pull out my phone.

I should have been close enough for our connection to warm and draw me forward. But the mate bond lay quiescent beneath my fingers. Either Thom wasn't as close as I thought or...

I refused to follow that mind trail to its obvious conclusion. Technology would come to the rescue as soon as I found a place secure enough to peer at the app again.

There. I ducked behind a pile of garbage that materialized into a homeless man sleeping in a puddle of his own vomit.

No, that wasn't a homeless man. That was Thom.

Chapter 9

My mate was breathing, but everything else about the situation was deeply wrong. Curled up in fetal position, Thom's vibrant masculinity had dulled. He seemed old, tired, vanquished.

With anyone else, I would have assumed they'd gone a bit overboard while vacationing, drinking too much then passing out. But Thom was a bartender well aware of the dangers of inebriation. He rarely consumed more than a single beer and he definitely knew his own limits.

Plus, he didn't reek of alcohol. If my nose was correct, he'd had no more than his usual, self-imposed quota.

No wonder I fell to my knees and shook him hard before second-guessing my actions. Wasn't it a bad idea to move someone with a back injury? Or was that a concussion? I wasn't a doctor. I didn't know what to do when my mate lay on the cold, damp pavement refusing to wake up.

Meanwhile, the slackness in our mate bond chilled me more than the fog settling deeper and deeper into the city landscape. Human voices passed by on the other side of the street, and for one split second I considered calling out. Asking for help so we could rush Thom to the nearest emergency room. I wanted to have every one of his vital signs monitored, to hire experts to diagnose whatever had gone wrong with him, to spare no expense getting him back on his feet.

I didn't, of course. Shifters couldn't afford to have our innards poked and prodded by humans. We couldn't afford to be comatose around two-leggers, either, since the latter would definitely freak out if Thom accidentally went furry upon waking.

Instead, I stilled my frantic thoughts and yanked out my cell phone. My sister had a doctor in her pack, a doctor who'd provided well-kid checkups for me on a regular basis then put my arm in a cast the year I got into a dirt-bike accident. And, sure, reaching that doctor would mean waking up two families since I was currently contacting the Fairwood pack only through a location-cloaked video chat on Mai's computer. For the sake of Mai's kids, I refused to let our continued connection enter the public eye.

Still, none of them would begrudge the waking. Even if it meant my nephew donned a cape and decided he was Midnight Man, a superhero allergic to bedtimes. Even if it meant my infant niece's tenuous sleep schedule was tossed out the window.

No one would complain about the wee-hours phone call...yet I found myself dialing up Charlie, my human friend back in Gate City, instead of my sister. After hitting voice mail three times, I was relieved when her bleary grumble finally emerged from the speaker. "Please tell me you didn't forget the time difference."

"I didn't forget. I have a medical emergency." I hesitated, then added, "Is your girlfriend there?"

"Yes, but..." Charlie sounded wide awake now as she tried to warn me what we both knew already. Nora was an EMT, but she wasn't aware of the existence of shifters. I couldn't draw her into that knowledge if I didn't want the Executioner breathing down her neck as well as mine.

"I won't spill any beans," I promised. Nor, I promised myself, would I let the tears prickling behind my eyelids fall to the pavement.

Because Thom's skin felt cool, our mate bond refusing to respond even when I tried to send a pulse of star-ball energy through it. Meanwhile, the silence between me and Charlie suggested I'd drawn the wrong straw this time.

After all, I'd treated her girlfriend badly the one time we'd met in person. And Chief Reed's territorial boundary meant I still hadn't managed to make that mistake up to Nora in person.

"Never mind," I started.

But Charlie had spoken at the exact same moment. "I'm trusting you," she warned.

With a rustle, the phone exchanged hands.

Turns out, I lied but nobody knew it. Not about keeping Nora safe—that part was a top priority. But tears? What did it matter if a few salty droplets fell while I tossed out symptoms and answered questions about pupils and vitals?

"I can't tell for sure without seeing him," Nora said at last, voice business-like. "But I'm guessing he's on Flunitrazepam."

When silence confirmed my ignorance, she clarified: "A tranquilizer. Date-rape drug. Roofie. Whatever you call it, he'll bounce back once he sleeps it off. Someone should keep an eye on his heart rate and breathing tonight, but otherwise..."

"Otherwise I should let you go back to sleep. And thank you from the bottom of my heart. I owe you a huge favor..."

And I lost track of Nora's sleepy farewell because Thom's eyes were finally opening. Ice blue or sky blue, they'd always been clear and penetrating in the past. Not so now. Instead, his irises appeared murky, like the deep ocean where light barely penetrated. "Foxy lady," he slurred.

"Let's get you back to the hotel," I answered, helping him up into a seated position.

"Or here's good."

I barely missed the puddle of vomit as Thom yanked me over onto his lap with a strength that belied his earlier bonelessness. His lips on my neck were sloppy...and they still sent shivers of pleasure cascading down my spine.

Shivers I wasn't about to succumb to. Drawing back far enough to recover my phone, I swiped over to a ride-hailing app and requested a lift.

The process took only a few seconds, but Thom's kisses had already faded. His head drifted down to land on my shoulder. "I feel like a bus ran over me," he rumbled, "then backed up and gave it a second try."

"You have a lot of experience with being run over by buses?" I countered, trying to keep my voice light. While I spoke, I rearranged us so I was the one sitting with his head on my lap.

Normally, Thom would have said something clever. But now he only hummed then went silent as I stroked my fingers through the spiky hairs at his nape.

And, slowly, I relinquished my hopes for the evening, replacing them with new hopes. Hopes that Thom would wake up tomorrow fully himself again. Hopes that I'd win enough Moon Trial contests so I could thank Nora in person. Hopes that I could achieve all of that without spilling any more blood.

For now, though, only one issue needed to be dealt with before I could let my mate sleep off the drugged haze that consumed him. "Do you know who did this to you?" I murmured into his ear.

At first, I thought my mate wasn't going to answer. His breathing had slowed back down to sleep cadence. His eyelids had drifted shut.

But then, finally, Thom rolled over so he could peer straight up at me. A hint of familiar ice crept into his eyes as he enunciated clearly. "My good-for-nothing brother."

"Your brother? I didn't know you had a brother."

Thom didn't answer. He'd fallen soundly asleep.

Chapter 10

I wanted to talk to my mate about this surprise family member. About how, despite the "good-for-nothing" modifier, "brother" had risen from Thom's mouth smelling bittersweet.

And no wonder. Raised by a human father, Thom had known nothing about werewolves until he hit puberty and shifted into wolf form for the very first time. Psychology 101 had taught me that family role models are essential to understanding facets of our own personality.

Thom had never met a werewolf relative...until now.

But long-hidden identity issues weren't going to be dealt with tonight, not with Thom slipping in and out of consciousness. Instead, the next hour was a comedy of errors as I tried to find a bed for him to recover in and failed miserably. At the hotel, the human desk clerk sent me upstairs to check in with the so-called Moon Convention organizers...who actually turned out to be more San Francisco guards, both of whom feigned ignorance when I asked for my keycard.

Not only did they feign ignorance, the buzz-cut guard on the sixth floor man-handled Thom back to the elevator when his card didn't work in the door that had been pointed out as belonging to the Reed pack. My explanation that *I* was the Reed heir fell on deaf ears.

On the next level up, the similarly burly but slightly longer-haired guard didn't even let me set foot on the carpeted floor he was in charge of. "No women," he growled, blocking me from following Thom as my mate swayed down the hallway.

"Look at him," I countered, pointing toward my mate. Thom was hesitating, one foot slower to fall than it had been a moment earlier. Lack of momentum added to the wobbliness of his legs and he appeared unlikely to make it to his destination. "He needs assistance."

The guard just shrugged and graced me with two bonus words tacked on the end of his previous statement. "No women, no exceptions."

Thankfully, Thom's room was the closest one and his fumbling fingers managed to get the door open with the keycard I'd dragged out of his pocket and placed in his hand in the elevator. And Rupert responded to my raised-voiced request to keep an eye on Thom with grumpy assent once I warned him that, without Thom to lend him consequence, he'd be eaten alive at tomorrow's contest.

Only once a litany of groans and complaints suggested Thom was being taken care of did I poke the elevator button for what appeared to be the women's floor. Downstairs, Mr. Buzz Cut was more amenable to chatting without Thom present. He was, however, just as adamant as before that he couldn't help.

"I can't open plus-one doors," he informed me.

"But I'm an heir, not a plus-one." I felt like I'd said this a dozen times already. No wonder Ember brought cupcakes to the Moon Trials to soften her path. "Could you check your list please?"

Shrugging, Mr. Buzz Cut did finally deign to pull out his phone. "Huh," he said after one long moment. "Plus-ones are all accounted for. Who are you again?"

"Kira Fairwood." Then, because I knew I wasn't getting anywhere without the caveat, I added: "Reed heir."

"Well, why didn't you say that in the first place?" Without waiting for my answer, Mr. Buzz Cut led me down to the far end of the hallway, feet moving far slower than his lips while he spilled woes about a girlfriend he adored but who seemed to enjoy jerking him around.

I was so tired my eyes had gone bleary, but the guard's keycard hadn't been inserted into my door yet. So I leaned against the wall and considered his problem. "Have you told your girlfriend how you feel about her so she doesn't have to act out to get your attention?"

"You're saying bring flowers to our hookups?"

"I'm saying if you call them hookups then it's no surprise she thinks she has to keep you on a leash."

And that was clearly none of my business because Mr. Buzz Cut's keycard suddenly found the slot in the door and he backed away with alacrity. Shaking my head, I stepped into a darkened room and was asleep before I hit the bed.

I woke to a bond writhing in my belly. It slithered between the folds of my intestines, slammed into my kidneys, then pressed my gorge up into my throat.

"Thom?" I sent the word down our mate bond silently, only realizing after I'd done so that I was utilizing a different connection than the one that had woken me. No, my tether to Thom hadn't been the one to set my heart racing. The tightness in my chest was due to another connection, one that had been quiescent for so long I barely remembered its existence.

My sole pack bond. The one I'd build to get Chief Reed off my back four months ago then left alone so as not to annoy the woman on the other end. Now, our connection warned that Willow was in immediate danger. And if I was reading the bond's information correctly, she was on the other side of the wall beside which I now lay.

Hurry, hurry, hurry said the seething in my belly. But I stilled myself instead, straining my ears for hints of the culprit.

My nose rather than my ears provided the first clue. Someone had been in my room recently. They weren't here now though. Instead, I followed the furry scent path through the bathroom and to a closed door.

We'd been given a suite? It made sense that the powers-that-be would have provided an heir and her plus-one shared housing since we were the same gender and thus apparently allowed on the same hotel floor. But why would an intruder come through my space to get to Willow's?

The why would have to be dealt with later, though, because the writhing bond in my belly promised my pack mate needed assistance *now.*

Which is when I made my mistake. I'd been pulling the door to my bedroom closed behind me, intending to turn the bathroom into a dark pocket that I could burst out of. But I'd released the knob just a trifle too quickly. The latch, which I'd thought was already engaged, snicked into place.

It was the tiniest sound, too low for a human to have picked up on at a distance. But a shifter? A shifter paying attention would hear that metallic click.

As if in response, a shriek broke the silence. That was Willow. I'd lost the element of surprise and she was in pain.

So I grabbed the second door knob, the one leading to Willow's room. Or rather, I grabbed for it.

But the side of the door slammed into my gut before my fingers could gain purchase. The knob bruised my ribcage, knocking my breath away.

A dark shape, taller than me but shorter than Thom, shouldered me in the neck, spinning me into the towel rack. The invader was gone before I had time to deploy my sword.

Behind me, my bedroom door slammed as the attacker fled into the hallway. Should I follow or soothe my pack mate?

Willow's sobs simplified the decision. Letting the magic of my sword seep back into my body, I padded into my pack mate's room and lowered myself onto the edge of her bed.

The moment my butt hit the comforter, however, she lashed out. Not effectively. More like a terrified, flailing child. "Get away, get away, get away!"

"It's me! Kira. I'm not going to hurt you."

The blows halted. Willow hiccuped, then muttered: "How can you say that when it's your fault he was here?"

"He? Who was it?"

Rather than answering, Willow spun away from me so she could hide her tear-streaked face in the covers. Her shoulders heaved and I did the only thing I could think of. I reached out to rub circles into her back the way Mai used to when I got myself into trouble that seemed insurmountable.

Only my fingers barely made contact before Willow wailed at approximately the volume of an air-raid siren. Outside our room, female voices started slow then rose into a cacophony that nearly matched the shriek of my pack mate. Within seconds, someone was pounding on our exterior door.

Ignoring everyone other than Willow and keeping my hands to myself this time, I tried to work my tongue around a question that sounded wrong no matter how I arranged the letters. "Did he touch you inappropriately?"

And, to my surprise, that straightened Willow's backbone. She whirled to face me, eyes glinting with the fury of an inner wolf that had seemed absent a moment earlier. "Is there any appropriate way to touch someone when she doesn't want you in her bed?"

"No."

"Then, yes, he touched me inappropriately." Willow was on her feet now, grabbing a fluffy terry-cloth robe off the headboard and tugging the tie tight at her waist. "And, no, he didn't do anything that would make you need to avenge my purity. Not that I have any. A secondhand pack princess is good for no more than being a plus-one, isn't that what you decided when you bought my plane ticket west?"

Before I could decide which part of the angry torrent to respond to, Willow had crossed the room and flung open the door to reveal a tidal wave of similarly dressed plus-ones. Apparently my guess had been right—this level was the one where all of the Moon Trials women had been situated. It seemed like every one of them pressed into Willow's room as a unit, encircling my pack mate and doing with their clucking and cooing what I hadn't been able to with the ultimate in shifter connections.

Speaking of which, our shared pack bond had gone lax now that Willow was safely inside the gaggle of plus-ones. Shrugging off a pang, I figured this was my opportunity to play to my strengths and find the invader. So I skirted the edge of the crowd and stepped out into the hallway. There, Pet and Ember stood on either side of the door, swords in their hands and postures mirror images of each other.

"What happened?" the cupcake baker asked.

"I'm not exactly sure." I peered to the left, where my door was once again closed. A savvy attacker, though, might have slammed it shut as a decoy before hiding himself in preparation for later awfulness.

Again, the urge to investigate set my feet tapping. Surely Willow would be safe with so many allies around her?

But as I took a step away from Willow's open door, our pack bond quivered. Willow might say she didn't want me here, but she didn't feel comfortable being left behind either.

Pursing my lips, I considered the two women in front of me, two women with whom I'd formed a tenuous connection the previous evening. "Would one of you be willing to sniff things out in my room? See if anyone's there and assess who might have passed through recently?" Because I'd smelled the intruder, but only enough to know he was a shifter. A longer consideration would be necessary to turn up identifying clues.

"I'll go." Pet shed her sleep shorts and top then shifted as easily as if we weren't standing in a public hallway.

A public hallway that was no longer devoid of menfolk. Because the stairwell door banged open and the dark shadow of the Executioner strode through it. With him came an overwhelming astringency, proof that the scent in yesterday's bathroom hadn't been left behind by the janitorial staff. His flat gray gaze held mine just long enough to send a shiver down my backbone, then he knelt beside something I hadn't noticed before.

A person, slumped against the wall where Mr. Buzz Cut had been standing hours earlier. From a distance, the man appeared dead, but the Executioner didn't hurry or exhibit any sign of compassion as he checked for a pulse. Instead, his fingers were clinical, his face emotionless. His floor-cleaner scent continued to clog my nostrils.

Then he plucked something small off the side of the man's neck and spoke loudly enough for me and Ember to hear easily. "Drugged," he rasped, flat gaze boring into me. "I don't suppose you know anything about this?"

I didn't, but the ease with which Chief Reed had backed down last night colored my answer. My alpha had been furious, then he'd dropped the issue in a very uncharacteristic manner. "No," I said, wincing as I noted how uncertain my own scent had become.

No wonder the Executioner's gaze pinned me like a butterfly in a lepidopterist's cabinet. His teeth glinted with the predatory intensity of a wolf on the hunt.

Chapter 12

Still, the Executioner didn't press the issue. Just stood there while Ember settled everyone down with an impromptu slumber party. "Gather round!" the cupcake baker called, dragging lingering plus-ones into Willow's room where, of course, they didn't all fit. As the Executioner used his keycard to open my door, laughing women promptly spilled back out into the hallway.

Pet was one of them, unabashedly naked as she reported, "No intruder present, but I wasn't fast enough to try for a scent profile."

Which left the guard currently snoring at the end of the hallway as our only data point. As far as I could tell, no plus-one army had sullied the odors in his general vicinity. Now, if I could just get past the Executioner, who hadn't been willing to let me move more than an arm's length from him since showing up...

I glanced in his direction, noting that his flat glare appeared to have refocused onto his cell phone. He tapped at the screen, inserted his keycard to unlock a door that was already open, then tapped the screen again.

Surely I could...

"No." The single word landed like broken glass beneath my feet and suddenly I was furious.

"Willow is my pack mate. If you're unwilling to do anything to figure out who hurt her, then at least let me smell around the guard whose drugging was clearly part of the setup."

One eyebrow rose, then the Executioner shrugged and provided the barest modicum of information. "No scent."

"Oh, so he drugged himself? Took a sleeping pill on the job to ensure he wouldn't be woken by plus-ones chattering about sleepwear?"

"Gala dresses, actually." This was Pet, who seemed to find me amusing as she leaned against the door jamb leading into a bedroom I wasn't likely to sleep in anytime soon. "Willow didn't pack one in the required pink, but they've got her covered. Everyone's pooling resources so any plus-one sent home tomorrow can help out those who stay behind."

As she spoke, the teenager motioned lazily and I was momentarily distracted by the flow of plus-ones heading in our direction. Several had left my suite when the Executioner unlocked the door and now they were returning bearing gowns that sparkled and flashed in shades ranging from pastel rose to a deep pink.

Meanwhile, my pack bond jiggled just the tiniest fraction, not with fear this time but with pleasure. Whatever the point of the gala was within the bigger picture of the Moon Trials, it gave Willow joy to think she'd look good at it.

Which meant it had been an oversight on my part not to research the wardrobe my plus-one needed so her stay in San Francisco would be more pleasant. I frowned then refocused on the point at hand. "Whatever they're discussing, the guard didn't drug himself."

For a moment, the astringency of the Executioner's scent faded. He cocked his head as he rasped out: "Tranquilizer dart."

Then, dismissing me as easily as he'd pinned me with that steely focus, he clapped his hands to draw the attention of every woman both inside and outside my suite. "You will all be locked in your rooms until after the next Trial," he rasped.

A collective groan of disappointment resulted in the tiniest twitch of the Executioner's cheek. His version of a smile? His subsequent words were no warmer, however. "Correction, in a room of your *choice*. Meals will be delivered by me personally. Do not fear. You will all be safe."

They'd be safe because I'd be there to watch over them, not because the Executioner had rejiggered the keycards so only he could unlock our doors. Which appeared to be what he'd been busy doing while staring at his phone, as evidenced by Pet's frustration when she regained the clothes shed in the hallway and still couldn't get back into her room.

As the Executioner let Pet in, I measured his height against the vague memory of tonight's intruder. This dark shadow of a man might be in the right ballpark and he'd also shown up surprisingly quickly both here and beside the dead man's body in the gymnasium...

The Executioner's reason to scare Willow, however, remained murky. Unless, of course, Chief Reed had bought his compliance.

Well, if anyone tried to harm my pack mate again, I'd be there waiting. I headed for my plus-one's room, then paused as Willow looked up from the women she was whispering with and demanded, "Get out."

Ember was the only non-plus-one who'd been granted entry to the room and she addressed me over the confections she was pulling out of a beeping microwave. "I'll keep an eye on things," she promised. "Take my room. You'll need to rest if you want to do well tomorrow."

"And you? Don't you need to rest?"

"In order to lose? Not so much." Then, not explaining that bombshell, she added, "Here, take a cookie."

The sweetness carried me across the hall then turned flavorless the moment the Executioner locked me into my borrowed room.

I tried to sleep, but Ember's bed was cold and vast without the mate I'd hoped would be there beside me. The text message waiting on my phone from my sister added to the emptiness as well.

"I never thought I'd go months without seeing my you," Mai had typed. *"This isn't a guilt trip, Kira, just a question. Staying apart—is it worth the consequences? Grub misses you. Aurora barely knows you. Some days, I feel like I've ripped out half of my heart."*

The time stamp was too many hours ago for me to risk replying with a video call, but it was clear Mai had been lying awake just like I was now, staring up into the darkness. Because she never would have let down her guard enough otherwise to so thoroughly bare her soul.

I rubbed the skin above my own heart as sympathetic pangs cut through me. Our sisterly connection felt so tenuous here in my solitary hotel room, as if memories of the past and hopes for the future were both frozen into a hazy, indecipherable mess.

It was just middle-of-the-night blues, I knew. Still, I couldn't quite talk myself into staying put. Instead, I dragged a pillow and comforter over to the floor-to-ceiling window that overlooked the city, leaned my forehead against the cool glass, and peered out.

Even in the wee hours, there were lights and movement below me. Fog blocked details, but I could imagine people traveling home to their loved ones after the late shift. Others starting their day early after kissing the foreheads of sleeping toddlers.

Seeing the bustle and knowing what lay behind it made me feel even more alone.

Only I wasn't. Another text popped up on my phone, this one a new addition to the group thread between the other female participants of the Moon Trials. *"Go to sleep, Kira,"* Ember had typed.

"How do you know I'm awake?" I couldn't resist answering. After all, the chatter had stilled across the hall at least fifteen minutes earlier.

"I didn't," Ember responded tersely, *"but I do now."*

Smiling, I couldn't resist scrolling up to check out the rest of the messages I'd ignored during the drama earlier in the evening. It was a discussion of Moon Trial strategies in which Ember had laid out each option in such pedantic detail she would have seemed Rupert-like if the tastes of chocolate and sugar hadn't still lingered on my tongue. In Ember's opinion, the best choice was to win the first contest with flair then obviously throw over the second.

"I'm winning all of them," Pet had countered.

"Understandable," Ember had texted back. *"With your history, I might feel the same way. You're right that if you win, everyone will toady up to you for a decade*

in hopes their heir will be given a leg up when you organize the next Moon Trials. But, look, you're rolling the dice. At least consider the comfortable middle. Hit the fifty percent mark with obvious ease and you'll always be considered a threat. Go any higher and you'll be on everyone's radar, which can be bad as well as good."

"I don't see why you're even here," Pet answered, proving that everyone other than me had done their homework regarding the private lives of their competition. *"With your father's support, you don't need this."*

"I'm here to build alliances," Ember responded easily.

"All the more reason to win."

"But I want honest friends, not sycophants."

The time stamps suggested Pet had needed to look up *sycophant* before answering. Then she'd proven her youth by inserting an emoji with hands up in a shrug.

"We're glad to be your friends, Ember," I typed, joining the conversation belatedly. Then the other issue that had been roiling around in my mind erupted into a question I hadn't really intended to ask her: *"You don't happen to know if Thom has a brother, do you?"*

"I didn't think so," Ember answered immediately, *"but I'll look into it."*

"Tomorrow," I suggested. *"After you sleep."*

"Tomorrow," my new friend agreed. *"After we both sleep."*

Turning my phone screen dark, I peered back out at a city that didn't feel quite so lonely any longer. And I pondered the options Ember had laid out for Pet.

I wasn't about to aim for an outright win at the Moon Trials. The fifty/fifty chance of death simply wasn't worth it. But if Ember was right and acing matches with flair gave winners standing long after the battles were over...well, maybe I could kill two birds with one stone.

Because my inability to spend time with my family gnawed at me. But if I proved myself a force to be reckoned with, perhaps I could become part of Mai's life again while still keeping Fairwood enemies at bay.

The trick would be performing well without descending into the behavior of a predator. The memory of the fallen shifter's face back in the gymnasium merged with the more distant memory of Willow's mate. Had today's victim's mouth been a bit wider than average or was I conflating the past with the present?

My dreams that night were of blood rather than desserts.

Chapter 13

I t felt like I'd only been sleeping for a few minutes when the whole floor was roused by the gray-eyed Executioner banging on doors. I followed the noise into the hall to find the storm cloud of a shifter offering a rolling cart of delicacies for the plus-ones along with two words for Ember, Pet, and me: "You're late."

By the time the three of us reached the hotel lobby, thirteen other contestants had already assembled. I didn't need Rupert's calculator to tell me what that meant. Unfinished fights yesterday must have been won and lost while the Executioner questioned every woman in the gymnasium bathroom. So some of these shifters should have looked as exhausted as I felt.

None did. Instead, they stalked from breakfast buffet to leaning stations, no one succumbing to the apparent weakness of actually *sitting* at a table. The air was so redolent with fur, I expected at least a few heirs to shift before vans showed up.

But I noted that only vaguely out of the corner of one eye because heirs weren't the only werewolves present. Instead, Thom's tall strength towered above Rupert only twenty feet away from me. I skirted growly heirs, my hand finding its way to Thom's forehead before I realized what I was doing.

Showing weakness. The one thing no heir could afford while at the Moon Trials. Sure enough, the scent of edged pleasure wafted toward me from every side.

Whatever. I found it hard to care about our audience when Thom's broad palm drew my hand down to slide across his stubbled jaw before settling onto his chest. Two hands above one heart, its thumping synchronized with my own.

"Good move," my mate rumbled, his eyes twinkling even as he let his shoulders slump downward theatrically. "Being underestimated could come in handy."

"So you're fine?" I murmured low enough that no one but Thom could hear me.

He nodded. "Sorry to scare you last night. I let down my guard around someone I considered family. Not the smartest move. I won't make that mistake again."

"You have nothing to apologize for," I countered. "We're a team. We watch each other's backs."

I knew Thom was fine when he graced me with the tiny hint of a smile no one else ever seemed to notice. "Like that hunt last fall when the rabbit tried to eat you? I totally saved your skin."

"Rabbits can be scary," I responded stiffly, barely managing to keep the corners of my mouth from twitching upward. "Didn't you ever read *Bunnicula* as a child?"

"I'm afraid my education in that department was sorely lacking." Leaning in closer, Thom dropped his voice until it was so low I felt more than heard it as he added: "Perhaps you could educate me at a later date?"

As he spoke, his fingers stroked the spaces between my fingers and I shivered. We had things to discuss. Thom's brother. Willow's late-night intruder. But all I wanted was to live in this bubble of silly memories and unrestricted physical access for one moment longer.

I wasn't given that moment. Someone blew another ear-piercing dog whistle and every heir except me surged out onto the street.

I had no choice but to follow. The Moon Trials were why I was in San Francisco, after all. So I reluctantly turned away from the man whose presence was headier than the beverages he served at his bar back in Gate City.

Well, I tried to turn away. Thom's fingers stayed twined through mine, his iron strength swinging me back around to face him as he thrust a napkin-wrapped bundle into my free hand. "Eat," he rumbled. "And stay safe."

I stole one more kiss then hurried outside to join the competition. I was the last one to board the second van.

During the ride to the next Trial location, someone I could have sworn hadn't been present yesterday regaled us with a long-winded monologue. He was roughly Ember's age, a good decade older than the average Moon Trials competitor, and his speech suggested he was in charge of today's fight.

I waited until it was clear nothing the shifter said was particularly worth listening to, then I murmured a question to the women flanking me on either end of the back seat. "Who's that?"

"Wylie?" Pet's eyebrows drew together.

"Kira missed the mixer," Ember reminded the teenager. Then, to me, "Chief Wylie won the previous Moon Trials. He told us last night that it wasn't worth his time to attend the first contest since so many heirs wash out."

Pet's assessment was more succinct. "Pompous windbag."

Which wasn't wrong. Our trip yawned endlessly as Chief Wylie nattered away about the historic footsteps we were treading in—his. Only when we turned off the still-dark highway did our host's canines glint and the topic turn more relevant.

"Today, we're going to have *fun*," he told us. "Each of you has been matched with an heir on the other van. Your first goal is to incapacitate your opponent. Your second goal is to assist your van mates. Because the winning team will be given a leg up in contest number three."

He lowered his voice conspiratorially as he continued. "But be aware that we're not isolating you from the wider world this time. This is a hunt among humans. Slip up and..." He drew one finger across his throat.

Beside me, Pet rolled her eyes then pulled out her phone. "The roster's up."

She was right. The app we'd all been told to download prior to arrival now had a new section unlocked and inside were name pairings.

I scanned the list, noting that we'd once again been matched in alphabetical order. Which meant...yep, Rupert was my opponent for the second Trial. One way or another, Thom and I wouldn't be together in San Francisco after this morning. I was suddenly glad I'd taken the time to steal one final kiss.

Only...that wasn't quite right.

"You have five minutes to call in favors," Chief Wylie informed us. "By mutual agreement, you can trade competitors with other members of your team. But first, one final note for one very special heir."

Dark eyes settled on me and stuck there, the wolf behind Chief Wylie's gaze hungry and his words apparently aimed at me personally. "Do try to please me. You'll be sorry if you don't."

My seatmates took Chief Wylie's words as a warning. After all, the Executioner had clearly earmarked me as a potential murderer and troublemaker. But the alpha's admonition had landed differently upon my skin.

His attention felt slimy, invasive. As if he was looking through my clothes in a very unshifter-like manner. With an effort, I shook off the feeling and tried to trade opponents...with zero luck.

The trouble appeared to be that I'd missed last night's mixer where, apparently, enough alliances had been formed to fuel a flurry of heated conversation. Without a similar history to trade on, everyone on the van rejected my approach. Or, in Pet's and Ember's cases, seemed too intent upon a previously planned path to meet my eye.

Shrugging, I took the opportunity to wolf down two bacon and egg biscuits—lack of sleep always left me starving—while Pet called three rows over in an effort to trade up to a contender she considered more worth her while. On my other side, Ember scrolled through names in the app, tapped a finger against her mouth, and muttered things like "bad idea," "yikes," and "well, *he'd* send me home in a body bag."

"Still planning to lose?" Pet's lip curled as she completed her negotiations and returned her attention to us.

"Yes, and..." Ember's eyes lit up as she spun to face me. "Your Rupert. How likely would he be to stab an opponent while she's down?"

"I wouldn't exactly call him 'my Rupert.' But let me check."

While I texted with the write-in heir who was bound to flunk out unless faced with someone throwing over the Trial on purpose, Pet continued to poke holes in our strategy. "That doesn't make sense. Kira, you haven't even asked who Ember would be trading you." She paused, pulled up what appeared to be a dossier on her phone, and hummed. "Well, I take that back. Damien should be easy. He would have lost last night if his opponent hadn't died."

And Rupert was on board also, or at least as on board as he ever was. *"Will you be a gentleman if your opponent tosses the contest?"* I'd asked him.

His response: *"I won't waste my energy on someone who's already lost, if that's what you're getting at."*

So— "You're on," I told Ember as the van slowed. We barely had time to input our swap before we were each handed tactical headsets and given a quick crash course on how to use them to engage with our team mates.

Then, in a pre-dawn suburban neighborhood with sprinklers running and the air sweet with flowers, fifteen werewolves and one kitsune started our hunt.

Chapter 14

The headset I'd been given was too heavy for a canine to wear easily, which I supposed was intentional on the part of our host. After all, we'd been dumped into a neighborhood full of three-million-dollar houses, not the sort of area where a human accidentally sighting something paranormal could be swept under the rug.

So I stuck to two legs while a map sprang to life in my goggles, the image filling a third of my vision. Seven glowing dots emerged to represent my team mates while, as best I could tell, the shifters from the other van weren't visible to us. Left guessing about our targets' locations, half of my team mates had opted to head east in a small wedge while two weren't moving at all.

I huffed out a small sneeze of frustration. Even though we were each meant to find an individual member from the other pack and force him to surrender, every man for himself wasn't going to win this battle.

It was a relief when someone took over managing our amoeba-like attack pattern. The only slightly unusual part was who had seized command.

"Fan out," Pet ordered, her age turning irrelevant as she proved herself an excellent tactician. "Report any shifter scent to the group along with the closest cross streets."

"You expect us to listen to you, kid?" a male voice growled.

Ember chuckled out a throaty purr and one of the glowing dots changed trajectory to obey Pet's suggestion. Following suit, I crossed the street and veered left, into an area where street lights were few and far between. There I caught a hint of fur that reminded me of Thom's signature aroma but darker. "Burnt cinnamon toast at Burgoyne and Montecito," I reported.

"That would be Karl and also first contact." Pet's voice came through tight and excited. "No more heel-dragging. Benedict, Lucas, get your asses in gear. We're going to *win*."

And it worked. Glowing dots spread out just as Pet told them to. One team mate headed in my direction, presumably to meet up with Karl, while other scents were reported and identified in fits and starts.

Then it was my turn. Old leather and whiskey was scented five blocks over. "Damien," Pet noted.

"What'd you do, spend all yesterday sniffing us and taking notes?" the same heckler as before demanded.

"Aren't you glad she did?" Ember rebutted.

Ignoring the banter, I ran. Through the reek of floor cleanser, which dulled the working of my nostrils but which I didn't report to my team mates. The Executioner's location was irrelevant to the contest since he wasn't a participant in the Trials. I could only hope he—and his scent—moved on to patrol somewhere else soon.

Meanwhile, the neighborhood had started stirring. A dog walker emerged from her house, the miniature furball erupting into a yapping hissy fit that only ceased when I was out of its sight line then started back up soon thereafter.

Which meant a shifter was trailing me. The Executioner, I guessed, when the dog yelped once before going abruptly silent. It probably took one sniff of the big, bad wolf and jumped into its mistress's arms.

Ignoring my pet-scaring pursuer, I turned in a complete circle. This was where Damien's scent had been reported. And my team mate was right—I caught a whiff of old leather and whiskey even through the Executioner's shock to my nostrils. Damien had been in this spot recently, but where had he disappeared to after that?

Padding up and down the street resulted in a quickly fading scent trail in both directions. Had Damien cut through a yard, risking an annoyed homeowner calling the cops on him?

No. A long, narrow well of darkness dropped off on either side of the street right where Damien's scent was strongest. A creek bed had been dug down below grade and concreted into a nearly invisible submerged alley. And while access was restricted by a chain-link fence, even a coordinated human could have climbed over the barrier and scrambled down.

I looked both ways then paused as someone strode around the corner toward me. It wasn't an innocent bystander or my prey however. Just the Executioner, leaning up against a telephone pole and watching me silently with those flat gray eyes.

Well, let him watch. I splashed down in ankle-deep water as Ember's voice came through my earbuds. *"Engage."*

At that instant, the view through my goggles expanded to fill my entire vision. We'd been told not to attack without verbal warning, a rule that my cupcake-baking buddy had obeyed to the letter. What we hadn't been told was that those not involved would get an up-close-and-personal view of each battle thanks to the headset we all wore.

Water seeping through my boots was now the only indicator of my physical location as the transmitted scene split in two. On one side, Rupert raised his sword, muscles tense and arms trembling. He was outclassed and knew it. Likely he didn't trust Ember to keep her word and lose on purpose. I was only 80% sure of that likelihood myself.

On the other side of my screen, Ember moved wolf-lithe while circling Rupert two-legged. The camera taking this in spun as Rupert kept her within his sights, jerking up and down when he stumbled slightly trying to keep up.

Then I was drawn back to my own skin for a split second as the scent of floor cleanser settled over my head like a shroud. It wasn't a physical touch, just the instant awareness that the Executioner was standing at the edge of the street peering down at me. His reek hunched my shoulders until I forced them to straighten. Let him watch. I was doing exactly what I was supposed to—focusing on Ember's fight.

And when I was finally able to ignore the dark presence above me, I grinned. Because my new friend was turning the battle into a non-lethal showcase of her abilities just as she'd promised. She sliced the air, took a running start, then used a retaining wall assist to leap up and over Rupert's shoulder.

The view turned even jerkier as Rupert cringed beneath her. His options for evasive action were basically nil.

No, this was Ember's moment to take down her opponent. She could have barreled into him or swiped low with her sword and cut deep into the shifter who was a passable swordsman but not anything like the athlete Ember was proving herself to be.

Instead, she ignored the opportunity and landed solidly, one leg in front of the other. Catching her balance, she paused...then collapsed theatrically.

"Ow, ow, oh no!" Dropping her sword, Ember lifted one hand to her forehead in a proto-swoon. "My ankle! It's sprained! I can't go on!"

Rupert padded toward her like a mouse being asked to pull a thorn out of a lion's paw. For one long moment, he seemed afraid to fight even a defenseless Ember. But then the tip of his sword pressed into her belly where a cut would mean not immediate death but a slow, agonizing descent into mortality.

"You surrender?" His voice squeaked up at the end.

"I surrender," Ember agreed, her tone far steadier than his was. Then, angling herself so she was speaking directly to his camera, she added, "And I'd like to remind everyone that invitations to my after-party will only be addressed to those who keep their noses clean. There will be cake, lots and lots of cake. Fight smart and fight fair and I'll see you on the other side."

A chatter of text messages from alphas and plus-ones erupted on the side of my goggles. Apparently Moon Trials participants hadn't been the only ones watching. Equally apparently, Ember's ploy had worked—more congratulations were heading her way than Rupert's.

Ignoring the byplay, Ember saluted us all then collapsed further, as if the sword Rupert was holding had struck deep instead of wavering inches from her skin. I shook my head, forgetting for a moment that the rest of the battles today and later in the week would be less theatrical. Ember was a class act and her loss had won me another day with my mate. I hoped to be invited to that after-party because I wanted to enfold her in a massive bear hug.

Then the moment was broken by one quiet word that came, not through my earbuds, but from far too close by in the creek where I lingered. "Engage."

Chapter 15

My goggles were still flashing the results of Ember's contest—apparently our team had been granted partial points for style—when moving air whistled past my face. I parried, or tried to. But my arms wouldn't move. They were pinned to my sides, something clenching hard and unyielding around my middle.

And now, too late, the goggles cleared to reveal Damien's goateed face inches from my eyeballs. If I wasn't mistaken, he was one of three shifters who'd been leaving the bar near where I'd found Thom last night. Which likely meant he'd been involved in the drugging. Could this be the brother of my mate?

My stillness as I considered the complete absence of similarities between the two men made Damien smile wider. Then he jerked the trailing end of the jointed metal lasso he'd used to incapacitate me. "Hadn't expected a fox to be quite so easy to rope."

I wouldn't have been if the Executioner hadn't hovered above me, drenching the stream bed in his overwhelming scent and masking the approach of another shifter. Had that been intentional? If so, it was yet more data pointing toward his guilt for last night's room invasion and possibly for the murder during the first Trial too.

I tilted my head back until I could see the Executioner's silhouette against a streetlight, then I dismissed the annoyance. Nobody ever said werewolf fights were fair.

And, the truth was that while Damien thought he'd vanquished me, I was far from defenseless. My star-ball sword was easy to shorten into a curved knife, perfect for sliding up under the lasso and sawing...

A jolt of electricity shot through me and Damien grinned wider. "You really think I didn't consider that? This here rope"—he shook it, slapping my stomach with the slack—"was a present from your alpha. Wonder what you did to piss him off? He sent it for whoever faced you down this morning. Gift tag said the red stuff is *hihi'irokane*, perfect for keeping foxes in line."

"Never heard of hihi-whatever," I gritted out. Still, my necklace was made of a reddish-gold metal that had originally been used to trap my star ball and which I'd later used to lock up Gate City's magic. Like the lasso, it had originated within the Reed pack, pointing toward a familiarity on the part of their alpha with kitsunes before the two of us ever met.

And that was an issue to ponder later. Right now, the important connection was between the metal around my neck and the metal clasping my hands to my sides. Sending my star ball sliding up to encompass the orb at my collarbone, I silently pleaded for assistance from the sentient being that resided in a fox skull underneath Thom's bar.

I didn't know exactly what I was talking to, but I knew it was powerful. After all, even the human military had taken notice of the unlikelihoods that kept cropping up in Gate City's vicinity. And that being had spoken to me months ago when I'd been granted the ability to harness its magic. *Keeper of the Gate*, it had called me. Surely it could help the Keeper out with a little lasso-loosening oomph now?

Unfortunately, I was now on the other side of the country. So I shouldn't have been surprised when nothing happened for so long that Damien raised an eyebrow. "Do I need to rough you up, or are you going to surrender already?"

Then the very faintest trickle of something seeped out of my necklace and into my body. Whatever it was felt just as electric as the shocking jolt when I tried to saw at the lasso, but considerably less painful. As if I'd completed a circuit and let power flow without cease.

"Oh, there was one more thing." Damien had let the free end of the lasso slacken while he gloated, but now he used it to drag me so close we were almost embracing. Lowering his head, hot air licked at my ear as he whispered, "Your alpha had a message he wanted me to pass along once you failed. Don't know what it means, but here's what he wrote—'I didn't have to use the blood.'"

"I didn't have to use the blood."

No, that was wrong. It had to be. Last winter, Chief Reed had trapped me by utilizing his superior knowledge of kitsune weaknesses. Freely given kitsune blood put me under his command the same way a more dominant werewolf could force a subordinate to follow his orders. He'd set me up, ordered me to kill his nephew...and I had.

The death grimace. The spurting blood. The awful crunch as my sword sliced through a neck from side to side...

I'd been racked by guilt until Chief Reed demanded a second vial of blood from me. Then it had all become clear. My hands had struck down Willow's mate—something I still hadn't been able to come to terms with—but Chief Reed's will had powered the action.

"You forced me to kill your nephew," I'd growled at him when that realization struck.

And Chief Reed had been so proud of himself that he'd become suffused in the saccharine scent of smugness. *"Oh, did you not realize? I do hope you haven't lost any sleep over that."*

But had Chief Reed ever actually said he'd used blood to force my action? Not in so many words.

Memory had caught me so hard in its grip that I barely felt Damien whipping the lasso again to refocus my attention. His words, though, snapped me back into the present at last.

"You're as spineless as your mate." My opponent was leaning in so close now that I could count the hairs in his goatee. "Once you're gone, it won't be as fun to play with the meat who thinks he's an alpha. But we'll keep playing. We'll..."

Usually, I would have laughed in his face. Thom was well able to take care of himself.

But my mate had wanted to be underestimated, a choice that might become even more important now that Rupert had won a second contest. So I swallowed down the bitterness of the past and fed into Thom's charade with a growled: "Don't mess with my mate."

I'd only pretended anger…at first. Then the trickle of electricity starting at my necklace overflowed into my body and suddenly I was furious.

I was furious with Chief Reed for shaking up an understanding of the past I'd just come to terms with. With the Executioner for using his scent to dull my instincts in this second Trial. With Damien for using a technicality to ambush me before threatening Thom.

I was furious at three men, but only one was present. Damien I could deal with. *Would* deal with. *Now.*

With supreme satisfaction, I watched the necklace energy merge with the lasso and turn the threads of metal subtly redder, like a coal pushed closer to the fire. I somehow knew that all I had to do was *want* and the lasso would obey me. Roiling emotion tempted me not to dally thinking through the consequences, just to act.

I acted. And the lasso ripped itself out of Damien's hands as easily as if he'd never been holding it. The loop spun back up over my head like a video of the past replayed backwards.

Then I was the one holding the lasso's free end. Damien was the one trussed up like a calf at a rodeo. That pang of remorse in my chest was overcome by the *hihi'irokane* vibration of excitement. This was what it meant to win.

And I wasn't finished either. When the loop securing Damien's wrists wrenched his arms toward me and his mouth opened in a proto-yell, I twitched one finger and a tendril of lasso slid down to gag my opponent.

"Can't have that," I admonished. "Not in a human neighborhood."

Damien's eyes were wide now. He didn't seem to like being on this end of the lasso as much as he had on the other. Shrugging, I cast the free end upward until it glittered in the pre-dawn glow of streetlights, looping through the railing above us and dragging my opponent up off his feet.

He tried to say something then. *I surrender!* Maybe. Or a plea to stop before his shoulder joints popped out of their sockets.

I spoke over him. "Can't hear you." And if I couldn't hear, I didn't have to stop either. I...

I lost some time after that. Lost track of what I was doing and why I was doing it. When I blinked back to myself, my right fist was sore and blood flowed from Damien's face down into the water beneath him.

He wasn't moving. I couldn't even tell if he was breathing.

My goggles pulsed with congratulations. I'd won.

Chapter 16

I'd won...and I'd lost. Because Chief Reed might have provoked me with his message, but he hadn't forced me to do anything this time. And Damien might have threatened my mate, but Thom would be the first to tell me he could stand up for himself.

Meanwhile, I'd turned a defenseless opponent into a punching bag. That was all me taking winning entirely too far.

Too far because, whatever role Damien had played in the drugging of my mate, Thom had bounced back by morning. I suspected the man dangling in front of me wasn't going to rebound nearly so fast.

Words tried to elude me, but I finally dragged out four. "We need a doctor."

Above my head, half seen through the text thread of congratulations pulsing across my goggles, the Executioner rasped out an answer. "He's not dead."

"Oh, you know that? Because you've come down here and taken his pulse?" I said as I forced unyielding muscles to do exactly that.

Thankfully, the wheeze of Damien's breath reached my ears at the same time I found the flutter of heartbeat at his throat. Which meant the Executioner was right. Still, being knocked unconscious wasn't as harmless as movies made it out to be. Best-case scenario, Damien had a painful concussion and weeks of recovery in front of him. Worst-case scenario, the damage might last far longer than that.

And my hands were shaking so badly I wasn't even sure I could lower the defeated shifter to the ground without causing additional damage. I needed to get Damien help then find somewhere safe and dark where I could lick my wounds without an audience.

Not yet. First, I appealed to the pride of the pack leader who I knew was watching. "Surely San Francisco is an established enough clan to have a medic on call if not a doctor. Maybe they have a nurse practitioner? A ten-year-old with delusions of grandeur?"

The reek of floor cleanser drew closer. The Executioner's rasp was colored by annoyance this time. "You only punched him once."

Still, the Executioner grabbed Damien under the armpits and jerked his chin, which I took to be my signal to unwind the lasso. I wasn't sure if the *hihi'irokane* would obey my wishes without whatever deeper energy I'd tapped into earlier, an energy that seemed to have helped push me past the edge of civilized behavior. But even though I kept my star-ball far from the necklace this time, the lasso slithered loose as obediently as a trained snake before retreating to wind around and around my forearm. The end tucked underneath itself and disappeared like an ouroboros swallowing its tail.

I shivered, fighting the urge to shake the metal loose the same way I'd shake off a tarantula crawling across my skin. To don my fur and run and run and run until I found the safe harbor of my mate.

As if he'd heard my desperation, Thom's name popped up on the text thread for the first time. His observation was off topic, out of character, and yet still very much himself. *"No one told me the plus-one dress code for the gala. Guess I'll be spending today hunting down a pink tuxedo. J."*

The final letter could have been a typo, but it wasn't. My stomach settled. We'd planned for this. Well, not for *this* exactly. But for a place to meet up if we needed to slip away from minders who stayed too hard on our heels. A place to go if I *needed* Thom the way I needed him right at this moment.

"Yeah, you track down that pink tuxedo," I murmured, hoping my voice would carry through. Then remembering the other person I had to contact before memories of this Trial could be suppressed along with my other dark regret, I raised my voice, hoping my string-puller was among the alphas who'd been invited to watch from afar. "Chief Reed, this is your report."

I spat on the ground, anger trying once again to cloud my vision. The fury didn't quite manage to overcome me this time, but my fingers were clenched into fists by the time Chief Reed's name popped up on the text feed.

"I'm proud of you, heir."

I'll bet he was.

I tipped my head to look up, trying to recenter myself. But the blood I'd spilled appeared to be expanding, flowing out to fill the sky while a roar followed it like thunder.

No, that wasn't blood. That was sunrise. And the roar was a throaty vehicle pulling to a stop on the street above us, the scent of fur emerging along with quiet voices. Chief Wylie, I hoped, had sent his best doctor to prove his pack's prowess. Damien wasn't my problem any longer.

He couldn't be my problem any longer. Not when my fingers, ears, and eyeballs were all failing me.

I dropped the goggles at my feet, not caring that the headset splashed instead of landing on dry concrete. Then I turned my back and strode away into the darkness under the street and out the other side, where water deepened and my boots sank into deposited mud and other effluvia.

I managed to keep my muscles from erupting into full-body shudders until I was out of sight.

In the end, I did turn fox, but only because the Executioner's scent stuck to my tail like a thistle burr. Whatever he wanted, I couldn't deal with it, not at this moment. So I ducked beneath an overgrown trellis at the corner of an otherwise perfectly manicured yard and shucked off my clothes, tying them up along with my cell phone and necklace into a bundle that my star ball could bind against my furry sides.

Only it wasn't my star ball that heeded my request. Instead, the lasso pinched my arm for one split second then it spun out and around my possessions, yanking them tighter and tighter until the result was barely larger than the phone at the center of the mass.

"You missed the boots," I murmured, feeling a little odd talking to an inanimate object. But how inanimate was the lasso really? Because a tendril came free from the packet and flicked itself against my soaked, muddy footwear dismissively.

"Okay, yes. But I might need them later."

The lasso ignored me and I caught another whiff of floor cleanser. The window of opportunity to get out from under the Executioner's thumb was quickly running out.

So I left the boots, tugging at my star ball until its electricity consumed me then spit me out into fox form. The instant I settled onto four legs, Chief Reed's lasso lashed out faster than I'd thought possible, tightening into a loop around my throat.

For a split second, I couldn't breathe. For a split second, blood filled my vision.

Then I shook off the memory, inhaled deeply, and accepted the collar. The lasso was simply binding my possessions to me as I'd ordered. There was nothing else going on.

Still, my feet were less sure than usual as I scampered up the trellis, across a fence, through three yards, and to the train that would take me back into San Francisco. And more frequently than I cared to admit, I shook myself in an effort to dislodge the collar that stubbornly refused to come off.

Chapter 17

Jmeant the Peace Pagoda in Japantown, a towering edifice that rose out of a tourist-filled square. Thom could have ended up there for any number of reasons—today, his cover was hunting a pink tuxedo.

For my part, once I spun back into humanity and accepted the lasso's movement from neck to arm, it was easy to lose myself amid masses of people who had nothing to do with shifters. Slipping between four huge concrete pillars topped by a flat red lintel on my way to the Peace Pagoda, however, the lasso abruptly came to life. It squeezed so tight I gasped, reaching out to steady myself against the cool concrete.

Then I was through, the lasso returned to slumber, and my mate's voice crackled to life in my mind. It felt like Thom had been trying to use our mate bond repeatedly, just waiting for me to come within hailing distance. As such, his words came through in a seemingly endless loop.

"...Left. Change of plans. Turn left. Change..."

An image supported the words—the door to one of the paired shopping centers that flanked the Peace Pagoda square. Along with the image came a sensation of caution, warning. Something had set my mate on edge.

I understood what when I caught a whiff of floor cleanser, not fresh but stale as if the Executioner had walked by this point half an hour earlier. Did he really have nothing better to do than haunt every part of the city I ended up in? And how had he gotten here before me? Had he seen through our veiled messages and ordered someone to follow Thom?

Didn't matter. My mate would know if someone was directly on his heels, and Thom was so close I could feel the tug on our mate bond like frothy waves drawing me into a sunlit ocean. I followed the tug through the indicated shopping center until I reached what appeared to be a bustling, Japanese version of a dollar store.

There, I ran into a roadblock in the form of three old ladies clogging the congested area between shop and checkout line. They were so slight I likely could have picked them up one by one and set each aside without winding myself. But I didn't, of course. Instead, I tried to slide past, only to have the entire mass of women wiggle sideways to block me.

"*Sumimasen*," I murmured the way I might have said *Excuse me* if they'd been speaking English. And one woman—her wisdom hump slowing her movement—turned in my direction, took me in, and erupted in a torrent of Japanese.

The words were far too fast for me to understand. But her gnarled finger reached out and tapped the lasso on my forearm. Now I picked out a single word that was newly familiar: *hihi'irokane*.

"You know what this is?" I started.

Before she could answer, the reek of floor cleanser slapped me. The Executioner had caught my trail or perhaps was just patrolling in hopes of stumbling across me. Either way, we'd be eye to eye momentarily if I didn't move deeper into the establishment.

Deeper into the establishment where my mate bond promised Thom lingered.

I didn't wait for an answer to my question. Instead, I used the opening the old ladies had finally provided and pushed my way down a narrow aisle crammed full of snacks I'd never heard of. Rushing out the other side, I fell into my mate's waiting arms.

We held the embrace for a breath-stealing eternity. I could have said I was listening to make sure the Executioner missed my scent trail, but that would have been a lie. No, I just needed to feel Thom's warm presence surrounding me before I dealt with the past.

But I couldn't lose myself for long. Regrets bubbled up within me then bounced like all surface thoughts did down the mate bond. Without me having to speak, Thom knew how horrified I was at my mauling of Damien. And I knew what he'd seen didn't strike him as cause for concern. Yes, I'd hit Damien hard, but it had only been a single punch. Well within the expected outcomes from the Moon Trials.

"My intentions..." I started, not quite knowing how to describe the flare of white-hot rage that had gushed through me. How anger had turned my world red, how I'd lost time in which I could have done anything.

"Thoughts aren't actions," Thom rumbled. "Take last night for example."

And his experiences in the city yesterday flowed over me the same way I'd shared my worries about this morning. I saw how he'd met his half-brother at the mixer I'd missed while locked away in that gymnasium bathroom. The sibling in question hadn't been Damien, but rather the burnt-cinnamon shifter I'd smelled but not sighted.

"Karl," Thom rumbled, the single word a growl. "He and his friends invited me out for a drink and I thought I was being welcomed into the family. Didn't expect to end up in a puddle of my own vomit."

"You want to rip his throat out." I was surprised by the intensity of emotion pulsing off my mate. In the past, Thom's human heritage had allowed him to bypass the werewolf need for claws and mayhem. Not so now.

Thom's voice went even deeper than usual as he bypassed my question. "I'm here to back you up, not cause additional problems." His words sounded like Gunner when he threatened bloody murder to protect my sister. And yet, Thom shrugged, and when he spoke again he'd regained the gentle rumble I knew best. "The point is, I *didn't* rip out Karl's throat. And you acted entirely appropriately even when goaded. Although..."

He reached out, one finger tapping the lasso coiled around my forearm. "Coincidence or instigation?"

"I had the same thought," I admitted. Dropping my voice for no particular reason since the nearby shoppers were paying us no attention, I added, "I can't get it off."

I'd tried after shifting back to humanity and regaining my clothes and other possessions. Striding from train to Japantown, I'd attempted to pry the lasso back into flexibility, but the chain-mail-like construction refused to unwind beneath my fingers. When I instead worked to brute-force it up over my hand, the lasso stuck at my knuckles and wouldn't budge.

"May I?" Thom rumbled.

"Be my guest."

Then his fingers were stroking down my arm and across the lasso. I shivered at the contact, watching the formation of goose bumps trailing the path of pleasure.

And the lasso that had refused to let go no matter how hard I shoved at it unwound the same way Pumpkin rolled over on his back to beg a belly rub. Thom crooned a wordless lullaby as he gently removed the metal from my person, wrapping it around his own arm instead.

"Here's another question for you..." His words ended in a grunt and I raised my eyebrows as I realized the lasso had clenched tight around his forearm.

"I can try to take it back," I offered.

Thom shook his head. "Leave it. My wolf rages frequently. I can handle whatever this thing throws at me."

And I believed him. That look in his eyes when he mentioned Karl had been murderous...and yet, this morning over breakfast Thom had been willing to turn himself into a weakling for the sake of future subterfuge. It took true strength for an alpha to hide in plain sight.

While I was thinking, Thom continued talking. "My question," he said, "is this—how do you know Chief Reed is telling the truth now?"

At that, I winced, lasso forgotten. "You heard what Damien said?" Because if Thom had heard, then everyone else had also.

My mate followed my logic easily without needing it spelled out for him. "Only those who know you well will understand the meaning behind it."

Willow would understand. And as if she'd heard me talking about her, my phone chimed with my plus-one's ringtone.

I wasn't done with this conversation, however, so I ignored the repeated ringing. "I don't know," I admitted. "When Chief Reed originally told me he'd drunk my blood, he did so in the form of a question. It wouldn't have smelled like a lie either way."

"Then you might as well assume the best until you know otherwise."

"Like you'll assume the best about your brother?"

Thom shook his head and I wanted to hear his response. But my phone had come to life again with the same ringtone as earlier. Willow wasn't the sort to call a second time unless time was of the essence, so I picked up. "Hello?"

"I need you." Her voice was choked. "Please."

Then the call cut off.

Chapter 18

For the second time in twenty-four hours, I reached inside myself in search of my one and only pack bond. I didn't have high hopes the connection would help since Willow was supposed to be at the hotel miles from here. But, to my surprise, our tether was hefty with proximity while also so brittle it seemed like one wrong move might crack it in two.

"Can't find her?" Thom's low rumble was backed up by his warm fingers sliding between mine. This physical comfort—so simple yet so impossible for us to achieve in the elapsed months since I'd become Chief Reed's heir—settled me enough to shake my head.

"Willow's close. I can get us there if…"

"…I watch out for trouble."

"The Executioner…"

"…is sniffing around. That's why…"

"…you moved our meeting point."

"Yep." I didn't need to see Thom's nod to know he was ready to go.

So as a unit, we hunted Willow while evading other hunters. Winding between tourists, we worked our way back out to the open square, crossed it, and entered the other shopping center. On this side, painted sea serpents writhed on the ceiling above us. Spices on the air reminded me of the meals our father used to cook in honor of our mother, the ones that never again graced our table after his death.

The single time I'd tried to recreate Japanese cuisine, my effort had brought Mai to tears. Had she stopped cooking my favorite meals for a similar reason after I broke our pack bond? Doubt coiled like a sea serpent inside my gut.

I only realized I'd stopped dead outside one of the several restaurants lining the hallway when Thom spoke. "In here?"

"Maybe." The pack bond did turn away from the main drag at this point, but I couldn't tell whether Willow was inside this restaurant or another without entering.

"Only one exit," Thom observed. "Unless there's a back way for staff."

His rumble helped me dismiss the past and focus on the present. Because even though my mate liked to think his mind was human, he'd chosen the dollar store for our meeting, I suspected, because of its two entrances. This restaurant tensed his muscles and we weren't even inside yet.

"You could watch the door," I offered, giving him an out in case lupine instincts proved overwhelming.

Thom snorted. "Not likely."

Together, we walked into the trap.

The restaurant should have been full of humans, but no one was sitting at any of the booths within our sight line. And the instant we made it through the door, a trio of burly shifters stepped out from behind the empty hostess station.

They all went for me, but Thom was there before fingers made contact. Using the lasso bracer to ward off blows, he tossed a suggestion back over his shoulder: "Run."

Okay, maybe my mate thought the single word was more than a suggestion. But I wasn't about to ditch him and Willow. Instead, I spun toward the scent of floor cleanser, finding the Executioner waiting in the shadows only three feet away from his bully boys. Willow, wild-eyed, was pressed up against the wall behind his back.

"What do you want?" I demanded, eying the distance between me and my plus-one. Was there any chance I could pull her away before the Executioner pounced? Unlikely.

"Your presence at the hotel," the thundercloud of a werewolf rasped. His scent grew even stronger, as if spitting out five words pushed him past his limit.

Meanwhile, out of the corner of one eye, I saw all three of the San Francisco shifters piling onto Thom as a unit. The glint of a blade caught light from around the corner and I pushed its mental image into Thom's mind. *"Danger!"*

He twisted away from the first stab, but his enemies weren't merely aiming for restraint. The second thrust raised a thin line of blood across the back of his neck. Meanwhile, I couldn't attack the Executioner with Willow so close to danger.

Sometimes, the smartest move is to give in while you still have energy left to fight.

"Okay, we surrender." I raised my hands to show their emptiness, nudging Thom through the mate bond to do similarly. For a moment, I thought he'd ignore my suggestion. He *heard* me, that part was clear. After all, he'd gone after the knife, his huge hand closing around the other shifter's wrist as they battled for control of the sole weapon. But he'd ended up underneath a pile of werewolves. Even if he got the knife, he wouldn't be able to keep it for long.

"When I told you to act like a wolf months ago, I didn't mean go full-on alpha," I chided, hoping the memory would push him out of the protective haze he seemed to have fallen into.

For a moment, I didn't think it had worked. My mate's only reply was a wordless growl.

But then he went boneless beneath the other werewolves. I held my breath, waiting until the blade disappeared back into a sheathe beneath somebody's shirt.

Only then did I meet the Executioner's flat, cold gaze. "Willow has no part in this," I promised. "Let Thom take her to safety and..."

"No." The Executioner's hand clenched down around my wrist, his momentum yanking me out of the restaurant before I could decide whether to plant my feet or fight back. Willow, unrestrained, followed close on my heels.

I cocked my head as I peered back at her, trying to make sense of the frantic phone call, the brittle pack bond. Realization struck me so hard I spoke it aloud. "You weren't coerced to be here."

In response, a spark of something hot and real flared down the pack bond toward me. "Why should I need to be coerced to reel you in?" Willow demanded. "You go feral and every plus-one is locked in her room when we should be preparing for the gala."

One of the San Francisco shifters snickered. "No greater danger than standing between a girl and her hairdresser."

Or between a widow and the fox shifter who had killed her mate.

Thom once again growled. I couldn't see him, but I felt that he'd been released. That he was about to do something decidedly unwise, likely because of the lasso he'd taken on for me.

"I have this handled," I pushed down the mate bond, hoping words would once again bring him back to reality. *"If you've got something better to do, feel free to do it."*

Thankfully, this time Thom was able to reply, even if he did disagree with me. *"You're currently restrained and about to be imprisoned."*

"When have I ever let that stand in my way?"

Our discussion before the Moon Trials hung between us, not needing to be repeated. Thom had laughed off my concerns that he wouldn't be able to stomach being treated like a plus-one rather than an alpha. Now, I could feel him shaking off heavy emotions the way a wolf might wring water out of his fur after swimming. And when he answered, his silent voice was once again full of humor.

"If you're sure you don't want help, that pink tuxedo is calling."

His words faded gradually as if Thom had veered away from the Executioner's contingent. And, despite the fact I was being marched back to the hotel like a kid caught out past her curfew, my belly warmed. This was why I'd been willing to mate with Thom when regular men left me cold and every other alpha raised my hackles. He could handle anything and he trusted me to do the same.

So I clued him in to the obvious just in case he'd missed relevant social cues during his limited time around other werewolves. *"Word to the wise: no alpha werewolf would be caught dead in pink."*

"My masculinity," Thom observed, *"doesn't feel threatened in any way."*

In stark contrast, my pack bond to Willow was sorely threatened, having dwindled down to barely more than a memory by the time we settled into the SUV waiting for us streetside. We rode back to the hotel in silence and once we stepped out of the elevator on our floor, my plus-one pushed herself into a horde of other women pouring out of their rooms. Her icy glare when Clipboard Lady materialized to hand me a folder of keycards pushed me back two steps.

The glare turned out to be contagious, too, quickly spreading to all of the other women. Now, I decided, was not the best time to address relationship issues with my plus-one. Instead, I tried one keycard in my door, got a red light, then had more success with the other card.

Once the automatically relocking barrier closed between me and Willow's fury, I considered washing my bare, filthy feet but decided against it. The huge bed called me and I was asleep before my head hit the pillow.

I woke an unknown amount of time later to the overwhelming reek of floor cleanser and the point of a knife hovering above my left eye.

Chapter 19

My hands had ended up beneath the covers while I slept, and the blade was far too close to give me time to disentangle them. So I acted on instinct. Lashing out with my star ball in its rawest form, I encircled my attacker's wrist and bent it backwards.

A woman's cry of pain halted me before I snapped any bones. Blinking, I focused at last on the face of my attacker. Not the Executioner but—"Willow?"

She'd collapsed in on herself, one hand cradling her injured wrist while the knife lay unused on the comforter between us. Meanwhile, the light above our heads toggled off then on again while the Executioner hummed wordless interest in the proceedings from closer to the door.

Ignoring whatever was going on in his head, I nudged the knife off the bed, waiting for the dull thud of it hitting carpet before I addressed Willow. "Look, I know you hate me."

"As if I don't have very good reason for that." She looked up and the splotches on her face, to my surprise, looked less like tears and more like fury. Dismissing me, Willow turned to address the Executioner. "I did what you wanted."

The shifter in question nodded once, padding closer so his astringent reek encircled me. I tensed, the lower half of my body still entangled in the covers. He was reaching for the knife and...

My star ball blazed into sword form, slashing through bedding, but the Executioner didn't attack. Just turned the knife Willow had threatened me with around once before sliding it into the top of his left boot.

Beside me, Willow took a deep breath then spoke again, her voice wavering. "You promised."

Another nod. The Executioner leaned toward me again, but I was finally ready. I'd wiggled both legs out from under the covers and was poised to spring...

I didn't have to. The storm cloud of a werewolf came close just long enough to snatch a single keycard off the bedside table before retreating. "One night," he rasped.

"Wait!" Willow was half off the bed, speaking to his back. "You're not going to arrest her? You said if the lights flickered it would be evidence that she'd used her fox magic yesterday in the gymnasium."

The Executioner shrugged, continuing toward the door. I should have kept my focus on him, the real and present danger, but words exploded out of me, aimed at Willow. "You set me up!"

I'm not sure why I was so surprised. I mean, attacking her mate's murderer with a knife was a reasonable reaction. Why, then, was making me look guilty of a different murder so far beyond the pale?

"You think I had no right?" Willow snapped back.

I shook my head. "You had every right last winter. But I've spent all of the intervening time trying to make it up to you."

"By pimping me out?"

My mouth, which had opened to address a very different expected response, clicked back shut. The Executioner chuckled as he stepped out into the hallway and shut the door behind him. Before I'd mustered words, I was alone with a furious female werewolf.

"Plus-ones," Willow ground out in the face of my incredulous silence. "That's what we're here for. Heirs share our keycards around to gain favors. You can't pretend not to know that."

I hadn't in fact known that, but the facts lined up now. The guards who were so unhelpful when I'd brought Thom back to the hotel last night. The heirs this morning who'd had favors to trade on after only one evening spent in each others' companies. The keycard that didn't work in my door but had been given to me as if it was my own.

Arguing my former ignorance seemed like a bad idea, so I pivoted. "Seriously? The issue has nothing to do with my tendency toward murder?"

"You think I care about that?" And Willow's facade of strength crumpled, her words descending into a choked mumble that I had to strain to understand. "Quentin was an abuser. I'm glad he's dead."

I blinked, rewriting the past. If Willow wasn't mad at me for killing her mate, then what had pushed her over the edge just now?

Only once her gaze dropped to the floor, the spot where her borrowed knife had fallen, did I get an inkling of the true problem. She was disgusted with herself for not having the gumption to stab someone she thought was her enemy, someone she thought was poised to steal away her free will yet again.

With that revelation came an easy solution. "You know more about kitsunes than I do," I observed. "I hadn't even realized the lights flickered when I pulled on my magic."

As I'd hoped, Willow's waterworks dried up in the face of my logic. "True," she agreed, voice noncommittal.

"So you know," I continued, "that when I swear an oath, I'm bound by it."

Willow nodded again, but her scent remained acrid with distrust. Until, that is, I made a promise so simple it couldn't be misconstrued.

"I won't let anyone in your room you don't want there," I told her. "When the Executioner returns your keycard—I assume the one that doesn't work in my door is yours, right?—I'll hand it over."

Willow's voice was small when she disagreed with me. "Plus-ones don't get their own keycards."

"This one does. And, next time you want to stab somebody in the eye, you're going to know what you're doing."

Which is how we came to spend the rest of the afternoon practicing self-defense and basic knife moves rather than primping for the gala. Most of the other plus-ones joined in, resulting in dozens of apples, a ham, and three roast chickens falling beneath their murderous assault.

By the time Thom showed up in his pink tuxedo to escort us to the waiting vans, the pack bond between me and Willow had become a true sharing rather than a forced connection. This time when I rose up in my seat to crane my neck at the view while crossing the Golden Gate bridge, Willow matched my enthusiasm. And after we disembarked in front of a huge, imposing mansion in the midst of wilderness I wouldn't have expected to find so close to San Francisco, she nudged me into my mate's waiting arms.

"You'll be alright?" I asked, even though music tugged my feet toward the dance floor while Thom's crazy pink tuxedo somehow managed to make him more rather than less enticing.

In answer, Willow hitched up her skirt to grant a glimpse of the knife she'd strapped to the outside of her thigh. "I think I can manage." She hesitated, then added, "Although..."

"Willow?" I prodded when it became clear no further words were forthcoming.

And she shook her head. "Later. Enjoy yourself. You deserve it."

I gave her another moment to change her mind. When she didn't, I met Thom's piercing sun-from-behind-a-cloud smile. "Shall we?" he rumbled, holding out his hand.

So we waltzed, my mate's strong palm pressed up against my shoulder blade and my heart lighter than it had been since I broke the bond between myself and my sister. Thom's head was so close to mine that he barely had to lean forward to murmur in my ear.

"You're always beautiful. But tonight you're radiant."

"Lack of guilt will do that," I answered, letting him spin me straight down the middle of the dance floor and toward the darkness beckoning between two columns at the other end. We passed heirs making deals involving sexual favors and their plus-ones. Older, equally dominant wolves who I thought might have been pack leaders brought in for the occasion. Servers with trays of colorful drinks and tantalizing canapés.

Ignoring all of it, Thom and I aimed for seclusion where we could celebrate alone.

Only those shadows turned out to be occupied. My mate and I caught the man's outline at the same instant, our forward momentum morphing into a whirlpool spin in place. I'd already started eyeing a different shadowed alcove when a far too familiar voice crept toward me out of the darkness.

"Mate bonds can be broken and recreated elsewhere," Chief Reed murmured to someone I couldn't see. "All I require in exchange is an alliance and one vial per month of her blood."

Chapter 20

The lasso on Thom's wrist clenched tighter while his hand on my shoulder blade turned into a claw—literally. My name hadn't been mentioned, but who else's blood did Chief Reed consume on a regular basis?

"An intriguing offer." This was Chief Wylie, our host here in San Francisco. "But she's yet to prove her abilities in fur form. Can a fox really stand up against a wolf?"

"She'll win the next battle," Chief Reed promised.

"If she does, then we have a deal."

Chief Reed and Chief Wylie might have a deal, but I had a mate who was about to go ballistic. The lasso writhed around his forearm and I could have sworn it nipped at my fingers. "Cool it," I told both my mate and the oddly animate metal, keeping my voice low so the older men wouldn't hear me. At the same time, I steered us subtly away from the alcove. Who said the guy was always supposed to guide the trajectory of the waltz? "I'm not about to break our mate bond. I'm afraid you're stuck with me."

My words didn't entirely ring true though. Because I knew my oath would force me to obey Chief Reed if he mandated action. And what was up with the mention of bonus blood? As far as I knew, Chief Reed already had one batch on ice to manipulate me with whenever he wished.

A loaded silence, then—"Lose the next Trial," Thom rumbled.

That did appear to be the easy way out of my predicament. But—"You're saying you don't want further opportunities to wrap your arms around me?"

Not to mention Willow, whose fate rested on me obeying Chief Reed's commands.

Thom's growl didn't lighten, but at least he was able to string more words together this time. "I'm saying we'll find another way. I'll create another way. The juice is no longer worth the squeeze."

I opened my mouth to answer, but our conversation wasn't fated to continue. Because steering Thom backwards without being able to see over his much taller shoulder wasn't a good idea now that we'd entered a busier portion of the ballroom. Or perhaps Pet had lined herself up for collision. Whatever the reason, we slammed into her, or she slammed into us, and a glass of red wine shattered on the ground at our feet.

"Excuse us," Thom rumbled, his human upbringing winning out over the lasso-induced anger. He released my hand in order to pull out a cloth handkerchief that matched the elegance of Pet's wardrobe. A twist of his chin and a flourish of his arm turned the offering into a courtly gesture that matched the ballroom ambiance.

One Pet didn't respond to in kind. Ignoring Thom's offer, she glared at me and spat out a single word. "Traitor."

Her reaction was oddly out of proportion to her wardrobe damage. Because, despite the massive amount of pale-yellow skirt offering a perfect canvas for splatter painting, only a few drops of liquid marred the hem.

Frowning, I considered the lasso. Could it send anger to someone it wasn't even touching? I doubted it, and at the moment the *hihi'irokane* object appeared entirely inanimate. No, this fury was all Pet.

No wonder Thom's voice turned steely as he answered for me. "Strong language for an accidental mishap."

"I'm not talking to you, *plus-one.*"

As Pet spoke, the music ceased. I could feel every eye in the room latching onto us as Pet dismissed Thom and lobbed a warning in my direction.

"You let down our team," she told me, eyes flashing. "Won your match then fled like a coward. So we'll all be handicapped when the time comes for the next challenge." She waved expressively at the wine on the floor, wine that *did* resemble a certain nightmare-inducing bodily fluid. "You'll see more blood soon, *traitor.*"

The threat would have been scarier if Pet hadn't currently resembled a kid playing dress up while Thom did a pretty miserable job pretending not to angle his wide shoulders between us just in case she transitioned from words to swords.

I, on the other hand, fully intended to fight my own battles. So my attention was focused elsewhere when the Executioner took advantage of the dramatic pause to strike with surgical precision.

It started with a note on a silver tray carried by a submissive werewolf. "Chief Faris?" murmured the young man sidling up to my mate's elbow. Thom, glanced at Pet one more time, unfolded the paper, then paled.

"What is it?" I sent down the mate bond.

"Who is the more relevant question. Answer: the woman who gave birth to me."

Despite my mate's evasive wording, his scent suggested curiosity, interest, perhaps even yearning. So I cut to the chase. *"The note's from your mother."*

"I suppose you could call her that. She wants to meet. Now. After ignoring me for three decades. Assuming she even wrote this. I wouldn't know her handwriting from a stranger's on the street."

"You wouldn't know your mother's handwriting, but you might know her scent."

Thom's eyes were hooded as he considered the slip of paper. He held it out a good distance from his body, pinching the note between two fingers like a filthy garment he wanted to discard. His gaze flicked to me, though, and he nodded. Then he raised the paper to his nostrils, sniffed, and his lips thinned.

"Well?"

"It might smell like family. Possibly."

And Thom would always wonder if he didn't answer this summons. So— *"Go,"* I told him. I could handle Pet's theatrics even if they weren't, as appeared likely, already over and done with.

Thom's jaw clenched. *"We haven't finished discussing our mate bond."*

"We'll have many years to finish that conversation," I countered. *"This may be your only chance to find the source of your X chromosome."*

The X chromosome—the one werewolf traits were carried on. Whether or not Thom was aware of that scientific factoid, his mixed emotions flew down the mate bond wordlessly. Yes, he was curious. But instinct told him to stay by my side until the issue of Chief Reed was dealt with. I was his mate and I was in clear and present danger. The wolf inside him refused to abandon me now.

Instinct likely would have won out if I hadn't nudged him in the opposite direction. *"You said you were here to back me up. Well, backing me up now means staying out of the limelight."*

And that did it. For himself, Thom wouldn't step aside. But for my sake...

He nodded once, square chin dipping in what might in an earlier era have been a bow. Then I was alone with a furious teenager...and an audience of dozens of werewolves.

Chapter 21

Thom's receding scent tried to draw my gaze after him. But I forced myself to focus just like I'd demanded he do. And I considered the young woman who was vibrating in front of me, shifting from foot to foot as she barely reined in her rage.

It had been rude to ignore her for so long. Not just rude but, to a werewolf, a gesture of dominance. No wonder Pet reeked of fur while I was pretty sure I caught the glint of a weapon through what appeared to be a slit in her skirt.

She might want to fight, but I didn't. Instead, I tilted my head subtly sideways, exposing my neck just enough to calm her inner wolf. Only once her eyes were once again human did I speak.

"You have every right to be disappointed," I told Pet, keeping my voice lower than hers had been. No need for every heir, plus-one, and alpha to be privy to this part of the discussion. "I understand you've had some trauma in your past that makes this contest more important to you than it is to the rest of us..."

"Some *trauma*?" Pet didn't bother speaking quietly, but the scent rolling off her this time wasn't anger. Instead, I caught a sharp bite of pain and saw the first hints of tears welling up on her lower eyelids.

Oops. Whatever history Ember had been referring to in her text thread must be a doozy. And a teenager in a fluffy yellow dress who experienced an emotional breakdown in this room full of competitive werewolves was painting a target on her back.

I could almost hear the echo of Thom's frequent admonition in my mind. *None of your business. Protect your own skin.*

And yet, no matter how much Pet tried to threaten me, she was still just a kid

So I took a chance and snagged her elbow, drawing her toward a different set of shadows that I hoped would be more conducive to conversation than the first had been. To my surprise, Pet allowed herself to be tugged into an empty alcove complete with a large window opening onto the outdoors.

Which should have meant the alcove was bright rather than dark. But while Thom and I had been dancing, night had fallen. Turning away from the window-turned-mirror, I took the girl's hand. "Talk to me."

In response, her fingernails bit into my palm so hard they nearly drew blood. Her voice was midway between fury and a sob when she tossed out words like a sword strike. "You have no idea what it's like to lose three sisters."

"You're right. I don't. But you do…?"

Pet nodded.

"I can't even imagine," I told her. Losing one sister, though… I'd feared that so many times it sometimes woke me in a cold sweat.

And it turned out all it took was the scent of my empathy to open the floodgates. "We didn't have any brothers," Pet confided, "but Dad kept hoping for one up until I was born. By then, my sisters were half-grown, raised to be pack princesses. They didn't know how to defend themselves. They were no match for power-hungry neighbors and mates who struck them. One is dead. Two wish they were. Well, one, I guess."

Her tear-stained explanation reminded me far too much of the world Willow came from and which I'd unwillingly become part of. A world where women were chattel and marriage was a crapshoot that might provide status or might turn your life into a horror movie with no end in sight.

Prying Pet's nails out of my palm, I squeezed her fingers. "You're afraid the same thing will happen to you."

"I'm not afraid." Pet's scent promised she wasn't lying. "I intend to win the Moon Trials, then I can be alpha in my own right after my father dies." Her voice cracked halfway through, though, and her scent turned wobbly.

"What aren't you telling me?"

Pet turned to peer back into the mass of werewolves we'd left behind us in the ballroom. No one was crowding close, but the teenager's gaze became hunted anyway. "Dad's here now," she admitted. "He's sure I'll lose. That's why I'm wearing this."

She swept her hand across the dress that really didn't appear to be her style. "That's why I lashed out at you. I need to prove to him that I can hold my own among heirs or he'll find me a mate. An alpha who'll become pack leader after him. But anyone strong enough to do that is an asshole."

"Not all alphas are assholes," I promised then pivoted topics as the scent of her disbelief slapped me in the face. "If you want to win, though, we'll make sure you win. I'll have your back at the next contest, not that you need my help or a leg up from the organizers. You're more prepared than anyone else here and your sense of strategy is impeccable. We..."

I paused as my phone rang with a tone I hadn't expected. Usually, Charlie and I texted each other multiple times a day for quick check-ins. But she rarely called and she knew the Moon Trials were all-consuming, that an interruption now could mean the difference between life and death.

Still, I *had* left her hanging, waking her up when Thom was drugged then never getting around to sending a follow-up. I held up a finger to Pet—"One minute." Then I answered the phone.

"They took her." This wasn't Charlie. The female voice was familiar but not instantly recognizable, especially when she sounded just as frantic as Pet had been a moment earlier.

"Nora?"

Charlie's girlfriend barked out an affirmative. Then—"They said not to call the cops. That *you* were responsible."

I didn't have to ask who had been snatched, but I did anyway. "Someone took Charlie?"

"That's exactly what I just said. Give me one good reason not to hang up on you and dial 911."

Chapter 22

"**D**on't do that." I wanted to explain why, but the scent of floor cleanser promised the Executioner had joined us in the alcove. No, that was wrong. There was no us to join. Pet must have slipped away the moment I accepted the call because the Executioner was the only one there now, the man whose job involved keeping the existence of werewolves secret through any means necessary, including killing the girlfriend of my best friend.

One dark eyebrow raised and I tried to force my open mouth to spin a believable lie so Nora wouldn't call in the cops to investigate Charlie's abrupt departure. An ailing, off-grid grandmother maybe. Or a mob connection that was enough to scare Nora but not enough to send her skedaddling to the FBI.

Both sounded just about as likely as the truth—that my friend and I had ended up on the wrong side of werewolves. So I went with the shred of honesty that wouldn't make matters worse.

"Listen to me. If you call the cops, you will die. Charlie will die."

"So you want me to, what, sit on my hands? Charlie was terrified."

Charlie never seemed fazed by anything. And Nora had no reason to trust me, especially when my answer was: "That's all I can say."

Silence yawned between us. The Executioner's acrid scent clogged my nostrils. Then a long sigh gusted out of my phone's speaker. "If she's not back here by nine a.m..."

Nine a.m. was too soon. I could barely travel across the country to where Charlie had been snatched in that time frame. "Nine a.m. two days from now," I countered. By then, I would have won one contest, lost another, and pulled as many strings as I had at my disposal to get my friend loose.

"Are we *bargaining* about Charlie's safety?"

"I swear to you, Nora, if she could talk to you, she'd say to leave it alone."

Another long silence during which the Executioner's scent sweetened into smugness. Then, to my surprise, Nora relented. "I'm trusting you because Charlie trusts you. But my girlfriend had better be back here safe and sound two mornings from now..."

"She will be," I promised, having no idea how I would make that happen. A dial tone was my only reply.

Well that, and the Executioner offering words without prodding for the first time ever. They grated in my ears like gravel, pricked like claws as they sidestepped down my spine. "I have an answer to your question from the airport."

I wanted to pretend I'd forgotten my question. But my sally while trying to get around the wall of werewolf yesterday bubbled up unbidden. *"Are you here to kill me or protect me?"* I'd demanded. At the time, I'd been so sure of my footing.

But solid ground had turned to shifting sands since then. So I wasn't surprised when that same glowering shifter's rasp now pressed down upon my skin like a not-so-gentle palm atop my head. "Kill you."

I wasn't surprised, but I was furious. "Me or my friend?" I snapped back. Because it couldn't be a coincidence that Charlie had been snatched at the exact same instant the Executioner came to a conclusion about the accumulating evidence against me. "Are you afraid to take on a kitsune? Is that why you're going after someone who can't even shift and defend herself?"

The Executioner blinked then offered one word in response to my tirade. "Plural."

"Plural?"

"Friends," he elaborated, and I wished now that he'd stuck to his initial threat. Because every word out of his mouth scratched holes into my composure, especially when his rasp continued. "Everyone you've spoken to since arriving in San Francisco is considered an accessory to your crime."

I spun, scanning the ballroom but knowing what I'd see already. Or rather, who I wouldn't see. Willow and Thom were both missing.

Meanwhile, the scent of floor cleanser grew even stronger as the Executioner took another step forward. "All are in custody to ensure your good behavior."

Only that was patently untrue. I'd been in contact with Chief Reed, and he was even now stalking out of the other alcove, a smug smile twisting up his lips. Bastard had made a deal about me and he very much wasn't in the Executioner's custody. "Not everyone," I said, pointing.

The Executioner followed my extended finger then shrugged as he clarified. "Everyone you care about."

Which was almost true, then became entirely true. Because my phone rang with the tone I'd never ignored until tonight. I declined the video call that was considered a safe contact because it was untraceable...as long as someone wasn't standing there watching me take it.

But Mai tried again. Decline. Retry. Decline. Retry.

The Executioner stood with arms crossed and flat eyes intent while he waited for the inevitable. The sad truth was, I couldn't fail to answer my sister. Especially when Mai should have been asleep at this hour, seizing every kid-approved hour of slumber.

"What's wrong?" I demanded as I caved and opened our video chat.

"Don't be scared," she greeted me, straight dark hair standing on end. A streak on her forehead looked far too much like blood for my peace of mind. "But there was an attack here tonight."

"Who's hurt?" And I forgot for a moment about the Executioner, especially when I caught sight of a *sword* slicing through the air behind my sister. "Watch out!"

"No one's been hurt yet," Mai answered calmly, twisting around to fend off her pint-sized offspring who'd apparently found a way to arm himself. "How about you put that down, Grub?"

"But I'm an heir like Auntie Kira!"

My favorite nephew *had* donned the cape I envisioned earlier and he was wearing nothing else except superman underpants. He jabbed a fist toward his mother while making the requisite sound effects. "Pow! Bam!" With his other hand, he extended a weapon that appeared to be far more real than his imaginary superpowers were.

I wanted to engage with my favorite kid. Wanted to suggest that heirs might defend their packs, but once the danger was past they let their parents tuck them into bed before they woke up their baby sister.

But I was putting every member of my family at risk with this contact. So I ignored my nephew for the first time ever. Ignored his bouncing around, trying to win screen time, while I tossed curt words at Mai. "Do you need me there?"

Mai's brow furrowed then she shook her head. "That's not why I called. The invasion is over. No biggie."

Out of the corner of my eye, I saw the Executioner's smile widen to reveal teeth already turning subtly pointy. Forcing my gaze away, I sped up the words I tossed back to my sister. "Mai. This isn't a good time. If you didn't call because you need backup, what *do* you need?"

The furrows in her brow deepened. The pit in my stomach expanded out to supernova proportions.

"I just didn't want you to hear about the attack from anyone else," my sister explained after a very long silence. "The Randolphs were the ones who invaded. I think you beat their heir last night and they were pissy? Whatever. We dealt with it. But I could see someone throwing that fact in your face at an important moment. I know how stressful those werewolf chest-beating competitions can be."

She didn't know. She had no idea.

And if I didn't want Mai to become intimately acquainted with the stresses of the Moon Trials, I needed to keep her in ignorance. "I have to go," I said with no preamble or sweetener. Then I hung up on my only family members and faced the werewolf who had already proven adept at blackmail. "You heard every word. She's not an accessory."

Another shrug. "Remains to be seen."

I held out my wrists. "So take me into custody. Lock me up and let my friends go."

"Disrupt the Moon Trials?" The Executioner shook his head. "You will compete until I say otherwise. Any effort to leave will be considered proof of guilt."

Guilt, said the man who was the judge, jury, and executioner for shifters whose crimes transcended pack boundaries. He'd doled out both judgment and punishment to my ex-boss seven months ago, the result rising behind my eyes in a flash of something that felt more real than memory.

Blood on Scarlet's arms. Terror in her eyes. She'd died and I'd done nothing to stop it. I couldn't let the same thing happen to Charlie, Thom, Willow, and my sister. Not ever and definitely not right now.

So I cleared my sandpapery throat until words were able to come out again. "What if I lose a fight and am forced out of San Francisco?"

The Executioner blinked. Once, twice. Then, finally, he answered. "I suggest you don't lose."

Chapter 23

To deter Chief Wylie's interest and maintain my connection with Thom, I had to toss the next Trial. To keep everyone I cared about safe, I had to win.

As if my indecision had been a summons, Thom's voice entered my head, deep and soothing albeit faint from distance. *"Give me the word and I'll be there with bells on."*

"You're not locked up?"

"Oh, I'm locked up alright. Didn't get to meet my long-lost mother either. I gather the note was a present from my brother, a way to draw me away from you." A burst of emotion surged down the mate bond along with the words then was squelched as quickly as it had started. The replacement imagery was more like the Thom I knew—he imagined himself as Bruce Banner bursting out of clothes and turning full-on Hulk. *"I don't have to stay where they left me,"* he finished, in case I hadn't gotten the visual's point.

My mate's response wiped the cobwebs out of my brain and allowed me to focus. Yes, Thom likely could break free of his confinement, but the long-term consequences of such an action wouldn't be pleasant. Not with the Executioner holding others hostage who were far less able to protect themselves.

Reluctantly, I gave the answer neither of us wanted. *"It's too dangerous to try to get everyone we care about out right now. Wait. Hold the line."*

A wordless rumble was my only answer, so I pulled out the big guns. *"You promised not to act like an overbearing alpha. Right now, that means cooling your heels."*

"Again?"

"Again."

Thom didn't like it. *I* didn't like it. But if I had to choose between possibly losing my mate bond due to a command from Chief Reed at an undisclosed later date or definitely losing everyone I cared about now, it was no contest.

Or rather, it was the impetus for a contest that appeared to have started without me. Because while I'd been holding difficult conversations in my secluded alcove, the ballroom appeared to have become considerably emptier. And I understood why when my phone chimed yet again.

This time, the alert came from the Moon Trials app announcing the third Trial. Rules were simple. We were to leave Chief Wylie's house four-footed with nothing but fur along for the ride. Those who chose to surrender had only to step back inside this same space. *"No blood on my floors,"* our host warned.

And when did the Trial start? Fifteen minutes ago. A quarter of an hour during which this morning's winning team had likely set up ambushes and scouted terrain in the wilderness around the mansion. When Chief Wylie had promised a leg up to the winners, he hadn't been kidding around.

"Shit," Pet snarled from halfway across the ballroom. She didn't bother finding a private place to disrobe, just dropped her dress into a puddle along with her cell phone and what appeared to be a pirate-level arsenal of guns, knives, plus a scimitar that I couldn't quite imagine had been hidden on her person. One eye blink later, she was furry and sprinting for the exit.

I wasn't far behind. Because the organizers had ditched alphabetical order at last, matching me up with Karl Hogan. Thom's half-brother. The one who had drugged my mate and left him on the streets of San Francisco without any interest in whether his sibling lived or died.

My teeth sharpened against my tongue even though I didn't intend to shift until I saw an open door in front of me. The Executioner might be forcing me to win a battle I'd be better off losing, but it would be a pleasure to trounce Karl.

Assuming I made it far enough to reach him. Because two male heirs brushed past me in the squeeze between ballroom and foyer. Their larger bodies spun my smaller one into the wall, proving they shared Pet's annoyance at ending up on the losing team.

Then they were past. I rubbed my shoulder, waiting until a gust of fur scent promised the duo had shifted before following them out into the entryway.

I'd expected to be alone there. After all, of the eight shifters involved in this third Trial, four had been given a head start. Then Pet and the bruisers had rushed on ahead of me.

Only there was still a werewolf lingering in the foyer. Rupert sat against the wall naked, head hunched over bony knees as he gave himself a pep talk. "That's the last of them, Rupey darling. It's safe to shift now."

He hadn't noticed me and my muscles vibrated with the urge to ignore his predicament. To deal with this Trial, free Charlie and Willow and Thom, then find a way to bribe Chief Reed out of forcing me into an unwanted mating.

It really should have been easy to dismiss the guy. Rupert didn't like me. I didn't like him.

"Remember," he continued his pep talk, "brains win over brawn every time. You can do this. Let's get it right."

I closed my eyes, reopened them, and accepted the inevitable. I wasn't walking out on him. Not when he clearly needed help and was a member of my mate's pack.

"Rupert?"

He didn't turn to face me. Didn't jump to his feet either. At first, I thought he hadn't heard, but then he spoke to his kneecaps.

"Shifting is difficult for me. I don't suppose you'd stay until I'm done?"

Back in Gate City, before being reeled into Chief Reed's orbit, I'd run with Thom's pack a heaping handful of times. As we arrived for each hunt, Rupert had been waiting at the designated spot already in fur form, which I'd written off as an unwillingness to fully immerse himself in a group of wolves he'd been thrust into against his will.

Now, though, I reconsidered the past in the light of new data. Rupert was the exact opposite of a dominant shifter and dominance tended to be linked to speed of shift among werewolves. As such, changing to fur was likely slow and painful for him. No wonder he'd given up his head start in favor of privacy at this critical time.

From the hunch of his shoulders, he seemed to expect the same snark that he usually dished out to flow back in his direction. Rather than caving to predictability, I sank down beside him. "Of course I can stay," I answered. "Is there anything I should do to help?"

"Just talk to me," Rupert answered through gritted teeth. Sweat was already beading on his forehead, but there were no other obvious signs that he'd started shifting. His teeth were flat across and hairs were no longer than humanity dictated on his forearms.

I considered suggesting that he just give up, go back inside the ballroom and forfeit the Trial. But being unable to shift fast enough to take part in this contest would be a black eye he'd carry with him the rest of his life. No, Rupert needed to turn wolf and I needed to help him get there.

To that end, I hunted around for a topic he'd find pleasant. "Tell me about your island."

And, just like that, Rupert's ears started lengthening and turning pointy. "It's a beauty," he answered. "Palm trees. Turquoise water."

"Huh."

"What?" The question was slightly garbled and no wonder since Rupert's jaw was no longer precisely human shaped.

"Well, I'd assumed Thom sold you a plot of land within his territory." Just like Ember's father had ceded Gate City to my mate, but with the purpose this time of giving Thom a way into a closed-door contest so he could back me up.

"Not everything revolves around your mate."

Rupert's legs were remolding themselves before my eyes, the transition so slow it must have been excruciating. But telling me off seemed to shield my companion from pain because his voice turned familiarly pedantic as he continued.

"I've planned this retirement for years. Acquiring the land was easy, but implementing a security protocol has proven more difficult. It pains me to admit that any stronger wolf could steal the island right out from under me with a bark of command. But now..." Words trailed off as his mouth became a snout.

"But now," I finished for him, "you're proving yourself. You've already made it into the top echelon of Moon Trials heirs, so nobody will think about messing with you as long as you shift and officially take part in contest three. You can walk out that door and back in again then retire in peace to your tropical island."

And Rupert—lupine but one of the smallest male wolves I'd ever seen—did exactly that. I watched his back to make sure no one was planning an ambush during his three seconds in the dangerous outdoors, and as I did so I was surprised to find that I already missed the future presence of this recalcitrant pack mate. Hopefully I'd toast Rupert at the Full Moon Saloon with all of Thom's pack in the very near future.

But as I unfastened two necklaces I usually carried with me even in fur form—one a gift from my mate, the other holding a fragment of Gate City's magic—I couldn't help thinking that Rupert might not be the only one absent from Thom's bar after the Moon Trials were over. Because no matter what happened tonight, I really couldn't win.

Chapter 24

Karl was everywhere. No, not the Karl I was supposed to be fighting. Instead, I was surrounded by the Bay Area fog I'd learned went by the same nickname as Thom's half-brother.

Wet air blocked moonglow and muffled sound, but scents curled around my vulpine face like beckoning fingers. There went the trail of the two bruisers who'd knocked me into the wall back in the ballroom. That other muddle marked the route of the previous four heirs to exit, one of whom I was seeking. And there was Pet's path, making a beeline for the darkest part of the encircling woods.

I'd intended to track Karl. He was, after all, why I was out here. But an oath tugged at my footsteps. My promise to Pet. *"I'll have your back at the next contest."* That plus my memory of the arsenal the teenager had ditched along with her clothing. Anyone who carried so many weapons wasn't comfortable fighting in animal form. Or perhaps she was aware of the reality that a young, female wolf was bound to be smaller than her opponent. As I well knew, size mattered during four-legged fights.

Turning toward the darkness, I ran just a little faster than was really wise.

Ran until I heard snarls and the crash of brush in front of me. From the scent of blood on the air I was almost too late, but I didn't shift and dive in with sword extended. Pet wouldn't thank me for fighting her battles overtly. If she really intended to stick the Moon Trials out until the grand finale, she'd spend the rest of her life playing with the big dogs. There needed to be no question she was the baddest wolf around.

So I ignored the wince-worthy yelp that I was pretty sure had come from Pet rather than from her opponent. And I circled the area the sounds had come out of, trying to catch a view of what was happening in the near pitch dark.

Pet and her opponent were up on a wooded hill, and as I ascended, fog thinned around me. Gradually, the darting forms of two wolves grew visible. One, smaller and more slender, was aiming for a war of attrition. She lunged, bit, then retreated. Lunged, bit, was almost caught this time.

The other wolf was slower, but he didn't require speed to win this war. All he needed was one slip from his smaller opponent. Then he'd have her on the ground, his bulk preventing escape...

As if my thought had created reality, Pet's left rear paw faltered as she sped in for another nip. She caught herself before it became a fall, but her recovery came too late.

The male heir had her in his grip.

He'd latched down on her ruff, but the battle wasn't over. The pair rolled in a flurry of snapping teeth and frantic snarls. Pet was fighting for her life now, thinking she had no advantages left to call upon.

Good thing she was wrong. Because there were ways I could influence the fight without having obviously taken part in it. Thom still wore the lasso, but its mere existence had given me an idea.

Shifting up to human form, I eyed the trees on all sides. This part of the forest was unmanicured, which meant there was bound to be...

Yes, there. A widowmaker dangled, a massive limb fallen from its parent tree but caught up in the canopy. If I lengthened my star ball out into a long, skinny rope, I could snag the limb and pull it down onto an unsuspecting werewolf. The hefty branch wasn't big enough to kill the male heir, but it would likely pin him long enough for Pet to gain the upper hand.

It wouldn't do much good, however, if I brought the widowmaker down on both of them.

So I waited, wincing every time Pet yelped. I couldn't quite see what her opponent was doing, but it had to be painful since Pet didn't seem the type to show distress for anything short of gaping wounds.

She also wasn't the type to give up. Just when I was about to ditch the idea of impacting the battle without seeming to be actively involved in it, Pet wriggled out from under the larger wolf. She was limping and he seemed bound to catch her again within seconds.

He'd have less luck with a huge tree limb slamming the wind out of him though. I jerked at my star ball and the widowmaker fell exactly where I'd thought it would. The larger wolf grunted as wind exploded out of him, then he gasped for air that refused to reenter stunned lungs.

Pet ignored him. Instead she spun, shifting into humanity as she turned toward me. "Who's there?"

The hardest part of the entire endeavor was drawing Pet far enough away from her fallen opponent so we could speak without him hearing. But I managed and she nodded once she understood what had happened. "Thanks," she said as she stripped flexible limbs off a small shrub.

"You realize that's poison oak," I couldn't resist telling her.

"Not allergic," she answered.

"And you plan to use it for...?"

"Restraints. Wilson won't forget this battle anytime soon."

She was already heading back to her opponent, a good idea since if we left him lying there much longer he'd probably get his breath back and restart the battle. I fell into step only to halt as the younger woman growled over her shoulder. "You're done here. We're even. Go find Karl."

The oath slid away from my muscles like unlocking handcuffs. But I still hesitated. Pet was a teenager about to drag a grown man through the forest using a vine as shackles.

As if she could smell my uncertainty, Pet's eyes flashed. "I don't need your help."

Which was exactly what Grub said the last time he wanted crackers from the top shelf. My pint-sized nephew had set a stool on the counter and used the elevated furniture to reach his prized snack box. He'd done it himself...and three minutes later, when he lost his balance and tumbled to the floor, I'd caught him in my arms.

Pet wasn't my nephew though. And Grub—plus several other people very dear to me—would be in the Executioner's sights if I didn't hurry up and find my own opponent.

Reluctantly, I left Pet setting up an allergic reaction for a larger werewolf. Shimmering down into fox form, I slid into San Francisco's fog hunting a were-wolf that shared the veiling water vapor's name.

Chapter 25

"Come out, come out, wherever you are."

The voice, like yet unlike my mate's, flowed through the fog toward me. Scents braided in and out of the shrubbery, flicking at my whiskers and puffing up my fox tail. Karl and at least two other werewolves must have passed back and forth through this spot just like Chief Reed had done in a different forest a week ago, repeating their meanders until trails became a mess of here-then-gone-then-here-again.

It was an effective strategy for ambush. But why would Karl call out, pinpointing his location?

Because he wasn't the only one hunting. By fixating my attention to my left, Karl hoped to cover someone creeping toward me from my right.

I leapt sideways just as teeth closed over the fur above my right shoulder. A tuft of hair pulled loose, momentarily stretching the skin underneath in an almost-rip that ached like a wasp sting. But the wolf had lost his bid for a more permanent tooth hold. He snarled, his dark bulk advancing through the clinging moisture. I took a step backward...

...into human hands. "Gotcha fair and square," crooned a male voice, dropping the final Rs more adamantly than Pet did so his words came out more like "faya and squaya." Not Karl then, since Thom's brother boasted the educated tones of a TV announcer.

Whoever the R-dropper was, his touch creeped me out and I struggled to break free. But my captor just chuckled, gripping my ruff harder while holding me out at arm's length. Fox paws paddled against nothing and I itched for fingers with which to fight back.

Luckily, unlike Rupert, I had no problem shifting. And unlike the werewolf gripping my neck, I was able to bring a weapon along for the ride even though, as mandated, I'd left the mansion with nothing but fur on my back.

In this case, the most useful weapon, I decided, was a razor-studded collar right where creepy guy's hand was. As predicted, he dropped me with a shout the instant I slithered into spiky humanity. Even two-legged, I had no problem landing on my feet.

Landing on my feet with my mouth open to decrease the odds. Because three against one wasn't so hot, even if I did have access to any weapon I could dream up while the werewolves only boasted what nature gave them. "I'm surprised you're here rather than hunting your own opponent, Griffin." I wasn't actually sure which of the two shifters close to me was Griffin, but the Moon Trials app had promised that was the name of Rupert's opponent for the third contest. The shifter of that name definitely had non-fox-related priorities. "Won't look good when you take all night and can't even find the wolf you're supposed to catch."

The man who was still cradling his sliced-open palm growled a question I didn't quite catch over his shoulder. Then Karl was there, the burnt-cinnamon aroma preceding him as he stalked toward us through the fog.

Like the others, Thom's sibling appeared as only a bulky shadow, but a bulky shadow so much like my mate it made my cheek twitch. Karl's voice was like Thom's also, although his words would never have come out of my mate's mouth. "I saw the weakling struggling to shift," Thom's half-brother promised. "He won't make it out the door, much less set you a wild goose chase."

"Oh, are you so certain?" I cocked my head and enunciated the next bit widely to ensure all three could catch the scent of truth on my tongue. "I saw Rupert turn wolf and walk outside myself."

What I didn't bother to mention—I'd also seen him about face and head back in three seconds later.

Griffin peered at me through the intervening moisture, or I assumed he did. I couldn't make out his eyes or facial expression, which felt like a major handicap at that moment. Still, clues came from scent also, and Griffin's scent was rife with fur even though he was fully human.

Then he wasn't human. Four-legged, he loped away from us without bothering with parting words. No wonder the wolf who'd recently tried to snag me in his jaws growled.

Karl was less concerned. "His loss. You think the two of us can't take down an itty-bitty fox?"

Then the real fight began.

Back when I was Grub's age, my sister learned to wield a sword from our father. Later, she'd passed the same lessons along to me. But the truly useful course in self-defense hadn't come until we moved in with the clan of Mai's mate Gunner. There, I'd been assigned a werewolf tutor who spent an entire year ambushing me in dark alleys with increasing numbers of pack mates. I'd quickly learned how to offset my weaknesses by playing to my strengths.

Top weakness? Size. Like Pet, I was too scrawny to risk hand-to-hand combat, or claw-to-claw as the case may be. And, let's be honest, fox teeth weren't long enough to break through the hide of a well-furred wolf anyway. It was better not to get too close.

But I was fast and my star ball was a major asset. As long as I didn't let myself become pinned, two against one wasn't terrible odds.

Especially when Karl stayed human. He'd fashioned a crude club out of a thick branch, which he used to block my sword strikes while the wolf harried me, lunging out of the darkness then disappearing back out of sight. But Karl's true weapon, I quickly realized, was the same as mine—a glib facility with words.

"I'm surprised even you would fuck a plus-one." He paused to spit at the ground, as if the mere idea tasted vile. Then he added: "A plus-one in *pink*."

The funny thing about insults is that they say more about the insulter than the insultee. Karl clearly had issues surrounding his own masculinity, so I tossed a dig his way while dancing out of the path of the charging wolf. "Jealous, huh? Still a virgin?"

This time, the club swished through the air with rage behind it. This time, Karl's words were even more foul. "I can't say I'm surprised my whore mother popped out a bastard," he growled, "but I thought even she was too good to spread her legs for meat."

And, okay, so that dig was a bit effective. *Meat* was my least favorite slur, especially when I knew the human being insulted. Big T—Thom's father—was ten times the man Karl could ever hope to be.

Still, I'd learned my lesson fifteen hours earlier. Losing my temper would hurt me more than it hurt Karl.

So I kept my tone light while swiping with words and sword at the same time. "Scientists are still debating the contributions of nature versus nurture. But you and Thom are an example that should close the book on that conflict at long last."

Karl didn't reply right away, which I took to mean his education was sorely lacking. But that didn't turn out to be true. Instead, I was the one who'd dropped the ball by not paying close enough attention to the wolf while digging into Karl's insecurities. And the wolf was no longer wolf.

Or at least I assumed as much when something hard came flying through the air to slam into my fingers. Feeling fled for one split second as the digits in question released their grip on my sword—my star ball. My lost weapon skittered through the air away from me, dragging my energy along with it. I felt like I was the one a widowmaker had just landed on.

Then Karl was spinning me sideways, twisting my arm behind my back while he slammed my face up against the rough bark of a tree trunk. "Are you a whore too?" he growled into my ear, burnt cinnamon a parody of my mate's enticing aroma. "I'll bet Thommy Boy bought a mate the same way he bought a territory. I wonder if he'll buy another after you're dead?"

Chapter 26

Rather than answering immediately, I tugged at my star-ball sword. It wasn't so far away that it was cut off from me entirely, but distance made influencing the weapon's location feel like slogging through a vat of cold molasses. Slowly, slowly it inched across the leaves in my general direction. All the while, I waited for the fingers of Karl's free hand to slide across my skin.

Because he was just the sort to use my nakedness as a power play. If my star ball didn't show up in time, I'd have to try for an elbow to the kidneys, but that would be tricky the way Karl was holding me out to one side.

So I tried for words again. "Oh, do you intend to team up to put me out of my misery? Two big guys managing to take out a woman half your size. That'll definitely make you look like the strongest wolves around."

To my surprise, Karl fell for it. "Go," he told his companion.

"You sure? I thought we had a deal."

"We did and we do," Karl promised. "Strings will be pulled to ensure you're matched with me or Griffin next time. I can see why you wouldn't want to lose to a girl."

So the nameless heir was smarter than the rest of us. He intended to purposefully toss the fourth Trial. Good for him.

And good for me. Because a trickle of warmth wrapped around my left ankle. I'd stalled long enough so the energy that had slipped away from me moments earlier suffused my body.

Now, Karl's nakedness wasn't a threat. It was an opportunity. Even the most dominant alpha gets a little antsy when a sword slices toward his unprotected dick.

I didn't slice though. Didn't make trouble either as Karl marched me back through the woods toward Chief Wylie's mansion. He bad-mouthed Thom the entire way and for one split second I considered losing this fight the way Nameless Heir intended to lose the next one. Not because I was afraid. No, the mere mention of my mate made me yearn to have Thom there beside me. The idea of being forced to break our mate bond...I winced, my feet refusing to take another step.

"Don't think you can pull that crap on me," Karl growled, shoving me toward the open doorway that beamed light out into a manicured garden. We'd already made it almost all the way back and I could feel eyes on us. Likely every pack leader, plus-one, and heir (minus Griffin) was peering out the windows, watching this final showdown.

Not that Karl was giving them much to watch. Luckily, I could fix that.

"Don't pull crap like what?" I asked. "Like this?"

I was fox then woman again so fast Karl was left grasping at air. Grasping then recoiling as I pointed my star-ball sword right at his family jewels.

"I recommend," I continued, "that you back through that doorway and surrender if you want to keep your teenie-weenie danglers attached."

Apparently Karl didn't approve of having the size of his reproductive organs maligned. Because he roared and tried to charge me.

I say tried because I had a sword and he wasn't even holding a tree branch this time. I slashed three quick strokes across my opponent's chest, digging in just deep enough to leave an arrow pointing south.

"Eh, eh, eh," I chastened. "Through the door or next time I'll aim at that minuscule thing at the tip of the arrow. With the guide, I *think* I can find it. Maybe. It *is* awfully small."

As I spoke I crowded him backwards. Karl only needed to take three more steps and he'd be inside, leaving me the victor...

I felt more than heard the moment dozens of eyeballs lost interest in our battle. A thunder of feet became louder then softer as if they were heading up the wide, sweeping stairs at the far end of the ballroom. Someone shouted. The Executioner blew his piercing whistle, hurting my ears even at a distance.

Okay, there wasn't any more time to play with my prey. "In you go," I observed, turning my star ball into a hooked cane that slid Karl's feet out from under him. He tumbled through the open doorway into the foyer and I followed, leaping over his recumbent form then continuing on past him. Across the now empty ballroom and to the stairs everyone else was disappearing up.

At the top, a long balcony overlooking the ballroom was crowded full of moving bodies. The mob parted for one split second, allowing my eyes to fall on a single crumpled form at their feet.

And beneath whoever had fallen, proof that someone had broken the primary rule of the third Trial. Chief Wylie's floor was covered in blood.

Due to my short stature, I couldn't see who'd gone down or how badly they'd been injured. I'd caught a glimpse, but that's all it had been. A fleeting image of splayed limbs and the vaguest impression of something grotesquely wrong. An image that tried to suck me into the past before the crowd closed up and settled me back down in the here and now.

Then the Executioner was striding toward me, the crowd parting before he got close enough to wave his hands and demand passage. Those flat gray eyes bored into me and I felt absurdly guilty for something I was pretty sure was none of my business. "This way," he ordered.

I looked over my shoulder. Nope, nobody behind me. Apparently I was the one being paged.

Usually, curiosity would have drawn me forward. But the blood on the floor was doing its darnedest to recall past events I'd spent a significant amount of effort repressing. So I hesitated and the Executioner reached out as if to grab me.

He'd latched onto me twice before, but both times I'd had clothing to shield my bare skin. His gaze already felt like cockroaches crawling across me, so I raised my hands and took a step forward. "Okay, okay, I'm coming. Keep your pants on." I did, however, keep my gaze trained shoulder height or higher as I preceded the Executioner through the crowd.

Well, I tried to keep my gaze up. But the scent of fresh human blood, nothing like the smell after killing a deer or rabbit, slapped me and I couldn't help myself. I peered down...at someone I'd never met before. A middle-aged man who'd still been very much in his prime when a cold-blooded killer ripped out his entrails and used them to weave a cat's cradle between two balcony rails.

My gorge tried to rise and I realized I'd made a mistake thinking the gory death during the first night of the Moon Trials was a to-be-expected event when too many werewolves from different packs were stuck in close proximity. That murder could have been a wolf mauling its prey, but this one wasn't. Instead, the body before me represented a very human display of passion, recompense for some awful wrong.

Either that or I was witnessing psychopath behavior. Whatever the motivation, after two deaths in fast succession I had a sinking suspicion there would be a third.

I was right. "Keep moving." The Executioner's rasp preceded his fingers pressing against my shoulder blade, his touch every bit as awful as I'd anticipated. Musings on psychopaths and psychotic breaks slipped away as I rushed to distance myself from what felt like maggots slithering across my skin.

Maggots slithering through dead and aged flesh. The aftermath of death, slow and relentless...

Shivering, I sped up and once again the crowd parted, seeming to know where we were headed before I did. We were moving away from death, however, so I was glad to obey this time.

Was glad until I wasn't. Because my feet hit an obstruction and I peered down to find a second body, this one of someone I recognized.

"Chief Reed," I murmured. Then I flinched because the scent here wasn't the same human blood that had overwhelmed me when I passed by the first body. Instead, my pack leader stunk of something eerily familiar—urine from a fox.

Chapter 27

This victim also wasn't dead. Chief Reed's eyes slitted open as I spoke and he whispered, "Space. My heir and I need space."

"You need a doctor." This was one of the burly guards who were ubiquitous at the Moon Trials. He knelt beside my pack leader, assessing the injured party.

But Chief Reed shook his head, pushing the guard away with feeble fingers. "No."

Unfortunately, the word had come out with too much intensity. Chief Reed doubled over as if to hide his coughing fit from the assembled shifters. One hand reached for his back, fingers coming away bloody. He clearly wasn't okay.

And, just as clearly, he wanted to speak with me before being treated by medical staff. So I took the spot the guard had occupied a moment earlier, naked knees landing in a puddle of fox pee. I didn't like this man, but I didn't want him dying alone either. "I'm here."

Closed eyes were my only response. Had Chief Reed faded past the point of comprehension? No. Another word came out on a breath this time, the same demand he'd led with. "Space."

Werewolves were unrelenting gossips, but the Executioner's flat stare was enough to cow our audience into moving away from us. "You too," Chief Reed said when only one man remained—the Executioner himself.

Dark eyebrows rose, then the shifter in question shrugged and retreated to the other end of the long balcony. That far away, wolf ears wouldn't pick up our voices if we spoke very quietly.

Not that we needed to speak to communicate. I reached out to pat the old man's hand, noting as I did so that his skin was papery. As if he'd aged three decades in an hour, or maybe Chief Reed's overwhelming presence had just covered up his true years in the past.

Vitality damped, he now looked nothing like the manipulative alpha who'd made my life miserable for one long season. Instead, he appeared to be shrinking into insignificance, a man far past his prime and ready to take his leave of life.

Pity softened my voice. "We're alone," I promised. "Who did this to you?"

"Couldn't see." Chief Reed's words were only a thread of sound I could barely hear as he turned away, fumbling in his vest pocket with one bloody hand. Trembling, he managed to pull something out, enclosing it in an age-ravaged fist. A deathbed gift? I prepared to act appreciative even though I wanted nothing Chief Reed had to give.

But I'd called that one wrong. Chief Reed's bloody fingers opened to reveal not some family heirloom but that same darn vial of my blood he'd been sipping from for the last four months. Before I could protest, he glugged all that remained, clearly preparing to force me into an action that would wreck my life and the lives of those around me.

Not just any action. Chief Reed's conversation with Chief Wylie leapt into my brain and I reacted on instinct, slamming both palms over my ears. If I couldn't hear the command to break my mate bond, would I still have to obey it? I had no idea. All I knew was that Chief Reed, who'd seemed to be at death's door moments earlier, ripped my left hand away from my head with such force I second-guessed my earlier analysis of his advanced age.

Second-guessed it more when I peered down the older man's fist. There was no difference in smoothness between my skin and his skin. No age spots. No sag.

I frowned. "That doesn't make sense."

"What doesn't make sense is allowing your pack leader to die when you can save him." Chief Reed's growl was no longer thready. Still, it hitched at the end as if his wound continued to pain him.

I had a crazy fox urge to sprint away from this man, never looking back. Instead, I stayed where I was and offered. "If you need help, let me call a doctor."

"The only thing I need," Chief Reed answered, "is another vial of freely given kitsune blood."

And, at long last, puzzle pieces snapped together, revealing a picture I couldn't believe I hadn't seen earlier. The sips of my blood used to force me into behavior that was purely malicious rather than overtly functional. Chief Reed's primary purpose hadn't been hazing. He'd been using my blood to boost his vitality, the wild-goose chases and other awfulness mere icing on the cake.

"I'm not the first kitsune you've fed from, am I?" I demanded, remembering the *hihi'irokane* in my necklace and the same metal making up the gifted lasso. Had Chief Reed run another fox shifter into the ground long before he met me? Had he used an oath to bind her then promised her freedom that never quite materialized, all in exchange for vial after vial of blood used to extend his own life?

If so, that could explain why he dressed as if he came from a bygone era. Why he seemed to care so little about the identity of his heir. Forcing me to kill his nephew then offering to marry me off to Chief Wylie—did it really matter who was in line to succeed him when he had no intention of ever turning over the reins of his pack?

"Not the first and not the last," Chief Reed agreed. His voice, I noticed, wasn't as pained as it had been a few minutes earlier. He seemed to grow younger right in front of my eyes as he jiggled the empty vial. "Heir, you are duty bound to give me blood when I need it."

But was I? The oath I'd sworn to Chief Reed lay quiescent in my gut at this moment. "You can command me to bleed," I realized, "but if you do, the blood won't be freely given. It won't do you any good."

In response, he leaned in closer. "I'll die without your blood. Do you want another murder on your conscience?"

For a split second, his ploy worked. The past slapped me in a wave of blood and gore. I'd done that. I'd killed his nephew. I'd…

Clenching my teeth, I refused the seduction of guilt, replacing it with the image of Thom's face instead. My mate wouldn't be with a murderer. I'd killed unwillingly then and I wasn't the one who was causing Chief Reed's death now.

So I shook my head and told the old man what he didn't want to hear. "Withholding aid isn't the same as pulling a trigger. If a victim leaves her abuser to die, who's really at fault?"

"I don't care who's at fault," Chief Reed growled, his eyes flashing. "I care who wins. And if you don't provide blood, the winner won't be you."

Then he raised his voice, turning it thready and pained as if he hadn't just healed himself at least partway. "Executioner! Get her away from me! I remember now who attacked me. It was this woman. My back-stabbing heir."

Chapter 28

The Executioner didn't run toward us. I had a feeling he never ran. But he walked fast and he'd be upon us in seconds.

Chief Reed took full advantage of the opportunity to lean in closer and hiss. "Last chance."

But his changed body angle let me see what he'd been hiding. My blood might have removed years from Chief Reed's apparent age, yet he still had a knife sticking out of his back with fluids of his own dripping off the hilt. And in the few moments since he'd chugged the contents of that vial, wrinkles had started reforming on his face.

All I had to do was leave this man alone and he'd die. Four months ago, that thought would have horrified me. But now I rose and spoke down to him with only a minor tremor in my belly. "You've worked so hard training me to be a predator. Are you surprised that your lessons stuck?"

Then, dismissing him, I turned to face the Executioner and laid out facts that I hoped were obvious. "Chief Reed is a manipulative bastard. You know I didn't do this. I was outside, fighting other heirs until just a few minutes ago."

The Executioner raised one dark eyebrow. "The scent?" he rasped.

"Hunters buy that stuff online all the time. Anyone could upend a bottle. Plus, foxes are small. Do you really think my bladder could hold anywhere near that quantity of urine?"

For a moment, I thought the Executioner had listened to me. His flat stare swept across the balcony to the other body. Back to me and away again.

Then his cheek twitched as he shook his head. "Occam's razor," he rasped. "Fox pee comes from a fox. You have personal ties to both alphas."

"I don't even know who that other man is!"

"Of course you do." This was Chief Reed speaking from the floor beneath us. He sagged lower with each word, but he wasn't too far gone to twist the metaphorical knife. "Chief Hogan is the father of your mate's half-brother. Understandable that you'd want to avenge Thom's dwindling honor, but don't you think you went beyond the pale this time?"

Then the Executioner's cold hands wrapped around my arms, his fingers like slithering leeches as they latched onto my skin. He marched me away from Chief Reed. Toward the body—Chief Hogan—and past it.

I could handle this, though. The Executioner might be taking me into custody, but he'd let me out for the next Trial. Once freed, I was sure I'd be able to find the killer in time to bow out of the final contest. Soon, my friends would be safe again.

Plus... Warmth flooded my belly as I realized what else would happen in the very near future. Without Chief Reed in the picture, I could return to Gate City. I could be Thom's mate and a member of his pack with no territorial boundary between us.

Only Chief Reed wasn't quite done wreaking havoc. "You're pleased, aren't you, heir?" He'd raised his voice to ensure I heard him and the strain was almost too much. But he squashed an impending cough in time to cast a few more words in my general direction. "Just like you were pleased when you killed my nephew."

As stick-it-to-you last words went, he'd made a hole in one.

Here's what most people don't realize about memories. They aren't photographs, to be taken out and pored over time after time with no resulting change other than the subtle fading of age. The same scene doesn't imprint on our retinas like a favorite movie to which we know all the lines. Instead, every time we access a memory, we change it just a little based on the person we are now.

And Chief Reed had done an excellent job of changing my current perspective. I barely noticed the Executioner thrusting me into a small bedroom because I'd fallen into a memory newly mutated in my mind.

Quentin leered, his too-wide mouth turning into a joker's smirk. He'd enjoyed forcing me to lock my star ball inside the hihi'irokane *necklace. He'd enjoyed about-facing from respectful to bullying once my wings were clipped. So why shouldn't I enjoy returning the favor in spades?*

"Don't let the old man mindfuck you." I spoke the words aloud, hoping they'd knock me out of the quicksand Chief Reed had shoved me toward. People I loved were depending on me to keep my shit together.

So I closed my eyes for one split second during which the past—or some version thereof—flashed through my mind's eye for the millionth time, both darker and harsher than previously. Then I focused on the room I'd been shoved into.

It was windowless and the door, when I tried the knob, was locked from the outside. I might have been able to finagle the locking mechanism with my star ball if I got desperate, although I'd always had a much harder time dealing with traditional locks than with the airy insides of a car door.

Padding deeper into the space I was stuck within, an en-suite bathroom provided no additional egress points although the decor had potential to be turned into weapons. Not that I'd need makeshift weapons. Because my star ball could become a sword much easier than it could be used to deal with that locking mechanism.

And, to my surprise, I had more assets than that. My luggage had been transferred here and so had the clothes I'd discarded down in the foyer.

Unfolding tonight's apparel with trembling fingers, I clenched my fist around the two necklaces I'd so reluctantly taken off earlier in the evening. This tangible link to Thom calmed me even though he appeared to be too far away for us to communicate via our mate bond. As I'd promised myself up on the balcony, Thom's humanity would never allow him to choose a monster as his mate.

"But how well does he really know you?" I could almost hear Chief Reed tearing holes in my mental armor. *"You've barely spent half a day together as a mated couple."*

Chief Reed was wrong. Thom and I had shared hopes and dreams, history and secrets despite the very real barrier Chief Reed had placed between us. We finished each other's sentences. We knew the dark pitfalls within the other's mind.

Fastening both chains around my neck, I held the dangling pendants tight for one long moment. Then I dressed and powered up my phone.

It was time to arrow in on the present, just as Thom would have expected me to. Messages flitted across my screen, the one from Ember the most intriguing since it came with a mass of attachments that appeared to be dossiers of all the Moon Trials participants. Her message, however, was on a different topic entirely.

"Pet won't listen," she'd typed, *"but I hope you will. The last two battles of the Moon Trials tend to get bloody and regrets can be brutal. Don't go there. Toss the ending and come to my party. I'll make spicy chocolate cupcakes just for you."*

As if I had a choice. The Executioner seemed intent upon seeing me involved in the grand finale before he doled out punishment for two and a half murders. Murders that weren't my fault but that mirrored another that very much was...

Blood once again tried to take over my vision. But I shook my head and stayed focused. I needed to pay attention if I didn't want more innocents being drawn into the Executioner's blackmail web. Step one—block the numbers of everyone I cared about.

To that end, I wore out my thumbs working through my address book. Ember and Charlie and Nora and every single member of the Gate City pack were restricted from contacting me. Even the underground video chat with Mai could be a source of danger to my family, so I reluctantly uninstalled that as well.

Only then did I open the dossiers Ember had sent me. Scrolling through page after page of information about werewolves who wouldn't have batted an eyelash at cold-blooded murder, I tried to draw connections that willfully eluded me. If the same person who went after Chief Hogan and Chief Reed tonight had killed the shifter in the gym during the first Trial, then the field could be narrowed to

Moon Trials heirs and plus-ones. Or possibly one of Chief Wylie's pack mates, although I'd gotten the impression he was rotating guards around, not putting the same ones on duty for more than half a day.

Something niggled at the back of my brain. A clue I'd taken note of without realizing its significance. But when I let my mind wander, I was back at Chief Reed's villa, my sword divorcing Quentin's smirking face from the rest of his body. In memory, a burst of satisfaction warmed my belly the same way it had tonight when I turned to leave Chief Reed bleeding out on the balcony above the ballroom.

I shook my head. No. That wasn't right.

Still, even though I wasn't sure whether I'd laughed at Quentin's death gurgle before horror overcame me, that was what I now remembered. And it was so late my vision swam when I tried to once again read tiny words on my cell-phone screen. I had to sleep if I wanted to solve this puzzle of murder and blood.

So I curled up beneath cold blankets, clenching my fist around Thom's amulet. And I slept without the nightmares I'd expected, fell deep into restorative slumber and stayed there until my phone chimed at the same moment someone tried to push through the accumulation of furniture I'd used to block the already locked door.

Chapter 29

F lipping back the covers, I sprang to my feet while ignoring the call that couldn't have come from anyone I cared about. After all, I'd been plenty thorough blocking numbers.

But while the call was irrelevant, the intruder at the door wasn't. With nowhere to hide, I padded forward, my star ball materializing into sword form as I prepared myself to face unknown danger. Whoever was trying to push their way in possessed strength out of the ordinary based on the way they were slowly but surely shoving a hardwood bureau, a heavy armchair, and a massive wooden trunk out of their way.

Then the slide ceased. "Chief Reed," called a voice I didn't recognize, although the scent crawling through the crack was more familiar. Salty fog. This was yet another San Francisco guard, his voice toeing the line between demanding and respectful. "May I come in?"

"Wrong room," I answered bouncing on my toes to wake up sleepy muscles.

"Right room," he countered. "My condolences on the loss of your alpha and apologies on being the one to bear sad tidings. But I have the right room, Chief Reed."

Chief Reed. A strange mixture of satisfaction and guilt went to my head like the bubbles of champagne combined with the morning-after hangover. I hadn't actually considered what role allowing my nemesis to bleed out last night would place me in this morning. Hadn't considered that I might inherit the gravitas of leader of a pack.

I didn't want the job, but I'd use whatever tools I had at my disposal to free the innocents the Executioner was holding hostage. And being a pack leader was definitely an asset among wolves.

So I dragged the wooden chest out of the way, letting the burly guard push the door the rest of the way open. Then I addressed the man whose shoulders filled the entire frame. "So, that means I'm no longer eligible for the Moon Trials? I can take my friends and go home?"

The guard shook his head in negation, not seeming particularly sorry to deny me. "Executioner says you're still an heir until you set foot in your territory for the first time as pack leader. No, I'm here because you've got a visitor. If you'll come this way..."

A visitor. My mixed emotions settled into the knife-edge of focus. The serial killer seemed to have a personal vendetta against me, as evidenced by the fox pee. If he'd come to gloat, I could use that to my benefit...

But I knew the moment I was ushered into a well-appointed sitting room that this wasn't the serial killer. A wisdom hump bowed the old woman down and her dark eyes reminded me of my sister's.

"Your young man asked me to come," said the old woman in Japanese, "but I didn't expect to spend all morning being driven out of the city. Pretty place, but I need to get back by lunchtime. Can we make this quick?"

So that's what Thom had been up to when he slipped away back in Japantown. Eventually, he'd purchased a pink tuxedo, but first he'd spoken to the old woman who'd caught my attention with her mention of *hihi'irokane*.

And while I would have liked to pick her brain, the minute she showed up at the hotel with my name on her lips she'd become yet another innocent to be used as blackmail against me. I turned to tell the guard I had no interest in speaking to this woman, but he was gone and the door had been closed in my face.

On the other side of the room, the old woman tapped her cane impatiently. "My grandson is a *hāfu* too," she continued. "Although I prefer the term *duburu*. Two cultures, not half of one."

I blinked, vaguely remembered language lessons translating the less common words. Both *hāfu* and *duburu* meant a person with one Japanese and one non-Japanese parent, although the latter was more complimentary. The old woman was being kind in her choice.

She was being kind and I was being rude. Despite myself, I settled into the facing chair and addressed her with a grandmotherly honorific. "*Obaasan*, you were good to come. But I'm afraid Thom was mistaken."

"Yes? You have no interest in the Japanese side of your heritage? And yet, you wear this." She reached out to tap the red-gold necklace with one gnarled finger. "*Hihi'irokane*."

My heart rate sped up at the word and I glanced over my shoulder to check again that the door was closed. No one appeared to be near enough to hear, and whatever damage I'd done by associating with this woman had been clinched the moment I set eyes on her. Throwing caution to the winds, I begged for further information. "You know about *hihi'irokane*? Tell me. Please."

"I know Niko made me play games just because of this. Staring at a computer screen." Her mouth pursed up as if she'd bitten into something sour. "Children should spend their time running around outside."

I'd heard older members of Gunner's pack say the exact same thing about my nephew and his youthful obsession with cell-phone apps. Apparently some gripes transcended cultures.

And that wasn't the point. "You know about *hihi'irokane* from your time in Japan," I prodded. "Maybe your own *obaasan* taught you?"

"Such an obsession with the old country." The woman in front of me shook her head. "No. I told you. *Hihi'irokane* is in my grandson's game. All he does is twitch his fingers then ask me about Japan. But this is a good place we live in. Niko is more American than Japanese. You are also."

"Says the *obaasan* who shops at Daisho and still prefers conversing in Japanese," I couldn't help responding. Because we hadn't been speaking English all this time. I'd only kept up with our back and forth because she'd spoken slowly as if used to enunciating clearly for new learners, or for a beloved child.

Still, there was no reason to turn my voice tart. I was reacting to the disappointment of realizing she knew no more about the red-gold metal than I did.

Before I could apologize, the old woman nodded, using her cane to push her way to her feet. "That's exactly what I mean. Don't look back like I did. Look forward."

As she spoke, she hobbled across the room, cane tapping loudly enough so the door opened just as she reached it. I guessed we weren't stuck inside after all. I could only hope the old woman was also released back into the city she'd come from with no ill effects.

I opened my mouth to offer my phone number, to tell her to call me if she ran into any trouble. After all, she hadn't provided any clues, but she'd come all this way to speak with me.

But further contact between us would create more problems for her rather than fewer. I swallowed down the offer even as the old woman swiveled to consider me.

"Don't walk through a gate unless you intend to return along the same path," she intoned.

Was that a metaphor? A literal warning? The massive concrete-and-wood structure I'd scurried through when entering Japantown rematerialized in my mind's eye. The lasso had sprung to life when I'd swerved to pass beneath the red-painted lintel on my way in, but the Executioner had marched me out in a different direction...

"Wait!" I called. But the old woman was already gone.

Chapter 30

S he was gone and my phone was ringing with the same unknown number that had tried to get through earlier. Whoever it was, they were apparently going to keep calling until I answered, so I obliged. "Hello?"

"Auntie Keeera!" My nephew's voice rang out of the speaker as if he was yelling into his end, which he likely was.

For one split second, love expanded my chest like a helium balloon. Then I pulled the phone away from my ear. Was it possible I'd forgotten to block my own sister or brother-in-law in my haste to protect those I cared about?

No, I knew both Mai and Gunner's numbers by heart and this wasn't either. Meanwhile, noises in the background were much different than I would have expected inside my sister's home or even elsewhere in her pack territory. A momentary roar could only be a bus passing. A babble of voices read as entirely human.

I needed to hang up so the Executioner couldn't harm my nephew, but if Grub was in trouble... "Where are you, sweetie?" I asked him.

"Here!" he caroled unhelpfully. "The plane came all the way to Fran Sanfisco! I'm an heir too!"

That couldn't be true. To hop on a plane alone, a kid would have to steal a parent's credit card, flash various officials that grin I'd taught him, and if all else failed use his greased-pig technique to slide past flight attendants. For most children, the task would be impossible. For my nephew...

"No, no, no, no, no."

I only realized I'd spoken aloud when Grub's cheery voice caroled out an answer. "Yes, yes, yes, yes, yes! We're going to have so much fun, Auntie Kira! Bam! Wham! Boom!"

I could just imagine him shadowboxing imaginary opponents in the territory of an alpha who had no reason to look kindly upon the kid's trespass. Getting Grub back into his parents' hands took priority over everything and I spun away from the door—newly locked behind the old woman—and toward the window overlooking Chief Wylie's garden.

From the second story, in broad daylight, I could see that we truly were out in the middle of nowhere. Manicured lawn abruptly gave way to the same forest I'd hunted through last night, a driveway curling off into the trees the only sign that we hadn't been dropped into an untrammeled wilderness. If I made it to those woods without anyone noticing, I could lose a tail then find a road, call an Uber and be at the airport within an hour...

That was worst-case scenario thinking, however. I still had hopes Grub might board a plane and return to safety under his own volition. After all, unlike his parents, I could usually get the firecracker to voluntarily squelch his lit fuse.

"Now listen up, young man," I said, donning the mock serious tone that often turned us into partners in crime rather than adult-to-be-ignored and kid-busy-ig-noring. "Your parents need you. What kind of heir runs off and leaves behind his little sister?"

"Rorora doesn't like adventures," Grub countered. "She likes to sleep and drool. She's boooring, Auntie Kira. But we're the two musketeers! Remember?"

I did remember. I remembered being a happy-go-lucky auntie who thought it was amusing to teach her nephew to wriggle in and out of trouble. I remembered the summer Mai went on a sugar-free kick at the same time I became momentarily carless due to a small escapade involving a tree and a fender. Four-year-old Grub and I had hitchhiked into town and gorged on ice cream...something I only felt comfortable doing because I knew my star ball and fox teeth would protect both of us if anything went cockeyed.

In contrast, my nephew on his own possessed no star ball and no fur form. He didn't seem likely to reach double digits either unless I acted like a parent instead of a bad influence now.

"Okay, look," I said, dropping the joking tone. "I'm going to tell it to you straight. San Francisco isn't safe for me and it definitely isn't safe for you. You need to go back into the airport and call your parents then get on a plane and…"

"I'll protect you, Auntie Kira!" Grub interrupted.

"I'm afraid you can't, kiddo. This is a big city and I'm not even within its boundaries any longer…"

"Hacker Man knows where you are!" he caroled. Then he rattled off an address that, from my vague understanding of the Bay Area sounded like it might match up with my current coordinates. "I'll go fast like a bunny," he added. "Don't worry, Auntie Kira! I'll keep you safe!"

"Grub! Stop that! Listen to me!"

But the kid had already ended our call.

I rang Mai up directly rather than taking the time to try to reinstall the obscured video chat. If the Executioner wanted to come after my family, he had plenty of ammunition already. And time was of the essence if, as I suspected, my nephew had used one of his dad's tracking apps to figure out my current location.

So I punched in digits I knew by heart and didn't bother with a greeting, just laid it out straight. "Grub's in San Francisco."

"Thank you for finding him!" Mai answered. Her voice was higher pitched than usual and I could only imagine how she'd been tearing her hair out while trying to find her oldest child. "You never answered on the video chat so I didn't think you got our message. We'll have someone at the airport waiting when he gets back here. I'm so grateful. In fact, I'd give you my firstborn if you didn't have him already."

Her laughter was slightly manic and it also cut to the quick. Because I didn't have Grub. I was calling Mai in hopes she could reel him back in.

"Don't be grateful yet," I answered, prying at the edges of the room's only window. It was the non-opening kind, just a big sheet of glass in a metal frame that didn't respond to attempts to separate glass from molding. I suspected I could kick the pane out, but not quietly. Guards would come running. "If I don't call you back in half an hour, you're going to have to find a way to get Grub out yourselves."

"Very funny." Mai's tone suggested she didn't actually think I was funny at all. "You helped create this monster. You're legally bound to control him."

"Don't you mean ethically?" I couldn't resist rebutting.

"No, legally. Grub and I forced you to sign a contract one night while you slept."

Sisterly banter was heartwarmingly enticing and I wanted more of it. I wanted to promise Mai the moon—and the safe return of her wayward child. But I couldn't. Instead, I firmed up my voice. "Mai, I want to help. But it's 50/50 whether I'll manage. You need to pull other strings and you need to pull them now."

The voice coming out of the phone changed from female to male. "What exactly is going on with you?" This was Gunner, his growl in my ear suggesting Mai had set the phone down between them.

"Nothing drastic," I answered, glad my brother-in-law couldn't smell the air I was exhaling. "Moon Trials stuff. I'm afraid it's going to take an effort to get away."

"An effort?" This was Mai, her voice unbelieving and her earlier relief no longer in evidence. "Then make the effort! This is your nephew, Kira. He's my"—her voice broke—"my baby. *Please.*"

I couldn't keep listening to Mai beg for something I had no way of providing. So I ended the call and clutched the phone in aching fingers. This was it. I was alone.

Or so I thought. Earlier, I'd strained to reach Thom down the mate bond and gotten no answer, but the force of my emotion must have bridged the distance in a way mere effort hadn't. Because I got the distinct impression my mate was unfolding himself from forced rest and preparing to do something drastic.

"I'm coming to find you," he observed. With his words came an impression of splintering wood, not a suggestion this time but his actual experience in the here and now. Pain seared a fist and a foot then a blur of motion spun down the mate bond.

I'd told Thom to wait and he'd waited until he couldn't bear to wait any longer. And now he was on his way to provide the exact assistance I craved.

Assistance that would go better with a little guidance. So I latched onto our mate bond and used it to send along every bit of information I had related to the endangered parties. *"If you can get Willow out then find Charlie,"* I ended, *"I'd appreciate it."*

Thom didn't answer directly. Instead, his growl turned gruffer. *"While you do what exactly?"*

"What I should have done from the beginning," I answered. *"I'm ditching the rules."*

I missed Thom's reply because I was too busy throwing a roundhouse kick at the glass then leaping backwards to escape the shards as they shattered like razor splash around me. Clothes went flying as I flashed vulpine, star ball seizing my cell phone and both necklaces almost without my conscious volition.

Then I was leaping through the jagged remnants of the window, landing just as I'd planned on the broad tree limb on the other side. Claws snagged bark to slow my descent just enough so I didn't bruise anything when I hit the ground still running.

And now, finally, Thom's words caught up with me. They were fading as if putting even this small amount of distance between us was more than our mate bond could handle. Or as if he'd finally reached the end of his rope dealing with my impetuous behavior.

"Don't do anything rash. Wait until I join you."

I couldn't wait though. Not with Grub traveling closer to danger every second. Not with the clock ticking down to Nora calling the cops about Charlie's kidnapping.

Instead, I listened to the shout from the room I'd recently vacated and stretched my legs longer. *"Remember how you told me to stop acting like a fox who thinks she's a wolf? I've officially stopped. Today, I'm acting like exactly who I am."*

Thom growled something wordless then forced his outburst into syllables. *"Kira, be careful of your own skin. Promise me."*

Ignoring my mate's demand, I sprinted toward the forest with hope buoying my footsteps. The guard peering down at me from the broken window was too late to catch up and I was on my way to save my nephew and...

The hand that snagged my ruff came from out of nowhere. The reek of floor cleanser slapped me one second too late.

I struggled against air as the Executioner lifted me up to eye level, considering me with a flat gray stare that bit like a wolf even though he was entirely human. "Good of you," he rasped, "to save me the stairs."

Then something soft and sweet-scented covered my nostrils just before the world went black.

Chapter 31

Thwump. Thwump. Thwump. Fast-moving air rumpled my fur and I tried to pry my eyes open. Both eyelids resolutely refused to obey me, as did my legs when I demanded they run.

Not that I could run when I was being carried. Carried then dumped unceremoniously on uneven ground far enough from the roar and wind that I could make out two different voices. Neither resembled the rasp of the Executioner. By scent, I gauged the pair consisted of yet more San Francisco guards.

"My money's not on this fox," one scoffed. The chime of a phone notification was followed by a hoot. "Look at this!"

Their words washed over me the same way the wind had. Buffeting but leaving no long-term residue. Instead, darkness tried to suck me under. Would have if the memory of Thom's ice blue eyes hadn't promised that I needed to pay attention. I needed to find a way to wake back up.

"Whoa!" The second voice was deeper than the first. "Somebody had a bone to pick with...who is that?"

"Fletcher kid. Griffin." A pause then a disbelieving laugh. "They say it's suicide."

"Well, sure. Who doesn't commit suicide by cutting off his own dick and shoving it down his throat?"

Griffin was dead? The R-dropping shifter who'd teamed up with Karl during the third Trial? If so, this added up to yet another murder of passion, assuming Chief Reed's less gory death had been a red herring intended to point toward me as the culprit.

My half-asleep brain gelled clues in a way I hadn't been able to earlier. Because the mode of death of murder number three painted an even clearer picture of motive than the second had.

Three murders to redress sexual misdeeds. Three sisters mated against their wishes. One heir with a vested interest. *Pet.*

I gave up on trying to open my eyes and transitioned over to drawing upon my star ball. Its energy would shift me to humanity then everything would become clearer. I'd...

...do nothing when magic refused to respond to my grasping advances. A hard boot nudged my belly, moving me further than I'd managed on my own since waking. "Think we should leave her here like this?"

"She wasn't going to win even if she was awake."

"But the stakes just got higher." This voice, I realized, was actually familiar. Chief Wylie had finally subbed back in one of the same guards I'd interacted with earlier. If I wasn't much mistaken, foot-nudger was Mr. Buzz Cut, the guard who'd asked my advice about his girlfriend. He must have liked what I told him more than I'd thought at the time because he continued to stand up for me now. "Look, they merged the final Trials since there are only three heirs left. First one to surrender is airlifted out alive. Second loser leaves in a body bag."

A surge of adrenaline shot through me, almost but not quite sufficient to tempt sodden muscles into action. If the final two Trials had been combined into a single contest, I needed to surrender ASAP. No way was I taking part in a battle to the death.

But the thought muddled in on itself. Yes, I'd surrender. After a nap. Mai had always told me it was important to rest up before a big match. Rest up and eat well. Protein would be a good choice. Or was I supposed to carb load? Had there been vegetables in her pre-fight meal plan? I couldn't quite recall.

As I drowsily fell into a past when I'd been a headstrong teen shielded from danger by my older sister, the deeper voice became muffled as if he'd turned away from me. "Not our problem."

Mr. Buzz Cut didn't argue but he didn't immediately follow either. Instead, fingers manipulated my muzzle, loosening the soft mask that encircled my snout. The tiniest trickle of fresh air invaded, cutting through the sticky sweetness that clogged my senses and dulled my brain patterns.

It was too little too late however. I was already sinking back into the darkness of slumber. This time, even the niggling reminder of Thom's demand that I be careful was insufficient to keep me awake.

Heat on my fur woke me. Heat plus an abiding thirst that demanded quenching. I tried again to pry my eyes open and succeeded...just in time to catch the glint of a sword descending toward my unprotected face.

Roll sideways! Now! This time, my body obeyed. The weapon bit into the ground where I'd been a moment earlier. Taking advantage of my opponent's effort to pry it loose, I found my feet and spun in a tight circle, assessing where I'd ended up.

I stood four-footed atop a wild, treeless headland with long cliffs leading down to a roiling ocean. Wind whipped my fur while waves crashed beneath us, but that wasn't the source of the roar and buffeting air I'd experienced earlier. If I had to guess, each heir had been ferried by helicopter to a different location in order to spice up this Trial with an element of hide-and-seek.

I'd slept through the spice and Pet had found me. She assessed her sword—only slightly dented—then raised it while circling in search of an opening. "In case you're curious," she observed, "Dirk surrendered hours ago. You were hard to find since you just *sat* here. But it's just us now. We might as well get this over with."

My mind remained muzzy from the drug, but I hadn't forgotten my blinding flash of insight earlier. In full sun, however, it was hard to believe that the kid in front of me was a cold-blooded killer.

It was hard to believe…and at the same time it wasn't. Because her stance had turned full-on predator, not bloodthirsty so much as determined. How I'd misgauged her so thoroughly was beyond me.

Especially after she'd bared her soul to me yesterday. *"You have no idea what it's like to lose three sisters,"* she'd confided. *"One is dead. Two wish they were. Well, one, I guess."*

She'd as good as admitted to taking out her third sister's tormentor. So, yes, Pet *was* a wounded child, but one with murderous intent.

Murderous intent and plenty of opportunity. She'd admitted to touching the fuse box back in the bathroom and had been one of only two other heirs with obvious access to the plus-one floor on the night Willow was frightened. Like Ember, Pet had banked on the mixer element of the Trials to help her achieve her goal. Unlike Ember, her primary motivation had been revenge.

And while the young woman had no reason to take revenge against me, she had every reason to win this contest. If I didn't want to join the ranks of her victims, I needed a mouth to speak with and a weapon to protect my naked skin. So even though the effort was nearly beyond me, I shifted upward into humanity, grabbing as I went for my star ball. Unfortunately, my magic felt as groggy as the rest of me. It fell back asleep the moment I achieved two feet.

Which meant I dodged unarmed the next time Pet attacked. Her thrust was controlled, calculated. It sliced through the air one millimeter shy of my belly, which I'd sucked in through pure instinct. Her secondary stroke *did* cut into me, raising a thin red welt along my upper arm.

"I have nothing against you," Pet continued. "But I intend to win, which means you have to die. Fight or surrender, but don't waste either of our time with this"—she waved one hand as if unable to come up with the word, settling at last on—"cowardice."

"Wasn't it cowardice to sneak into an innocent plus-one's bedroom to take the spotlight off your true targets?" I asked, testing my hypothesis while doing my darnedest to shake some sense into my snoozing star ball. Foxes can be lazy, but we weren't lazy when it counted. *Come on, come on, come on,* I demanded, but my star ball refused to wake back up.

My words had struck their target however. Pet faltered just a little. "You guessed. How?"

So many clues, most of which came down to—"Geography."

And Pet shrugged off her initial reaction, stalking toward me as she answered. "So I have yet another reason to ensure I'm the only one walking out of this Trial."

Okay, that wasn't what I'd been going for. I dodged another wicked blow and softened my voice. "Listen to me. Doing whatever it took to save your sisters was totally understandable. But you're done. That battle is over. Put down the weapon and I'll help you figure out how to get around your father. I'll…"

"You're such a do-gooder." Pet's sword swiped toward me and I leapt backwards…

…onto a ledge of earth that crumbled beneath my bare foot.

Fox reflexes should have saved me, but whatever drug the Executioner had used to knock me out was still working its way through my system. Both muscles and star ball wobbled inside my skin, worse than useless. I stumbled backward instead of forward and...

To cut a long story short, I fell. Into the wind that rushed up from the ocean. Toward craggy boulders exposed by low tide. There would be no cushioning water to splash down into. No lasso with a mind of its own to save me now.

Still, I flailed in search of something to grab hold of. A tuft of grass in one fist provided a millisecond of hope until the whole clump tore out by the roots. A rock bit into my other palm, staying anchored long enough to spin me around so I slammed belly first into the side of the headland. Then my final handhold pulled loose and there was nothing left to grab.

Nothing for me to grab, but someone to grab me if she wanted to. And, apparently, she did. Pet's fingers clamped down on my left wrist, our contact the only thing that kept me from plummeting toward the rocks hundreds of feet below us. I peered up into eyes that appeared lupine and I couldn't help asking, "What are you doing?"

"Keeping this fight fair." Pet's voice was strained as she tried to pull me up, the effort making little progress. "I intend to win by the sword not by *gravity*."

She wasn't strong enough to drag me all the way to safety, but the stabilizing support allowed my feet to settle against the side of the headland so I could start walking my way up toward her. One step. Two. Half a dozen more and I might be able to throw my torso across the edge and shift my center of gravity from vertical to horizontal.

At which point I half expected Pet to stab me in the back. Maybe some words would help prevent that?

"Did you ever wonder," I panted, "whether winning the Moon Trials is all it's cracked up to be?"

Pet's answer was brief. "No." Still, she kept leveraging me upward. Four steps complete. Four more to go.

"I'll bet it's lonely at the top," I huffed, trying to get ungainly legs to make another effort. But they rebelled, reminding me that gravity wanted me to move in the opposite direction. Of all the times for my body to go on strike.

"Maybe Ember was the smart one," I panted out while willing strength into soggy muscles. "Build enough alliances and you don't have to keep other packs petrified. What if we followed her lead and refused to kill each other? Had each others' backs for the next decade? Wouldn't that make your life better than going it alone?"

Okay, I'd told Thom I was going to act like a fox and here I was mouthing lupine platitudes. But they weren't really platitudes. The mere fact that I hadn't fallen to my death proved that wolves had something going for them. And the truth was, I *liked* acting like a wolf. Especially when the wind whipped my bare legs one last time then was blocked by soil as I rolled over to stare up at the sky.

Well, at the sky and at Pet, sword extended. "Get up," she growled, clearly uninterested in my offer of pack and friendship. "Then fight me. I intend to win fair and square."

So we fought. I managed to rematerialize my star-ball sword and hold my own while Pet proved she'd been playing nice earlier. Once we were both armed, the kid gloves came off and she slashed with such skill I started feeling like a chopping board. Armor would have been nice. *Clothes* would have been nice. But a little blood loss never hurt anyone, right?

The trouble was, I only managed to channel half of my lagging energy into the sword fight. The other half was still focused on talking Pet out of a battle where winning by the rules would equate to a long-regretted loss. "I'm not just saying this to save my skin," I continued. "I killed once in haste and now regret it at my leisure. Don't do that to yourself…"

My argument trailed off as a beloved voice yelled my name into the wind. "Auntie Keeera!"

Really? Had the kid tracked me all the way here using that cell-phone app from his father?

Pet took advantage of my faltering attention to nearly evade my defenses. Her teeth were sharp within her human mouth as she added the weapon of words. "If you have to talk, that means you're not good enough to win. I—"

Whatever she'd intended to say, I'd never know. Because if Grub was here…well, it was time to ditch reason and end this fight the dirty way.

So I used the tool I'd swiped up while lying on the ground staring at a sky the same color as my mate's irises. I'd hoped I wouldn't have to descend to subterfuge. Had hoped I could find a way to convince Pet it was a good idea to name ourselves co-winners.

There was a time for hope and a time for reality. If Grub was here—reality won.

To that end, I swiped at Pet's knees, knowing she'd bend to parry. The stoop shouldn't have been a danger to her. After all, my own sword was down low, blocked by her weapon. I had nothing to attack her unprotected face with…or so she thought.

My opponent's eyes widened comically when I slapped the drug-infused mask over her nose and mouth. Her frantic attempts to rip the obstruction away, in contrast, had no humor behind them.

Her first blow rocked me back on my heels and I barely managed to seep my star ball into my skin in time to grab Pet's wrist and prevent her sword from slicing into me sideways. I'd been banking on the drug acting as quickly on her as it had on me, but the mask had been sitting out long enough for volatile chemicals to become airborne and waft away in the relentless breeze. It might take minutes to work. It might not work at all.

Still, the mask had folded itself shut when it fell away from my snout. And something must have remained within those folds because Pet struggled for only a few seconds. Then she went limp so quickly I barely managed to ease her to the ground before she could stab herself with her own sword.

At which point, I forgot about murder and Moon Trials. Because my nephew was running up the rise toward me, cheeks pink and—was that tear puffiness marring his chubby cheeks? I only realized I was growling when the kid slammed into my body and started vibrating along with me. "Auntie Kira," he murmured, nuzzling in closer. "You sound grumpy."

"Of course not, kiddo. How could I be grumpy when hugging my favorite Grub?" I forced my voice to sweeten as I stooped to encircle his body in mine, all the while scanning the spot he'd materialized out of. The lay of the land was such that I couldn't see who was coming up the hill after him. But someone had to be. Someone had caused those tear stains.

Pet's willingness to murder for family suddenly made much more sense.

Regaining my full height, I eased my body sideways so Grub was behind me and my sword was once again at the ready. Then I calmed my breathing and I waited for danger to strike.

I didn't have to wait long. A wolf bounded toward us, female if I didn't miss my guess.

"She's the one who saved me," my nephew piped up, peeking around my hip to consider the oncoming four-legger. "Well, the big man in the pink suit did, but then the meanies grabbed him and *she* drove a really cool truck to get us here. It went vroom! It was red and sparkly!" His voice turned indignant. "They told me I was gonna have to wait in the truck, though. So I jumped out the window! Just like you woulda, Auntie Kira! Now I can help you! Pow! Bam! Boom!"

There wasn't time to argue that it was okay for me to jump out of moving vehicles but not okay for my nephew to do likewise. Because the female wolf—Willow,

I realized as she sped toward us—wasn't alone. She was running flat out away from nearly a dozen San Francisco wolves.

I wanted to fight. I craved the opportunity to win back Grub's smiles and chastise the beasts who had stolen his happiness.

But for the second time during the Moon Trials, surrender was the only viable option. So I lowered my sword and donned the widest smile I could muster. "Chief Wylie! Nice of you to come pick us up in such a timely manner. Great Trials. Five stars, definitely. I'll write up the review as soon as we get home from the airport and unpack."

I had little expectation that the bristling alpha would respond to my verbal diarrhea. But, to my surprise, he shifted upward until he loomed above his sea of wolves. "It will be my pleasure," he answered, "to give you pleasure."

The words should have come across as chivalrous. They didn't. Instead, the sharp scent of lust forced its way into my nostrils. Chief Wylie's eyes ranged over my nakedness and even Grub picked up on the subtext.

"Don't you look at my auntie like that!" The kid wriggled free before I could grab more tightly onto him. Snatching up Pet's sword two-handed, he swiped it in a wild arc that seemed most likely to cut off his own foot.

"Whoa there, tiger." I sidled in front of my nephew, even though the effort meant approaching Chief Wylie closer than I really meant to. I wasn't on my own, however. Willow had settled into our little cluster and was now pacing me step for step, ruff raised and fangs bared. Human, she'd seemed afraid of her own shadow. But, lupine, she'd come into her own.

Unfortunately, one wolf and one woman weren't going to make much headway when we were so seriously outmatched. So I was grateful when Chief Wylie attacked only with words.

"You'll have to share, of course," he continued, his glance dropping from me to Pet, who was still sprawled comatose on the grass between us and the headland. "Amusing that both your pack leaders would offer their heirs as mates on the exact same night. At first, I was conflicted. How could I choose between such a tender morsel and a woman genetically predisposed to age like fine wine?"

Yuck. I winced, which was a mistake. Not because of Chief Wylie's smug grin, but because it clued my nephew in to the fact that I wasn't handling this situation as well as I pretended to be. Sliding out from behind me, he charged with sword raised and a berserker roar of: "Meeeaaaannnnieee!"

Luckily, Grub's legs were shorter than his temper. Willow and I surged forward in tandem to cut him off from danger yet again, managing to slide back in front of my bloodthirsty nephew before he could make contact with Chief Wylie. But our abrupt forward charge must have come across as an attack.

Because the San Francisco clan surged forward in tandem. Willow and I were left desperately defending while trying to prevent Grub from getting swallowed up by wolves taller than he was. My sword flashed so fast, I lost track of the motion. It was simply spin and cut and lunge and stab and do it all over again until muscles burned and the world narrowed down into a tiny sliver of ever-moving fur and Chief Wylie's smug and repeated laugh.

Without Willow, I would have gone down in the first minute. Even with her help, there was no way we'd be able to save Grub, let alone ourselves. Because my nephew refused to retreat along the edge of the headland where he would have at least been protected on one side by the nothingness of the cliff face while hunting a crevice large enough for one small boy to hide within. Instead, he talked smack at the top of his lungs, throwing out insults that didn't entirely make sense and would have had me chuckling if the rage on lupine faces hadn't warned that these snubs might be his last.

"Take that, banana face!" Grub caroled. And: "Doo-doo head doesn't know his big toe from his tonsils!"

As he yelled, we retreated. Step by step our trio was forced to the edge of the headland as Chief Wylie's lupine tide advanced before us. His wolves had clearly been told not to cause me permanent damage because they snapped their jaws shut at the last minute rather than crunching through my leg bones. Still, I had less faith they'd steer clear of wounding Grub and Willow. So I fought until my wrists felt like overstretched rubber bands and my legs quivered like jello. I wouldn't last much longer. *We* wouldn't last much longer. Not without reinforcements that seemed highly unlikely to materialize.

Even Grub's enthusiasm had started lagging. "You fight like a," he paused for several long seconds before finishing, "a farting microraptor."

Unfortunately, there were no flatulent dinosaurs, or help of any other sort, on the horizon. So I dug deep inside myself instead. Dug up rage that had turned me into a monster during the second Trial. Grasped for the vicious satisfaction I'd felt when leaving Chief Reed to bleed out on our host's balcony. Went so far as to pull up the memory of hacking through Quentin's throat months ago, before black and white of morality had morphed into so many shades of gray.

The memory rose, fuzzy and faded. All I seemed able to recall now was the sour taste of bile, the sickness on my tongue at having been forced into murder against my will.

Still, I faked it. Roared out anger I didn't feel and heard that rage echoed by Grub's little-boy voice and Willow's lupine howl. Together we'd fight until we couldn't, a moment that was creeping up on us far too fast.

Then a vision of male perfection in a rumpled pink tuxedo barreled up over the rise.

Chapter 34

Thom had never looked more beautiful than he did in that moment. Every ounce alpha, he radiated strength that almost made the off-balanced battlefield feel balanced. One side of his mouth quirked up into a crooked smile...then the intense vitality of his being collapsed in on itself.

I blinked. This was a different man now dragging his way toward us as if one of his legs was injured. His broad shoulders had folded toward his ribs and his chin nudged his chest. Meanwhile, his voice quavered as he called out: "Chief Wylie. I've come to beg a favor."

Until that moment, I don't think any of the San Francisco wolves had known Thom was present. The rustle as they spun to face the danger at their back transitioned into yips resembling snickers. Shifters who never would have stepped out of the way of an alpha now parted to let Thom approach their pack leader without hassle or obstruction.

For his part, Chief Wylie flashed wolf-sharp teeth as he verbally engaged. "A favor you say. What do you want?"

"Reed territory," Thom told the ground, his words spilled over themselves like frantic puppies. "Of course, you don't need to part with much. A strong pack leader like yourself will keep everything except the scraps. Able-bodied wolves. Riches. I don't expect those." He swallowed audibly then continued. "But the land itself. I'd buy it. I'd offer all the money I have saved up."

Chief Wylie's huff of laughter was so quiet every San Francisco wolf leaned forward to ensure they caught his answer. "I'd heard you bought territories. A sad state for an alpha. What if I want more than cash?"

"Then I'll give you something considerably more valuable." Thom's voice had dropped also. But where Chief Wylie's quietness reeked of power, my mate's words seemed to be imploding into near soundlessness. It took him two tries to spit out his counteroffer. "I can promise...a broken mate bond."

"Thom!" I couldn't help myself. I knew this was a ploy. I knew from the way Thom had smiled at me before crumpling up his body so it resembled a beaten submissive's. He was playing on the other alpha's arrogance.

My head knew that but not my heart.

Pain roiled through me as Thom failed to respond to my outcry. Of course he couldn't explain aloud. But via our mate bond...

I forced words down the tether pulled taut between us. *"What are you doing?"*

No answer. He'd shut our connection all the way down.

Thom was thirty feet away from me now, twenty feet away from Chief Wylie. His path into the crowd of San Francisco shifters had closed behind him. If something went wrong, he'd be trapped, one lone wolf unable to battle his way to freedom.

But nothing went wrong, not then at least. Instead, Chief Wylie's nostrils flared and he motioned in my direction. "You've hurt this fox's tender feelings. A little more of that and I won't even need to bargain for a broken mate bond. Better hurry up before I decide I don't need what you have to give."

And Thom took one final step forward then straightened like a bent sapling released from an obstruction. The scent of alpha musk roiled off him as he opened his mouth and I understood in that moment what he'd been up to.

He'd needed the scent of my desperate refusal to back up his playacting, a bid to win proximity he couldn't have gotten any other way. Because just like our mate bond, alpha commands were impacted by distance. Once close enough to Chief Wylie, Thom had a real chance of barking the other pack leader down.

The trouble was, we'd both forgotten my hotheaded nephew. Grub darted out from behind me, Pet's sword raised above his head as he yelled out a wordless battle roar.

He was past me before I could grab onto his slipperiness. Past Willow and slamming straight into Chief Wylie's knees.

And the San Francisco alpha was ready. His broad palm settled underneath Grub's chin before my nephew got in a hit or Thom managed to spit a single word out. It wouldn't take much strength to slam that hand upward and snap a neck not yet hardened by age. Wouldn't take any time at all—less time, perhaps, than an alpha command would require to seize hold of the older man's muscles.

No wonder Thom's teeth clicked shut. No wonder he didn't try to evade when a wolf beside him turned human, wrenching Thom's arms behind his back then smothering my mate's mouth with a meaty palm.

Even if Thom had wanted to, he couldn't order Chief Wylie to surrender now.

No wonder Chief Wylie dismissed Thom as he considered me. "Kneel," he demanded, "and break your bond."

Thom's blue eyes were frozen fire pleading with me to ignore the order. The lasso writhing around his forearm suggested a cascade of anger was building up inside.

But for Grub, I'd do anything. My knees slammed into the earth.

I'd obeyed the first part of Chief Wylie's demand, but I still hoped I could talk my way out of the second. "I thought you wanted Pet as well as me," I observed. "Pretty sure her father won't sell off his daughter to a pack leader who already has a mate."

"Who said I intended to do anything other than fuck you?" Chief Wylie answered, his voice pleasant even though his words weren't. The lasso around Thom's arm was so tight now that my mate's skin had reddened. Soon, I suspected, Thom would be tempted into action that would get my nephew killed.

And still Chief Wylie continued to bait us both. "*Your* alpha is dead, little fox, and you're sloppy seconds. Good for nothing but a side piece at this point."

As he spoke, his palm forced Grub's chin up a little higher and my nephew whimpered. I held my breath, hoping Thom could rein in the lasso's anger in a way I hadn't been able to.

Silent stillness was my answer. Silent stillness until Chief Wylie snapped out. "Stop stalling. My patience is running thin."

His scent backed up that claim, as did his history. Harming a child was likely no big deal to a pack leader who'd won the Moon Trials a decade ago. He'd proven willing to kill then. He appeared just as willing to kill now.

And at any second, the lasso might tip my mate over into violence. Violence that would spill over and harm my nephew.

I had to do something. The only thing I could think of was obeying Chief Wylie's mandate.

So—*"I'm sorry, Thom,"* I sent, fumbling for our mate bond only to have it evade my fingers. Thom was doing something to the tether, or I was doing something to it. Whatever the reason, I failed three times before managing to clamp down on the invisible yet very tangible connection that lay between the two of us.

As I struggled, the wind picked back up. Or perhaps that roaring in my ears was just foreknowledge of what would happen when I broke our mate bond to save my nephew. The upcoming emptiness was unfathomable.

But Chief Wylie had pressed Grub's chin up yet higher and tears were sliding down my nephew's cheeks now. Thom's fingers were white from blood loss on the arm the lasso strangled. And I held tight to our mate bond with one hand while latching down with the other in preparation for ripping my most precious connection apart.

The crazy shriek that rose from behind me was so unexpected it almost yanked my hands in opposite directions and finished that severing. Instead, I froze as a gawky shape spun through the air, aiming for Chief Wylie's back.

Chapter 35

The attacker was Pet, awakening and diving to the rescue. Which would have been wonderful if her angle was such that she was able to see the danger Grub faced from her actions. Instead, it seemed she didn't know that all it would take was an unintentional jarring of Chief Wylie's wrist and my nephew wouldn't be able to engage in high-spirited high jinks ever again.

I went from kneeling to sprinting in a millisecond even though physics promised I was too far away to influence the outcome. But I had to try. Grub owned a piece of my heart. Of my sister's heart. And, in his own right, the kid was a firecracker who deserved to explode whenever and on whomever he jolly well pleased.

Out of the corner of my eye, I heard a grunt. Saw something red-gold fly through the air faster than my legs could carry me. But it wasn't flying toward Chief Wylie, so I didn't pay any attention.

I did, however, notice the grass blades beneath my feet freezing one millisecond before my mate's deep voice demanded: "*Freeze!*"

Everyone froze except me. Ignoring the fact that wolves and two-leggers alike had lost the ability to move more than their lungs and their eyeballs, I shoved my way through the throng on the way to my nephew.

Or rather, toward my nephew and mate. Because Thom had gotten to Grub first. Huge hands disentangled tiny limbs from the alpha's rough hold with a gentleness I'd felt on my own skin far too infrequently. And as he worked, my mate rumbled out reassurance. "Our little superhero is in tip-top condition," he promised. "Here."

The warmth of Grub's body sliding into my arms was matched by the heat of Thom's glancing touch. Our gazes locked for one split second while I demanded, "How did you know you could break free without Chief Wylie snapping Grub's neck?"

Thom shook his head. "Didn't," he rumbled succinctly. "Your lasso took matters into its own hands. Or should I say teeth?"

Because the lasso was slithering across the battlefield toward us. Ignoring me, it wound its way up Thom's leg and latched back onto his forearm. Creepy...yet it had saved my nephew by, I gathered, biting the shifter who had restrained Thom.

"Thank you," I told the lasso while watching Thom hoist Pet over one shoulder and Willow over the other.

Ignoring the fact I had just spoken to a hunk of metal, my mate observed, "Exit will be tricky. I gather alpha commands fade with distance."

"You gather?" I shook my head. "I think we're well past the point where you can pretend to be a good old country boy with no concept of your true heritage as an alpha werewolf."

Thom shot me that crooked smile and shrugged, his gesture made more impressive by the dead weights draped over each shoulder. Then he led the way out of the frozen shifter-scape as adeptly as a dancer might traverse an empty stage.

Unfortunately, he'd been right about the command fading. He dropped behind the moment we hit open countryside, but still the ominous rustle of no-longer-frozen werewolves materialized within seconds. "Smart ideas?" Thom asked.

"Nope." I hesitated, torn between clinging to Grub and materializing my sword. "Perhaps unfreeze Pet and Willow..." I started. Then I lost all words as a horde of moving bodies came rushing toward us over the hill.

The scene that met our eyes should have been ominous. If we'd been outnumbered before, we were now lone boats adrift in a vast sea of warriors.

But these newcomers weren't San Francisco wolves. I didn't know any of the huge beasts speeding toward me, yet their scents didn't boast the salty-fog overtones of locals. They instead reminded me of inhaled steam off chocolate cupcakes pulled fresh out of the oven, an aroma I associated with...

"Ember," I murmured one moment before a human-form shifter crested the rise behind the chocolate-scented werewolves. She nodded at me then addressed Chief Wylie over my shoulder.

"I forgot my favorite cupcake tray. Hope you don't mind me dropping by to retrieve it."

The San Francisco alpha spluttered something wordless, unsurprising since Ember wasn't carrying any baking paraphernalia. Instead, there was a sword belted at her hip and a grizzled wolf pacing her step for step.

The older wolf's gaze slid across me and I froze despite myself. This was a predator who rivaled even the Executioner in the realm of raw alpha power. Thom might have been able to bark down Chief Wylie, but this wolf could have told us all to hop off the nearest cliff and we wouldn't have even considered refusing until we were already midair.

Only, the hulking beast did nothing of the sort. Instead, he licked Ember's trailing fingers as if he was a family dog demanding affection. She patted his head absently then turned her attention to Grub, who'd started wiggling in my arms.

"Somebody's been missing you," she observed, gesturing back over her shoulder.

We all looked, of course. Looked at Mai and Gunner and half of her best warriors, plus Thom's second and several other familiar Gate City faces, all of whom were racing to catch up with Ember's army. A complicated tangle of emotions struck me so sharply I nearly lost my footing. Because my intention all these months had been keeping loved ones out of danger. Instead, my fumblings appeared to have tempted my sister and friends into trespassing on the territory of an alpha who'd been strong enough to win the previous Moon Trials.

But that tangle of emotion? None of the components included regret. Foremost, in fact, was hot-air-balloon joy buoying me up until I thought I'd float rather than jump off that nearby cliff.

Because this was my family. We were meant to be together. Mai, as usual, had been right.

"Mommy!" Grub called, snatching a long dagger from a frozen Pet. "Lookee! I'm winning the Moon Trials! Wham! Bam! Boom!"

At which point, Chief Wylie finally found his voice. "Good of you to join in this celebration of the Moon Trials' conclusion. But the final battle is not yet over. Two heirs still stand."

He was deflecting. Which was understandable given the fact that the wolf at Ember's side—her father?—could have taken over the entire San Francisco pack without the need for bloodshed. Plus, if a fight broke out, we were now the ones poised to win.

We were poised to win...and I was poised to lose. Because Thom's freeze on Pet had finally faded. She slid off my mate's shoulder and came down facing me, yet another dagger clutched in each hand.

Her arsenal was impressive, but of course I could turn my star ball into any weapon I needed. Unfortunately, daggers weren't the problem. The problem was will.

Trouble being, I was no more willing to harm the teenager now than I'd been the last time we did battle. She, on the other hand, had proven that deaths didn't lie heavily on her conscience.

"Go to your parents," I told Grub, shoving at his hind end. I'd gotten myself into this. Somehow, I was going to have to find a way to finish it without my nephew caught in the crossfire.

Only...Pet was turning away from me and using her daggers to menace another. "You got that wrong," she countered Chief Wylie's pronouncement. "Trials are over. Ended in a tie."

Chapter 36

I don't think Chief Wylie would have been able to argue if Ember's father hadn't appeared to forget our standoff and instead wandered off to stalk grouse in the shrubbery further back from the cliff edge. The grizzled wolf dropped to his belly and slunk along the ground with an intensity of focus that seemed all out of proportion with the cluster of fat birds waddling along in front of him. No wonder Chief Wylie's teeth sharpened as he shook his head at Pet.

"As the host, I make the rules. And my rules are simple. Only one contestant walks out of the final Trial alive."

Except it turned out that Ember's father hadn't been ignoring us after all. The grouse flew, the grizzled wolf spun, and his growl turned the air ten degrees colder. I wasn't the only one rubbing goosebumps off my arms.

No wonder Chief Wylie's gaze dropped to his shoes as he tilted his head away from the other pack leader in instant submission. "Apologies. I misspoke. I congratulate you both on your tie."

"We won, we won!" Grub caroled, hefting his stolen dagger and barreling toward Pet.

"Not you, little one." One hand came down on my nephew's head to hold him in place while the other gently disentangled her weapon from his fingers. "Next decade, you can compete in the Trials. I'll make sure you have a fair shot."

Next decade. I met the teenager's gaze and nodded appreciation. Not that I expected to co-host that contest. Because...

"Kira?" Thom's broad hand slid onto the small of my back as the entire mass of us started away from Chief Wylie's pack mates. Our opponents hadn't followed, yet the warmth of my mate's proximity didn't manage to thaw the chill that had come over me. No wonder Thom continued to nudge me verbally. "What did I miss?"

I shook my head rather than speaking a lie he would smell immediately. And I throttled down our mate bond also, just in case my thoughts were so loud they hopped from my head to his.

Because this wasn't over. Yes, the Moon Trials were done and Chief Wylie appeared willing to let us all make our way to the airport without being hassled. But Charlie was still in the clutches of the Executioner, who had warned me that leaving San Francisco would be considered proof of guilt.

Proof of guilt for murders I now knew Pet had committed, a fact I might have considered sharing if that same teenager hadn't saved my nephew and stood up to Chief Wylie on my behalf. I owed Pet and my kitsune magic wouldn't let me turn her in now even if I'd wanted to. No, I'd need to deal with the Executioner myself.

I had no way to contact him though. So I let myself be swept up in the tide carrying us away from the salty-fog tang of the San Francisco werewolves. When we reached the road, I bid farewell to Ember and her father, who had chartered a plane and landed much closer to our wild battlefield than the international airport toward which the rest of us were headed.

"I'd let you guys hitch a ride across the country," she told us, "but I suspect it's better if you run the official gauntlet."

"Gauntlet?" Thom's palm tugged me a little closer into the strength of his body. He'd draped his pink suit jacket around my shoulders while rumbling out a promise of more clothes back at the vehicles. But if this was to be our last hour together then I preferred flesh on flesh.

Pet appeared oblivious to anything except the Trials' aftermath as she took over the explanation. "Losing heirs tend to hang out at the airport to greet the winner. It's neutral turf so Chief Wylie can't kick them out. They'll want to gauge our level of injury. Decide whether we really are worth bowing down to for the next decade."

That made sense, and was likely the most important part of this whole ordeal for Pet. "I'll make sure they know you were the true force to be reckoned with," I offered.

"No," the teenager countered. "We won together."

Did Pet realize she'd hammered yet another nail into my coffin with her words?

Thom's blue eyes pierced me but he didn't ask what was wrong a second time. Instead, he sorted out borrowed vehicles, cramming me, himself, my sister, Mai's mate, and Grub into the back seats of a minivan driven by his second while Willow rode shotgun. My nephew refused to sit down as we wound our way back through beautiful countryside I wasn't able to appreciate, but I didn't care. Because his perpetual motion and chatter made me forget, for a short while, what lay ahead.

"Auntie Kira said it wasn't fair to leave Rorora behind," Grub informed all of us while evading his father's grip and clambering up to lie on his belly atop the headrests.

Mai raised one eyebrow the same way she used to when I refused to abandon my fox skin for days on end as a child. "Oh, that was the one thing you did wrong, huh?"

"Yep," Grub answered happily. "But I'm a good big brother. Next time, Rorora can come too."

"We'll see about that, mister." With a speed strike worthy of a cobra, Gunner rolled his son down into his lap and started a tickle fight so intense that a winded Grub finally allowed himself to be strapped down beneath a seatbelt. And I basked in proximity to family I hadn't seen in person for far too long.

Sooner than I wanted, though, we were pulling up to the airport. Our baggage had arrived before us, a lone San Francisco shifter waiting amid the pile of luggage with eyes on the ground and scent muted submissively. Willow and I donned enough clothes to be human-friendly then we made it through security with only one small hassle when the *hihi'irokane* lasso almost refused to leave Thom's arm to pass through the scanners. On the other end, it leapt onto my skin so quickly the human screener frowned and opened his mouth as if to call up reinforcements before shaking his head and dismissing what hadn't made rational sense.

Then we were on neutral turf with a couple of hours to kill before our flight carried us back east. As Pet had warned, several of the other heirs lingered, eying us as we embedded ourselves in the flow of moving humans. But it was the scent of floor cleanser that captivated my full attention. The Executioner was here, waiting to pounce.

I was so intent upon the scent that Thom's raised voice made me jump. "Karl. I have a bone to pick with you."

Following my mate's gaze, I found his half-brother nursing a beer inside a half-enclosed seating area. Tension was evident in each sharp contour of his body's shape.

For a moment, it appeared Karl was going to pretend not to have heard. But he was the weaker wolf, as I'd already guessed, so I wasn't surprised when placating words matched his eyes cutting down and to the left. "Forgive and forget," he muttered. "It's what brothers do."

Days ago, Thom would have leapt at the implied invitation. Now he rumbled out a correction. "Brothers? I don't think so. I had all the family I needed long before I met you."

As he spoke, the mate bond between us surged with truth of Thom's assertion. The way he saw it, his human father measured up in all the ways that mattered, providing two parents' worth of nurturing during his childhood. Later, Thom had created his own pack and his own way of being an alpha werewolf. And as the icing on the cake, he had me beside him, my chocolate-and-hot-pepper personality making his life both sweeter and full of an unexpected kick.

Or at least Thom thought he had me. I, on the other hand, needed to turn myself in if I didn't want Charlie's life to be snuffed out by an angry Executioner.

Luckily, Karl wasn't content to let Thom's dismissal end matters between them. "Join me," he wheedled, pushing out the neighboring stool with one booted foot. "We'll talk about it."

Thom might not need more family. But resolution? We all need resolution. He took a step forward while I took a step backward...and our intertwined fingers brought us both up short.

"Kira?" Thom turned away from his brother to question our separation.

For my part, I peered into blue eyes I wasn't sure I'd ever see again and I almost couldn't bear to pull free. But I had to, so I made an excuse. "Your chat will go better without an audience."

And mine also. Thom would never allow me to turn myself in even for Charlie's sake.

Luckily, my mate's attention was on his half-brother, so he missed the tremor I almost but didn't quite manage to keep from impacting our mate bond. Our fingers slid apart then I watched long enough to see the brothers' stiff postures ease incrementally. I doubted they'd ever be friends, but perhaps Thom would get something out of time spent with a sibling who was also a wolf.

For my own part, I just hoped Karl kept Thom busy enough not to notice that I followed the scent of floor cleanser deeper into the maze of the airport. The Executioner waited within a mini-museum exhibit. In the dim seclusion of the winding pathway that led away from the airport and everyone I'd followed there, his flat gray eyes fell on me as heavily as lead weights.

Chapter 37

The Executioner didn't speak immediately, however. Just wandered deeper into the exhibit, until the piped-in background noise of a historical dock reenactment covered up the distant hum of the airport proper. The walls here showcased images of Japanese immigrants, a topic that might have interested me if my entire body hadn't vibrated with tension. As it was, all I could think about was the tasks I'd left unfulfilled.

Grub and Aurora would grow up without an aunt who loved them. Willow wouldn't be nurtured into the pack-leader status I thought she might be capable of achieving. Charlie's girlfriend would never understand that the monkey wrenches I'd thrown into her relationship had nothing to do with her sexuality or ethnicity and everything to do with keeping her safe from undercover magic.

Thom...I couldn't even think about Thom right now or I'd lose my nerve. Instead, even though the first shifter to speak often cedes the upper hand, I broke the silence. "I'm turning myself in."

The Executioner turned to face me, head cocked. Only after the museum noises cycled through a jerky halt and restart did he rasp out: "You're turning yourself into what?"

The faintest hint of a crinkle at the corners of his eyes suggested he intended his response as humor. His subsequent change of subject made equally little sense. "There are only three Japantowns in the United States," he observed sounding nearly as pedantic as Rupert. "San Francisco boasts the oldest, unsurprising given their long history as an entrance point for Japanese immigrants. I wonder what percentage of those immigrants were kitsunes?"

Coming from a formerly monosyllabic man, three sentences amounted to a doctoral dissertation. I frowned, trying to understand what he was getting at. "Several?"

"Likely." He pointed at the image of famous personages blown up to much larger than life size on the wall beside us. "And yet, the expat community is known for a sculptor, a poet, and an athlete. What does that say to you?"

"That the Socratic method is an inefficient way to get your point across?"

Those minuscule eye crinkles deepened, then the Executioner's nostrils flared. "You're frightened."

No point in lying about it. "Terrified," I agreed.

The heavy weight of the Executioner's interest struck me harder for a moment then eased as he turned his eyes away. "You think I intend to punish you for the Moon Trials' murders. But your human friend has been released. The true culprit has been found."

Charlie was safe? For an instant, I was ecstatic, then I found myself peering back over my shoulder even though I knew all I'd be able to see behind me was a bend in the exhibit. "Pet," I started, but the Executioner spoke over me.

"Griffin Fletcher left behind a suicide note in which he claimed responsibility for the other deaths. You weren't aware of this?"

A folded square of paper emerged from the Executioner's pocket and I half expected it to smell of fox pee. Instead, baking soda flaked off the surface, the most basic method of disguising scent.

Blaming the murders on a dead man was clever, but the job was rushed and I couldn't quite imagine the Executioner had fallen for it. "You believe the note is legit?" I asked carefully.

"What I believe is irrelevant." The Executioner's rasp mellowed into something closer to a purr than to his usual mimicry of a rusty handsaw. To my astonishment, those eye crinkles migrated all the way down to the corners of his mouth now. "Fletcher's mate has confirmed the note's authenticity. I believe you know her sister? Petunia Kirkpatrick, your co-winner at the final Trial."

The Executioner was no idiot. He'd connected the obvious dots, followed each clue back to its source the same way I had. And he'd evidently come to the same conclusion as well.

Pet might not have operated under the auspices of official werewolf law, but she was right to stand up for defenseless sisters. She'd acted out of desperation until the trajectory of her life made desperation unnecessary. As the co-winner of the Moon Trials, she would have no reason to resort to murder to keep her family safe in the future.

In other words, Pet was unlikely to reoffend. So why not take her age and extenuating circumstances into account and let her off the hook?

It all made sense, except for mercy coming from a man known only as the Executioner. Now, though, he turned away to jerk his chin toward a dark lump on a windowsill in the grainy black-and-white photo in front of us. "I suspect historical kitsunes did the same thing as modern ones," he murmured. "They hid their existence and were misjudged when they dared to step out of the shadows."

I blinked. "Are you apologizing?"

Rather than answering, the Executioner turned away. "Come, I have a question for you to answer."

"So ask," I called after his retreating back. The dock sounds cycled through another glitchy end and beginning while I considered the image of the possible kitsune hiding in plain sight in long-ago San Francisco. Then I turned to leave the past in the past and follow the Executioner out into my future.

While I'd been consumed by the likelihood of imminent death, my family and friends must have dispersed throughout the terminal. Because the only friendly adult in sight as I emerged from the exhibit was Mai. She waved at me...and accidentally gave Grub the opportunity to slip free of her usually firm grasp.

"Pretzels!" my nephew exclaimed, hightailing it across the terminal faster than such short legs should really be capable of moving. Mai rolled her eyes and started to follow, only to pause when the Executioner cleared his throat and managed to catch the attention of every shifter nearby.

The throat clearing transitioned into words rusty with saw-blade intensity. "Kira Fairwood," rasped the scariest shifter I'd ever met, "the Lawkeepers lost an important asset when you exited our organization. I would like to offer you a replacement position working with me."

I blinked. Everyone knew the Executioner hunted alone. He neither wanted nor needed a partner. Doling out death was apparently a solitary pursuit.

And, of all the jobs, this was the least up my alley. Or was it?

Because the Executioner had proven during the Moon Trials that he didn't act precipitously. That he punished only the truly deserving. Still—

"You might not approve of my methods," I countered. By which I meant I wasn't going to torture anyone no matter what they proved guilty of.

I didn't realize until the closest heir flinched and the air around me filled with the sharp tang of fear that my words could be misconstrued in the opposite direction. That I could have been saying I liked more blood, more suffering than even the Executioner could stomach.

Those crinkles around the Executioner's eyes deepened and he spoke before I could backpedal. "I'm certain we can work something out."

He'd thrown me a major bone, which was why I had to be honest in my reply despite our audience. "I also can't commit to a full-time gig. I have a lot on my plate right now."

"Noted. Any other requirements?"

The Executioner's foot was tapping and nearby shifters were doing their best to subtly drift away from me. Talking back to the Executioner wasn't wise and they had no wish to be caught in the inevitable crossfire.

Up close, though, I could see that the terrifying man who'd made my Moon Trials ten times worse wasn't angry. He was just finished with this conversation. He'd likely spoken more words today than in the entire past year or maybe even decade.

A partner would understand that fact and let him off the hook gracefully. So I shook my head in answer to his question. "I won't keep you. I know you're busy."

The Executioner was gone before I finished my second sentence. Which was a shame because I could have used his scare factor for what came next.

Or so I realized when Grub's high-pitched voice carried from a good distance away. "Who are you?"

My attention spun to the burly werewolf who'd grabbed the boy's arm. Grub's assailant was a stranger, but his identity didn't matter. What he represented did.

"I'm your worst nightmare, puppy," the much larger shifter growled. "Shouldn't have been walking around by yourself all alone."

Chapter 38

The manhandler was five times Grub's weight and a hundred times more dangerous. No wonder Mai and I both saw red.

Well, I was only guessing Mai saw red, but her actions bore that out. Because she ignored all social norms and hopped up onto the top of a sunglasses display that blocked the direct path to her child. From her elevated perch, she'd be able to run along the peak and reach Grub no more than a minute later than I would arrowing straight from where I currently stood.

And both of us would be far too late. Because the werewolf in question had knelt down to Grub's level, looking to outsiders like a kindly adult while hissing menace into the child's face. "Where are your mommy and daddy, puppy?"

Grub's eyes widened. For all that he wasn't old enough to shift, he could still smell intention and I could only imagine the garlicky bite of predator rolling off the man who held him in his grasp.

No wonder Grub's voice shrank as he swiveled his head frantically in search of a mother who was no longer visible, all while trying and failing to pull away. "Um. I dunno. But..."

"Well, that's too bad, isn't it?" The werewolf's hands bit down harder as he straightened, yanking my nephew up along with him. He intended to take the kid away somewhere dark and secluded where no one would hear his screams.

I'd halved the distance between us by this point, but I was still too far away to save my nephew. And just as I tried to thrust even more speed into my muscles, a crowd of humans came gushing out of a newly arrived plane between me and the drama. They were tired, dragging rolling suitcases that turned my path into an obstacle course. I wasn't going to make it and neither was Mai.

I wasn't going to make it without magical assistance that is. My star ball prickled beneath my skin even though showcasing magic in front of all these weary travelers would put me right back on the Executioner's shit list. But I'd do whatever it took to save my nephew.

Turned out I didn't have to. "My aunt's right there!" Grub piped up, pointing toward me. His attacker's gaze rose, met mine through the intermittent passage of humans...and that scary werewolf released his hold on Grub so fast my nephew went tumbling to the floor.

Formerly scary eyes grew even wider than Grub's and his Adam's apple bobbed as he swallowed. "My mistake, Executioner's Apprentice," he said, projecting his voice just enough to ensure I heard it. He'd clearly been a member of the audience the Executioner and I had spoken in front of moments earlier.

"I prefer Death Junior," I countered just as the sea of humans between us thinned. Then I was running and so was Grub. We met in the middle, the kid's leap and my lowered arms hefting him aloft in an instant. He hugged my neck in a stranglehold as I glared at the werewolf backing away from us. "I think you owe the kid a pretzel."

"Two pretzels," Grub muttered into the underside of my jaw just as his mother landed lightly beside us. A few watching humans exclaimed before apparently deciding that jumping off sunglasses stands wasn't worth raising a fuss about. Because no one bothered us as I continued to stare Grub's attacker down.

"How about two dozen?" The werewolf's backwards steps sped up and he bumped into the counter before realizing he'd reached it. Half turning while still keeping me in his view field, he ordered, dropped a hundred dollar bill, then skedaddled without waiting for his pretzels to be served up.

Which was fine. Mai, Grub, and I were glad to take ownership, scarfing down a quarter of the hot, bready twists while watching a plane take off. Then we caught up to Gunner, Thom, and Willow, who easily consumed the rest.

And all the while, I couldn't help grinning. Because my existence was no longer a source of danger to my nephew. Instead, I'd finally gotten what I wanted. My name alone protected those I loved the most.

Thom noticed my change of mood, of course. His approval slid down our newly reopened mate bond as we settled into cramped airplane seats ahead of my sister's family. *"Everything good again?"*

"Better than good," I answered, my thigh brushing up against his thigh. The foreknowledge that Chief Reed wouldn't be building walls between us in the future made it possible to table the excitement that flushed through me at my mate's proximity. It also dulled the ache from farewells that ensued once we reached our connecting airport.

"Does this mean you'll finally stop being a stranger?" Mai asked as we hovered at the dividing line between two arms of the B terminal. Her gate was to the right and mine to the left and both planes had already landed. We couldn't stand there forever, but we also weren't quite ready to step apart.

"Yep," I assured my sister. "this means you're going to become thoroughly sick of me. I'll give Grub and Aurora so many crazy ideas you'll beg me to stop visiting."

"Ideas like what, Auntie Kira?" Grub demanded, using my hands to accelerate his bounces into leaps that would have done a jackrabbit justice.

"Adventures and mischief and wild capers," I told him, turning the little boy's final spring into an elevated hug before pulling my sister and her mate into our huddle. The trick was an old one that came back as easily as if it hadn't fallen out of my repertoire during recent months. Only firmly gripped by both parents could we count on Grub staying put once I turned my back.

This time, though, I wasn't parting from my family solo. "We'll see you next weekend," Gunner said, meeting Thom's gaze over my shoulder as our hug disbanded.

I turned, eyebrows raised, to find my mate nodding. And as Mai, Gunner, and Grub ambled away from us, the warmth in Thom's blue eyes made it easy to ignore the emptiness left behind by receding family members.

"Next weekend?" I prodded.

"Favors," Thom rumbled by way of explanation. "I offered the Full Moon Saloon to Ember as her party venue. That way you owe her nothing. Plus, she gave me free rein to invite whoever I like."

"Nice move." I melted into a hug that felt just as warm yet entirely different from the one I'd just shared with my family. "Still, I'm glad the shindig's not until next weekend. Because I have a lot to deal with cleaning up Chief Reed's messes first."

"Says the new Chief Reed. Speaking of which." Thom's blue eyes glinted. "Any chance that hard border boundary could be softened just a little?"

"For you, it could be turned entirely permeable."

Which is when our embrace morphed from sweet to spicy. Thom's lips descended onto mine and for a good long while I forgot about packs and parties. All I noticed was his hands and my hands, the scratch of beard stubble against my soft neck and the firmness of an alpha's touch tracing the curve of my hip.

"Get a room," muttered a harried passerby.

Not too many hours later, we did.

Epilogue

"**Y**ou're stalling."

I looked up from the duffel bag I'd packed and repacked three times in order to consider Willow. She held herself subtly differently than she had a week ago when we'd touched back down on the east coast and headed off together to reclaim her uncle's mansion. Her shoulders were straighter, her head higher. And rather than prickly snark, a bite of alpha protectiveness colored her tone.

Willow was almost ready to pick up the reins of pack leadership, having already aced the tasks I'd set her as my second. It didn't hurt that Chief Reed's most recent forged birth certificate—his method of hiding his lack of aging from nosy humans—meant Willow was the previous alpha's closest living relative and now owned the thousands of acres stockpiled before his death.

That was step one. Step two involved gradually distancing myself from this mansion on a hill until Willow became de facto pack leader. I had high hopes the plan would come to fruition in the very near future...which didn't explain the odd emptiness in my stomach when I considered my much-anticipated return to Gate City, the home I'd chosen for myself.

"Yep, totally stalling," I acknowledged, upending the bag over my bed yet again. Out tumbled the few possessions I'd accumulated while acting as Chief Reed's heir, each present and accounted for. The hollow nagging at my gut had nothing to do with a forgotten toothbrush or hat.

Willow began rolling my t-shirts into stiff logs that left even more room in my bag for emptiness. Her words were just as economical. "You intend to be late to your own party."

"It's not my party," I countered, wrinkling up my nose as I smelled the lie in my words. Okay, so maybe the first part of tonight *was* my party. My welcome back to Gate City after months away, an hour for revelry as a pack before Ember and the other heirs showed up to eat cupcakes and build alliances, hopefully without a side of murder.

We packed in silence for one long moment, during which time I realized that I wasn't the only one stalling. Willow had something she wanted to say.

"Just tell me," I demanded as I stuffed the rest of my clothes in the bag unfolded. I mean, who really cared if they ended up wrinkled on the other end?

Willow frowned, and for a moment I thought she wasn't going to admit to whatever was bothering her. Then she bit her lip and spilled. "So, I should have told you this earlier. There was another kitsune. Long before I was born, or at least that's what the whispers say. We knew Chief Reed never aged. We knew he had odd items like this one." She reached out and tapped the *hihi'irokane* lasso that resolutely refused to budge from my forearm. I got the distinct impression it woke up at the intrusion, but Willow must not have noticed because she kept talking. "I'm telling you now because I think Chief Reed's excessively long life had something to do with Gate City."

It would have been handy to learn all of that *before* the old man roped me into giving him so much blood that I almost became stuck walking in the legendary kitsune's footsteps. Still, I shrugged and let Willow off the hook. "Water over the dam. Thanks for the heads up."

Because the queasiness in my stomach had settled. The red lines on my right arm where I'd spun the lasso far too many times trying to pry it off my skin stopped itching.

My instincts had been trying to tell me I was walking into danger returning to Gate City with a *hihi'irokane* lasso affixed to my body. Problem acknowledged, I zipped up the duffel bag and swung it over one shoulder before heading down the mountain.

One teeny tiny premonition wasn't enough to keep me away from my mate.

The Full Moon Saloon was Gate City's favorite watering hole. Who doesn't love cheap drinks, werewolves mingling with humans, and a magical artifact in the crawl space underneath?

Today, though, the sign on the front door read "Closed" and the back lot was nearly empty. In contrast, fox ears confirmed that the interior was hopping. Thom had likely told his pack mates to show up on foot, leaving the nearer parking spaces for out-of-town visitors due to start arriving in half an hour.

Proving my guesswork correct, two familiar shapes strolled around the corner as I pulled my car up beside Thom's truck. Charlie glanced toward me then away again, proving she wasn't quite ready to forgive and forget. But when she pulled open the door to the Moon Room, interior lighting illuminated Nora's wide eyes and dimpled smile...plus the moon medallion dangling from a chain around her neck.

Looked like the awfulness with the Executioner hadn't dragged that pair apart but rather pushed them closer together. And Nora seemed to be taking the existence of the paranormal in her stride.

Even better, Charlie peered back over one shoulder just before the door slammed shut behind her, gracing me with an eye roll deeply familiar from our many years of friendship. That eye roll meant, *"You screwed up."* It meant, *"You're gonna have to grovel."* It also meant, *"Yes, I'll forgive you in the end."*

No wonder I hopped out of my car with a spring in my steps.

By the time I made it inside, the pack's interest had glommed onto its newest member. So for a split second, I was able to take in the space I'd missed so much without anyone noticing I'd arrived. Today, the long windowless room was lit by colored lights while throbbing music intertwined with an occasional howl. Drinks flowed freely and shifter and human alike slid around each other with wild movements that were both like and unlike dancing. Everyone here was a member of Thom's pack or soon to become one, which warmed the air with the ease of familiarity and connection.

Well not quite everyone here was connected. I frowned at one glowering shape in the corner. Trust the Executioner not to understand that you don't show up at a party before the designated hour.

Then Thom's blue eyes met mine from the far side of the room and I forgot all about our premature party guest. Because my mate's mouth had quirked up into a secret half-smile he saved for me alone and my blood, heart, and stomach warmed to a boil.

Or perhaps Thom's smile wasn't so secret, not tonight at least. He must have sent an alert down the pack bonds because every gaze locked onto me one millisecond after his did.

Not just their gazes. Something struck my gut at the exact same moment, knocking my breath away. It wasn't a weapon however. No, this felt like Grub headbutting me to demand affection.

I looked down and caught the faintest glimmer of a pack bond worming its way through my defenses. *Who?* Tracing the tether back to its source proved impossible because I was being bombarded by another and another and another. Each curled around me, intertwining and weaving me up into a net of welcome.

Tears pricked my eyes. I hadn't expected acceptance when I walked through this door. Not after I'd drawn the pack's alpha into trouble repeatedly. Not after I'd failed to set foot in the Full Moon Saloon for four long months while Chief Reed held me under his thumb. And definitely not after I rushed back to that old wolf's lair to help out Willow after the Moon Trials rather than touching base with these people who deserved my attention just as much.

With these *friends*, rather. Because newly formed pack bonds were matched by hollered greetings from Thom's second, from the human woman Bertrand hoped would become his mate, from Dixie Lee's tween daughter who now had a fox just like mine inside her, and from the young couple who'd found a safe harbor in Gate City despite her family's disapproval.

Thom's human father didn't just call a greeting. Big T drew me into a bear hug and whispered something in my ear that sounded suspiciously like, "Welcome home, daughter."

And I was so warmed by the gesture that I missed the moment the lasso uncurled itself from around my forearm. I only caught the motion out of the corner of my eye as the bite of something digging into the back of my neck made me slap at my skin then grab at the metal one moment too late.

Because one end of the lasso's flexible length had opened up and swallowed the *hihi'irokane* orb that locked down the magic of the Gate City artifact. Tearing the necklace off me, the lasso shot across the floor far faster than even a living object should have been able to move.

"Grab it!" I called to werewolves who were instead leaping away like elephants fleeing the horror of a mouse attack. Pumpkin, who'd hitched a ride back to the Full Moon Saloon soon after Chief Reed's death, was the only one who moved toward rather than away from the lasso. But even our orange tomcat was too slow to catch up.

Because the golden streak had already slipped underneath the rolling cabinet that hid the artifact's trapdoor. A boom, a flash of light, and the trapdoor opened itself in flying shards of wood carried outward by billowing gusts of oily black smoke.

My sword was in my hand and half the werewolves were on their way to going furry by the time a shape rose up out of the dark vapor. Thom was the one who reached the site first though. He cocked his head then stretched one hand down to help what appeared to be a naked young woman up out of the pit.

"I'm Thom," my mate introduce himself, as if this was someone he'd met on the street rather than a stranger who clearly hadn't been beneath the bar one moment earlier. "And you are?"

I couldn't see the woman well, could only make out the wildness of her hair as she shook her head. "I don't know." Then she flared her nostrils and recoiled. "You're a wolf."

"No one here is going to harm you," Thom started. But the woman had already attacked.

Her fingers raked across my mate's face, drawing blood that she sucked into her mouth while spinning away from him. "Don't follow me. None of you."

Every werewolf except one froze, the blood-assisted command turning Thom immobile and most members of his pack by association. Pack bonds didn't bind me the same way they did the others, though, so I could have given chase.

I didn't. Not when Thom stood there glassy eyed and immobile. I thrust energy toward him down our mate bond and was relieved to find strong fingers already flexing by the time I reached his side.

"Not the party surprise I'd expected," my mate rumbled, peering down into the pit. I leaned in beside him, finding nothing except stone and shards of bone that had once been a fox skull. If I didn't miss my guess, the prickle of magic that used to imbue this space had fled along with the strange naked woman. Woken, perhaps, by me passing one way through the Japantown gate without going back?

"I suppose," my mate continued, "we're going to track her down and fix whatever's broken?"

He seemed willing but I found I wasn't. "Nope." I shook my head. "A wise man once told me that I didn't have to look out for everybody around me. Plus, it seems that task has already been claimed."

Because the Executioner wasn't a member of Thom's pack so he hadn't been forced into immobility by the strange woman's blood consumption. Instead, as I peered out through the open back door, it looked like his long legs might catch up with Thom's fleeing attacker in short order.

Two weeks ago, I would have rushed after them to protect an apparent innocent from the Executioner's glowering awfulness. But since the Moon Trials, I trusted that enigmatic werewolf to dole out justice with a fair and careful hand.

Plus, the strange woman had scratched my mate. I bared my teeth and slid both of my arms around Thom's neck in the universal posture of a woman demanding a slow dance.

"That what you want?" Thom rumbled, repeating the first words he'd ever spoken to me.

This time, I wasn't tongue-tied. This time, I answered easily.

"Yes," I told my mate. "This is exactly what I want."

JapantownSF
NO OVERNIGHT ... ALLOWED
... IN PLA...
... USE ... S OR
... SIDE OF ... ANCE
... THANK YOU ...
COOPERATION

San Francisco

I was lucky enough to get to visit San Francisco while plotting out *Moon Duel* and I thought you might enjoy some location photos to ground the events in place.

Japantown

Me entering Japantown through the official gate, photo credit Jay Williams.

Previous page: My brother beside the Peace Pagoda.

*The sea serpent painted on the ceiling where the scents drew Kira
back to her past.*

*Okay, so Kira didn't go into the bookstore. But I
did and I barely managed not to buy all the books
in languages I couldn't speak.*

Mountain View

Concrete-lined stream in Mountain View.

Point Reyes

Kira's final showdown took place along these windswept cliffs.

Broke Truck
Lost Pup
Aimee Easterling

Broke Truck, Lost Pup

This short story is set when Thom is sixteen years old.

The craziness started like a run-of-the-mill Country Western song. My truck broke down. My dog—well wolf—pushed out of my skin. And the first werewolf I'd ever met—myself excluded—offered the hand of his daughter in marriage.

Okay, so maybe the story wasn't such a cliché.

Before the proposal, I actually thought maybe he was a real, wild wolf. He looked more like one than I had when I first shifted in my bedroom back in Gate City and watched myself in the mirror, trying to walk like a wild thing and instead tripping over my own two feet.

I hadn't gone furry much since then. It was tough enough to be a teenage human, let alone a teenage wolf.

But when the truck I'd built out of junkyard parts wheezed to a halt, fear that I might have cracked the cylinder head woke the slumbering animal inside me. Those jeans that fit a little too tight but just right ripped off me. The window I'd rolled down to feel the breeze against my face turned into the perfect exit strategy. And I'd run and run and run in no direction in particular, without human words or purposes in my head.

Then he appeared. Twice my bulk although not much taller than me at the shoulder, moving like he'd been born in the forest. He cocked his head, lifted one leg, and peed in a manner that I could only call pointed. Two eye blinks of complete stillness, then he shifted upward into the form of a guy in his prime, ripping me into humanity alongside him.

The sudden shift hit me like a gut punch. Instinctive fear prickled my naked skin as I folded in half around the pain in my center. This guy exuded power and danger like no person I'd ever met before and I wasn't even able to straighten my spine enough to watch for his teeth to turn back into wolf fangs before they sank into my unprotected flesh.

Luckily, he seemed to find me too amusing to attack. "Not very good at trespassing, are you?"

With an effort, I managed to force my chin up so I could meet those scary eyes straight on. "This is Faris land," I choked out. "Has been for over two centuries."

I'd known that, even under the spell of my wolf, which was why I'd run this direction. Dad took pride in the fact that he hadn't sold an acre of the old homestead his who-knew-how-many-greats grandfather had claimed back in the late 1700s.

So, no, I wasn't trespassing. This guy was.

His head cock looked so lupine that for a moment I lost track of the fact we were both furless and entirely naked. "Territory has nothing to do with deeds and titles," he informed me after one long minute. "A smart wolf gets permission from the alpha whose land he's walking across."

Alpha. The word nearly pulled my wolf back out of me and I didn't realize I was stalking in a circle around the self-proclaimed alpha, growling softly, until his hand shot out and grabbed my shoulder.

"Cool it, pup."

Something about those words forced literal cold into my muscles. Or maybe froze them. I found myself unable to take another step and the growl died a squeaky death inside my throat.

Which meant the man could have let me go, but he didn't take his hand off my shoulder. From anyone else, the gesture would have felt like a threat or—given our lack of clothes—something sexual. But my wolf was soothed. It curled up inside me and I found I could once again manage human thought.

Dad always said: when in doubt, be polite. This time, I paid attention to the admonition. "Sir, I don't have the foggiest idea what you're talking about."

"You don't, do you?" He leaned in closer as if he intended to bite me, but instead his nostrils flared wide.

Now his hand didn't feel quite so soothing. It was, I realized, awfully close to my throat. And had his firm grip moved four inches over, it would have cut off my airflow.

Fear woke my wolf again, but this time I didn't let it consume me. "I'd appreciate you removing your hand," I said, the words coming out stiffer than I'd intended but without the growl the wolf tried to force into them.

The hand in question moved so fast I wasn't able to avoid it. Went for my head...and tousled my hair before retreating out of my personal space.

"I like you, pup. You're welcome to join my pack."

I didn't have to think about that offer, just shook my head. Sure, it might be confusing to be the only person I knew who had a wolf inside him. But Dad and I were a team. I wasn't about to ditch my lone parent for some stranger I'd met in the forest. "No thanks."

It wasn't until the stranger hummed that I remembered how that cold I'd felt in my muscles earlier had frozen me. If I didn't miss my guess, this guy could literally force me to do whatever he wanted me to.

Like leaving Dad in the lurch.

"Look," I started, but he spoke over me.

"Traditions matter to you."

I nodded, not quite sure where he was going with this but glad that the subject seemed to have turned away from his earlier offer.

"Good. It's a time-honored tradition for a strong alpha to trick an up-and-comer into marrying his daughter."

Marry? I'd just landed my driver's license last week. And I really, really wished my truck hadn't overheated because now would be a great time to have wheels to carry me away from this disaster.

Outrunning the guy who'd just offered to become my father-in-law wasn't going to work, so I tried a question. "Is it a trick if you tell me about it, sir?"

He shrugged. "Ember will like you better once you're alpha of a territory. Do you have a dollar?"

I spread my arms wide, demonstrating the obvious. We were both buck naked. Our clothes, let alone wallets, were nowhere in sight.

"Well, a rock will have to do." He jerked his chin. "That one's pretty. *Pick it up.*"

My muscles obeyed him without my permission, bending me down to gather a rock that looked like all the others. Again without any conscious volition on my part, I held out the rock, which the other man snagged out of my hand, sniffed, then balanced on top of his head.

"Good choice," he said, as if he wasn't emulating a naked circus clown. "In exchange, I'll give you a territory. Twenty-five miles in every direction from this point. Sound good?"

Unlike his previous order, this discussion wasn't forcing actions upon me. So, with a silent apology to Dad's admonitions to respect my elders, I proceeded to talk back. "Sir, I'm not marrying your daughter."

"Not unless Ember asks you to, *obviously.*" He cocked his head again, which somehow didn't manage to dislodge the rock. "Now I'm the one trespassing. What are you going to do about it?"

This lesson—my first—in being a werewolf was approximately as befuddling as my calculus homework. "Pee on a shrub?" I guessed.

That lightning-fast hand lashed out to strike me on the shoulder and I had my fists up before I realized it was just a sign of affection. The rock on his head tilted but didn't fall off.

He nodded as if I'd finished the math problem correctly. "Do that."

Then, without another word, he twisted in on himself and became that huge wolf again. Only, this time, there was a rock resting on top of his head, a rock that stayed steady as a ball cap while he loped away from my family's property—my new territory—and toward what I assumed was his own.

When I returned to my truck, it started right up. Its head wasn't cracked, although I couldn't vouch for my own.

Because I was alpha of a territory being groomed to appeal to another alpha's daughter. I didn't meet the woman in question for more than a decade, though, long enough for the rock-balancing wolf to fade into foggy memory.

But that's another story and not really my own to tell.

USA TODAY BESTSELLING AUTHOR
AIMEE EASTERLING
SLAYING SOLSTICE
A NO FOX GIVEN SHORT

Slaying Solstice

December 13, 3:13 pm

Grub: These r the presents I wnt. Slay with real reindeer. Gaming system. World peas.

Kira: You don't ask for much, do you?

Grub: k, I wnt these 2 [Link to 1,000 Piece Turkish Delight Collection]

Kira: Ask whoever's reading you The Lion, the Witch, and the Wardrobe what sarcasm is.

Grub: ...

Grub: ...

Grub: Does that mean I dnt gt Turkish Delight?

Kira: Your mom said I could only buy you one present. And, just so you know, Turkish Delight sounds yummy but it tastes like dirty socks.

Grub: Ew! Whoz socks?

Kira: Your dad's. After he's gone hunting with the pack and forgets to shower before putting them on because there's a disaster that keeps him too busy to change clothes for three days.

Kira: So, what do you say? Gaming system? What kind?

Grub: If I had a slay, I cud run w/ the pack not stay hom w/ the puppies til I'm big enuf to shift. Rudolf is fast!

Kira: How about a huge box of candy that actually tastes good? I could talk your mom into believing that's a single present.

Grub: Slay

Kira: Kid, you drive a hard bargain. I'll see what I can do.

December 22, 5:45 am

Mai: WHAT DID YOU BUY MY SON?!?!?!

Kira: A slay

Mai: I'll slay you if you don't tell me whether this contraption is going to get him killed.

Kira: Relax. That's a top-secret prototype hoverboard from the Base next door. Charlie says it has some kind of fancy protective buffer thingummier the scientists cooked up to keep you from falling off. Magnetic hyper-resonance something-or-other.

Mai: English?

Kira: Tell Grub it's a sleigh and he'll be thrilled. It's totally safe.

Kira: Maybe don't let him hold the baby while he tries it out
though.

Kira: And put him in a helmet and knee pads.

Mai: Sounds like a disaster waiting to happen.

Mai: Your punishment for whatever he breaks first is taking care
of the kids next weekend so Gunner and I can get a minute to
ourselves.

Kira: Wouldn't miss it for the world.

Mai: Love you.

Kira: Love you too. Happy solstice!

THE
ALPHA
PUZZLE
A NO FOX GIVEN SHORT
USA TODAY BESTSELLING AUTHOR
AIMEE EASTERLING

Chapter 1

I'd do anything to win one of Kira's smiles. Yes, even though she doled them out as easily as the mayor tossed candy off a parade float. Every single one was far sweeter than any food I'd ever put into my mouth.

There was one special smile, however, that no one but me ever saw. Kira graced me with that smile now as we leaned against the bar together, watching Willow charm the socks off my pack by solving every single puzzle they threw her way.

Apparently, keeping her head down and putting up with a thoroughly unpleasant mate plus a scum-of-the-earth pack leader had given Willow plenty of time to become a pro at everything from rubik's cubes to old-fashioned bent-nail tangles. And now that she was the alpha in charge of the clan next door, my pack loved the challenge of trying to find a puzzle the formerly timid woman couldn't solve.

"She's ready," Kira said as Willow somehow managed to get all of the same-colored marbles lined up along two interlocking tracks, working so quickly the glass clacked.

"Ready?" I didn't stick my nose into Kira's business unless she asked for help, so I couldn't be certain. But my understanding was that Willow had dealt with all the hurdles in her path already.

She'd gotten over the death of her mate. She'd won the support of hidebound underlings who initially couldn't imagine obeying a female leader. And, as this evening proved, she was well able to make friends while keeping large numbers of her pack mates in line outside their territorial boundaries.

My brows drew together. "Ready for what?"

Instead of the smile that had warmed me earlier, Kira shot over that consoling glance she often tossed in my direction when my human heritage tripped me up in the werewolf arena. "Holding her own among less friendly alphas, of course," my mate answered. "I think she's ready to make her debut, but only if you're willing to host?"

The imploring expression Kira turned on me now took my breath away while filling me with almost unbearable gratitude. Gratitude that Kira had come into my life plus, if I was honest, a cascade of more earthly emotions relating to the apartment we shared upstairs.

When I was able to speak again, I found myself agreeing without bothering to ask what exactly I was agreeing to. Which is when Kira bit her lip and started to backpedal.

"We'll definitely want to hold the gathering outside city limits in case things go cockeyed. And don't bring Ava or Lily or Eli or…"

"Stick to shifters who can handle themselves in dangerous situations. Got it."

Only that was apparently wrong also. "No. You have to look strong if your strength is going to rub off on Willow. Which means surrounding yourself with pack mates who clearly need your protection…while not really needing your protection."

It was a puzzle, just like the sliding-tile puzzles Willow was able to solve at a glance but which I, as a child, had tended to pop apart then put back together the easy way. As an adult, I gave puzzles like that a very wide berth.

But I'd do a lot for one of Kira's smiles. And she was gazing up at me as if she expected me to do the pack-leader thing and know exactly who would look weak while actually being well able to take care of themselves. "On it," I promised while making a mental note to call my brother-in-law and pick his brains first thing tomorrow morning.

Kira's smile this time was full of mischief and promise. Immediately, I re-arranged that mental to-do list.

I'd call Gunner *second* thing tomorrow morning…

Chapter 2

W ith Gunner's help, I sent out invitations that were just polite enough to guarantee attendance without sounding obsequious. I limited each visiting alpha's entourage to half a dozen. And I handpicked the precise number of my own pack mates to boost our stature without making me look like I was hiding behind my clan.

As the apparently-but-not-really-weak attendees, I chose my father and Dixie Lee. Both were human, both had plenty of experience dealing with unruly werewolves, and both had someone present who would rip out the throats of anyone who gave them so much as a dirty look.

So the evening should have been going well, but it wasn't. "Act like you're enjoying yourself. Or at least lean," my brother-in-law Gunner suggested as he handed a beer to me, another beer to Kira's new boss, and a third to the alpha who'd traded over part of his territory to me when I was a clueless teenager, taking as his only prize a useless rock. I felt nearly as clueless now, although glad to be surrounded by friends. Between the four of us, we could handle any overt problems.

Too bad the current problems were less than overt.

Still, I relaxed my muscles the way my brother-in-law suggested and took a sip from my bottle while perusing the shabbiest party I'd ever hosted. I'd set up cornhole, figuring that was the sort of game even werewolves couldn't fight over. And they weren't fighting precisely…they'd just turned it into a contest of aerial keep away involving wolves plus my mate and her sister in fox form whizzing through the air trying to catch bean bags in their mouths.

Half the time, the leapers ended up slamming into bared-fanged guards rather than making it to the cornhole boards. Blood hadn't been spilled, however, and Kira was enjoying herself. I could tell by the way her tail twitched as she landed on the back of my lupine second, using Bertrand's height to vault herself closer to...yep, she'd caught a bean bag and was now carrying it in her mouth toward her side's goal.

One fox being chased by six growling wolves was bad for my blood pressure, but I trusted Kira to know her own strength. So I turned away with an effort and considered the next issue facing me as host—food.

The trouble was, human gatherings had taught me that a party is only as good as the snacks on offer. And everyone seemed to be grabbing hot dogs and marshmallows out of the packages then stuffing them into their mouths cold rather than using the provided sticks to roast the offerings into campfire delicacies.

"Don't werewolves believe in s'mores?" I muttered under my breath.

Gunner frowned, not understanding my question, but Kira's boss followed my gaze and rasped out one of his rare answers. "We cremate our dead. I assumed the bonfire was intended as intimidation."

Apparently our guests had made the same assumption. Because the fire I'd built for ambiance and as a roasting venue was being given as wide of a berth as the alpha who was supposed to be the guest of honor.

And that was the real problem. No alpha had challenged Willow, but none of them had spoken to her either. Which was the exact opposite of what should have happened when a new pack leader was given an opportunity to meet her neighbors on neutral turf.

In contrast, the other alphas had been wandering off in groups of two or three all evening to negotiate pack-leader-type trade deals, two of which I'd taken part in myself. The first alpha to approach me had asked whether I'd take on an unruly wolf who deserved a second chance but would be skinned alive if he stayed in his current territory. Yes, of course I would. The second alpha shot me sly glances while insinuating that I might turn over some of my spare females in exchange for an extension of my southern hunting grounds. The answer to that had been a resounding "Hell no."

I'd been so furious after the latter conversation that it had taken me a while to notice that Willow was only being approached by pack mates of those of us leaning against this rail fence and watching the proceedings. Considering the matter now, I got the distinct impression Willow was being treated as more of a pawn than a power.

Which gave me a wild, Kira-like idea.

I pushed off the fence rail and stopped leaning. Heading toward the bonfire, I made a pit stop beside my mate, who'd accomplished her goal and was now panting on the ground in human form, clothed in a very skintight gown she'd created out of her star ball's magic.

I gave her a hand up then filled her other hand with what I'd been carrying. "Hold my beer?" I asked.

Chapter 3

I'd hoped my question would win a smile and I wasn't disappointed. Kira's grin promised she'd caught my mimicry of the redneck archetype so many of the neighboring alphas liked to slot me into.

I could only hope the alpha who'd asked me to trade women like chattel would be among those falling into the stereotyping trap.

I didn't pause long beside my mate, however. Instead, I continued on to where I was clearly visible against the glow of the bonfire, at which point I called, "Willow, come here."

My words snapped like a whip but didn't actually command her muscles. Still she shot me a slit-eyed glare then stalked over to my side.

"Anyone got a rope?" I asked next, purposefully using poor grammar to add to the redneck effect. My father jerked his chin in an offer to head back to his truck and find the supplies in question, but I waited instead until one of our visitors came up with what I'd requested. Accepting the rope, I sawed it in two with my pocketknife, knotted one end of the first length into a loop around Willow's right wrist then the other end of the same rope around her left wrist, ignoring the smirk that was trying to break out over her face as I worked.

Of course she'd know the classic rope-handcuff puzzle. I'd found it described on the internet, intending to pull it out at our next inter-pack get-together. I hadn't actually fully understood the solution, but the setup was simple enough.

Knot each end of a single rope around the first person's wrists. Do the same with the other person after looping the second rope through the first. The result was a seemingly unbreakable connection, two people bound together with no obvious way to escape.

It would be a good showcase of Willow's intelligence. A good way of shoving shit into the acquisitive alpha's face without doing him physical harm.

Assuming he took the bait.

"Who wants to compete with this woman?" I called, lifting Willow's arm in the air as if she was livestock.

Willow got the hint and started playing along. She tugged at the rope I'd tied around both of her wrists, preventing them from moving more than shoulder-length apart. Twisted her face up into a pained scowl.

The visual was impressive—woman in bondage. I could just imagine the asshole alpha salivating into his drink.

Sure enough—"What's the prize?" someone at the back of the crowd demanded.

No, not someone. It was that same acquisitive alpha.

"What do you want the prize to be?" I countered.

"Her," he responded, just like I'd known he would.

I stroked my chin as if deep in thought. "What do you think?" I asked Willow, keeping my voice low enough so a nearby human wouldn't have been able to hear. I was playing on the fact that everyone present knew I'd been raised far from other shifters. Perhaps some of them would be stupid enough to think my own exceptional hearing hadn't clued me in to the fact every werewolf within a hundred yards could pick up on my words.

"What do I think about what?" Willow hissed back, acting upset even though I could smell her amusement. Good thing smoke from the fire dissipated that scent before it traveled very far.

My own part in the charade was harder to manage, but I managed to glower as I demanded, "Are you willing to void the debt you owe me by taking this chance?"

Willow and I both knew she didn't owe me a debt. If anything, she owed Kira a debt. Or perhaps Kira owed her a debt. Whichever way the debt had originally flowed, the two of them now considered their budding relationship built on a firm foundation of friendship.

Despite that fact, Willow let her voice rise a little as she demanded, "Is that the only way to clear my debt?"

"Afraid so."

She turned her face toward the flames, which was a good thing since the joyful sparkle in her eyes would have ruined the effect otherwise. Her shoulders slumped as she told the fire. "Then, yes, I guess I have to agree."

Chapter 4

The asshole alpha pushed shifters out of his way in his haste to be the one who won the right to take part in the contest. He agreed to the rules I laid out—no severing the rope in any way, no untying the knots, whoever found a way free first won ownership of the other.

I knew Willow would make short work of the puzzle, so I asked them both another question also. Just to ensure the asshole alpha didn't later call foul.

"Have you successfully completed this puzzle previously?"

They both shook their heads, then spoke when I demanded it so they could smell the truth on each others' breath.

"No."

"No."

I tied a second rope around the asshole alpha's right wrist. Looped it between Willow's rope and her body then knotted the free end around his right arm. They were ready to begin.

Only someone was clearing his throat behind us. I turned to find the middle-aged alpha who'd given me my territory sipping some sort of cocktail with a pink umbrella and what appeared to be a strawberry carved in the shape of a rose on a second toothpick skewer. His name was Wolfie, but I couldn't quite talk myself into using such a childish nickname for a man who was either crazy or terrifying or just really enjoyed playing the part of trickster. Mostly, when I spoke to him, I managed not to use his name.

"You promised entertainment," he said.

"This isn't entertaining?"

Wolfie shrugged. "A couple of ropes? Ownership of a woman? I propose we raise the stakes."

Before I quite knew what was happening, we'd all agreed to a third outcome. Branches were piled leading out from the bonfire on either side of Willow and the asshole. Gasoline was sloshed across the wood. Fire licked down the length, nearly surrounding the contestants. The only way out was through a small gap where Wolfie and I now stood.

"If the fire burns faster than you work the puzzle," Wolfie said, not bothering to raise his voice despite the crackle of flames on either side of us, "then you have the option to surrender. Give up and you're owned by our host instead."

Wolfie tipped his beer bottle in my direction then wandered away back into the crowd. He'd created mayhem and now seemed to be...stalking a mouse beside the marshmallow bags?

That left me back in charge of ensuring both contestants agreed to the changed rules. It was hard to tell in the orange glow of the bonfire, but I could have sworn I saw fear in the asshole alpha's eyes when I peered into them. Still, when I asked, "Acceptable?" he nodded and Willow nodded too.

"Then begin," I intoned.

The flames made it hard for most of the audience to see clearly, which is likely why Kira ambled up to join me in the small gap between fiery borders. Heat turned her cheeks red, but she didn't back up as the asshole alpha proved his assholishness, struggling with the ropes in such a way that he nearly tipped both himself and Willow into the flames.

Then the asshole's elbow caught Willow's chin. A crack of bone against bone. A female cry of pain.

The act was unintentional, but still my wolf rose up behind my eyes. I growled and took a step forward.

"Wait," Kira told me, the slightest pressure of her hand on my arm enough to make me stop in my tracks.

And I waited. Because my mate was right. This was Willow's time to prove herself, not her time to be rescued by me.

Unfortunately, Willow was dazed by the blow. She was also so outmassed by the asshole that she had no way of manipulating the ropes even once she shook her head clear and tried again to free herself.

And every moment the flames licked higher. A spark landed in Kira's hair and I smothered it with my palm. "Step back," I suggested.

"They can't step back," she countered.

Which was true. Another spark had flared alight on the back of the asshole's shirt, the looped ropes preventing him from slapping it out. Willow coughed as she tried to win a little slack in her own line, failing as the asshole began spinning in a tight circle that drew her unwillingly along for the ride.

Then it was over. "I surrender!" the asshole howled, his face human but the words bringing to mind a wolf with a tail between its legs.

Or perhaps the contest wasn't over. "Well I don't," Willow countered.

She did something subtle with one of her fingers. Then she was free.

Chapter 5

Kira stepped aside to let Willow pass through the ever-shortening gap between pillars of flame, but I stood my ground. I waited as fire licked up the asshole alpha's back, until his eyes had to be stinging even more than mine were. Then, when he still didn't speak, I stated the obvious. "You lost."

"You didn't accept my surrender!" the asshole countered, voice shrill.

"Not to me. To her." I jerked my chin in Willow's direction just in case the alpha was slow as well as an asshole. And, predictably, he came up with an even less palatable reply.

"A man can't be owned by a...woman!"

Only a tiny pause suggested that he'd originally intended a different final word, one that began with C. Once again, my wolf tried to take control of me. This time, I let it out.

"Perhaps you'd like to rephrase that. A *person* can't own another *person*."

My wolf snapped my human teeth sharply as we finished speaking. And whatever the asshole saw in my eyes made his own wolf rise rampant within his human skin.

This was the exact sort of lupine pissing match I'd never understood previously. But with Kira behind me clucking over Willow's bruised chin, I couldn't imagine stepping down.

Luckily, I didn't have to. Turned out the asshole *was* afraid of being burned. And as the fingers of flame on his back turned into a raging inferno, his eyes slowly faded from wolf back to human. His head bent sideways, neck bared, as he choked out, "Alpha. You're right. A person can't own another person."

I let him pass then. It would have been cruel not to. Still, as he brushed past me, my wolf spoke one last time.

"I don't own you. Neither does Willow. But you're not welcome here, now or ever. Take your pack mates and go." Then I smacked him on the back several times to put out the flames, not bothering to rein in my strength.

The asshole left without complaint or bluster and the party looked up after that. Willow ended up encircled by a ring of alphas impressed by her bravery in the face of the fire. Wolfie caught his mouse and skewered it on one of the roasting sticks to char off the fur before crunching it up like hard candy.

And Kira smiled so wide the reflected glow of the bonfire made her human face almost vulpine. "This is the best party ever," she murmured, as we stood together hand in hand watching werewolves mingle the way werewolves mingle.

"You're right, as always," I agreed.

Character

Ava – Dixie Lee's eleven-year-old daughter

Bertrand – Thom's second-in-command

Big T – Thom's father

Charlie Raven – Kira's closest human friend

Chief Reed – alpha of the territory northeast of Gate City

Chief Wylie – alpha of San Francisco who won the last Moon Trials

Colin – young werewolf in Gate City

Damien – Moon Trials participant

Dixie Lee – human bartender at the Full Moon Saloon

Eli – human who likes to hang out at the Full Moon Saloon

Executioner – Lawkeeper who deals with high profile issues…often by putting the offending parties to death

Griffin Fletcher – Moon Trials participant who is mated to one of Pet's sisters

Grub – Mai and Gunner's six-year-old son

Gunner Fairwood – Mai's mate and Kira's brother-in-law

Hank – trusted member of Thom's pack

Ito – member of Kira and Mai's grandmother's honor guard in the Moon Marked series. By the time *No Fox Given* begins, he has married Jessie Raven

Janet Allegra – military wife whose death instigates events in *Full Moon Saloon*

Jessie Raven – Charlie's twin sister

List

Kaito – member of Kira and Mai's grandmother's honor guard who ended up in a coma at the end of the Moon Marked series. He was sent to a care facility in Gate City when it became clear he wasn't going to wake up

Karl Hogan – Thom's half brother and a Moon Trials participant

Liam Randolph – heir to the Randolph pack and a Moon Trials participant

Lily Randolph – A new member of Thom's pack

Mai Fairwood – Kira's sister

Nathaniel – Lawkeeper tailing Kira and Thom in *Full Moon Saloon*

Nora – Charlie's girlfriend

Penny – Jessie and Ito's six-year-old daughter

Pet (Petunia) Kirkpatrick – fifteen-year-old Moon Trials participant

Pumpkin – big orange cat who lives at the Full Moon Saloon

Quentin – Chief Reed's heir and Willow's mate

Rupert Rumfelt – Kira's annoying Lawkeeper coworker and later a Moon Trials participant

Scarlet – Kira's Lawkeeper boss

Smoke – problematic member of Thom's pack

Thom Faris – the proprietor of the Full Moon Saloon and leader of the Gate City pack

Willow – Quentin's wife

Big T
Charlie
Ava
Grub
Willow
Thom

From the Author

I hope you enjoyed Kira's story! Next up, the Executioner and the amnesiac steal the show in *Wolf Trap*, a sneak preview of which begins on the very next page.

Meanwhile, if you'd like to be the first to hear about new books and sales on my backlist, I hope you'll sign up for my email list at www.aimeeeasterling.com. As a bonus, subscribers gain access to plenty of fan-only extras, including photos of several of the locations included in this series.

Speaking of fan-only extras, you won't want to miss the tangible goodies that go with this series and others. Head over to my website to join the excitement.

Thank you for reading! You are why I write.

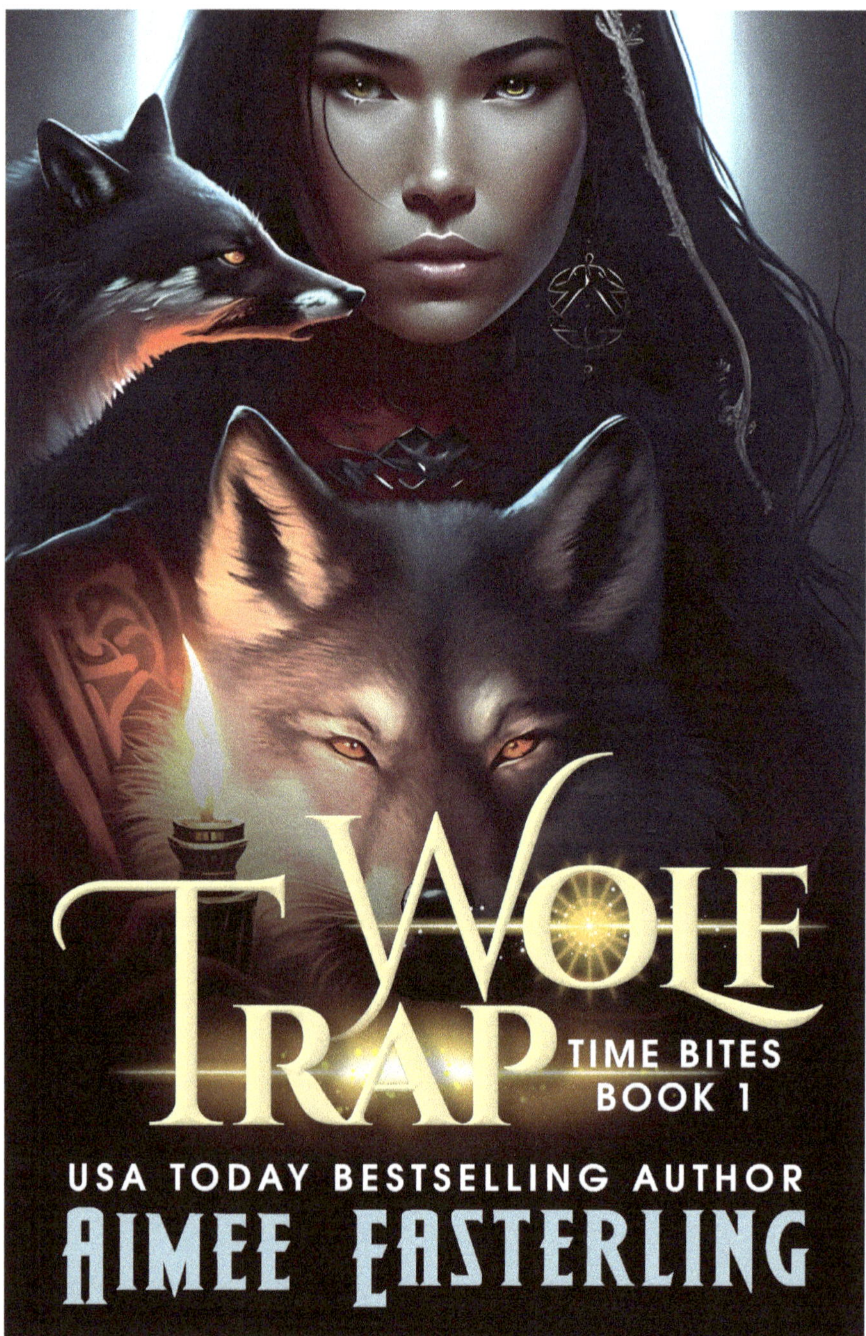

WOLF TRAP
TIME BITES
BOOK 1
USA TODAY BESTSELLING AUTHOR
AIMEE EASTERLING

Wolf Trap Excerpt

*F**lee! Scary Guy!!* demanded the scrawl of black ink up the inside of my left arm, the words at just the right level so my opening eyes couldn't help but fixate on the written advice. Blearily, I noted that my sleeve had been pushed up to reveal even more tiny letters decipherable only because they matched my own handwriting: *Light sleeper!!! Get out now!!!!*

I blinked away grit and tilted my head to consider the situation. Scary Guy didn't look particularly scary. His head rested on the neighboring pillow, my breath just barely fluttering his long, ebony lashes. Equally dark hair atop his head was mussed as if he'd tossed and turned in the night, and no wonder since his broad, fully dressed body indented the covers rather than resting beneath them. Still, he'd managed to curl protectively around me while never quite touching the lump I made beneath the luxurious duvet, all while wearing a formal lounge suit that had not been made for sleep.

In other words, nothing appeared to have happened here last night. Nothing that would risk my standing in society...other than our completely inappropriate proximity without benefit of a chaperone, of course.

Still, if I couldn't trust my own words, what could I trust? The marked-upon arm was stretched up under my head and sound asleep, but I eased it down in preparation for a sneaky exit.

Or, rather, I tried to.

Something soft yet unyielding held the arm in question exactly where it had been when I awakened. Something that made no sense, then suddenly did as my understanding of the world twisted on its axis, unlocking knowledge that felt at the same time old and brand new.

The item restraining my motion was a *sex toy*, the mere phrase making me blush. Absurdly fluffy pink handcuffs wrapped first around my wrist then around the bed frame. I'd been locked very gently yet very firmly in place.

The puzzle of last night—why was I here? Who was Scary Guy?—tickled my mind like a sword umbrella found in a thrift shop with a price tag far less than a collector would have paid for it. But my racing pulse demanded flight rather than puzzle-piecing, so I focused instead on potential tools within easy reach.

Lamp on a bedside table. Alarm clock with huge glowing digits that tried to consume my attention with its marvelousness but which I ignored as unhelpful. Drawer that I guessed from the hotel-like atmosphere might hold branded stationery and pen.

No flexible wire was in evidence, and I couldn't quite recall what I intended to do with the item if I found it. But I trusted the shred of memory promising a solution, so I kept searching. Perhaps if I was very lucky the hotel would have splurged on one of those newfangled retractable pens...

After one quick glance to ensure Scary Guy was still sleeping, I bent my body slowly, slowly, away from him then eased the drawer open to reveal exactly what I'd expected. *Bingo.* Not only information about my location—"Lexington, Kentucky" was helpfully typed beneath the hotel name on the expected stationary—but also the exact item I needed to free myself. Tucking the ballpoint beneath my chin, I let muscle memory guide me as I unscrewed the top from the bottom and tapped out the metal spring.

Straightening even a small part of the curved wire was a bear with Scary Guy asleep on the bed beside me. Each time I moved, his breathing hitched and I froze. But eventually I held a length of semi-straight metal pinched between thumb and forefinger. Eventually, I was ready to work myself loose.

Hairs prickled on the back of my neck as I turned my back on Scary Guy completely this time. The posture was necessary to reach the handcuff, but a niggling memory promised that long eyelashes were false advertising. The man sleeping on the bed beside me was a predator and if I woke him...

Quieting my breathing with an effort, I inserted the wire into the hole then bent it into a V shape. Out it came then in at a different angle. *Twist. Click. Success.*

I grinned then froze as Scary Guy moved on the bed behind me. I couldn't tell whether his eyes had opened. Could only feel the possessive weight as a huge hand slung itself across my shoulder and neck.

The touch should have been distasteful or worrisome, but his skin smelled like lemon-meringue pie. Sweet and tart with furry undertones.

Werewolf, my foggy memory suggested. *Alpha. Danger!*

I scraped the lining of my brain in search of further information but found nothing I could put words to. Just oddly mixed emotions and a complete absence of tangible puzzle pieces.

Meanwhile, behind me, Scary Guy's breath had eased back into the regular susurration of slumber. He was unaware of my imminent escape...for the moment at least.

*Enough puzzling,*I warned myself. *On task, please.*

With the full use of all my fingers, it was simple to unlock the other handcuff from around the bed frame, even though I had to be fastidiously slow now that Scary Guy's heat pushed into my skin through layers of fabric. The hotel had very helpfully chosen a bed with a slatted headboard, which meant I could move the handcuffs down the line, reattach them, then....

The pink fur was so soft that Scary Guy didn't wake when I slid his wrist into the unlocked side of the restraining device. He didn't wake when the latch clicked shut. That success made me cockier than I should have been.

Easing a pillow into the space beneath his arm where I'd reclined one moment earlier, I crept out of bed and came erect on high-laced boots. No wonder my toes had complained so adamantly. It would have been entirely inappropriate to undress last night, but surely I could have at least slid off my footwear?

I paused to consider...and a huge hand lashed out to clamp shut around my billowing skirt fabric. "Wait," Scary Guy rasped, the single word as harsh as sandpaper against my skin.

I was caught. Then I wasn't.

Lunging sideways, I used the release of spring-like tension in one leg to rip myself free of my captor's grip. "I'd rather not," I rebutted, dancing out of reach then continuing toward the window that offered escape into night just on the cusp of dawn.

The crash behind me could have been the headboard being ripped apart or just a display of temper. I didn't dare slow to check. Only once I'd pushed the window open and slammed my shoulder through the screen—such a shame to ruin astonishingly fine craftsmanship—did I dare turn back to assess the situation I was leaving behind.

Flat gray eyes bored into mine and now I understood the nickname I'd scrawled up the inside of my arm. This man *was* scary. Not because of his size and his muscles but because of the emotionlessness behind those pupils as he patiently wriggled the headboard slat back and forth and back and forth again. Brute force hadn't broken the wood but it wouldn't be long before patience won him free.

Still, I found myself succumbing to the temptation of the puzzle rather than fleeing. "Who are you?" I demanded.

The tiniest crinkle of humor formed on either side of his otherwise emotionless eyes. "Tell me your name and I'll tell you mine."

That seemed like a fair trade so I opened my mouth to oblige him...and found nothing where my identity should have been. No given name, no family name, no knowledge of who I was and why I was here in this hotel room.

A lightning bolt of terror spun through me. Then, on its heels, something I could cling to. A female voice slicing through the fog of memorylessness like a remnant of previously uttered breath.

"You are strong. You can do this."

The sounds didn't quite match the words, but I understood them anyway. And even though I still didn't know who I was, the remembered voice of my mother was immediately recognizable. I knew on an instinctive level that her belief in my abilities had buoyed me up in the past. If I so chose, I could let that maternal trust buoy me up now.

The first ray of early morning sun struck my back like the warmth of maternal kudos. A sharp whistle from the street almost jogged more reminders loose inside my head.

Almost, but not quite.

"No idea, huh?" Scary Guy's rasp was louder than it had been a moment earlier. And while he hadn't shared his name, I somehow knew this man wouldn't raise his voice without good reason.

He was covering something up. The sound of slowly splintering wood maybe?

I didn't wait to find out. I jumped through the window—first floor, thankfully—and obeyed my own instructions. Feet against pavement, I fled.

Keep reading in Wolf Trap!

www.ingramcontent.com/pod-product-compliance
Lightning Source LLC
Chambersburg PA
CBHW040803010826
48981CB00042B/559/J